Born in Ohio, Stephen Smoke started writing when he was ten years old, typesetting his own sports magazines and selling subscriptions to family and neighbours. Having a passion for music, in 1972 he moved to Los Angeles to become a rock-and-roll star, but turned to producing words instead – becoming head writer for 'Hollywood Live', a live comedy show. In 1979 he founded *Mystery Magazine*, which he published until 1982. Now a screenwriter and feature film director, he has written fourteen previous novels.

Stephen Smoke still lives in Los Angeles, with his wife Margaret Lam, and a black shar pei named Ace.

Also published by Headline is his previous novel, PACIFIC COAST HIGHWAY: 'A fast-paced thriller . . . Smoke keeps the surprising turns of plot coming' (*Publishers Weekly*)

Also by Stephen Smoke

Pacific Coast Highway

Judgment Hour

Stephen Smoke

HEADLINE FEATURE

First published in Great Britain in 1994
by HEADLINE BOOK PUBLISHING

First published in paperback in 1995
by HEADLINE BOOK PUBLISHING

A HEADLINE FEATURE paperback

10 9 8 7 6 5 4 3 2 1

ISBN 0 7472 4533 9

Typeset by Avon Dataset Ltd., Bidford-on-Avon, B50 4JH

Printed and bound in Great Britain by
Cox & Wyman Ltd, Reading, Berks

HEADLINE BOOK PUBLISHING
A division of Hodder Headline PLC
338 Euston Road,
London NW1 3BH

For Margaret
Without whom none of it would make much sense

ACKNOWLEDGMENTS

I would like to thank Peter Lavery, my editor at Headline, and Fran Pomerantz, Michael Blaha and Stan Corwin for their friendship, patience and contributions.

PROLOGUE

It just didn't work anymore.

The rules he had grown up with, abided by, no longer applied. Order and justice, even a conscientious attempt at justice, seemed to be a quaint notion from another time and place.

Feelings. Feelings were important now. How a person felt was more important than what he thought. People felt angry. They felt victimized, fearful, discriminated against and lonely. People didn't think much these days, anyway. Didn't know how. TV did that for them.

These were strange times, thought Carnie as he took a pull off his beer.

'There have never been times like the ones we're living through today,' said Kyle Talbot, popular radio talk-show host. 'Moral relativism has destroyed this country. "Everything is relative," people say. "Nothing is really good or really bad," people say. Well I have news, ladies and gentlemen. There *is* evil in this world. There *are* bad people doing bad things. The time has come to snap out of that Sixties numbness and recognize what's happening in this country. The killer is at your door. Are you going to open that door and let him murder your family, rape your wife and daughters, and say that there is nothing *inherently* bad about that action? That everything is relative? That you have to take into consideration the cultural background and childhood of the killer? No. You *know* that it is right to defend your family against violence. Against evil.'

Carnie sat in the dark room, the only light coming from the amber radio dial. The only sound, Kyle Talbot's voice.

'You know what's right and you know what's wrong. It's wrong to molest a child. It's wrong to knowingly hurt another person merely for your own pleasure. But these days when someone takes a stand against evil, he is crucified by the media. Many have stood against evil, and many have been crucified. That doesn't mean that their actions against evil were wrong, only that those actions were misunderstood. But what is misunderstood today becomes clear in time. What is right is not always what is popular.'

Carnie nodded. In the darkness. In reverence.

'To recognize evil and do nothing about it makes cowards of us all. This country is drowning in drugs, illicit sex, perversion, greed and corruption. And this evil continues to exist for one good reason.' Talbot paused for dramatic effect. 'Because there are no consequences for doing evil. We are a nation aware of personal rights, but completely ignorant of our responsibilities. We have become a country under siege by "decibel journalism"; shout loud enough, get in someone's face enough, people eventually believe that what you're saying is true.

Or they become too afraid to call it a lie.

'There are those among us who are not used to shouting; not used to making waves. We've always played by the rules. But I am here to tell you that in America in 1994 the rules have changed. And if you don't know the new rules, you will perish, along with everything and everyone you love.'

The man nodded. Shifted in his chair. And set down his bottle of beer.

Right next to his .357 Magnum.

ONE

'What size do you wear?'

'Ten.'

'Let's see what we've got here . . .' Jeremy Dern started sifting through piles of sneakers for a pair with a size 10 tag on it. Strange job for a person such as himself, thought Jeremy, not for the first time. Cleanliness. He was like Felix in *The Odd Couple.* Hated dirt. Germs. Washed his hands every time he touched money. Friend of his, metaphysical type, said that was the reason he was always broke: 'You think money's dirty, therefore you push it away from you.'

Jeremy didn't buy all that psychic mumbo-jumbo. He was broke because he never went to college, never developed a skill and, at twenty-nine, had spent the past five years being kept by some guy who was married and kept insisting he was bisexual instead of gay.

'Do you have any preference?' said Jeremy, keeping his head turned away from the customer. He wrinkled his nose as the smell of used sneakers polluted his nasal cavity.

'Pardon?'

'Any special color?'

'No,' said the man.

Jeremy figured his compulsiveness had some kind of medical name, but he wasn't sure exactly what it was. He'd seen a program about it on 'Donahue'. Some female psychiatrist on the show had said there was a kind of compulsive disorder that made a person wash his hands after touching money, after touching anything he thought was dirty – even doorknobs. This compulsive behavior made the person go back home to check if he had turned off the oven, left the stereo on – weird shit like that. That was himself, thought Jeremy. So fuckin' what.

'Here we are,' said the clerk with a propped-up smile, as he stood with a pair of used Nikes, size 10, blue on white, no holes, half the tread intact.

'Thanks.'

'Don't you want to try them on?'

'No.'

Jeremy nodded. *He* wouldn't have wanted to try them on either.

The man paid with cash and took the shoes, the tattered gray winter coat, the soiled but serviceable gloves, and walked out of the Salvation Army store, a bell above the door ringing once as the door opened, then again as it closed.

Jeremy looked down at the crisp twenty in his hand. Strange, he thought. Crisp money. Crisp *twenty*. People who came into this store, who bought used clothes, they usually paid with cash, but in small bills. Money they'd received on the street – begging, doing odd jobs. The bills they offered were old, dirty, written-on. Maybe a crisp one-dollar bill.

Maybe even a crisp fiver during the Christmas holidays. But a crisp twenty? In April? A twenty was the kind of bill a person got at a bank. Most customers, especially Jeremy's customers, didn't go to banks, didn't have checking accounts.

Jeremy stuck the twenty in the drawer.

And went to the back to wash his hands.

'What size do you wear?'

'Ten.'

'You gonna to be wantin' poles, too?'

'Yeah.' Every year Matt Baldwin promised himself that he would go down the Convention Center in downtown Los Angeles for the big 'after-season' ski equipment sale. He never did, and he knew he probably never would.

Matt loved Tahoe. He hadn't skied around the world, but he had skied in California, Colorado and Tahoe. For him, Tahoe was the best. But it had less to do with geography than it had to do with people. Or experience.

Ten years ago he had spent a week in Toledo, Ohio, on business. Before he arrived, people from his office – Matt worked out of the FBI's West Coast office in West Los Angeles – had told him things like, 'I spent a month in Toledo one night.' Toledo had a bad reputation. He wasn't looking forward to going. By the time he stepped off the plane, he was hoping he could wrap up his business in about three or four hours.

But after a week in town, hanging out with the

people he met, he had a completely different impression of Toledo. A guy at the desk at the hotel where he was staying turned him on to a coffeehouse, The Morning Glory, where he met a number of people – several guitar-player/poets, dancers, comedians, writers, actors, students, and a lot of nice, and very real, people. When the week was up, he actually considered taking a week's vacation and staying on another seven days.

People. Experience. That's what really made you feel something about a place. Unless you were in the real estate business.

'That'll be eighteen dollars a day – skis, poles, boots.'

'Fine,' said Matt. He handed the goatee-bearded young man his American Express Gold Card. It wasn't a pride thing – the Gold Card. It was a question of keeping himself honest. He had to pay the Gold Card's balance every month. That way, things didn't get out of hand – as they had before.

'How long you want these for?'

'Three days.'

For three days the man had loitered around the security building in Chicago, two blocks from the Four Seasons. The last time he was in town he had eaten a late supper at an expensive restaurant there. Tonight he sipped cheap whiskey and huddled in a cardboard box, trying to take some of the sting out of the wind off Lake Michigan.

'Eh, Carnie . . . you done?' said Willie, a black man

with a salt-and-pepper beard. It was *his* box.

Carnie handed the old black man the nearly empty bottle of whiskey.

Willie wiped his mouth with a dirty glove, a glove without any fingers left in it, and smiled a yellow grin. 'So they call you Carnie 'cause you was with the Carnival, eh?'

'Sure,' said the man in the tattered gray coat, soiled gloves and Nike tennis shoes. He had made up the name. It seemed appropriate. There were several ways to spell the name – Carnie, Carney (like Lansford the baseball player) were two. But the man had not spelled his name. He was playing to a strictly phonetic-pronunciation crowd in this part of town. With a sense of painful irony, the man realized that spelling, in *most* parts of town, was one of the many disappearing fundamental tools with which he had grown up. The number *4* passed for the word *for*. *Nite* for *night*. And with a great number of the officially-educated, the word *ask* had to be spelled *aks* – phonetically, of course – as in 'I'd like to *aks* you a question'.

And when he brought up such things in mixed company, that is, with women and his more liberally-minded male friends, they said things like 'Communication is communication, regardless of how the word is spelled'. They said that he was making a mountain out of a molehill.

They didn't understand. They did not see the erosion. They just didn't *get* it.

'Can I ask you somethin' personal, man?'

Carnie just looked at the man hard for a moment.

Willie shrugged, and finished off the whiskey, which Carnie had bought and given to him as a sort of rent. Willie had told a friend that afternoon that he was 'leasing' his space to some crazy guy. Some guy who used to be with the carnival.

Carnie turned his attention back toward the entrance to 221 North Superior.

He looked at his watch: 10 p.m.

It wouldn't be long now.

Matt checked his watch: 10 p.m.

It wouldn't be long now.

'Have you ever seen these guys before?' asked Jim.

'I saw them twice, actually, but that was back in the Seventies,' said Matt.

Jim Sample and his attractive wife Amy sat in a booth with Matt at Caesar's Tahoe. The Moody Blues were playing. 'Nights In White Satin', 'Ride My Seesaw', 'Question of Balance'. Those Moody Blues. Matt remembered getting stoned in college and listening to the Moody Blues, figuring they had discovered a map to the cosmos, and the mind, and that, like some kind of treasure hunt, the meaning of life could be discerned from the lyrics. If you listened long enough. Got stoned enough.

Things changed. Matt stopped getting stoned, cut his hair, and joined the FBI. And the Moody Blues became a pop band that felt comfortable playing at Caesar's Palace.

When the drinks came, Matt grabbed the check

and raised his beer in a toast. 'Thanks, Jim,' he said.

Jim and Amy clinked glasses, and Jim said, 'You're welcome.'

'It's been great,' said Matt, setting down his beer glass. 'One more day.'

'Hate to go back.'

'All good things must end,' said Amy philosophically.

Matt didn't like to think of it like that. Things changed, but they didn't have to end.

The Moody Blues finished 'Nights In White Satin'. Matt remembered that the last time he saw the band he was so knocked out he couldn't move from his seat for nearly ten minutes after the concert ended.

Tonight he just got up and walked out before the lights came up.

The pizza delivery van pulled up in front of 221 North Superior. Carnie looked behind him and checked Willie. The man was curled up in the corner, head down, his hands wrapped around an empty whiskey bottle.

Carnie stepped out of the cardboard box, the wind blowing his hair as he staggered across Superior in the general direction of the pizza van. All the time, Carnie's peripheral vision took it all in. No one on the street. Just the pizza man. And Carnie.

'Hey, man, I ain't eat in two days.'

The pizza man turned to see the bum crossing the street. *Fuckin' bums. Shit, they know I've got change on me.* 'Fuck off, man.'

'C'mon, man. Don't be that way.'

The pizza man was around the front of his truck, when Carnie caught up with him.

'Look, man, I don't give money to—'

It happened in an instant. The pizza, which was inside a warmer, hit the street with a dull thud. The delivery man, who Carnie figured to be in his mid-twenties, heard a gurgling sound – heard it before he recognized it was coming from his own throat. By then, his world was turning black. The delivery man would live, but he would not be eating solid food for a few days.

Carnie caught the man as he fell and jerked him into a nearby alley.

In less than sixty seconds he emerged from the alley, wearing the delivery man's hat and coat. He scooped up the pizza from in front of the truck, and headed for the front door.

He stood under the security camera and pressed the buzzer. After a moment, he heard the door lock buzz open, and he walked into the lobby.

He watched the numbers in the elevator light, then go dim . . . light, then go dim. His heart was beating fast. Not from fear. Exhilaration.

The doors opened.

As he walked down the hall, he walked the walk of the righteous. Courage that came from the knowledge that God was with him. That he was, in fact, doing the right thing.

He pressed the bell next to the apartment door. He could hear loud music and voices coming from the other side. The man was not alone. Still, Carnie was not afraid.

The door opened and a Latin man in his twenties ushered Carnie inside. The music was rap. There were lines of white powder on the glass coffee table. No need to hide it from some fuckin' pizza lackey.

Four men: all Hispanic. Three women: two white, one Hispanic.

Arthur Camacho stood in one corner of the room, his arm around a blond. She wore a black dress that hugged her like a short cocoon. She was kissing him, her eyes dreamy and doped up. Camacho was smiling and sipping a beer.

Carnie set the pizza-warmer down on the table, and reached inside. When he withdrew the semi-automatic weapon with the silencer, two of the men had their backs to him. Carnie pulled the trigger and began spraying.

In less than ten seconds, six lives were extinguished. Camacho stood against the wall, untouched. Except by the fear which kept him frozen in place.

Carnie walked over to Camacho who started to raise his hand. Carnie grabbed Camacho's wrist with his left hand and leveraged Camacho painfully to his knees. Still holding Camacho by the wrist, Carnie kicked him twice, breaking several ribs on the right side of the man's chest. Then, planting his foot against the back of Camacho's neck, he pinned him to the floor.

'Whatchu doin', man?' screamed Camacho, blood

starting to trickle from his mouth.

'Taking out the garbage,' said Carnie.

Then he put four bullets into the back of Arthur Camacho's head.

Matt Baldwin sat on the hood of his Jeep Cherokee, picking his way through a blues progression in G on an old Martin guitar, looking up at the clear night sky above Heavenly Mountain. Earlier in the day he had skied to the top of Heavenly, from which, if you turned to your right, you would be skiing into Nevada. If you turned left, you came down the mountain in California. In late April the snow was wet and heavy, even at the top of the mountain. He had almost decided not to come, because he knew the conditions would probably be this way. But he'd had such a great time here in late January. Then Jim and Amy's two-bedroom time-share condo with a view of forever had suddenly become available and, well, there were more reasons to come than to stay at home.

While the skiing hadn't been as good as in January, he'd still had a great time. Jim liked to drink beer, play cards and talk loud. Matt liked that, too. But at times, without a companion, Matt felt like a fifth wheel.

Laurie, Matt's wife, had decided not to join him, even though when the trip was originally planned she had marked it on her calendar. And Jarod, his stepson, wanted to come, but he had finals and a ballgame.

Matt reached into the cooler and removed a cold bottle of Samuel Adams. He took a bite out of this 'barley sandwich' and breathed in a tank of clean air.

He started fingering a little slide country-rock on the Martin, and mumbled some lyrics to an old Blind Faith song. For a moment in time it was just the stars and the Silence – Silence with a capital S. The hum of the city died slowly. For the first two nights the Silence rang so loud in Matt's ears that he had felt as though he might get the bends – it wasn't easy going down this deep into Mother Earth. City sounds – cars honking, tires screeching, TVs blaring, boom-boxes thumping, trucks huffing and puffing, voices threatening – were white noise spewing from the perpetual-*emotion* machine called LA.

But the Silence . . . The Silence was like a giant heartbeat in the womb of the world: felt more than it was heard. As he stood on top of Heavenly, earlier that afternoon, he had felt connected to the mountain, the earth, the sky, even the stars . . . And when he went to sleep at night, the mighty engine of the universe hummed in his ears. Resonated in his heart. Pulled him like some invisible ebbing tide into a cosmic sea that seemed foreign, yet mysteriously familiar.

Matt was not normally given to such thoughts. In truth they were not so much thoughts as they were feelings. Even so, he knew the feelings would go away when he left the mountains and surfaced back into LA.

He leaned back against the windshield, looked up at the sky, and started playing a slide guitar version of the country blues song 'New York City'.

Matt usually got up by seven, regardless of when he finally went to sleep; which, last night, was a little after two. From his chair in the living room, where he sat drinking a cup of fresh-brewed coffee, he could see for about seventy miles.

Jim Sample gently opened the bedroom door and poked his balding red head outside. 'You up already?'

Matt decided not to answer the self-evident question. 'What's goin' on?'

'You wanted to see me spray that stuff on my head.'

'Yeah?'

'I'm ready.'

'Great. I'll get the camera for some before-and-afters.'

Ten minutes later, Amy was directing traffic. 'Put some papers down so it doesn't get on the furniture.' Matt put down the Sunday *San Francisco Chronicle* over the furniture immediately surrounding Jim, who sat on a kitchen chair in the middle of the living room.

'You ready? asked Amy.

Jim nodded.

Amy started spraying a reddish brown substance from a can onto Jim's head. In a couple of minutes, after the 'set spray' had been applied over the original spray, Jim was a new man. If not a new man, then a man with more 'hair' than before.

'So? What do you think?' asked Jim.

'Looks great, man,' said Matt.

'Well?' Jim looked to his wife for an official verdict.

Amy walked over to her husband, and looked down upon his head. 'It looks like you've got paint on your head.'

Jim looked up at his wife, his face turning the color of his hair. 'Does this mean I can't use this stuff?'

'No, honey. If you like the way it looks, wear it. But if you're planning to go out in public . . .'

Afterwards, coffee, strong coffee, was poured for everyone. Jim and Matt had Danish, and Amy munched on a blueberry muffin.

'. . . and in Chicago, police have no clues in the murder of Mexican gang leader Arthur Camacho . . .'

'Un-fucking-believable,' said Jim, looking at the TV, which was tuned to CNN. 'I heard about that guy two weeks ago. What a scumbag.'

'What?' said Matt, turning his attention to the TV.

'Yeah, that guy, Camacho. He was some kinda' hot shit two weeks ago. Killed a cop in Chicago. Cops had him dead to rights, but he got off on some technicality. Then he sold the rights to his story to some movie producer for fifty grand. He was on some talk show, laughin', talkin' about how the American dream was all wet. Yeah, he made that joke, and the host and the audience laughed their asses off.'

They all stared at the TV. At the bloody scene in Camacho's apartment. Arthur Camacho wasn't laughing anymore.

'I'll bet one of the dead cop's friends killed that guy,' said Amy.

'Who the fuck would blame him?' said Jim.

Matt found himself riveted to the screen. Not so much by what he saw, the lure of real-life death and fresh blood, but by what he did not see. There were no wailing mothers, wives or sisters. No outraged community leaders shouting into the cameras. In fact, the only on-camera interview was with the dead police officer's widow, who said that she believed in God. She was sure that God had done what the justice system had failed to do.

Matt knew that God had not pulled the trigger. Which did not mean that the person who actually pulled the trigger wouldn't say that God told him to do it.

In the late twentieth century, God got credit for more murders than Jack the Ripper.

As he continued to watch the story of Camacho's death unfold, and the reaction to it, Matt began to get an odd feeling in the pit of his stomach. It was that feeling people referred to when they said their 'gut' told them something or other. This was not the first story like this Matt had seen. He knew the mood in the country. Working for the FBI, he knew it up close and much more personally than most people.

But he didn't like to talk about it. His life was spent crawling through shit. Today he was on vacation. He had clear blue skies and a snow-covered mountain to lift him above it all.

For a while.

Today Heavenly was his only challenge.

Hell could wait until tomorrow.

TWO

Kyle Talbot sat drinking expensive Scotch in a dark corner of the working-class bar. Not only was he an on-air personality, he was also part-owner of WLVG, a Las Vegas radio station. For the past fifteen years and three marriages, Talbot had lived the life of a man whose appetite for the rewards of success had always outpaced his achievement. During that time he had flushed dozens of dreams down a seemingly bottomless toilet of last chances. Yet somehow he had survived.

'I wan' another drink,' said the blond.

'What?' said Talbot, as though being shaken out of a light sleep.

'I wan' another drink.'

Talbot snapped his fingers in the general direction of the bartender, then put up two fingers and made a circle.

'Sometimes I don't think you really respect me,' said Cassie. The blond. It seemed to her that she had forever – at least, since she was thirteen – been known as 'The Blond'. With a capital B that stood for boobs and that rhymed with . . .

'I *don't* respect you,' said Talbot, polishing off his Scotch.

Cassie wrinkled up her face like James Cagney

had just screwed a grapefruit onto the end of her nose.

'Don't look so hurt. What the hell do you think we're doing together?'

'I love you.'

'Is that so?'

'Yes,' said Cassie, giving it her best righteous pout.

'And that's what you tell your friends?'

'Of course.'

'Is that what you told Irene?'

The bartender delivered the drinks, and left.

'What do you mean?' said Cassie, her confidence melting like a candle in a firestorm.

Kyle initiated his Scotch and smiled. Cassie wasn't sure why he was smiling, but then, Kyle wasn't completely sure either.

'Irene told Buddy that you were with me because of my money and power – maybe he used the word influence,' added Kyle, juicing up the smile another notch.

'That's terrible.'

'What's terrible? That you said it, or that Irene told Buddy?'

'How dare you spy on me?' said Cassie.

That was all the answer Kyle needed, but he really didn't require any confirmation. And he wasn't angry.

'Neither of us respects the other. I think you're attractive and I love fucking you.'

'Well, I never . . .' said Cassie in a huff. But she would sooner finish her drink than that sentence.

'And you want me because I can pay the rent and

the car payment, and because people in Las Vegas know who I am. Big fish, little pond – but, hey, at least you're catching something, right?'

'I never thought of it like that before.'

'Yeah,' said Kyle, as he messengered some more Scotch to his long-suffering liver. 'Don't sweat it. Sex and money. People pretend like it's some kind of sin to get together with someone for sex or money. People do it all the time. They just give it other names.'

Cassie looked up from her white Zinfandel. Twenty-two years old, new car, her name on a one-year lease of a two-bedroom condo. Her mom and dad worked two jobs, sometimes two apiece, and they still lived in the same shithole on Cherry Street. They played by the rules. Always had. Probably would have the rules etched on their tombstones, thought Cassie bitterly, as she washed down a few memories with the blush wine.

Cassie had already learned that the rules didn't apply to her. Nature had kissed her and, for a time, her beauty would be a magnet attracting all the creature comforts her parents dreamed of but could never attain. Not through playing by the rules, they couldn't.

Even now, as she sat across the table from a man she greatly admired, but whom she did not love, she felt the palpable power of her sex. She had lied to this man. This influential man. He had caught her in that lie. Caught her saying that she was using him. Yet so powerful was the man's attraction to what lay between her legs, that he had dismissed the indiscretion philosophically, constructing a logic that made her actions sound understandable, almost admirable.

'Eh, Kyle!'

Kyle looked up and saw Ellis Handy coming toward him.

'I think I'll go to the powder room,' said Cassie. She stood, leaned over and kissed Kyle on the cheek, then disappeared down a flight of stairs before Handy arrived at the table.

Handy, who was Talbot's partner in the radio station, owned, among other things in Las Vegas, the mortgage on Talbot's house – a fact that Handy frequently brought up whenever the two men argued. But lately all was right with the world, mainly because their new talk-show format was going through the roof. *Top Forty* hadn't worked. *Easy Listening* had bombed. The worst was *All Sports*. But, after a shaky start, this talk radio format was starting to pay off.

Especially Talbot's show. Over the past six months, the local show had been picked up and syndicated to twelve national markets including Los Angeles, Chicago, Detroit, San Francisco, Atlanta and New York. Not Rush Limbaugh. Not yet, anyhow.

'Good show tonight.'

'Thanks. You wanna drink?'

'Sure, I'll have a beer.'

Kyle waved toward the bartender, who knew what to bring.

'So, you talk to that guy in Philadelphia tonight?'

'Yeah,' said Handy with a sigh. 'He's really excited about the show. He liked the tape, loved the press kit I sent him. And the reviews—'

'He's not on board.'

'Not yet, but soon. Just hang in there.'

'I've been hanging in there for fifteen fucking years.'

'But we're close this time, Kyle. I can feel it.'

'Yeah, that's exactly what you said when we changed from rock and roll to country and western.'

'This is different. We're really making money this time.'

'We need to make a lot of money, otherwise you and I are going to have to go out and get real jobs.'

At forty-five, Kyle had been around the track more times than Carl Lewis, and he knew that his options, like the years, were slipping by without much to show for it. Ironically, he was perfectly suited for his new job – conservative talk-show philosopher/host. He was frustrated with life, with work, with government, with politicians – President Souther in particular – with gay activists, feminist activists, environmental activists, activists of virtually every color and stripe. He believed the world needed fewer activists, or blame-mongers as he called them, and more real leaders who preached the gospel of personal responsibility. And he said so on his show every night.

The Kyle Talbot Show was a hit from the beginning. It had started as a local show, with less than twenty thousand listeners. But from the first night, he knew that he was hitting a nerve. And just by being himself. Not trying to be a DJ, faking being twenty-something hip, or putting a twang on every voice-over commercial, like he did during the station's country-and-western incarnation.

Now he was just telling it like it was. And the predominantly white, working-class audience ate it up. Someone was finally putting lyrics to their sad songs.

But Kyle was nervous. He knew that this would probably be his last shot. In fact, before the show had started turning a profit in syndication, he was looking into buying a fast-food franchise with his brother. With his brother's money, mostly.

Kyle knew it could all turn to shit overnight. Fads came and went. Conservative moods could turn moderate, or even liberal, given the proper circumstances – or improper circumstances, depending on your point of view. Kyle was betting things would get worse in this country before they got better. And if they stayed bad long enough, Kyle just might use the situation to get rich.

But he had to play his cards right. No mistakes. Not now. Build the syndication audience. Deliver for advertisers, schmooze at the conventions, maybe hire a PR guy. There was plenty of work to be done.

What he really needed was a miracle. Something to set him apart from the pack. Something to focus the national media on his show.

Kyle had long ago stopped counting on a miracle.

But, he kept reminding himself, that didn't mean it couldn't happen.

THREE

'A sex marathon?' Charlie Stratton's beer arm froze in midair. And it took a lot to stop that motion.

'Why the hell not?' said Jackie Baer.

Matt drank his beer, as he sat in the corner of the Brentwood Hamburger Hamlet, hoping that their conversation was not being overheard. Baer used to be with the FBI, until he quit to make his fortune. First, he opened a mud-wrestling emporium. Made a mint. Then he opened up a nude country-and-western bar in Texas, with the gimmick of shooting squirt gun rifles at naked women's crotches – the women being inside a Plexiglas cage. 'Shooting Beavers' was what he'd called the place.

Matt and Charlie had shaken their heads at that one, too. Jackie didn't care. He made another ton of money.

'I got the idea when I was running this marathon in San Diego,' said Jackie, his voice filled with a tone of enthusiasm akin to a minister sharing a heartfelt revelation with his flock. 'Endurance, health, great-looking bodies, cable sale – maybe the Playboy Channel. Whaddya think?'

Matt cocked his head, nodded, figured it was better that his old buddy didn't know what he really thought, and said, 'I dunno.'

Charlie's mug still hadn't made it to his mouth.

'I figure condom manufacturers could pick up the production costs. Great advertising. Hell, I could promote the shit out of this thing.' Jackie raised his hands as though holding a banner. 'The Great American Sex Marathon.'

'Could call it the Great American Fuckoff,' said Charlie after taking his swig of beer and becoming animated again.

'Ah, you're just jealous. This could be big. I mean, you think Geraldo wouldn't go for this in a big way? Fuckin'-A, he would. You start off with about a dozen great-looking couples, and the couple that's left at the end of . . . whatever, is the winner. Kind of a Tantric kinda thing, you know. Endurance.'

'Training for it sounds like fun,' said Charlie.

'Hell, Charlie, I didn't know you could still get it up. I heard . . . well, never mind.' Jackie smiled into his beer mug, and winked at Matt out of the corner of his eye.

'Asshole.'

Just then the big-screen TV near their table filled with the images of several body bags being carried out of a building and loaded into an ambulance. The news anchor was saying, 'And police have no clues in the execution-style murders of Arthur Camacho and his friends.'

'Not fucking likely to get any clues, either,' said Baer.

'What do you mean?' asked Matt, even though he knew.

'What the fuck do you think I mean? Guy kills a cop, makes a mint selling the story to the movies, he winds up dead like that . . .'

'Like what?'

'What's the matter with you? You been off the planet or something?'

'He's been in Tahoe,' said Stratton.

'Whatever. Whoever killed Camacho was a pro. Maybe even more than a pro.'

'You mean a cop?' said Matt.

'Makes sense to me. Which means they're never going to turn up anything. No time, no way, no how.'

'What about a public outcry?'

'You hear anything? I don't. This is a guy even his mother didn't like. The apartment was littered with so much cocaine, you needed snowshoes to get into the place.'

'What about his friends? They were innocent victims.'

'Innocent? The girls were hookers and his pals were all known drug dealers.'

'Sounds like the perfect set-up. Like someone wrote and directed the whole scenario.'

'Like I said, we're dealing with a pro here.'

'You said a cop. I don't know any cops who are professional killers,' said Matt, trying not to let his irritation get the best of him.

'I didn't say that. All I'm saying is that in a just cause, under the right circumstances, a cop might be the perfect assassin.'

'Not a good cop.'

'Hey, get off your fuckin' moral high horse, man. Two guys come into your house, one of them holds a gun to your head while the other one gets your daughter to give you head, then fucks her in front of you, there's nothin' the courts can do to those guys that'd ever make things right again.'

Matt didn't have a daughter, but he'd heard this argument, or arguments like it, many times before.

'Tell you what, pally,' said Baer. 'Some ass-wipe blows you away, then tries to sell your bones to some fuckin' Hollywood piece a' shit, I guarantee you the guy ain't gonna spend that money.'

'I'll drink to that,' said Stratton, who would drink to anything, including the sound of himself breathing.

'To what?' asked Matt.

'Camaraderie.'

The three friends clinked mugs and drank.

'So, what the hell's goin' on with you and Laura?' asked Baer, purposely changing the subject.

'Laur*ie*,' said Stratton. 'She's corrected me on a number of occasions.'

'She's fine,' said Matt.

'Tell her I said hello.'

'Sure.'

'I don't think she likes me much.'

'She doesn't know you.' But Matt knew that Laurie *didn't* like Baer. Ever since he asked her if she wanted to pick up some extra money hot-oil wrestling at one of his clubs. Matt figured Baer got off lucky with a hateful look.

''Nother round?' said Baer. He didn't bother looking at Stratton, who started chugging his beer so that when the next beer was delivered it didn't look like he was drinking with both hands.

'Nah, I gotta go,' said Matt. He tossed a five on the table, said goodbye to Fran, the manager, and left.

Carnie cut into the skin, and the blood started running . . .

Into the saucepan.

He squeezed the last drop of red juice out of the blood orange. The shallots, salt and pepper and dry Sauternes were already in the pan. While it cooked, he ran a rolling pin over the blanched almonds, grinding them into fine crumbs. Then he put the crumbs on a tray, which he stuck into the 400-degree pre-heated oven.

When the almonds were ready, he dipped the halibut filet, one side only, into the flour, the beaten egg, and, finally, into the roasted almond crumbs. Then he put the filet into a skillet sizzling with butter and vegetable oil. One minute on each side. When that was done, he put the skillet into the oven for five minutes.

While the halibut cooked in the oven, Carnie checked the saucepan on the stove. The mixture had been reduced to a thick sauce. The last act was to stir in a stick of softened sweet butter.

A few minutes later, Carnie sat down in his dark living room, hit the button on his remote control for the radio, AM, and set down the remote. He picked up the small half-pitcher from the tray, and poured the blood-red sauce onto the breaded halibut. *Beurre blood.* Blood-orange sauce. That's what the French called it.

Carnie called it delicious.

A commercial came on the radio. Some guy was talking about 'Know your rights. You may be entitled to compensation from your employer'. Carnie tuned out the rest of it. He knew it by heart.

Rights. Fuckin' rights! People knew their rights, but they didn't have a clue what their responsibilities were. Carnie knew it from both ends. Usually the short end. Rights . . . He had fought for them in Viet Nam and in the United States. He'd been wounded twice in 'Nam, twice in New York, and once in Los Angeles. In every battle in Viet Nam he was fighting for the same thing – America. He wasn't some shit-kicking idiot with straw sticking out from under his hat. No, the threat to America had been real, then.

And it was real today.

In fact, Carnie believed the threat was more real today than ever. In the old days the enemy had a face, and it was always different from his. Today, the evil was more insidious. It spoke his language, sometimes – not always – looked like him, and it walked the streets of every city in the country.

Carnie was a soldier in the real war. More people were murdered each weekend in five major cities – forget the whole country – than in the last major war in the desert.

Murdered! Not killed by cars, cancer, or by accident.

Murdered!

The enemy walked among us, thought Carnie, even though they wore no uniforms. Yet they were destroying this country more efficiently than any external enemy he had ever encountered.

But a growing number of people were beginning to stand up; to draw a line in the . . . dirt, in the *scum* that had begun to pollute this country, like filth collecting in stagnant water.

The halibut was succulent.

People sat in their living rooms watching the violence spill into their lives through a TV screen. For a time, the garbage had threatened to drown Carnie. Night after night the bodies piled up, the ranting and raving ratcheting higher and higher. Volume. Impact. What you said mattered less than how loudly you said it. It seemed to Carnie that the planet was spinning out of control.

The phone rang and Carnie picked it up, 'Hello.'

'Hi,' said the woman with a gravely, sexy voice. She didn't talk that way on purpose – not the gravely part anyhow. She got *that* from genes and from smoking three packs of Camel cigarettes a day until she was thirty. The sexy part, well, that was on purpose. With certain people. With Carnie.

'Hi.'

'When'd you get back?'

'Few hours ago.'

'Everything okay?'

'Everything's fine.'

'You busy?'

'I'm eating.'

'I mean later.'

'Whatcha got in mind?'

'A little line dancing over at the Neon Corral.'

Carnie's first instinct was to say no. He was tired. He was always tired after . . . After it was over. But he said, 'What time?'

'I'm easy.'

'Ain't that the truth,' said Carnie goodnaturedly. He did not mean any disrespect.

'Be nice.'

'I am. Come by around nine-thirty.'

'See ya.'

'You look good, baby,' cooed Annie.

Lots of people thought Carnie looked like Dwight Yoakam, the country and western singer. An older Dwight Yoakam. Tonight Carnie had on his banana-colored Frye boots, a pair of tight jeans, a blue and black checked work shirt, a Stetson cowboy hat, and a light brown leather 'long rider' coat. The Fryes were ten years old, his third pair in twenty years; the hat was eight years old, a present from his father. The only real affectation was the long rider coat. But he had the look and the swagger to pull it off without looking like a wannabe.

Carnie had grown up blue-collar, working class. His father Arthur – sometimes known as Artie, but nobody called him Art – worked climbing poles for

Kentucky Bell Telephone. Tall and lanky, quiet until he'd had a few beers, or when the Cincinnati Reds or Bengals were involved, Artie was proud of his son. Proud when his son quarterbacked Lexington High to the state championship. Proud when his son came back with two purple hearts from Viet Nam. Proud when his son chose the profession he did because he wanted to make a difference in a world that desperately needed people to care about making a difference.

Artie had been in the ground two years now, and Carnie still missed talking to him.

Carnie liked this place. It was a West Los Angeles vision of what a shit-kicking, line-dancing, two-stepping, beer-drinking, Stetson-wearing bar ought to look like. Carnie knew what the *real* thing looked like, smelled like, fought like and drank like. The Neon Corral wasn't it. It wasn't close. But it was close enough for a Monday night when Kentucky was too far away.

'I missed you,' said Annie.

'Yeah?' he said with a smile, as he healed his dry throat with a dose of Bud Dry. He knew she would have rather he said that he missed her, too, but he also knew that she wasn't going to pout about it either. That was one of the reasons he liked her.

'Everything go okay?'

'Went fine.'

'Good, baby.' She didn't know much about the man, but she liked the feel of him. He was solid. A take-me-the-way-I-am-or-not-at-all kind of a guy.

Most men would be anything you wanted them to be just to get in your pants. That had been Annie's experience.

'You're lookin' mighty good yourself, darlin',' said Carnie, purposely moving the conversation away from matters he wished to remain private.

She brightened. 'Thanks.'

And she did look good. Annie Caine was a photographer for a west-coast publisher of nature books. She had first met Carnie here one night at the Neon Corral. They had talked and two-stepped together until the place closed. Even though she had suggested it, they had not gone back to her place. Not that night anyhow.

Before Annie started taking pictures, she had made a living on the other side of the camera. She had an eye for beautiful things. She thought Carnie was beautiful in a way she could never quite explain to him.

Carnie liked this place because it was full of noise, full of non-threatening laughter and music. Not that there wasn't an occasional fight or brawl, but Carnie was never threatened by that kind of violence. To him, bar fights were not threatening.

'You want to go to Arrowhead next weekend?'

'I don't think so,' said Carnie.

'Why not?'

'Business. Things are picking up.'

'That mean you'll be out of town again?'

'Probably.'

'Look, honey, I'd really like to go with you. I can

pay my own way, and you know I can keep myself occupied.'

'Nope. Ain't no place for you where I'm going.'

There would be no argument about it.

'You wanna dance?' said Carnie after a while.

Annie didn't answer. She just set down her beer, to mark her place, so that no one would take their table, and followed Carnie to the dance floor.

The dancers already there had formed a human merry-go-round, so Carnie and Annie got on and took a ride: two-stepping and shuffling to guitar and fiddle music that sounded more like Garth Brooks than Earl Scruggs.

For a moment the world was in balance, thought Carnie. Gone was the contentiousness of what had come to be considered everyday life. Here, amid the sights and sounds of country and western music, an attractive blond on his arm, Carnie was reminded of a better time. A time when he looked out toward the future and saw only hope and prosperity. And in that vision was the cohesive principle of justice. A belief that truth would always, eventually, triumph.

Carnie noticed a black man at the bar, and the little red light went on. Not many blacks in the Neon Corral. Not that many rednecks either. But there were a lot more rednecks than blacks.

'What's wrong?' shouted Annie over the music.

'Nothin'. Let's dance!' he shouted back.

It took nearly an hour to happen. If Carnie was

surprised about anything, it was that it had taken so long.

For the trouble to start.

Annie and Carnie turned their heads toward the sound of people yelling, and a bar stool hitting the ground. Carnie stood and put his arm on Annie's shoulder, a silent instruction for her to stay put.

'You fuckin' piece a' black shit!' screamed the white man.

'Back off, man!' warned the black man.

The blond who had been dancing with the black man now hid behind him.

'What's goin' on here?' demanded Carnie, his voice comfortable with authority. The swagger, the demeanor, the look: he wore it like a tailored suit.

'I don't like seein' no black man dancin' with a white girl. 'Specially a *young* white girl,' sneered the white man.

'She's with me. I brought her.'

'She should be with her own kind,' spat the white man.

'He's right about that,' said Carnie to the black man, who grew physically more tense at that remark.

The white man smiled at Carnie and said, 'Let's kick his motherfuckin' ass back to South Central.'

The white man made a move.

Carnie stuck out his arm and caught him in the chest, stopping him cold. The white man looked more stunned than physically hurt.

'What the fuck . . . ?'

'Back off,' said Carnie. Without the hint of a smile.

'I'm gonna fuck him up.'

'You're gonna have to go through me first.'

The white man tried to think of something to say. No words – no words he could back up – came to mind. Finally, he just walked away, muttering idle threats.

'Thanks,' said the black man.

'You better leave,' replied Carnie.

'But I—'

'And don't come back. I don't like you. I'm not your friend. I'm not your protector. But a man doesn't deserve to die for not using common sense.'

'What do you mean?'

'A black man doesn't go into a redneck bar with a white woman. Just like a white man doesn't walk around in certain parts of this city at night.'

'But it shouldn't—'

'I'm not talking about what should or shouldn't be. I'm talking about what *is*.'

The music had stopped, a hundred people in the bar were silent, as though waiting for another shoe to fall.

'I'm not going to be intimidated into not coming back here,' said the black man, as he took his girlfriend's hand and started toward the door.

'You know what they say about people who make the same mistake twice?'

The crowd made a path for the black man and the blond as they left the club.

The music picked up again, and people started dancing.

The white man who had initiated the confrontation looked at Carnie curiously. 'I don't know whether you're a hero or an asshole.'

Carnie didn't bother to answer. He could not have cared less what the man thought about him.

When Carnie went back and sat down with Annie, there were three beers lined up in front of him,

'Everybody wants to buy you a beer.'

'Not everybody,' said Carnie, as he sipped one.

'You were incredible. So brave.'

'Not really. I just don't have anything left to lose.'

'That may be why you're dangerous, but that isn't why you went over there in the first place.'

Carnie didn't say anything.

'Is it?'

'No.'

'Then why?'

After another swig of beer – and a silent toast to a man named Artie – Carnie said, 'I guess I still believe I can make a difference.'

FOUR

'Hi,' said Laurie. She looked up from the couch where she sat surrounded by folders and legal tablets.

'Hi.'

'You have a good time in Tahoe?'

'Yeah, it was fun. Jim and Amy said to say hello.'

'That's nice. You eat yet?'

'I'm fine. I'll make myself a snack.'

Matt leaned down to kiss his wife, and she kissed him back perfunctorily. He walked into the kitchen, removed a Samuel Adams beer from the fridge, then came back into the living room.

Laurie's Brentwood townhouse – Matt had moved in after they were married – had cost her $275,000 back when $275,000 was real money. She had been able to buy the place with her half of the sale of the Encino Hills house she had shared with her former husband.

She had met her ex-husband sixteen years ago, when they were both in high school. She had helped put him through law school, then he had helped put *her* through law school. And, of course, there had been their son, Jarod.

As well as a string of mistresses her husband had found to pass the time, while she struggled to catch up with his success amidst fading opportunities in the overcrowded corridors of the legal profession in late twentieth-century Los Angeles.

The living room had a fake fireplace, a real Persian rug, a couch and matching chair, a new CD stack, a side table on which was prominently displayed a photograph of Laurie's late grandfather riding an ostrich, and a three-foot-high wooden replica of a valet, hand extended. Its palm served as a place to rest a drink – which Matt did as he sat down in the stuffed burgundy chair.

'You look tired,' said Matt.

'I am. This case is driving me crazy.'

Matt didn't ask. Just took a drink of his Samuel Adams and waited.

'Every day it's the same old shit. My client's mother gets tanked up and holds court outside the courtroom, saying that the trial is a racist plot against her son and that she'd sooner kill herself than accept a plea bargain. A *racist* plot!' said Laurie incredulously. 'Her son killed another black kid at a funeral. Put a gun to the victim's head and blew the kid's brains all over the casket. And it's on video tape! I'm trying to save her son from the death penalty, and she's trying to get him on a talk-show.' Laurie sighed and shook her head in frustration. 'Sometimes . . . sometimes I just don't know what I'm doing anymore.'

'Most people don't know what they're doing.'

'What do you mean?'

'Don't worry about it. Just do the best you can.'

'I wonder what that *is* anymore. Sometimes I think I'm on the wrong side.'

'Everyone's entitled to a competent defense. Innocent until proven guilty, and all that. That's what separates us from other societies.'

'Our society's in ruin,' said Laurie with a cynical smile. 'Or haven't you been watching TV lately?'

'I guess a lot's happened since I went skiing,' said Matt with a smile. 'So, what do you wanna do?'

'What do I want to do, or what am I going to do?'

'Where have I heard this before?'

'Don't give me a hard time, okay? I'm really busy here.'

Matt sighed. Suddenly it was all back to square one. 'I thought maybe a few days apart . . .'

'Would what?'

'I don't know. Maybe . . .'

'Maybe what?'

Matt looked his wife in the eye. 'Two weeks ago you said you needed some space. From experience, I know that's just another bullshit term for "I want outta here".'

Laurie ran her fingers through her hair. She looked weary. 'Don't read something into this that isn't there. We're both just burning the candle at both ends.'

'Now you're speaking in clichés. Maybe I just better pack.' Matt put his beer to work, then set it back on the wooden valet. 'Are you happy?'

Laurie looked at her husband as though he had just asked her some esoteric, unanswerable question. 'That isn't the point.'

'Isn't it?'

'No, it isn't. People aren't happy twenty-four hours a day, seven days a week. That doesn't mean they ought to give up.'

Matt nodded. He recalled seeing a very famous actor on cable talking about the joys of reading and enjoying Shakespeare. He concluded his message by saying that 'If it isn't fun, it isn't worth doing'. Matt had heard that theory many times over the past twenty-five years. He'd learned it when he was in college in Ohio and even believed it for many years.

Then one day he realized that he had not always believed this and, in fact, no longer believed it. Even though it sounded so . . . politically correct, with just the slightest scrutiny, the theory was revealed to be utterly inane. Most, if not all, of the things that meant something to Matt, he had usually achieved at the expense of long hard hours and sacrifice.

He recalled a conversation with the woman he had lived with just before he married Laurie. Near the end of their relationship, Sarah had said, 'If we have to work so hard on our relationship, then it must not be worth it.' She had also said that she wanted 'space'.

When they got together for lunch a couple of years later, Sarah admitted that she had been having an affair at the time. Matt thought it funny the words people used to fill in the blank when they couldn't tell the truth.

'You happy half the time?' he said.

'What do you mean?'

'I mean, nobody's happy *all* the time. You happy *half* the time?'

'I don't know. I never thought about it.'

'Friend of mine, a psychologist works for the Bureau, he has this theory. Says nobody's happy one hundred per cent of the time. He says that if a couple is happy more than seventy per cent of the time, then it's a good marriage.'

'Seventy? Why not seventy-five?' said Laurie skeptically.

'You can quibble about numbers, but you know what I'm saying. A person might not know the difference between seventy and seventy-five, but they know the difference between ten and seventy.'

Laurie shook her head and turned away. 'I don't think about marriage like that. Lots of people aren't happy. They still . . .'

'What? Stay together? Is there something admirable in that? Do they give out gold watches for marital longevity?'

'Maybe they ought to.'

'We're not trying to change the world. We're talking about you and me and Jarod.'

'Don't bring him into this. He's not your child. You're under no obligation to stay with me because of him.'

Matt sighed and shook his head slightly. 'I don't know whether you said that to make me feel good . . . or to make me feel really bad.'

'What's going on here?'

'I don't know,' said Matt. 'Maybe I'm just trying to save our marriage.'

'Maybe it doesn't need to be saved.'

'You tell me.'

Laurie looked at her husband. Her husband of seven years. She knew that he loved her. But, for the first time in their relationship, they were both questioning whether or not loving each other was going to be enough. Over the past year or so they had grown apart. Sex had been less frequent and less passionate. Both their jobs seemed thankless, and both mainlined society's desperation like junkies sitting on a mountain of smack. It seemed like it would never end and, like a horizon, you could never see beyond it.

Sometimes she thought their jobs and their commitment to those jobs would bury them. Or, at least, their marriage.

'I really think you're making something out of nothing,' said Laurie finally.

'You think so?'

Silence.

'I've got to work on this motion,' Laurie said.

'Right. Guess I'll turn in. I'm kinda tired.'

'Skiing can do that to you.'

'Maybe next time you can join us.'

'You know I'm not much of a skier.'

Matt thought about telling her that wasn't the point. But he figured she probably already knew, and he was done arguing for the night. Done trying to capture the *real* truth – whatever the fuck that was these days. He loved Laurie and he believed, wanted, needed to believe she loved him.

That was enough. For tonight.

But he knew that it would not be enough for tomorrow.

FIVE

'Well, at least you didn't break your leg,' said Sam Johnstone. He was a fireplug of a man, with a flat-top and a solid gut that extended amply over his belt. It was a gut that could still take a punch on a drunken dare, and hold up better than most. Johnstone was often told that he looked a lot like Mickey Spillane, the mystery writer, in the old Lite Beer commercials. He was not particularly interested in skiing.

'Skiing's fun, Sam. You oughta try it sometime.'

'Yeah.'

Sam threw a file across the desk toward Matt.

Matt picked it up and opened it. Inside were newspaper clippings: 'MAN CONVICTED OF RAPING AND MAIMING YOUNG GIRL IS MURDERED.' He scanned the article. William Rascone, an itinerant electrician, was sentenced to thirty-years-to-life in prison for raping a seven-year-old girl, hacking off her legs with an axe, and leaving her in a ditch to die. Because of his model behavior in prison, plus the fact that he had not actually murdered the girl, he was released after serving slightly less than eight years. According to the file, someone figured that wasn't enough. Rascone's hacked-up body was found in a ditch just outside Bellevue, Washington, where Rascone had moved after his release from prison. Police said they had no suspects. When asked by a reporter if there was anyone who would want Rascone dead, an unidentified official said, 'Everyone.'

Another clipping read 'GANG LEADER MURDERED BY DRUG OVERDOSE.' Artimus Carlisle, a Dallas drug dealer and gang leader, was found in an alley, a syringe sticking out of his arm, which was filled with 'enough heroin to kill a Brahma bull,' the coroner said. The article went on to describe how Artimus Carlisle had recently gained nationwide notoriety when a local woman went on TV to call attention to the drug problem in her neighborhood. She had allowed a television crew to videotape through her window, capturing drug deals and prostitution taking place. The TV station did little to conceal the woman's identity, even though she had requested anonymity. In fact, it was very easy to figure out the house where the camera had been located from the video later broadcast.

Two weeks later, the same woman's house was firebombed and she was burned to death. No arrests were made, though it was clear who was responsible. Not only had the gang taken out the 'troublemaker', but the very fact that the police made no arrests terrified other neighbors into silence. Within a month the neighborhood was back to normal: normal meaning that drugs, gangs and prostitutes ruled the streets.

However, all that had changed a couple of weeks ago. Artimus Carlisle's murder provided a tonic to a neighborhood paralyzed with fear. No one stood up to take credit for Carlisle's death – no one wanted to go to jail – but it was generally believed that one neighbor, perhaps a couple of neighbors, had decided to take matters into their own hands. This act of violence had encouraged other neighbors to stand up against the suddenly vulnerable gangs. One gang member was even quoted saying, 'We never figured they'd do somethin' like that. Scary shit, man.'

'Okay,' said Matt, closing the file and putting it back on the desk. It contained more clippings, but he had the gist of it. 'So people are fighting back.'

Johnstone shook his head and poured himself a glass of water from the silver pitcher his wife had given him two Christmasses ago. 'I don't think so.'

'Your "little man" acting up again?' said Matt, referring to the nickname Johnstone had given to his own intuition. Johnstone had started referring to it thus after watching the film '*Double Indemnity*' one weekend, in which Edward G. Robinson, ferreting out insurance fraud, referred to his intuition as 'my little man'.

'Big time. And it's not just *my* little man. Something's going on, Matt.'

'What are you talking about, exactly?'

'Vigilantism.'

'Nothing new about that, Sam. Frankly, I'm surprised we don't see a lot more of it. The cops can't protect people anymore, and everyone knows it.'

'There's a difference between protecting your family in your home and going out to commit murder.

Self-defense has always been legal.'

'So, where are you going with this?'

'I don't think this is the work of vigilantes.'

'But you just said—'

'I think it's the work of *one* vigilante.'

'Then he's all over the place, literally. He's in Washington, Dallas . . . I don't know,' said Matt, shaking his head.

'Don't you think it's strange that in each case the police have come up empty? No suspects, no arrests?'

'Maybe they're not looking too hard. Frankly, in these particular cases I can understand that.'

'Maybe there's no evidence for them to find.'

'What do you mean?'

'I mean maybe somebody just figured out the perfect, absolutely-fucking-perfect crime. Maybe he doesn't live in the same part of the country as his target. Maybe he knows the local cops will never find any connection between himself and the victim. And maybe they're not going to try that hard, anyhow.'

'Pretty smart.'

'More than smart, Matt. He's good, real good. You don't travel across the country, kill somebody, and get away with it time after time without knowing what the fuck you're doing.'

'What are you getting at?'

'What I'm getting at is this.' Johnstone paused for emphasis. 'I think the guy we're looking for is . . . one of us.'

'FBI?' said Matt incredulously.

'Not necessarily. But law enforcement. He knows what to do, and what not to do. He can get in and get out without being seen. He knows surveillance, electronics, disguises, paper trails, weapons.'

'This is all conjecture.'

'Yes and no.' Johnstone leaned forward on his elbows. 'You and I are not having this conversation.'

'Officially.'

'Exactly. As you know, I was in DC last week. One night I had dinner with the Director. He's very concerned about all this.'

'The file?'

'He's concerned about what it means.'

'And just what does it mean?'

'If we're wrong, nothing. If we're right, and we don't do something about it, it could mean the beginning of the end of law and order in this country.'

'Maybe you're overreacting a little. You said that when Souther was elected President.'

'Maybe. In any case, the Director wants us to find out.'

'Don't tell me – my name just happened to come up.'

'You're qualified. Best qualified, for my money. Serial killer expert. Eighteen years with the Bureau. You're as street-smart as they come. We want you—'

'Who's we?'

'All I can say is that persons at the highest level of law enforcement are in on this decision.'

'This is the plausible deniability part, right?'

'Look, Matt, you know the drill.'

He did. He knew exactly who Johnstone had spoken with, who was in on this. But just in case things went south, he could never name names to cut himself a deal. At certain levels, loyalty had a tendency to work more one way than the other.

'So I'll be on my own.' It was not a question.

'Not completely.' It was not an answer. 'Look, Matt, the Bureau will be here for you, but we don't want the public to put this thing together. Right now, people are chalking up this rash of seemingly disconnected vigilante incidents to "the mood in the country". If they found out it was the work of one man, they'd probably elect the fucking guy president. What we're trying to do is defuse the situation before it gets out of hand.'

'What do I say when I show up and some loyal-yokel sheriff tells me to fuck off?'

'Have him call here. It isn't like we're cutting you off. It's just that we don't want official Bureau involvement. We don't want it to get out that the FBI is looking for a vigilante who's executing America's most wanted.'

'So what am I supposed to tell them I'm doing there?'

'Be creative. Our only other option is doing nothing. And, if we're right, sooner or later someone's going to put it all together, anyhow.'

'One more thing.'

Johnstone shifted in his chair. He knew what was coming.

'You want me to bring this guy in?'

After a moment Johnstone leaned back in his chair and said, 'If you can.'

'I see,' said Matt, nodding. In fact the last thing Johnstone wanted was for Matt to bring this guy in. 'What if I say no?'

'You won't.'

'Why do you say that?'

'I know you, Matt. For as cynical as people think you are, you want this guy as bad as we do. And for the same reasons.'

'I'll let you know,' said Matt. He stood and headed for the door.

'When?'

'I've got to talk it over with Laurie.'

'Absolutely not.'

'If you know me as well as you think you do, you know I won't do it any other way. Don't worry, I won't tell her everything.'

Johnstone sighed and gazed at Matt. He thought about giving him the speech – the need-to-know, plausible deniability speech – but he knew Matt wouldn't buy it. Matt would *do* it, but Johnstone knew that he would do it on his own terms or not at all. And Johnstone wanted Matt, wanted him badly. He genuinely felt that Matt Baldwin was the best person in the Bureau to handle this case.

'Tomorrow?' said Johnstone finally.

'Maybe,' said Matt, and he walked out of Johnstone's office.

Johnstone picked up his phone and dialed an

unlisted number in Washington, DC. It was answered by a man – not by his secretary.

'I think he's in,' said Johnstone.

'I feel very uncomfortable about all this.'

'All what? We haven't done anything.'

'Not yet.'

'Look, I don't want to put any pressure on you.'

'Really?' said Laurie sarcastically.

'I don't want you to feel guilty,' said the man. 'I want it to be good, special.'

'You want what to be good?'

'The lovemaking.'

'You mean the sex.'

'Laurie, if this upsets you, I understand—'

'You damned well better. I've never done anything like this before. I feel . . . I don't know, like I'm losing control.'

'Sometimes that's good. You know, most people think they're in control when they're really not.'

'Spare me the soft-headed psychobabble. Maybe I don't know when I'm *in* control, but I sure as hell know when I'm not.'

'How does it make you feel – not being in control?'

Laurie shook her head and picked up her glass of wine. She sighed and drank some cheap Chardonnay. 'It's frightening.'

'And exciting.'

'It is exciting, Frank. You're exciting. But that's not surprising. The big difference is that *you've* got nothing to lose.'

'Is that so? What about my heart? Odds are, you're not going to end up with me. Even if you leave your husband.'

Laurie set down her glass and looked the man hard in the eye. 'Don't ever try to con me, Frank.'

'But I—'

'Save it. That might work on the twenty-year-old secretaries in the office, but I deal with professional liars five days a week.'

'Are you calling me a liar?'

'You were trying to manipulate me. Maybe I can't stop what I'm doing, but at least I'm aware of what I'm doing.'

'Tell me. I'd really like to know.'

'You know exactly what I'm doing here, Frank. Matt and I are having problems. We talk around things, but we don't deal with the core of what's wrong. You listen, you're attentive, you're attractive, you want to get in my pants, you're younger than I am . . . It's all very flattering and I'm vulnerable.'

'I don't want to take ad—'

'Don't even say it, Frank. Say what you mean.'

'I want to fuck you real bad.'

'See how refreshing honesty can be?' Laurie looked at her watch. 'I gotta go.'

Frank reached over and touched Laurie's hand. 'When will I see you again?'

'I'll call you.'

She stood and walked out of the restaurant.

Frank watched her as she walked away. How could anyone let that get away, he thought.

* * *

'So, are you going to do it?' asked Laurie.

'I think so,' said Matt. He had told her enough for her to understand the time commitment involved, without telling her exactly what he was going to be doing.

Matt had been out of town on extended stays more frequently over the past two years than ever before. However, he didn't mind that as much as he used to mind even small amounts of time away from Laurie and Jarod.

The past few years had taken their toll on the couple. They each had grown – unfortunately not in the same direction. Something was missing.

Passion.

They had both wondered aloud, and in the silent darkness before falling asleep, where that passion had gone, and whether they were demanding too much of their relationship. Was this the way it was with all relationships after a while? Even the good ones?

Matt knew that Laurie had fallen in love with him because of his passion. His passion for his work, his passion for music, for life and, most of all, his passion for her. He could not get enough of her.

A year ago, Matt and Laurie had gone to see a marriage counselor, a woman, who had told them to 'feel good about your fantasies. Feel free to express them. Together'.

Matt and Laurie had written down, separately and secretly, their top three fantasies: the mental-image scenarios that *really* got them hot. The marriage counselor had told them: 'Declare a week of passion and fantasy. You deserve it.'

Each night for six nights, Matt and Laurie, on alternate nights, revealed one fantasy which – the counselor had predicted – would arouse the other partner.

It turned out to be an amazing week. Lots of sex. Lots of candles and wine. But in the clear light of day it became obvious that all of the fantasies involved other people.

Eventually, about a month later, the new-found sexual euphoria wore off. Matt came to a conclusion: fantasy was good. But passion was better.

'When do you have to decide?'

'Tomorrow.'

Laurie nodded. 'Do what you think is best,' she said. Which was a lot like saying nothing.

But then, thought Matt, people often said such things when there was nothing left to say.

The door opened and Jarod walked in, carrying a large blue Nike bag. He was dressed in gray sweats, black Reebok basketball shoes, and a sweaty blue-and-white New York Yankee shirt. Matt had given him the jersey with Jim Abbott's number on it.

'Hi,' he said, and tossed his bag on the foyer floor.

'Laundry night,' said Laurie. She stood, kissed her son on the forehead, and started up the stairs. 'I'm going to be up till two or three. You two have a good time.' And with that she disappeared up the staircase as though ascending into a private realm. A place

Matt could not go. A place Laurie was heading to more often now.

Jarod went into the kitchen, came back with a Diet Pepsi, and slumped down in a chair opposite Matt.

'How's it going?'

'Coach worked our asses off tonight.'

Matt smiled, remembering. Remembering a time when *his* biggest problem was a baseball game. Sure, there had been parental and peer pressure. At the time, the week of any game had seemed like the most stressful week of his life.

But a week he would give anything to experience just one more time.

Jarod sipped his soft drink and looked at his stepfather. 'You okay?'

'Sure, why?'

'You don't look okay.'

'You ask too many questions.'

'My mom's a lawyer, my father's an FBI agent. What do you expect?'

Matt was struck by Jarod's use of the word *father*. Not stepfather. Matt had told Jarod that he realized he was *not* his father, and that he would not try to replace his real father except to the extent that Jarod wanted him to. Matt could not have loved Jarod more, had he been his own flesh and blood. He was a great kid, and the fact that Jarod used the word 'father' always made Matt feel good.

'So, are you okay?' repeated Jarod.

Several answers skittered through Matt's mind.

Some of them were acceptable; none of them was the truth. At fifteen years old, Jarod could tell a lie from the real thing. For the most part, anyhow. And Matt didn't want to lie. Still, he knew that he *would* lie to Jarod if it would shield Laurie. But Matt did not believe this to be such a case.

'No. I'm *not* okay. I'm going to be spending a little more time away from home for a while.'

'Because of your job?'

'Of course. What else?'

Silence. A considered silence. 'You're away for your job all the time . . . but you never usually say that you're going to be "spending a little more time away from home".'

'Let's not get caught up in semantics.'

Jarod shook his head. He wasn't smiling. 'This has nothing to do with words. I think I understand what you're saying.'

Matt knew that Jarod *thought* he knew what his stepfather was talking about. Kids never really knew for sure – just like juries never knew the *real* truth about any crime because they never actually saw the actions they were judging.

But Jarod was growing up as fast as he could. He knew about sex, but he didn't really understand his mother's relationship with Matt. He knew that Matt and his mother had been together for more than seven years. He knew that he loved his mother. He knew that now, after some time, he really did love Matt. But, lately, he wasn't really sure that Matt and his mother loved each other.

'Are you and my mom going to split up?'

'Why would you ask me such a question?'

Jarod shook his head and looked away. 'I dunno.'

Silence. They both knew why Jarod would ask such a question.

Matt made a decision. 'Look, your mother and I are going through something now . . .'

Jarod didn't ask what. At fifteen years old, living in Los Angeles, he had learned that part of the etiquette of communication was knowing what questions not to ask – and when.

Now was such a time.

'So where you goin'? Or is that a secret?'

'Not a secret. I just don't know yet.'

Jarod looked up at Matt, with sincere eyes lit with the kind of innocence that was usually dead these days by the time a person reached sixteen. 'You be back by Friday?'

'I'm going to try.'

Jarod nodded, looked away without trying to play to Matt's weakness. He understood. At least he was *trying*.

Silence – in that room. Outside there was the sound of traffic humming by on Barrington. The sound of metal wind-chimes clanging together on the patio.

But there was no sound from upstairs. Where a mother worked. A wife labored.

And a lover hid.

'I gotta take a shower,' said Jarod. He stood and walked upstairs.

In the silence Matt could hear Laurie's footsteps in the room above him. He could hear Jarod running the shower.

Matt sat alone until after midnight.

In the darkness.

Wondering when and by whom the rules had been changed.

SIX

Matt hadn't been to Chicago in about three years. When he was in Chicago he always stayed at a place called Stacey's. It wasn't the Four Seasons, but it was only a couple of blocks from there. Stacey's was a five-story hotel built in the Twenties. The original Stacey's great-grandson, Peter Stacey, ran the place now. The bar was a virtual cops-and-robbers Hall of Fame. There was at least a dozen pictures of Al Capone, and three-quarters of the photos were of cops past and present. There was even a picture of Dennis Farina, the Chicago cop turned actor. Peter Stacey liked cops, liked talking with cops.

The bar was all mahogany, no windows, always dark, always open – three hundred sixty-five days a year. During Matt's first visit there, Peter had given him the royal tour, attaching names to the faces in the photos, and pointing out bullet holes in the ceiling, one behind the bar, and two in the bar itself.

Today Matt sat in a corner by himself. He looked at his watch: 5 p.m. A man in a suit walked into the bar, looked around. Matt raised his hand and the man walked over to the table.

'Baldwin?' said the man as he sat down.

'Yeah.'

'Carlucci. Call me Chuck.'

Carlucci looked to be about fifty, thick face with jowls just starting to drag down a face that had probably looked chiseled most of its life. He still had a thick head of hair, although gray frosting was starting to show. He was a little over six feet tall, and under two hundred pounds – barely. He removed a beige trench coat and draped it over an unused chair at their table.

'Thanks for coming.'

'Did I have a choice?' Carlucci smiled quickly to take the edge off the words.

'You always have a choice, Chuck. Even with the FBI.'

Carlucci smiled. He didn't believe that, not completely, but there wasn't any point in arguing. 'I know why you're here.'

'Really?'

'The Camacho murder.'

'Why would you think that?'

Carlucci smiled again. 'Let's make a deal. Don't treat me like a moron, and I won't treat you like some asshole coming in here to piss all over my turf.'

Matt smiled. 'Sounds fair. But if I'm going to level with you, I need your word that it goes no further.'

'Okay.'

'We think that Camacho's murder is connected to other murders around the country.'

'Other vigilante-type murders?'

'Yes.'

Carlucci nodded. 'Makes sense. Camacho's murder was professional. Perfect.'

'So you already considered the possibility?'

'It crossed my mind,' said Carlucci, looking at Matt and trying not to smile.

'Tell me about it.'

'Not much to tell. Didn't surprise me that somebody whacked Camacho. He was scum, and he made the mistake of rubbing people's noses in it.'

'What do you mean by a mistake?'

'Things are changing in the Nineties. I don't have to tell you that.'

The bartender ducked under a slat in the bar and set a Scotch down in front of Carlucci. He hadn't ordered, but apparently at Stacey's he didn't have to.

'People know we can't protect them anymore. They're taking things into their own hands. It's natural. And the courts, some of them anyhow, are cooperating.'

'What do you mean?'

'In the old days, some guy comes into your house, you gotta kill the guy, shoot him *face-on*, otherwise he comes back and kills you. Or you went to jail if you shot him in the back – like it wasn't self-defense. Nowadays, you shoot somebody in your house, you walk. Period. Least that's what's happening here. And you know what?'

'What?'

'That's okay by me. Some guy comes into my house, it's a risk I want him to take seriously.'

'But that's different than going out, hunting someone down and killing him.'

'Some people need to be hunted down. Look, you and I both know that, once you toss out crimes of passion, most murderers and child molesters are going to kill or molest again. Let's say you happen to nail one of these sons-of-bitches. Who the hell knows how many lives you just saved?'

Carlucci took a drink.

Matt thought about asking him if his judgment was getting in the way of solving the case, but he decided it was not appropriate, and wouldn't improve his relationship with the detective.

Carlucci set down his drink. 'In case you're wondering, I still know my job. I've been busting my ass trying to find this fuckin' guy. You know why?'

'Why?'

'The guy's a pro. I don't like the feel of it. Some guy blows the head off some guy who raped and killed his seventeen-year-old daughter, I'd do what I could to look the other way. Hell, I might even give the guy instructions. But a pro? I don't like it.'

'Got any leads?'

'Not really.'

'Camacho killed a cop.' Matt just let it sit there.

'You're thinkin' it was another cop did it? Yeah, I know, I heard it all before.'

'If you found out that it was a cop, a cop you knew, what would you do?'

'I knew the cop Camacho killed. Not well – but I knew the fuckin' guy. And to answer your question, your *real* question, no, I wouldn't give him to you.' Carlucci smiled. 'But you already knew that.'

Matt didn't respond. There was no need.

'But I don't think it's a cop. Not a Chicago cop, anyhow. I'd have heard things. Frankly, if I thought that was the case, I wouldn't be sitting here now with you.'

Matt knew that was true. 'So what *do* you have?'

'The delivery man – but he didn't get a good look at the guy.'

'What else?'

'Photographs of seven dead people.'

'How'd he get in?'

'Posed as a pizza delivery guy,' said Carlucci with a straight face.

'And you told me that if I treated you right, you'd level with me!'

Carlucci tried not to smile. Covered it by taking a sip of Scotch. He set the glass down and said, 'We wondered about that. Obviously the killer had to know that Camacho was expecting a pizza.'

'Maybe he tapped the phones.'

'Maybe he had the guy under surveillance. Maybe Camacho had a pizza delivered every night.'

'Of course, you checked this with the pizza place?'

'Of course,' said Carlucci, taking pride, professional pride, in keeping pace with the big-fucking-deal FBI. 'They had delivered to that address before, but . . .'

'But?'

'Not for two weeks.'

'That doesn't play. Unless . . .'

'Unless he ordered a pizza from *someplace* every night.'

'Surveillance would give you that information.'

Matt knew there was another possibility, but it was not his job to tell Carlucci everything he knew – rather to get Carlucci to give him all he had.

'When can I come by and look at what you've got?'

'Anytime.'

'Tomorrow morning?'

'I get in at nine.'

'What will you tell your men?'

'About you?'

'You'll have to give them some explanation.'

'I don't know how they work things in the FBI, but here in Chicago, if I tell my guys to cooperate and not ask questions, that's what happens.'

'There will be speculation.'

'Can't stop a man from thinking. All I'm saying is that *I'm* the only one who knows why you're here. I gave you my word. That should be the end of it.'

Matt knew that was the end of the conversation.

Carlucci tossed down the remainder of the Scotch, stood and shook Matt's hand. 'See you tomorrow,' he said, and he turned to go.

A few minutes later Matt walked to the bartender and asked for the check. The bartender said it had already been taken care of. Matt nodded. He had not seen Carlucci pay, but he knew the tab was covered. One way or the other.

Matt went into the steak-and-potatoes restaurant next-door. He had eaten there before and, besides a generous cut of prime rib, the creamed spinach was what kept him coming back for more. That and the *real* drinks. Nothing out of a spray-gun or a box.

He seated himself at a corner table, where he ordered an Absolut vodka martini and a regular prime rib, medium rare. He had seen the large prime rib. Perhaps Dick Butkus could eat such a portion all by himself, but Matt knew that he could not.

As he sat drinking his martini, the radio was playing in the background. A talk-show host was saying, 'I have an item here, folks, that is going to break your heart . . .'

'. . . A woman from a little town just outside of Las Vegas is in jail tonight, charged with attempted murder,' said Kyle Talbot on the radio. 'Yesterday, Betty Womack walked into a courtroom and raised a gun toward a man on trial there, fired several shots, then was apprehended by guards before she could kill him. What's so bad about that, Kyle, you say? Well, let me tell you what's so bad about that.'

Carnie hit the volume button on the remote control, and the Garth Brooks song disappeared. He took a sip of beer and stared through the darkness at the stereo stack. Listened to the voice on the radio.

'She's a woman who looks a little like my sister. Probably looks a little like your sister, too. She's a mother who cares, really cares, about her children. Lotta people don't care about their children these days. But this is a woman who is willing to put her life on the line for her children. Not in some theoretical circumstance, but in real life. When she walked into that courtroom yesterday afternoon, she was willing to sacrifice her own life for the life of her child.'

Carnie sipped his beer and focused on Talbot's voice.

'Her husband had died in an accident five years ago. Two years ago, Betty met Angus Trent – in church,' said Talbot, almost spitting out the last word as though it tasted sour. 'Trent befriended Betty and became the local scoutmaster. Lots of dinners, lots of barbecues, lots of . . . trust between the two.

'And how did Trent repay that trust? According to charges filed against the man, Trent molested Betty's two sons. Both of them. Is this hysteria? Are these charges made by a woman scorned? No!' shouted Talbot dramatically. 'Trent had been arrested and convicted of child molestation before. Once? Twice? No, four times before. Four times!' Talbot played the dramatic pause. 'And yet the man was not only released to walk among law-abiding citizens, he was not required to make his prior record known to local authorities, and he was hired as a SCOUTMASTER!' screamed Talbot into his microphone.

Carnie took out a pen and paper from a drawer next to the chair in which he was sitting, and started making notes.

'Let me describe a tragedy to you, folks. If Betty Womack is convicted of attempted murder, she faces more time in jail than the child-molester would have if he had been convicted of molesting her children.

There's something wrong with that, people. Very wrong. You and I know that if Betty Womack believed that the justice system would deal effectively with the child-molester, if she believed that the system would protect her children, or at least hand down a *fair* punishment, she would not have felt that she needed to do what she did.

'But what is the alternative?' Silence. 'And we'll be back . . .'

Carnie hit the mute button as the commercial came on, picked up the phone and dialed a number.

'Delta Airlines,' said a voice on the other end of the line.

'I'd like to get some information on flights to Las Vegas.'

'What do you think?'

'Great show,' said Cassie, 'You really had me going.'

'I had myself going,' said Talbot, popping the cork on the bottle of a California Cabernet Sauvignon he had ready and waiting in his office. It was a ritual. End of the day. Making a decent buck. Drink a decent Cabernet. He deserved it. Of course, his dentist told him the Cabernet was turning his teeth red. So he had purchased, from the same dentist, a thousand-dollar whitening treatment. And charged it to the station. Big fucking deal.

'You want your mail?'

'No, you take care of it.'

'It's getting like . . .'

'Yes?'

'Like more than I can handle.' Cassie smiled widely.

'That's what I like to hear. You want some wine?'

'Sure.'

Talbot nodded, and poured some wine into a Styrofoam cup. 'Here.'

'Thanks,' said Cassie as she retrieved the cup.

Talbot poured himself some wine, tasted the rich Cabernet, and looked at Cassie, a beautiful blond half his age who would later, willingly and worshipfully, perform acts of sex upon him that his ex-wife used to refer to as 'perverted' when she could bring herself to speak of them at all. This was the good life, thought Talbot.

There was no therapy like success. He had worked all his life for this moment.

And he was willing to do anything now to make sure it didn't go away.

'How long will your husband be out of town?' asked Frank.

'I don't know. It doesn't make any difference. I'm with *you* tonight, and that's all that counts.'

'Not really.'

'What do you mean?' asked Laurie, pulling the covers up over her small, taut breasts.

'I mean that you're *not* with me tonight. Not really.'

Laurie sighed and sat up against the headboard. 'What are you trying to say?'

'I'm saying that you're not going to be here *all* night.'

'I've got to go home. I do have a son, you know,' she said irritably.

'I know. And you also have a husband. All I'm saying is that you're not really going to be with me all night. You'll be with me until you think it's time for you to go home and take care of your kid and wait for a call from your husband.'

Laurie threw off the sheet and started to get out of bed. Frank grabbed her by the arm and pulled her back.

'Don't pout,' he said.

'I'm not pouting.'

'You do that when you don't get what you want.'

'Do I . . . ?' It wasn't really a question. Laurie knew she acted that way. Matt had told her a hundred times. So had her first husband.

'Where is all this going, Laurie?'

'What do you mean?'

'You know what I mean. You're married. You want a roll in the hay with me every once in a while. What else is there?'

'What do you mean?' she repeated.

'Pretend I'm not stupid,' said Frank. 'I hope that isn't a real stretch for you. You've got a marriage and a son. On the surface, things don't look desperate. And then there's me. You come over here, we both get our oil changed.'

Silence.

'What more do you want?' said Laurie finally.

'I've thought about it – you and me together. But I try not to let myself think about it too long. It's not healthy.'

'Is that what you want? For us to get together?'

'I don't know.'

'Well, you damned well better figure it out. I never said I was going to leave my husband.'

'Do you still love him?'

'Yes, I do.'

'But you're *in* love with me. There's a difference.'

'You sound like a character in a bad romance novel. I have a good marriage, a son, a career and responsibilities. This is sex, pure and simple.'

'It's pure, all right, but it's not that simple. We're addicted to each other. You know it, and I know it.'

'Addictions aren't good things, or haven't you heard?'

'My only addiction is you.'

'All it takes is one.'

Laurie rushed into the house and picked up the phone. 'Hello,' she said.

'Hi, it's me.'

'How's Chicago?' She sat down on the couch and took off her earrings with her right hand.

'Just get home?' said Matt, ignoring her question.

'Yeah. Just walked in the door.' She didn't offer an explanation.

'I called earlier.'

Laurie looked at the answering machine. No messages. 'You didn't leave a message.'

'I just thought I'd call till I got hold of you. Or until I went to sleep.'

'It's two hours later there, right?'

'Yeah. Almost midnight.'

'It's not even ten here,' said Laurie, even though she knew Matt was aware of that. She was trying to make the point that she really wasn't late. Not *that* late, anyhow.

'So, how was your day?'

'Usual horseshit. I've got a meeting with my client's mother tomorrow. In the best of all worlds I could just tape her mouth shut for the next few weeks, and everything would be okay. But I don't think she's going to go for it. How about you? Getting anything done?'

'Still getting oriented. I talked with the chief of detectives today.'

'They always love to see the FBI,' said Laurie sarcastically.

'He's okay. We're not going steady, but I think he'll do what he can and keep his mouth shut.'

'I love it when you talk that way,' said Laurie, grinning in the dark. In spite of herself. In spite of the fact she still smelled of another man's body.

'Really?'

I really used to, she thought. But she said, 'Yeah,' adding quickly, 'Look, I've got to prepare for my meeting with Mrs Jenkins tomorrow morning.'

An awkward silence.

'Well, I really gotta go,' said Laurie.

'Okay.' After a slight hesitation, Matt said, 'Goodnight.'

'Goodnight.' Laurie put down the phone. Quickly.

When the door opened ten minutes later, Laurie jumped.

'Hi, mom,' said Jarod, tossing down his gym bag before closing and locking the door. 'How come you're sitting in the dark?'

'Matt just called.'

'How's he doing?'

'Okay, I guess.'

Jarod turned on a lamp and made to sit down in a chair opposite his mother.

'Put something down on the chair. You're soaking wet.'

Jarod took a dry towel out of his bag, laid it over the chair, and sat down.

'Does he think he'll be home for the game on Friday?'

'I don't know. I didn't ask him. You know he will if he can.'

'Yeah.' Jarod sat silent for a minute.

'Mom . . . ?'

'Yes?'

'I've noticed that things between you and Dad have been – I don't know – a little different.'

'Than what?'

'Than they used to be. You don't seem very affectionate toward each other.'

Laurie searched the social glossary for the right words and said, 'Look, honey, I'm not going to lie to you. Matt and I are going through a tough time right now, but it's nothing that should concern you.'

'What's going to happen?'

'I don't know. But whatever happens, you'll never lose Matt's love, or mine. That'll never change.'

'Yeah,' said Jarod, looking away from his mother. Knowing that things always seemed to change. Knowing that his mother was making a promise she might not be able to keep. His real father now lived in New York. Jarod still loved him, and he was sure that his real dad still loved him, but things did change when he had moved out. And they were never the same again.

Jarod stood, walked over to his mother, leaned down and gave her a kiss. ' 'Night, Mom.'

'Goodnight, honey.'

Jarod started to walk away.

'Jarod?'

'Yes,' he said, turning back toward his mother.

'Please don't worry about this. I really think there's a good chance Matt and I will get through this thing . . . together.'

'I hope so, Mom. I really do.'

As she sat alone in the living room, her feet tucked up under her, Laurie tried to convince herself that she sounded more confident than she felt.

SEVEN

Pete Carboni lived in an apartment near the University of Chicago. He shared the place with two roommates, both of whom were out when Matt arrived. The place was decorated with bookshelves made of stained planks and cement blocks. The coffee table was a large cable spool. There were posters of REM and the Spin Doctors on the wall, along with several large color posters of two identical twins with immense breasts in various stages of undress.

Carboni was a good-looking kid, late teens, with dark features and a Roman nose. 'I haven't been back to work – delivering pizzas – since it happened,' he said, referring to the night he was knocked unconscious and had his clothes stolen, and Arthur Camacho had been murdered. 'Lawyer says I ought to be able to collect a bundle.'

'From whom?'

'I dunno. He's workin' on it.'

'What do you remember about that night?'

'Not a whole helluva lot. Like I told the cops, I get out of my car, walk around the front of my car, head toward the building, then, bingo, somebody hit me from behind and next thing I know I'm wakin' up in the alley.'

'You ever deliver pizza to that address before?'

'Once or twice. But not for a couple of weeks at least.'

'Was there anything that you remember about the person who hit you? Maybe a smell, some sensation that registered just before you went down?'

Carboni shook his head. 'Nah. When I came to, my jacket and cap were gone. I was a little rocky, so my first thought was that the homeless guy took my stuff.'

'The homeless guy?'

'The guy in the box out front. But he took off when all the cops came.'

'What did he look like?'

'Like a homeless person.'

'Black? White?'

'He was black. An older guy. Had a gray beard.'

'What was he wearing?'

'I don't know.'

'Think about it. It might be helpful.'

Carboni squinted his eyes a little, and tried to remember back to that night. He started shaking his head. 'Nothing really comes to mind.'

'Was he wearing glasses?'

'I don't think so.' Carboni stopped shaking his head. 'Wait a minute. He was wearing a scarf. Kind of a long scarf – that's why I remember it. It was red with little white balls hanging off the end of it. I thought that was kind of peculiar. Looked like a little girl's scarf.'

'How about a hat?'

'Yeah.' Carboni closed his eyes and sifted through

the cloudy memories. 'I think he had on a Bulls' cap. You know, Chicago Bulls. Da Bulls,' he added, mimicking a famous Chicago-area pronunciation of these two words.

'You ever see him before?'

'Maybe, but I didn't have any reason to remember him.'

'Did he say or do anything else?'

'No, he just looked scared.'

'Of what?'

'Coulda been scared of me. I mean, like I said, the first thing I thought when I staggered out of that alley was that the guy took my clothes. I don't know, maybe he was just scared of the police – the sirens were blaring.'

Maybe he was scared of something else, thought Matt.

'Just what is it that you're tryin' to say, Miz Baldwin?' Tyrena Jenkins was one of the largest women Laurie had ever seen – at least in person. Tyrena was turned out in a floral print dress that, with poles appropriately placed, could have served as a small tent. Laurie was amazed that she was even thinking such thoughts, because she was always conscientious about never saying negative things about other people's appearances – she had spent her own teenage years on the Renoir side of the beauty scale, and had never forgotten how thoughtless and hurtful people could be.

But Tyrena Jenkins was different. At least she

seemed so to Laurie. Besides being around three hundred pounds, her hair was dyed blond with reddish tips, she had two gold teeth that showed whenever her mouth was open – which was all the time. She never shut up, and her voice was so loud that last week, during one of her daily 'press conferences', Laurie could hear that voice as soon as she entered the courthouse. The courthouse entrance was down two floors and halfway around the building from where Tyrena was holding forth, and she wan't even shouting. That was the woman's natural voice.

'What I'm trying to say is that your daily press conferences aren't doing your son any good.'

'Says who?' There was a threat in her voice. She almost seemed like some female, and much larger, Mr T saying, 'I pity the fool . . .'

'It's my opinion—'

'Look, I'm payin' *you*!'

That was not entirely true, since Laurie was actually a court-appointed attorney, and the government was paying her. But she had been around the track before with Tyrena about how the government was supposed to work for Tyrena, and the government's money was really her money, even though she had never paid taxes in her life. It was a losing battle and, gauging Tyrena's mood, Laurie didn't sense that this was an appropriate time for a civics lesson. So she let it slide.

'You're paying me for my expertise, for my skill as a lawyer. I'm trying to do the best I can for your son and you're making my job more difficult.'

'I don't care about that, I just care about gettin' my son home.'

'I don't think I can get your son home. At least, not as soon as you might want.'

Tyrena started shaking her head. 'Don't give me that bullshit about no plea bargain. We want justice.'

'For what?' Laurie looked the woman straight in the eye.

'What do you mean?'

'For what? For five hundred years of slavery? For hundreds of years of racism?' said Laurie, quoting from Tyrena's voluminous press clippings.

'Exactly!' said Tyrena, her gold teeth gleaming in the afternoon sun that streamed into the office from the window behind Laurie's desk.

'This trial is not about that.'

'It is to me!'

'It isn't to anyone else. There's another black woman in that courtroom who wants justice, too. She wants to see the man who blew her son's brains out punished.'

'That's not my problem,' said Tyrena, shaking her head from side to side.

'Maybe not. But it *is* your son's problem. And, as his lawyer, it's my problem too. If you continue to tell your son, and the press, that you will never accept a plea bargain, your son will go to jail for the rest of his life, and maybe even be put to death. They have him on videotape walking over to this kid and pulling the trigger. Your son murdered someone. There is still a penalty to pay for murder in this state. It's that simple.'

People these days thought lawyers were magicians. That they were capable of proving wrong was right, and up was down.

Tyrena Jenkins was praying for just such a miracle for her son. And for the first time that Laurie could remember, Tyrena Jenkins was silent. After a moment she said, 'What'll they do to my boy if you make some kinda deal?'

'He's going to jail. When all the smoke clears, if he's good in prison, he could still be out in ten years.'

'Ten years?' Tyrena said softly, her face going a little slack and suddenly showing its age.

'He's twenty now. When he gets out he'll be in his early thirties. He can still get married, have kids. At least you know he'll be coming home. Someday.'

'Ten years,' said Tyrena again. She was shaking her head, tears in her eyes. 'I don't want to lose my son for ten years.'

Laurie didn't think it was the right moment to point out that the victim's mother had lost her son forever.

'It's either ten years or maybe the rest of his life. He'll do what you tell him.'

Tyrena smiled, through her tears. 'Yeah, he's a good boy that way. Never talks back.' Then a glaze fell over her stare and she repeated, 'Ten years,' as though it were some kind of esoteric and evil mantra she had just learned. Words that had the power to save.

'Will you talk to your son?'

'Yes.'

'And stop talking to the press?'

Tyrena nodded.

In a way that Laurie did not completely understand at the moment, she almost felt bad about breaking the woman's spirit. Tyrena lived for the daily spotlight, thrived under it when others would have withered. For the first time in her life, people were listening to her.

Now she sat there silent, realizing that the only thing required of her now was to surrender. To convince her son that he should be grateful to go to jail for only ten years. This wasn't the way she had wanted it to end.

Tyrena stood. 'Miz Baldwin?'

'Yes?'

'Do you mind if I go out your back door? There's a coupla TV crews outside the front door. I told 'em to wait.'

'Of course.'

Tyrena started for the door.

'You know, we're really on the same side here. You know that, don't you?'

'Yeah.' Tyrena smiled a sad smile. 'For the first time and probably the last.'

And with that she was gone.

Leaving Laurie standing there thinking that Tyrena was probably right.

Matt spent most of the afternoon walking around an area ten blocks square, using Arthur Camacho's building as the center point. There were more homeless people than he would have thought. But then, most people tried not to see bums on the street. Bums always wanted something. On their way to a movie in Los Angeles recently, Matt and Laurie had been accosted by a homeless man. Because Matt had not had any change – he had used it all for a meter – the guy had yelled obscenities at him about Laurie. It was strange, Matt had thought at the time. If the guy was just some regular, drunk suit-and-tie, Matt would have confronted him. But the guy was 'homeless'. It was like picking a fight with a cripple – at least in Matt's eyes.

But the experience had changed him. He was starting to look at homeless people differently.

Matt had observed a growing cynicism among his peers in recent years. Among his friends there was a tendency to pretend that certain people and things didn't exist. In the Nineties people had been ripped off so many times by so many scams that they found it difficult to believe anyone they didn't know personally. Maybe that was just a way to rationalize not giving a needy person some help, Laurie had suggested one night over drinks at I Cugini.

Maybe nobody knew anything about anyone anymore, thought Matt, as he walked along Michigan Avenue. But today, while looking for a homeless man with a Bulls' cap and a red scarf with white balls hanging off the ends, he saw a lot of pain – a lot of desperation. And he realized that if he had to look at that much pain and desperation every day of his life, he might go mad.

It took him nearly three hours to find Willie Oliver. Matt first noticed him panhandling just outside a Woolworth store. He seemed to be doing okay.

'Hey, how you doin'?'

Willie looked up at Matt warily.

Matt withdrew a ten-dollar bill. 'I'd like to talk to you.'

Willie looked Matt up and down. 'You ain't no gay boy, now, are ya?'

'No.' Matt handed Willie the ten and said, 'Let's go across the street and get something to eat.'

After only a slight hesitation, Willie reached out, snatched the tenner and they headed across the street, the wind blowing small whirlpools of snow around them as they walked.

'How'd you find me?' asked Willie. He was already into his second cheeseburger with everything on it, as well as Matt's helping of fries. He had also worked the catsup and mustard over pretty good.

'The pizza delivery man gave me a description. The scarf and all.'

'Good thing it's still cold. Otherwise you'd never a found me. These are my winter clothes,' he said, tilting his head toward his scarf and brown overcoat.

'Sometimes you get lucky,' said Matt, sipping a cup of hot coffee, black.

The two men sat in a booth at a hamburger joint. Two women in the booth behind Willie kept peering at him and wrinkling their noses as though Willie was ruining their meal. Maybe he was, thought Matt. He smelled pretty bad.

'You saw this man – the guy who robbed the pizza delivery boy?'

'Sure did. Saw a lot a him, actually.'

'What do you mean?'

'I mean, he stayed at my place for 'bout a week, on and off.'

'What do you mean, stayed at your place?'

'He slept in my box, man.'

'In your box?'

'I live – well, I used to live in this big Maytag washer box. In the alley opposite the Superior Arms. Where that drug dealer was murdered.'

'How'd you know about that?'

'I read the papers. Okay, I don't buy 'em, but I read 'em.' A look of fear flickered on Willie's face. 'I had nothin' to do with that, man. Nothin'!'

'Don't worry, I know that you're not implicated in the murder. But this other man, what did he look like?'

'White guy. Couldn't get a real good look at his face.'

'Why?'

'Guy didn't shave. Not like me, I got a beard, you know. But he hadn't shaved in about a week or so. And he had this hat.'

'What kind of hat?'

'Stocking cap, you know? Blue. Kept it pulled down over his ears, sometimes even down over his eyebrows. Like either he was real cold, or he was hidin' or somethin', you know?'

'Had you ever seen him before?'

'He started hangin' 'round a week before the murder. Before that, I never seen him before.'

'How did he . . .' Matt didn't know exactly how to phrase this '. . . end up moving in with you?'

'That was kinda' strange, you know? I mean, it was my place. He just kinda came in and made himself at home. Almost like he dared me to throw him out. 'Course I wasn't gonna do that.'

'Why not?'

'This guy was a tough guy, man. You been on the street, you can tell, you know?'

Matt nodded.

'I never did believe he was no homeless dude. He was just masqueradin', you know?'

'What makes you say that?'

'He didn't have the look.'

'What look?'

'He didn't look hungry. He didn't look beaten down, you know? He wasn't interested in survival. Survival's my life. I hustle for a few bucks and I spend it the same day on food.'

And booze, thought Matt. Partly because this was a stereotypical observation, partly because Matt saw the telltale signs on the man's face. All that, plus the fact that he had seen the man conceal a pint bottle in his overcoat pocket as they walked across the street.

'I don't know what this guy did all day. All I know

is that whenever I was around my place, he was there, lookin' across the street, watchin'. I guess it all makes sense now. He was casin' the joint, right?'

'What did you call this man?'

'Carnie. Like a carnival, you know?'

'Was that his real name?'

'Who knows?'

'Did he say that he had ever been in a carnival?'

'No.'

Matt figured he knew how 'Carnie' bought his way into Willie's home. A nightly bottle of whiskey would have covered the freight. 'What happened that night?'

'Well, when the pizza guy drove up, Carnie got real interested.'

'Did he seem surprised?'

'Surprised?'

'Did it seem as though Carnie might have been expecting the pizza man?'

Willie pondered that for a moment.

'I mean, when he saw the pizza guy, did he immediately spring into action?'

Willie nodded his head. 'Yeah. Maybe he knew the guy was coming.'

'What happened then?'

'I watched Carnie walk across the street, hit the pizza man from behind, and drag him into the alley.'

'Where were you at that time?'

'At first I was in my box, but when I saw Carnie do that I got out of the box and . . .'

'Yes?'

'Well, I didn't know exactly what to do. I mean, maybe he was gonna come back for me. But he didn't. He came out of the alley next to the building wearing the delivery guy's hat and coat, carrying the pizza.'

'Then what?'

'Somebody buzzed him in. I was like frozen, you know? I didn't know what the fuck to do. About five minutes later, Carnie flies outta there like a bat outta hell. He's runnin' down the street and I never saw him again.'

'But you didn't stick around.'

'Hell, no. When all those cops come around, I knew that was someplace I didn't wanna be, you know?'

'Yeah. Is there anything else you can tell me about the guy. I'd really like to find him.'

'No shit, but I ain't seen him since that night.'

'Did you ever see him talking with anyone else?'

Willie thought about the question, and then his head started nodding. 'Now that you mention it, I saw him with some Mexican guy.'

'Did you recognize the other man?'

'Hell, no, they all look pretty much alike to me,' said Willie with a grin. 'He was young, though. Looked like mid-twenties to me.'

'How many times did you see Carnie with this man?'

'Couple, three times. I'm not sure.'

'You think you could identify the man if you saw him again?'

'I dunno.'

Matt recognized the answer. It wasn't that Willie

wasn't sure; it was that he wasn't sure what was in it for him.

'If you'll take a ride with me to look at some photographs, I'd be grateful.' It was the closest thing Willie was going to get to an offer in this lifetime.

'How grateful?'

'Well, I don't know if you appreciate good Scotch, but I'd be happy to buy you a bottle of Glenlivet.'

The word hit Willie like a bracing tonic. He looked as though someone had just handed him a Publishers Clearing House check. 'Sounds cool.'

EIGHT

There were slot machines in the Las Vegas airport. Sirens. Lights flashing. Coins falling into metal collectors – dumped into plastic cups. Plastic cups that were, to some, like tiny holy grails. But as a rule the cups were as empty as dreams. At least, that was the way Carnie had always seen Vegas.

He took a cab from the airport. He was dressed in a black sport coat, black T-shirt, jeans and Frye boots. He spoke only when the cab driver spoke to him. Seems the cabby had once been a popular lounge singer, on the verge of hitting the big time. That's the way the old dreams played themselves out now, anyhow. Then something happened. Something always happened. The excuses kept you sane, kept a little voice in your head telling you that you 'could've been a contender'. Kept you going while you drove a hack.

The cabby drove past Carnie's destination, the Flamingo Hilton, but he told Carnie he wouldn't charge him for the mistake. It was a scam. Vegas was a scam. But Carnie didn't mind. He was thinking about something else.

He checked in under an assumed name, presented ID that matched the fake name. He'd even managed to get himself an Honors Card with the fake ID.

Tonight he used the card to get a room on the 'honors floor' – the twenty-fifth, overlooking Caesar's Palace. From his room, the million neon lights looked like a Disneyland version of the promised land.

The room was spacious and included a matching couch and chair, a king-sized bed and an entertainment center. There was a large vanity area, but Carnie didn't think he'd be needing it. Not tonight, anyhow.

He lay down on the bed and hit the remote-control power button. The TV came alive.

'. . . Lawyers for Angus Trent said that he will be filing a civil suit against Mrs Womack. This will be over and above the criminal charges that have already been filed this morning. In a related development, Mr Trent's lawyers said that he has been approached by several producers regarding the film rights to his story, but that he will not be making a decision on any movie deals for at least two weeks. In other news . . .'

Carnie hit the off button and the television went black. The room was lit from the reflection of the neon sea outside the floor-to-ceiling windows. He looked at his watch and turned on the radio next to his bed. Then he punched the AM button, and searched the dial.

'. . . vigilante justice. That's all it is.'

'And just what do you think the punishment should have been for molesting two young boys? Destroying their lives? Robbing them of their childhood?'

'I don't know. I—'

'No, I want an answer,' said Kyle Talbot.

The caller was silent.

'Two years?'

'I don't know.'

'What exactly is the going rate for destroying a child's life?'

'You don't even know if the man was guilty. The most famous child-molestation case in history turned out to be just a bunch of hysterical parents, media and therapists. Not a single defendant was found guilty of a single charge. What if one of those parents had gone into the courtroom and killed one of those innocent defendants?'

'Just because you're not convicted doesn't mean you're not guilty.'

'That's outrageous!' said the caller. 'Our system of justice says that a person is innocent until proven guilty.'

'And when a person is proven guilty, then what? Three out of four convicted felons don't even go to jail. Is that justice? Is it justice to let a convicted child-molester out on the street after a few months of "counseling" at the taxpayers' expense, and turn him loose on our children? Is that justice? How many chances do we give people who continue to harm our families and destroy our children?'

'I don't know exactly—'

'I can tell you one thing – it's always at least one more chance than they give the victim.'

'That's really not fair—'

'I've got to break here. You're listening to the Kyle Talbot Show. Live in the US of A. Call us now at 1-800-555-K-Y-L-E. For those of you in Clyde, Ohio, that's five-nine-five-three. And we'll be back.'

Carnie stood, walked to the window and looked out over the Vegas Strip, which looked like a single giant pinball machine: bright, flashing, fluid.

He wondered where Angus Trent was. Wondered what he was thinking. Was he thinking about a movie in which he could tell his side of the story? Was he thinking about which actor would play him? Or was he thinking about Betty Womack's two boys, and what it was like touching them?

It was impossible to get into the mind of the insane. Carnie knew this. He had dealt many times with crippled minds. Minds that seemed to function normally, but which were wired wrong. Somewhere in the labyrinth of circuitry, wires were crossed, creating a mental short-circuit that sputtered and flared in the darkest part of the human soul. It was a black place where logic could not survive. Where sanity was sucked into the madness. A place where a rational mind entered at its own peril.

Angus Trent had a crippled mind and he spread the darkness that haunted him. Spread it like a cancer. Spread it to children who had no defense against Trent's disease. Someone must stop that epidemic. Someone should have done so before.

Carnie would make sure Angus Trent infected no one else with his plague.

* * *

Matt sat under a photograph of Al Capone, talking with Willie Oliver who was savoring a glass of Glenlivet over ice – this being on top of the bottle Matt had promised him, which rested neatly in a pocket inside Willie's jacket.

When Matt saw Chuck Carlucci standing at the entrance of Stacey's bar waiting for his eyes to adjust to the darkness, he waved him over. He had asked Carlucci to bring from five to ten photographs of Latinos, including photographs of the two Latino gang members murdered at Camacho's place.

Matt did the introductions all around – he had already explained how he tracked Oliver down. If Carlucci was impressed, he did a good job of hiding it when speaking on the phone.

'I came here on my own,' said Willie.

'I understand that, Mr Oliver,' said Carlucci.

It was odd, thought Matt – not for the first time – that it was usually the innocents who felt a need to confess, or at least to endlessly state their lack of guilt. Tough guys, real tough guys, knew enough to keep their mouths shut . . . and let their lawyers do the lying.

Carlucci spread the photographs out in front of Oliver, who took his time looking them over. Matt and Carlucci realized this wasn't because he was having any trouble making up his mind. Oliver had probably never been to Stacey's before – not in a very long time, anyhow. And he had probably never been there with one of Chicago's finest and a guy from the FBI. A guy from the FBI who had just happened to buy him a bottle of Glenlivet. No, this was a moment to be savored, and Oliver knew that when he walked out of there, he was walking out of there for good. Who the hell knew, maybe he could even milk it for a second round?

'Hmm . . .' said Oliver.

Carlucci and Matt exchanged glances. And waited.

Occasionally, between hums, Oliver would sip his Scotch. Matt knew the score. He raised a hand towards the bartender, then pointed toward Oliver.

Finally, Oliver pointed to one photograph. 'That's the guy.'

'You're sure?'

'No doubt about it.'

Matt knew that was probably true. He had noticed the way Oliver reacted when that particular photograph had been laid upon the table ten minutes ago.

Carlucci scooped up the photographs, and the three men talked for a while. Matt and Carlucci would not be able to confer until Oliver left, and he wasn't going to leave before he finished his drink.

'How many times did you see this man?'

Matt left the questioning to Carlucci. Respect. Turf.

'Coupla times maybe.'

'When did you see him with this . . . this Carnie guy?' Carlucci hated saying the man's name. Every time he said it, it was as though he was playing the killer's game.

'Like I say, a coupla times during the week before

the murders. He'd usually meet him in the alley next to the building. Out of sight, you know. Like they was trying not to be seen.'

'Yes. Did Carnie ever talk about this man with you?'

'No.'

'And he never mentioned the man's name?'

'No.'

'Well, I guess that's about it,' said Carlucci, noting that Oliver had drained the last drop of Scotch from his glass. 'I appreciate it,' he said, holding out his hand.

Oliver shook hands, stood, thanked Matt with a wink and a subtle tap on his jacket, right over the pocket where the Glenlivet lived. Then he left.

'Let me guess,' said Matt. 'Oliver ID'd one of the dead guys in Camacho's apartment.'

'Bingo.'

Matt wasn't waiting for a thank-you, and he knew that none would be forthcoming. What had just happened would ultimately take the case out of Carlucci's hands, and he knew it.

'That answers a lot of questions.'

'What's the guy's name?'

'Diego Rodriguez.'

'Now we know how the killer knew a pizza was coming. Rodriguez probably ordered it, right on schedule.'

'And just about anything else the killer would have needed. Obviously, Rodriguez was conned,' said Carlucci, waving his hand futilely over the photograph of the man Oliver identified.

'How long had Rodriguez been with Camacho?'

'Few years.'

Matt wanted to word this correctly. 'Was he . . . connected in any way to—?'

'He wasn't one of us. He's got a sheet you'd need a speed-reading course to get through in a weekend. And as far as I know, he wasn't an informant.'

'Yet someone got him to give up Camacho.'

'Could have been a lotta people. The mob. Some rival drug dealer. Maybe he was into some loan shark who told him if he didn't give up Camacho, he'd kill his family.'

'Maybe,' said Matt. But none of Carlucci's theories rang true. 'What about his family?'

'He's got a girlfriend who still lives in the neighborhood. She was the one who came down to ID the body.'

'Got her address?'

Carlucci thought about saying that he had already talked with the girlfriend. But then, he had already talked with the pizza delivery guy, too. So 'Yeah,' was all he said. 'Call me in the morning and I'll give you her address.'

'Thanks.'

'So, when are you planning on leaving?'

'Why?'

'No reason. Just curious.'

Silence.

'He's gone,' said Carlucci, referring to the killer.

'I know.'

'You know somethin'?'

'What?'

'I'm glad you're bringing him in, and not me.'

Matt didn't have to ask why. He knew. The asshole who killed a fellow cop was dead. No trial. No lawyers whining to a crowd five nights a week about how the cops stepped all over poor little altar-boy Camacho's rights. No TV movie. In fact, there was nothing Carlucci was sorry about regarding Camacho's death, except maybe that he hadn't done it himself.

'Think you'll catch this guy?' asked Carlucci after he finished his beer and set down the empty glass.

'I'll get him.'

'Do me a favor, okay? Wait at least a week.'

'Why?'

'There's an election here next week. You catch the guy before then, they might elect the fuckin' guy mayor.' Carlucci didn't move for a moment. He just looked at Matt, who couldn't tell if Carlucci was smiling or not.

Carlucci stood and shook Matt's hand. 'Call me in the morning. I'll dig up Rodriguez's girlfriend's address.'

'Thanks.'

Carlucci just nodded and headed out of the bar.

Matt finished his drink, left a twenty-dollar bill on the table, and walked out into the chilly night. He jockeyed the brown scarf, one Laurie had bought him for his birthday a few years ago, into position to ward off the cold. Suddenly he felt very alone. He walked by himself in a city where he was unknown. Looking for a murderer most people did not want found.

He remembered when he and Laurie had first gotten together. His work had often taken him out of town. Back then, he would walk through towns where he knew no one, but he never felt alone. He was connected. To Laurie. To Jarod. He was a part of something that transcended, was greater than, what he could see.

Tonight, as he walked the windswept streets of Chicago, Matt could not remember ever feeling more alone.

'President Souther's at it again, folks,' said Kyle Talbot on the radio.

Carnie sipped his Bud Dry as he sat there, lights off, in his Flamingo Hilton room. The lights from Caesar's Palace across the street painted his room in light and shadows.

'I'm telling you, this man has absolutely no concern for the people of this country. He's sacrificing our children's future on the altar of his own political career. Mr and Mrs Middle America, you'd better brace yourselves for what's coming. Because the President doesn't respect you. He thinks you're powerless. You don't hang him in effigy, you don't burn down buildings, you don't march on Washington hand in hand, singing songs. You're stupid. While you're stupid enough to stay at home, work your nine-to-five jobs, raise your kids, pay your taxes and vote, every other special-interest group is out in force. And because you're not, the President and his people think you're schmucks.

'You know why they think you're so stupid? Because you outnumber all those wackos, you pay most of the taxes, and you've got absolutely no clout. What in the hell do you think would happen if fifty million middle-class taxpayers took a couple of days off work and went to Washington? You could shut this country down without firing a shot.

'But you won't do it. And they know you won't. President Souther is not afraid of you. But let me ask you a question, folks. What if you did? Do you think the President would become more responsive to your needs?

'And we'll be back.'

Carnie sat there drinking beer, the phone cradled between his shoulder and his ear. 'You're next,' a voice had told him a couple of minutes ago.

The sound of Kyle Talbot's voice filled the room. As Carnie drank. And held on the phone.

'Hello, Las Vegas,' said Kyle Talbot. 'Our hometown.'

Carnie reached over and hit the on/off button on the radio. He knew the routine. There was an eight-to-ten-second time lag between live conversation and what went out over the air.

'Hi, Kyle.'

'Your name, sir.'

'I'd like to talk about what's happening with Betty Womack,' said Carnie. He didn't want to give his name – even a false name. Not yet.

'I'm glad we've got a caller from Vegas,' said Kyle. 'What do people – I mean the *real* working-class people – think of what's going on here?'

'I don't like it.'

'How would you characterize the mood in Vegas?' said Talbot. He held up his coffee cup with a photograph of himself stenciled on the side, and Cassie sprang into action.

Carnie set down his Bud Dry. 'I don't know exactly. I think there's this idea that maybe if the good guys start shooting back, maybe the bad guys will think twice.'

'Well put. Well put. I think you're right on the money. Saying you've had it up to here doesn't really cut it anymore. People have had it up to here for years. What most people don't realize is that, for the most part, we're dealing with criminals – with drugs. We're not dealing with people like you and me. Yeah, yeah, yeah, I can feel the tidal wave of hate mail coming in over that remark. But ask yourselves, folks, don't you really, in your heart of hearts, think criminals are different from you? You know the laws. They know the laws. You're under pressure, they're under pressure. You have to feed a family, make a car payment, a mortgage or rent payment. And yet somehow you find a way to live your life without going out and putting a gun to someone else's head.

'You know what the difference is between you and some criminal? *You* know what's right and what's wrong, and you act accordingly, no matter how painful that may be to you personally. *You* play by the rules – even the ones you don't like. You're responsible. Get it? The criminal knows his rights. You and I know our responsibilities. That's what separates us, folks. Pure and simple.'

Kyle paused for what he figured would be a considerable amount of gratuitous high-fiving among the initiated around the country.

'So, Las Vegas, what do you think we ought to do with Angus Trent?'

'In my opinion, he has given up his right to live among respectable people.'

Kyle paused a moment. He was the ringmaster. He knew how to run the circus. And he also knew when to rein it in. 'What exactly do you mean by that?'

'I mean the man should die.'

'I agree with you, Las Vegas. But they don't have the death penalty for child-molestation. Not that I—'

'He should die, anyhow.'

Cassie set down a fresh cup of coffee in front of Kyle. He seemed not to notice her. 'So, what exactly are you suggesting?'

'The man's death would solve a lot of problems. There would be no civil suits against Mrs Womack. Her children would recognize that when someone hurts them, that person – not the parent trying to protect them – will pay the price. And . . .'

'Yes, Las Vegas?'

'They won't have to watch the whole story on some TV movie from the perpetrator's point of view.'

'You make sense. You really do. But vigilante justice still isn't legal. Not even in Las Vegas.'

'Maybe it oughta be,' said Carnie, polishing off the rest of his Bud Dry.

'Yes, well, we appreciate your comments. And we'll be right back after this message from your local stations.'

Kyle slid his chair away from his microphone, and sat staring at the console.

'What's wrong?' said Cassie. She sat down next to him.

'Nothing,' said Talbot, dismissing her question. But he was thinking how he might have just been talking to some kind of gun-toting cowboy nut who was in the mood for a little frontier justice, and how maybe he should have milked the guy some more. Good radio. People liked that shit. Especially people who listened to *The Kyle Talbot Show*.

Carnie felt good. This was not the first time he had gotten through to talk with Kyle Talbot. He wondered if Talbot recognized his voice. Probably not. So many people called the program. How could a person keep track?

Carnie got up off the bed and walked to the window overlooking Caesar's Palace. He looked out upon the city again. And wondered . . .

Where was Angus Trent?

And did he know that he was a dead man walking?

NINE

Louise Hansen lived near the University of Chicago, not far from Pete Carboni. But when Matt Baldwin called at her address he was told that she was staying for a while with her aunt in DeKalb, about an hour west of Chicago.

About ninety minutes and six toll booths later Matt pulled up his rental car in front of a large two-story house set back from the street about thirty feet. It was large by Los Angeles standards. In DeKalb, which was known for being the home of Northern Illinois University as well as the home of the inventor of barbed wire, this gray two-story was about the same size as the rest of the houses on the block. Matt noticed the yard, not that it was anything special – just that it was a yard. A person didn't see many lawns in Los Angeles. Matt and Laurie lived in a condo that carried a ticket of just under three hundred thousand dollars. From the look of the two-story in front of him, you could fit about three condos into this place. And *he* didn't have a square foot of yard. He used to say that he was glad he didn't have to take care of a yard, but that was just a rationalization. He really *wanted* a yard.

A woman who looked to be in her mid-forties

opened the door and stared Matt in the eye. She wasn't smiling. 'Yes?'

'I'm looking for Louise Hansen.'

'She's not here.'

'I think she is,' said Matt, having noticed the beat-up Corolla deep in the driveway, almost behind the house. 'She is staying with you,' said Matt. It was not a question.

'So?'

Silence.

'She doesn't want to talk to the police.'

'I'm not the police. I'm with the FBI.' Matt removed his ID and showed it to the woman, who looked it over carefully. When she was done, Matt pocketed his ID. 'Look, I think I understand why she doesn't want to talk to the police. I'd just like to ask her a few questions, then I'll leave her alone.'

The woman gave Matt a don't-treat-me-like-an-idiot kind of look.

'I'll do my best to keep her out of it. I know she's not involved. Helping me is the best thing she can do for herself.'

The woman didn't look convinced, but she looked as though she was convinced there weren't any other viable options. 'Wait here,' she said and shut the door.

A couple of minutes later a young woman reopened the door and led Matt into a living room just to the right of the foyer. She sat down on a flower-print couch, and waved Matt toward a matching chair.

Louise Hansen looked to be in her early twenties. She had shoulder-length blond hair, large breasts, large hips, and freckles on her face. She was wearing jeans that had probably fit her better when she'd bought them than they did today, a nondescript white blouse that hung over her stomach, and tennis shoes.

'I don't know anything,' said Hansen.

'Then why don't I tell you what I know?' Matt knew that he had little leverage here. And Hansen did not look intimidated. After all, he reminded himself, she had been Rodriguez's girlfriend, so she did not come to DeKalb by way of never-never land. 'I think your boyfriend, Diego, was set up. I'm just trying to figure out who set him up.'

'Right,' said Hansen with a sneer. She reached over to a side table, picked up a pack of Pall Malls and a Bic lighter, and lit one up. She blew a plume of smoke into the air, and it floated to the ceiling like an unanswered prayer.

'Why do you say that?'

'Are you serious?'

'Yes. Who do you reckon set Diego up?' asked Matt.

Hansen looked at Matt, trying to gauge his ability to hurt her. After a moment she said, 'Who the fuck do you think?'

'I don't know.'

'Really?'

'Really.'

'The cops, that's who. I mean, it's pretty fucking obvious, don't you think?' said Hansen, peppering her language with the expletives she must have picked up from living with Diego Rodriguez.

'Why?'

'Because Camacho killed a cop, that's why. People take care of their own. Gangbangers and cops, you know what I'm sayin'?'

Matt nodded. He knew. But he also knew something Hansen didn't know. 'How well did you know Diego? His business, I mean.'

'Diego told me everything. He and Arturo – Camacho – they went way back. Diego, he was willing to do a lot for Arturo. But he never killed nobody.'

'You're sure?'

'I'm sure. Look, I know you think I'm a stupid bitch for hanging out with some spic.'

Matt did not respond. Not because he didn't have an answer. Not because he didn't have a good and truthful answer. He just knew that he didn't have any answer that Louise Hansen would believe.

'Diego was a good guy,' she continued.

'He was arrested for selling drugs seven times, robbery six times, murder twice, rape twice.'

'And how many times was he convicted?'

'Twice.'

'See,' said Hansen as though she were Perry Mason making a pivotal point.

'No, I'm not sure I do.'

'The hell you don't,' she said, sucking a drag off her Pall Mall and running her hand through her dirty blond hair.

'If you think there's some kind of conspiracy going on with the local cops, I've got to tell you that I don't know anything about it. I work out of Los Angeles. I've only been here a couple of days, and quite frankly I don't know what you're talking about.'

Hansen breathed in some smoke through her nose, 'They thought Arturo killed a cop, okay?'

'Did he?'

'Who the fuck knows?'

'I still don't know how your boyfriend got involved,' said Matt, even though he had a pretty good idea.

Hansen again did the little huff-and-puff with her Pall Mall, then said, 'They set him up.'

'They?'

'The cops!' said Hansen, playing teacher to a schoolboy who wasn't paying attention.

'What did they have on him?'

'Nothin'!' she said, as though the sheer volume of her response would be enough to convince. 'It was a fuckin' sting, man.'

'I'm listening.'

Hansen tapped her ashes into a clear glass ashtray, next to a plant Matt figured was getting closer to death the longer this interview continued.

'Everybody knew that Diego would've been a three-time loser . . .' she began.

'You're saying that the cops set up a sting that would put Diego in jail for a long time?'

'You got it. It was a drug bust. Completely bogus. I told Diego it would've never held up.'

'How long ago?'

'Maybe a week before Arturo was murdered.'

'What happened?'

'I'm not sure exactly. All I know is that it had something to do with some cop posing as a homeless person. He set Diego up but good. It wasn't like it was a small-time bust, either. Diego was sitting there with a lotta dope.'

'And . . .'

'And the guy whipped out a badge, arrested Diego, read him his rights and, while he was driving him downtown, they made a deal.'

'What kind of deal?'

'The cop said that if Diego would cooperate – set up Arturo – then it would be like nothing happened, you know?'

'So why do you smell a setup? Diego's selling drugs and he gets caught—'

'Diego was *out* of the drug scene. He knew what it took to stay out of prison. We were planning a life together. Kids, the whole nine yards.'

'So why was he still hanging out with Camacho?'

'He wasn't.'

'Maybe I'm missing something.'

Hansen looked at Matt, not as though he was stupid, but as though he was ignorant. There was a difference, and it was a difference they both knew.

'Diego stopped hanging out with Arturo since the last time he went away. The only reason he contacted Arturo was because this cop put pressure on him to "renew old friendships". He didn't want to, but if he didn't he was going back to prison.'

'So why did Arturo all of a sudden take him back?'

'You're really not from around here, are you?' said Hansen. 'The last stint Diego did in prison was because he kept his mouth shut about Arturo.'

'So Diego was supposed to feed information to this cop in return for burying the drug charges?'

'Exactly.'

'Diego told you this?'

'Yes.'

Matt knew that she wasn't going to go to the authorities with her story. What was she going to say? The authorities were the ones who had made the deal. At least, that's what she thought.

That was not what Matt thought.

'So what now?' asked Hansen.

After a moment, Matt said, 'I'm going to try to find the guy who set up Diego.'

'Right,' said Hansen, not bothering to conceal a sneer. 'Like you give a fuck.'

'That's my job.'

'Nobody wants to know the truth. Least of all the cops.'

'You're wrong.'

'Cops set up Diego, then they killed him to cover their ass. They took care of their own, and that's the fuckin' truth.'

Matt thought about saying lots of things. Some of them would sound like the truth, some of them like something else. But there was no point in arguing. *None* of his explanations would sound like the 'fuckin' truth'. Not to Louise Hansen.

* * *

Carnie sat in the Winners' Circle bar at the Paddle Wheel Hotel and Casino, drinking a Bud Dry, watching Angus Trent and his young man pull one-armed bandits for fun. All the while Carnie listened to what he considered to be good country and western music played by a band wearing black Stetsons. He considered country and western to be one of the last kinds – perhaps the only kind – of music where any white man over eighteen years old wasn't made the object of ridicule or rage.

In country and western videos, adult white males were depicted as worthy, likable, even attractive individuals, regardless of how much money they made, how politically correct they were, or how many trees they'd saved in the rain forest this month. Also, country and western was unique to the American landscape. It was not that it was racist – Carnie knew of no C&W songs portraying blacks or any other minority in a negative light. In fact, Carnie owned two Charlie Pride albums. What made the music attractive to a white man, thought Carnie, was that it was the only sort that *included* white men. Except polka music, which he hated.

In the background, the band was playing Dwight Yoakam's 'Ain't That Lonely Yet'. Carnie knew that he was beyond lonely – and had been for some time. Ever since Sandra Ann had been taken away from him, there had been a place inside him that could not be filled. Since that lonely and endless night, he had become a man devoid of feeling. Something,

something numb, now beat in the place where his heart had been.

The guys with the Stetsons stopped playing.

Carnie looked over at Angus Trent and his young stud. Life seemed so incredibly, excruciatingly unfair. This convicted child-molester frolicked with his lover, a kid who did not love – probably did not even like – Trent. Frolicked. Lived.

While Betty Womack rotted in jail, her kids in a foster home.

My God, who's in charge in this circus? thought Carnie. He had tried his best to stop asking himself such unanswerable questions. They were not good for the head, for the soul. Either you had faith or . . .

Or you did not. And if you did not, then you did not believe in God, or that there was a balance to the madness. A balance to the violence. A balance to the acts of people like Angus Trent.

And if you had no faith . . . if you no longer believed in God, then you were not bound by the old sanctions that warned against vengeance.

For Carnie there was only truth. And the truth was that someone should pay. Without a God – a God who would ultimately mete out appropriate justice – Carnie was left realizing that if he himself did not reap some measure of justice, those who did wrong would never be punished. Ever.

And he was not thinking of Mickey Mouse wrongs, but the kinds of wrong that could not be argued – the kind of wrong that had been done to Sandra Ann . . .

Someone *had* to pay.

And if there was a God, Carnie knew that He would understand.

TEN

Matt checked his watch as he ran toward the green Hotel/Motel sign on a cement island just outside the United Airlines terminal. He managed to dodge the exhaust from a Hertz bus and fell in behind three Japanese men in tailored suits. He flagged down the Park One bus, got on and picked up a free *USA TODAY*. The Angels were losing, the Dodgers were losing, and there had been more murders in LA and New York during the past week than in all the declared wars around the world. In other words, it was business as usual.

By the time Matt collected his car, drove to Westwood – which was located between LA proper and Santa Monica – parked his car and arrived in his office, it was nearly 6:15.

'I'm glad I caught you,' said Matt as he walked into Sam Johnstone's office and sat down in the chrome and brown-corduroy chair. It went well with the prints of ducks and hunters, or so Johnstone's secretary claimed.

'Where the fuck else would I be?' said Johnstonc. It was more a complaint than an answer.

It took Matt nearly thirty minutes to brief his boss about his trip and to give him his conclusions.

'So if this guy really isn't a Chicago cop avenging

a fellow officer's death, who do you think he is?'

'I don't know. Maybe he *is* a cop – just not a Chicago cop. Maybe he's an ex-cop. Maybe he's just somebody who knows about cops. Maybe he's just someone really bright who's read up about cops. Any way you slice it, it's trouble.'

'You think the Chicago cops know what's going on?'

'I'm not sure. I'm sure most of them would buy Camacho's killer a trip to Hawaii if they could find him. But I really don't think one of them killed Camacho.'

'What if one of them did?'

'Then he'll probably get away with it.'

Johnstone ran his big right hand over his face, pulling his nose, then dragging his hand down across a sandpapery five-o'clock shadow. 'You know, I almost wish it *was* a Chicago cop. Because, if it was, it's one less chance that we're right about this being some national vigilante. And, frankly, some guy kills a cop, I could give a fuck about catching his killer, you know what I mean?'

Matt nodded.

'But that isn't the way this thing is shaping up, is it, Matt?'

'I don't know yet.'

'*Nobody* knows yet. What I'm asking is: how do you see it? I trust your instincts. That's why I wanted you to handle this.'

'Our guy picks his shots. He goes in and does what the community wishes the lawyers and judges had done, and gets the hell outta there. But he's not some crazy vigilante.'

'What would you call him?'

'A brilliant vigilante.'

'Why don't we keep that quote away from the press?' said Johnstone sarcastically. 'First time a vigilante gets some favorable national publicity, they'll start selling guns at the 7-Eleven.' Johnstone was silent for a moment. Assessing options. 'What are you going to do now?'

'Wait. He's not done. I'll see his signature again soon, and I'll go after him.'

'As long as the press doesn't get hold of this, we've still got an edge.'

'Which is?'

'He thinks he's smarter than we are.'

Matt looked at his boss. 'He is.'

Matt didn't drive straight home. He knew Jarod's game was being played at a field on Barrington near Pico.

It was the fourth inning when Matt arrived. Jarod was playing shortstop and his team was behind by one run. The bases were loaded, one out. Matt took his seat in the stands behind a woman whose son was currently batting. Her son hit a ball up the middle, past the pitcher, who dove for the ball and missed. Jarod went to his left, snagged the ball in the webbing of his glove just as he crossed second base, stepped on the bag and threw to first base for the double play. End of the rally, end of the inning.

Matt was on his feet, screaming Jarod's name and pumping his fist in the air. As the woman in front of him screamed something at the first-base umpire.

'You looked like Ozzie Smith out there,' said Matt later, as he sat on the hood of his Jeep, while Jarod changed out of his rubber spike shoes into tennis shoes.

'Some guy said the local papers got a photo of the double play.'

'It was a great play, Jarod. Not many kids your age could've made it.'

'You really think so?'

'I know so. Helluva play. Really.'

Jarod smiled. He was aware Matt knew baseball better than most of the fathers – who knew more about their children's 'right to play' than they did about how to play the game.

'I didn't expect to see you,' said Jarod.

'Why?'

'Mom said you probably wouldn't be back until late, or maybe not even till tomorrow.'

'I wanted to be here.'

Jarod smiled. 'Thanks.'

'So, you want me to give you a lift home?'

'No, I'm going over to Steve's house for a while. Besides, Mom said she was gonna be late again.'

'You really were fantastic tonight. In fact, you reminded me of someone out there.'

'Really? Who?'

'Me. About a million years ago, I made a double play like that to win the city Little League Championship.'

'No kidding?'

'No kidding. I never forgot it. A wise man once told me that one of the keys to life is appreciating things when they happen, because they never come again.'

Jarod nodded his head and smiled an innocent smile. He understood the words, but he didn't really understand what they meant. But then, thought Matt, he himself hadn't either when his grandfather had said the same thing to him. 'The night I made that play, the papers got a picture of the first baseman catching my throw to end the double play. I made the play, and all he did was catch the ball. Can you believe it?'

'Lucky for me the coach's wife got it on video.'

Matt laughed – at himself as much as anything else.

'See you at home.'

'Right,' said Jarod. 'Dad?'

'Yeah?'

'I really appreciate you makin' the time to get here.'

'Nothing in this world more important, kiddo.'

'See ya later, Dad.'

Jarod put his spikes in his knapsack, put the knapsack over his back, got on his bike and pedaled off and away into the dusky evening. As Matt watched him go, he could see the ghosts of another time and place pedaling alongside him.

Matt phoned Laurie from the car, but there was no

answer. He drove up Barrington, past the softball field where a game was going on, past four lighted tennis courts, and into the subterranean garage. He parked the Accord and took the elevator up to the courtyard. One of the halogen lamps along the footpath had burned out. He made a mental note to speak with Stephen about it. Stephen was the president of the homeowners' association. Which meant, essentially, that for one year he was everybody's slave.

Matt stopped when he heard a noise from the alcove leading to one of the condos. He backed into the shadows and let his eyes adjust. There, about thirty feet in front of him, a man was kissing a woman passionately. Desperately probing her mouth with his tongue, his hands grasping greedily for one last sensation of intimacy. It was a lover's touch. A *new* lover's touch, thought Matt; he knew that there was a difference. He remembered what it was like to wrestle in sweat with a new love. He knew what it felt like.

He knew what it felt like . . . with the woman kissing the man in the shadows.

Laurie kissed the man again, turned, put her key in the door and started to walk inside. The man reached out, grabbed her arm, spun her around again and kissed her.

Then he left. And Laurie walked inside.

Matt walked out the shadows. Slowly. Stunned. Shaking.

He walked out to the front gate, looked through

the wire grating. Watched the man get into a black Porsche, gun the engine and drive off. Made a mental note of the license number.

'Matt?' Laurie turned around, surprised, as Matt walked in the front door.

'Who did you expect?'

'Nobody, I just . . . I just didn't expect you home . . . now.'

'I got lucky,' he said, setting his briefcase down next to the hat-rack Laurie had bought him in Santa Barbara for his fortieth birthday. He put his keys on top of the briefcase. 'I told Jarod I'd try to make his game tonight. I really wanted to be there.'

'That's nice.'

'You seem nervous.'

'I'm just . . . I dunno, it's been a long day.'

'You want a drink?'

'Sure.'

Matt walked over to the bar in the corner of the living room and poured them each a Glenlivet, neat. He handed her the drink. 'What shall we drink to?'

'I don't know.'

'Why don't we drink to us?'

'Sure. Why not?' Laurie clinked glasses with Matt, and they drank.

'Jarod was great tonight.'

'Really?'

'Made the highlight reel. You should've been there.'

'I . . . ah, couldn't get away.'

Matt nodded. 'Uh-huh.'

Silence.

'Look, I'm beat,' said Matt. 'Jet-lag. I think I'll call it a night.'

'I've got some work to do before I turn in.'

'Sure.'

Matt turned and started to walk upstairs. Then he turned back. 'Your lipstick's smeared.'

Laurie put her hand to her mouth reflexively. 'I've been rubbing my nose a lot. Allergies, I think.'

'Uh-huh. Goodnight.'

'Goodnight.'

Matt walked upstairs. Without kissing his wife. The wife he had not seen in two days. The wife he had not held in two days. The wife he had seen being held ten minutes before by another man.

Laurie downed the rest of her Scotch in a single gulp and sat down on the couch. She was still shaking.

ELEVEN

'You in already?' said Lloyd Garland.

Matt looked up from behind a wall of paper. He had tried his best to bury himself in his job this morning. Tried to shut down the crazy pictures tearing at his brain.

Lloyd Garland would be working with Matt on the vigilante case. Johnstone, who was in Washington, DC more than he was in LA, had left for Washington this morning. Matt had asked for, and received, permission to recruit Garland, a friend whose work and discretion he could count on.

Garland stood a little over six feet, and weighed a thin one-eighty. He was happily divorced, into computer golf, the stock market, Asian women and running. Unfortunately, he was also into smoking a pipe.

'What's all this?' Garland sat down in the chair in front of Matt's desk.

'I've been pulling information on all the vigilante activity around the country for the past year.'

'And?'

'There's a lot of pissed-off people out there.'

Garland took out his pipe, already filled, lit it, and blew the smoke away from Matt. As though that made a difference. Matt knew his office would smell of cherry tobacco for a couple of days now. But, unlike most people at the Bureau, most people in contemporary and politically correct society, Matt didn't care. In fact, even though he didn't smoke anymore, he didn't mind the smell of the tobacco. So Matt's office was about the only place in the building Garland could smoke. Garland's secretary had complained to him about his smoking, citing city and Bureau regulations. And most of the other agents were either ex-smokers or non-smokers.

Matt could count on an almost daily discussion – or smoke break – with Garland. Sometimes more than that.

'I've done a few preliminary sorts,' said Matt, leaning back in his chair, happy for the opportunity to focus on the investigation. 'First, in these files there are no murders done with the same weapon. Second, I've ruled out all cases where there is a direct connection between the victim and the assailant. In most cases, even if the assailant has public opinion behind him, he's still doing some jail time.'

'In the old days, you walk in and find your wife fucking some other guy, you blow him away, the courts would call it justifiable homicide.'

Matt was silent.

'Matt?'

'Yeah?'

'You okay?'

'I just lost my train of thought. Anyhow, after you take out the cases where there was some kind of connection between the victim and assailant, and cases where the assailant has been in jail for the past year, there's not that many cases left.'

'How many?'

'Twenty-five. Then I did another sort – how many of the twenty-five were national cases?'

'What do you mean by that?'

'Cases that had national visibility. Some of the cases were carried nationally only after the victim was murdered. What I was looking for were cases in which victims were high-profile enough to get national coverage before they were murdered.'

'National coverage?'

'Network news, CNN, USA TODAY, that kinda thing.'

'How many did that leave you?'

'Seven. Including Camacho in Chicago.'

'Interesting. But you still don't have anything to tie them together.'

'I know. Fact is, I've got shit.'

'And maybe you're wrong anyhow.'

'Maybe. And you know something, Lloyd? I hope I am.'

Garland sucked on his pipe, careful not to inhale all the Special Blend #39. Also careful enough to inhale enough of it to make it worthwhile. 'You still think you're on to something?'

After a moment, Matt said, 'Yes.'

'So, where do you go from here?'

'I'm going to sift through the seven cases, contact the detective in charge of each case . . . then wait.'

'What if he's finished?'

Matt smiled. 'No chance. If I'm right, he's killed and gotten away with it, so he probably believes God is on his side. That his sword is the righteous sword of His vengeance. Why should he stop now? It isn't like he's going to have a shortage of targets.'

'True.' Garland's pipe went out. He tapped the ashes into a Grand Canyon ashtray he had given to Matt a year ago – 'for the office'.

'Well, I'd better be getting back,' said Garland. He stood, smiled, and left the room.

Matt checked his watch. There was no point putting it off any longer.

The law offices of Benson, Weinberg and Stahl were located in Century City. The centerpiece of Century City – so named for its proximity to 20th Century Fox studios – was a pair of skyscrapers. These twin towers would be dwarfed by the Trade Center towers in New York, but they were very impressive by Los Angeles standards. In LA anything over twenty stories passed for a skyscraper. In many ways Los Angeles was a city that aimed low and usually hit the mark, thought Matt, as he rode up to the thirty-fifth floor.

The doors opened into a single lobby. Apparently, Benson, Weinberg and Stahl occupied this entire floor. Matt walked up to the front desk.

'May I help you?' said the pretty blond receptionist, flashing the whitest teeth he'd ever seen.

'I'd like to see Frank Jacobsen.'

'Do you have an appointment?'

'No.'

The blond's smile disappeared. She looked at Matt as though he might be trying to get through her to sell magazines to the partners. Part of her job was keeping out the riff-raff.

'I'm sorry, Mr Jacobsen doesn't see people without an appointment.'

'I really wish you'd tell him I'm here.'

'I'm sorry. Does he knew who you are?'

'Not exactly.'

'Then, there's no way—'

'Tell him the husband of the woman he's been fucking wants to see him.'

The blond's lips moved, but no words came out. She thought about saying, 'I beg your pardon?' but she had heard Matt clearly, and didn't want to hear those words again. She curved her lips into a tight-lipped smile and said, 'I'll be right back.'

'Tell him personally. Otherwise, I'm going to tell everyone on this floor, and I doubt if that would be too good for Frank's corporate image.'

The blond stood up and left the room.

Matt paced around the reception room. Frank Jacobsen. Attorney at Law. The license-plate check had led Matt to the lawyer. It was dangerous to fuck around with a cop's wife. Even an FBI agent's wife. Everybody knew that.

Most everybody, that is.

The blond walked back into the reception room, with her fake smile still working. 'He'll see you now. Last room on the left.'

'Thanks.'

The blond held the door open, and stepped aside as Matt walked past her and down the hall. The last door on the left led to a conference room. He walked in and closed the door.

'Look, I don't want any trouble,' said Frank. He looked real nervous.

In the center of the room was a long conference table, ringed by twelve chairs.

Matt walked over to Frank, grabbed his burgundy tie and yanked it up about four inches, so that Frank was standing on his toes. Then Matt grabbed Frank by the belt buckle and midget-tossed him across the conference table's smooth surface. Frank disappeared off the other end of the table, like water spilling over a cliff.

Matt walked over to where Jacobsen was getting to his feet, looking a little pale. Using the burgundy tie for leverage, Matt jerked the lawyer to his feet.

'You just made the mistake of your life, mister,' said Jacobsen in a high-pitched voice.

'Why's that?'

'Because I'm going to sue your ass from here to the end of time.'

'No kidding. What about the drugs in your house?'

'What are you talking about? I don't do drugs.'

'What about the drugs in your car?'

'You can't frame me.'

'Why not?'

'You're a cop.'

'So?'

'That's illegal.'

Matt smiled. 'That's a somewhat ironic comment coming from a lawyer.'

The comment didn't seem to bother Jacobsen. 'What do you want?'

'I want you to stop fucking my wife.'

'What does your wife say about it?'

'I'm talkin' to you.'

'It takes two to . . .' Jacobsen thought about saying 'tango'. But the look in Matt's eyes convinced him that the cliché might be inappropriate here.

'What if I still want to see Laurie?'

Matt hated the way the man seemed so comfortable with his wife's first name. Of course, he knew that Jacobsen was light years progressed beyond a first-name basis with Laurie, but still . . .

'Then I'll be back.'

Jacobsen didn't follow Matt out of the conference room. But he did look relieved to see him leave.

Riding down the elevator, Matt noticed that his hands had stopped shaking. But his insides were still churning. He knew that Jacobsen was probably on the phone to Laurie right now.

He knew what leverage he had over Jacobsen. But he had no idea what influence, if any, he still had over his own wife.

'Your wife called while you were out,' said Sarah, Matt's secretary of four years. She always referred to Laurie as 'your wife', rather than by her first name for two reasons: first, it seemed more appropriate in a business setting; second, having met Laurie a couple of times, she preferred not calling her by her first name, anyway.

'Uh-huh,' said Matt as he picked up a stack of five messages and walked toward his office.

'She sounded a little upset.'

'Thank you, Sarah,' he said, not bothering to turn around. He shut his office door behind him.

He sat down behind his desk and looked through the messages. He was not going to call Laurie back. This was not a conversation he intended to have over the phone.

The first message was from Lieutenant Earl Carpenter of the Dallas Police Department; he was returning Matt's call.

'I want you to understand that this is all off the record,' said Matt, when he had Carpenter on the line.

'What you mean is that you don't want me spreading the word around that the FBI is looking into our vigilante murder.'

'That's right. Is there anything new on the case?'

'Nope. And, quite frankly, the public doesn't seem too upset about Mr Carlisle's murder.'

'What about friends or relatives of the woman Carlisle killed?'

'All had alibis – iron-clad.'

'Maybe they hired somebody.'

'Maybe. Not likely, though. We checked it out, as much as we could. Didn't get anywhere with that.'

'How public did the case get after the woman was killed?'

'We got letters from as far away as Switzerland. When a drug dealer kills an old lady, then tries to sell his story to the movies . . . that's the kind of thing the media likes. Kinda ghoulish, if you ask me.'

'Switzerland? Then CNN carried the story?'

'Yep. We had CNN, USA TODAY, all three networks, plus about two dozen other media types hanging around for a while. It was pretty pathetic, really: all these people kissin' up to Carlisle like he was some kinda hero or somethin'. What he was is a cowardly punk who put his gun upside some eighty-year-old woman's head and blew her brains out. They were suckin' up to Carlisle because they needed him. He was the center of the story. They wanted to know all about his childhood, what his favorite music was, what kind of movies he liked. Like he was a rock star instead of a murderer. What kind of a society creates heroes like that?'

'You've lived with this case for a while now, what's your take on it?'

'I think the guy who took Carlisle out was some good-ole-boy who just said enough is enough. Lotta folks feel that way, but they don't have the stomach for the deed.'

'And you believe the family and friends of the woman Carlisle killed knew nothing about it?'

'No. But I'll tell you one thing: they're happy as hell about it. When Carlisle walked on that technicality and laughed in their faces, I figure the whole town woulda been deaf and dumb if the lady's son woulda blown Carlisle's head clean off, then and there. Figure it woulda been a tough case to prosecute without a witness . . . you know what I'm sayin?'

Matt knew exactly what Carpenter was saying. He decided not to ask him if he was playing dumb right now. If he was, Carpenter certainly wasn't going to tell some FBI agent he didn't know, and didn't have to talk to anyhow.

'I appreciate your cooperation.'

'Baldwin?'

'Yeah?'

Silence.

Then the Dallas detective said, 'You know about the note?'

TWELVE

'How dare you?' said Laurie. Her tone was a mixture of rage and indignation. She sat on the couch, while Matt paced the living room.

'Isn't that *my* line?'

'We're adults here, Matt. He could sue you.'

'I've been fucked around by lawyers before. Come to think of it, so have you.'

'That's not fair, Matt.'

'Maybe I just don't know the rules of this game.'

'You're lucky he didn't call the police.'

'I think Frank's lucky we don't live in Texas.'

'You should have come to me. After all, this is between you and me.'

'Gee, I hope I didn't screw things up with you and Frank,' said Matt sarcastically. 'Sorry, maybe that was a bad choice of words.'

'Nice to see you have a sense of humor about this.'

'Well, I don't! But what the fuck else am I supposed to do? What's the proper etiquette these days when you find out your wife's been sleeping around? I really don't know.'

Laurie and Matt both took deep breaths. Matt sat down in a chair. Laurie sat down on the couch opposite him. She shook a Marlboro out of a hard pack, lit it with a gold lighter, set down the pack and the lighter, inhaled, then blew a cloud of curling blue smoke into the air.

'Do you want a divorce?' said Matt finally.

'I don't know.'

'Do you love me anymore?'

After another puff, she said, 'I don't know.'

She did not ask if he still loved her. Matt figured that was because it didn't matter to her one way or the other.

'We need to talk about it.'

'Why?' she said, a look of defiance flickering in her eye.

'Why?' asked Matt incredulously. 'Because it's important. At least it's important to me. We made a commitment to each other, and I'm still holding up my end of the bargain.'

'Bully for you. So does that make me some kind of slut?'

'No, but it does mean that I deserve some answers.'

'We don't always get what we deserve, darling.'

Although the words stung, Matt knew why she said them. She had always said the best defense is a good offense; she lived by that rule in court. But she wasn't in court now, and Matt wished that she would have some compassion. Because his heart was being ripped out of his chest and shredded by her sharp tongue.

'Why are you so angry?'

'Because I know how angry you are,' she said, unwilling to reveal herself, only to react.

'Because of what I did to Frank?'

'Yes.'

'So you think I'm angry with you, too?'

'Of course.'

'I'm not angry, Laurie. I feel . . .' He searched for the word, but words seemed inadequate to describe his feelings. He was drowning in the silence, and no life lines were being tossed.

'I'll pack a bag,' he said finally. 'I can stay with Charlie for a while. Maybe we just need some time.'

Laurie said nothing. She puffed on her Marlboro. Matt couldn't tell if he saw a tear in her eye, or if the smoke was just getting to her. When Matt was halfway up the stairs, Laurie said, 'What should I tell Jarod?'

Matt thought about it for a moment. He had always leveled with Jarod about the tough things – sex was usually the main subject where tough answers were required. But he didn't want to put Jarod in an awkward position. Especially since they didn't know how things were going to work out. Chances were this . . . thing would resolve itself and life would eventually get back to normal. If Jarod knew the whole truth now, before Matt and Laurie worked it out, it could turn into a situation of trying to put the genie back into the bottle.

'I already told him I'm going to be in and out of town for a while. Just tell him I had to leave town again right away.' It made sense. It happened all the time. Jarod had heard that explanation for Matt's absence many times.

'Okay.'

'We've got to talk, Laurie. *Soon*. I can't leave it like this.'

'Like what?' she said, the hostile tone returning to her voice.

Matt came back down the stairs and stood in front of her. 'Don't pull that shit on me. I'm not some fucking jury you're trying to fool. I'm not intimidated. We had an explicit, not implicit, agreement – no sex outside our marriage. You broke that agreement. So don't try to cloud the issue. I'm not at fault here.'

'And I am?' she said, trying to hold her chin high.

'Yes. Damned right you are!'

'So you're just going to walk out, full of righteous rage, and expect me to come crawling back to you?'

'I expect you to work with me to resolve this.'

'Because I owe you an explanation?'

'You don't owe me your life, you don't owe me undying allegiance, but, yes, you do owe me an explanation.'

'Maybe I just—'

'Don't say it, Laurie. I want an explanation, not a colorful exit line. This is real life here . . . *our* life. When you're ready to talk, you can reach me at Charlie's or at the office.'

'What if I'm never ready to talk?'

'If you don't call me in a week, I'll figure that's an answer . . . of sorts.'

'One thing, Matt . . .'

'Yes?'

'Let's keep Jarod out of the line of fire.'

Matt just looked at his wife and pondered the

peculiarity of her remark. In the years Matt had known Jarod, he had done his best to shield him from harm, emotional as well as physical. For Laurie to consider that Matt would even think of acting otherwise was an indication of how far out of touch they had become.

Matt did not respond. He walked upstairs, packed a bag and walked out. By the time he closed the door, Laurie hadn't moved. Except to light another cigarette.

'I can't fuckin' believe it,' said Charlie Stratton. 'But you know how I feel about these things.'

Matt knew how his friend felt about 'these things'. Charlie Stratton was Matt's oldest friend in the Bureau. They had known each other for fifteen years. They had weathered Matt's first divorce, the death of Charlie's son Mark, Charlie's divorce, Charlie's heart attack, Matt's wounding in a shootout in Crenshaw, Charlie's stab at AA and his subsequent readmission into mainstream society as a 'maintenance alcoholic'.

'The four things that led to the downfall of this country occurred during the Sixties. Fuckin' Sixties,' said Stratton, as though speaking the name of the Anti christ at a revival meeting. 'Started with the fuckin' Beatles.' Stratton took a sip of beer and held it out toward Matt. 'You sure you don't want one?'

Matt shook it off. The two men were sitting on Charlie's patio, next to the pool. It was a small pool, but a pool nonetheless. Still impressive: more impressive to talk about than to swim in. Charlie sat with his feet up on a lounger that separated the two men. Matt had his legs crossed, and he was facing the pool, which looked as though it could use a cleaning.

'Number one, drugs. Can't argue with that. Number two, the pill – sex without consequences. No responsibility. Am I right?'

'You're right, Charlie,' said Matt, only half listening. He had heard the gospel according to Charlie at least a hundred times before.

'Number three, abortion. A liberal fail-safe. You wanna fool around, chances are, you use the pill, you can fuck around as much as you want, and you got no responsibility for it. But even if the woman gets pregnant, now you're *still* off the hook. And number four – and this is where I'm bringin' it back to your situation here – easy divorce. I promise till death do us part, but, on the other hand, if it doesn't work out, then I'll just get divorced. More "no responsibility" kind of thinking. Drugs, the pill, abortion, easy divorce. They all changed the shape of this country and they all sent a very clear message: do what you want, have a good time, whatever happens you're not responsible. Bottom line: no responsibility for your actions.'

Maybe he was just getting older, or maybe it was because of what he was going through, but even though Charlie's moral inventory did not explain away all of society's ills, Matt was getting to the point where Charlie's list could no longer be passed off as merely the ravings of a right-wing lunatic.

'You're sure I won't be in the way here?' said Matt.

'Hell, no. You can use the guestroom for as long as you need it.'

'I really appreciate this.'

'We do for each other. That's what friends are for, right?'

'Right. I think I'm gonna turn in.'

'Linens and towels are in the bathroom closet. Liquor cabinet is open for business . . . except for the Armagnac.'

'Understood.'

Matt left his host sitting by the pool. He didn't feel like he was imposing. He had let Charlie stay at his place for four weeks when Charlie had been tossed out of his house by his wife. Matt figured he was good for up to four weeks. But he knew that, long before that, he would need a plan.

Thank God for the job, thought Matt, as he lay in the tiny guestroom, which was even smaller than the pool. There was a phone next to the bed. Matt was not planning to use it. And he knew that Laurie would not be calling him. Not tonight.

Maybe not ever.

He had a Levelor life, he was Levelor blind / With a turn of a wand he could close off his mind / Shut out the light, keep the darkness inside / Like it's some kinda friend, not just a place to hide.

For Carnie, country and western lyrics were

elegant in their simplicity. A person didn't need to be a Rhodes Scholar to figure out what they meant. They came straight from the heart – or a bottle. In either case, they had the ring of real life lived, not contemplated, or recycled from some Hollywood perception of the way life fit neatly into two hours, a tub of popcorn and an overpriced soft drink.

Carnie sat on the bed in his room watching a country music awards show. Garth Brooks was singing 'Somewhere Other Than The Night', Carnie's favorite Garth Brooks song. The drapes were wide open and the Vegas Strip, which glowed like a dozen neon suns, cast shadows on the wall and ceiling. Circus shadows: dark spots that took on specific shapes the more he looked at them. The more he looked at the darkness that had fallen across this country, the more clearly he perceived the villains. And the heroes.

Carnie thought that the media, the mainstream media anyway, had clouded a fairly simple issue. You could walk up to someone at an ATM cashpoint, put a gun to his head, blow the guy away, and have the whole thing captured on video. Then someone somewhere along the line, usually a lawyer or agent, would end up pitching the other side of the story on the evening news. News people loved that kind of 'sexy' talk. The camera loved controversy. Before you knew it, people were marching out in front of the police department and describing the shooter as a political prisoner, a victim of racism, or a poor little rich kid who was molested by his decadent parents.

Carnie lived in a much simpler world. Even in his darkness, he could see the light. There were far fewer gray areas. His philosophy recalled a more traditional time when people could discern right from wrong. Now that seemed an impossible task.

For some. But not for Carnie.

The phone receiver was wedged between his ear and his shoulder. As someone at the other end came on the line and said, 'You're next,' Carnie hit the mute button, and Garth Brooks went silent.

After a moment, Kyle Talbot said, 'Hello, Las Vegas, you're on the air.'

'Hi, Kyle. You and I talked about Angus Trent yesterday.'

'Yes, I remember you. I certainly hope that *Mr* Trent's civil rights haven't been trampled on by you or the local constabulary.'

'Nope.'

'Well, that's the best news we've had all night.' The sneer in Talbot's voice could almost be seen, even over the radio. He sipped from his Kyle Talbot Show coffee mug. Tonight Cassie, whom he could see through the window preparing yet another pot of coffee, had been kind enough to put a shot and a half of Christian Brothers brandy in his cup. He set the cup down. 'What can I do for you tonight, Las Vegas?'

'What do you think of Angus Trent, Kyle? Really.'

Talbot drummed his fingers on the console for a moment, then said, 'I think he's scum. I think that it's a damned shame that because *he* molested a child, some decent law-abiding mother with no criminal record – who *knew* that the justice system was merely going to slap this jerk on the wrist – is now going to jail. I think it's just another example of how the justice system has broken down, and how upside-down this world has become.'

'I think something's going to happen to Trent.'

'I do, too. I wouldn't be at all surprised. He's out on bail, right?'

'Right.'

'Walking around, probably signing autographs and holding interviews, giving *his* side of the story. Boy, *there's* something the public needs to know,' said Talbot dramatically.

'I really think something's going to happen to Angus Trent,' said Carnie again.

There was something in the voice that stopped Talbot dead. He wasn't sure exactly how to respond. Did he really understand what this man was saying?

'What do you mean by that?'

'I'll call you tomorrow,' said Carnie and hung up.

'And we'll be right back, folks.' Talbot hit a button that killed his microphone. He waved to his partner, Ellis Handy, who was sitting on the other side of the glass, talking with the station's sales director.

Handy walked in with a Styrofoam cup full of Rolling Rock beer.

'Shut the door.'

Handy did so.

'Did you hear that?'

'I was talking to Andy. Why?'

Talbot thought about laying it all out to Handy, but thought better of it. Maybe that guy was just some loser talking out of the empty end of a Jack Daniels bottle.

But then again . . .

'Never mind. But if anything happens to Angus Trent, I want you in here on the double.'

'Why?'

'Maybe we're about to get the miracle we've been praying for.'

'*You're* in a good mood tonight,' said Cassie, as she handed Kyle Talbot a glass of Jack Daniels and sat down on the bed next to him. She wore a scarlet and gray Ohio State Buckeye football jersey, nothing underneath.

Talbot sat at the head of the huge custom-made waterbed, propped up against three large pillows, his attention focused on the big-screen TV a few feet from the foot of the bed. He had received the waterbed in return for a few radio spots a couple of years ago. The waterbed company was struggling, and the station, as usual in those days, was running in the red. Something was better than nothing. It was a paper transaction. It had cost Talbot nothing, and he hadn't had to drop a dime in Uncle Sam's hat either.

'Did you hear me?'

'What?' said Talbot.

'I said it seems like you're in a pretty good mood tonight.'

'I am.'

'Well, you know—'

Talbot held up his hand for her to be quiet. 'I want to see his.' *Headline News* came on. The top story was about the decline in home sales. Talbot hit the mute button. It wasn't there. Not yet, anyhow. Big-time murder always took precedent over government statistics.

'What are you looking for?' said Cassie, rubbing her bare, twenty-years-younger-than-he-was tanned legs up against his hairy thighs.

'A meal ticket, baby.' Talbot downed a healthy dose of liquid anesthetic and smacked his lips. 'A meal ticket.'

The Ruby Slipper was a Vegas bar in a mini-mall, with a twenty-four-hour coin-operated laundry on one side and a burger joint on the other. Carnie sat in his rented Fiesta, watching and waiting.

This was the second night in a row he had tailed Angus Trent to this bar. A car pulled up in front of the bar and three men got out. Carnie got out of his car quickly, and walked inside with the other three men.

'If Dante had been reincarnated as Jessie Helms, and he rewrote his vision of Hell, the Ruby Slipper Bar would be the movie version of the book.' The quote was framed in big letters, and hung just inside the door. It was attributed to the *Las Vegas Tribune.*

The Ruby Slipper was dark, and it took a minute or two for Carnie's eyes to adjust. Even though he knew what to expect, basically, he was not prepared for the sight of two men kissing passionately in a booth near the door. He tried to hide his disgust. He sat down at the bar between two customers who seemed to be alone. One was wearing black leather pants that seemed a little snug – as well as a little young for a man who looked to be in his forties. The man to Carnie's left was wearing a suit, and looked like any other nine-to-fiver. He was staring into a broken mirror above the bar, trying to catch someone's – anyone's – attention.

Across the bar, Carnie saw Angus Trent holding forth, signaling the bartender for another round of drinks. Three young men sat at his table, laughing, drinking and occasionally whispering to each other.

Carnie ordered a beer, no glass. In this bar he'd drink from the bottle.

'Hi,' said the man dressed in leather.

Carnie nodded.

'Haven't seen you in here before.'

'First time.'

'You from around here?'

'I work down the street.'

The look on the leather man's face curled into an awkward, forced smile.

It was a pitiful and desperate smile, thought Carnie.

'Really? I live a few blocks from here. Me and my . . . well, my wife moved out a couple months ago.' The muscle-less smile came back for an encore. 'For obvious reasons. For years I'd drive by here and . . .

Of course, I knew what this place was . . . I knew what *I* was. So, finally, I took the big leap and came in here last week.'

'That's nice,' said Carnie. He didn't mean that. He just couldn't think of anything else to say.

'Oh, hey, look, don't think I'm trying to pick you up, okay? I'm just making conversation. I know I'm not any James Dean or nothin' like that.'

'No, it's not that,' said Carnie, again not knowing what else to say. Wishing the guy would just shut up. Yet, in spite of himself, he felt sorry for the man.

'No need to explain. It's the leather, isn't it?'

'Pardon?'

'I'm too old and too outta shape for a leather outfit. I'm just making a fool of myself.' He shook his head and stared down at his drink.

Across the room, a drunken Angus Trent got to his feet. He smiled, waved at the bartender to hurry up that round of drinks, and stumbled off toward the restroom.

Carnie set his drink down, without looking at anyone, pushed himself off the stool, walked around the bar and headed toward the restroom, too.

The men's room at the Ruby Slipper was cleaner than most bar restrooms Carnie had been in. That surprised him. For some reason, he'd thought that it would be filthy.

Carnie took a wooden wedge out of his pocket and, in a quick easy motion, stuck it between the door and the floor. He then gave it a surreptitious kick with his heel.

Angus Trent was pissing into a urinal two down from where Carnie stood. Carnie turned his head toward Angus, who was already looking at him.

'Hi,' said Angus.

'Hi.'

Carnie turned his eyes back toward the wall in front of him. It was papered with a pattern of ruby red slippers, over which had been written scores of first names, phone numbers, limericks, and the blueprints of what could only be described as hieroglyphic wishes and dreams.

Trent walked over to the sink, pushed a silver button, and sprayed his hands with pink soap. He lathered up under a stream of water, and turned his attention back toward Carnie.

Carnie shook his penis, put it back in his pants, zipped up, and walked over to the sink next to the one Trent was using.

Trent turned the water off and looked over at Carnie, smiling.

'Hi,' said Trent, again.

'Don't I know you?' said Carnie.

'I don't think so.'

'No, I'm sure I know you.'

The smile started to melt from Trent's face.

Trent turned his face away, pulled a paper towel out of the dispenser, and said, 'I don't think so.'

It was the last thing Angus Trent ever said.

THIRTEEN

On a clear day, Matt could see the Pacific Ocean from his office in the Federal Building in Westwood. It was a clear day and the sun was dying in the water, but he couldn't now see the Pacific because Lloyd Garland's pipe smoke was obscuring the view.

'Of the seven cases that fit the parameters, the same note was left at four of them,' said Matt.

Garland looked at the fax copies of the notes. On all four the message was the same: *'We reap what we sow.'*

'Why weren't these released to the press?'

'First, none of the separate police departments knew about the notes discovered by the others. Second, it isn't unusual to hold back a key clue from the press. Third, in isolation, because all the victims were obviously hated by so many people in the communities in which the various murders occurred, such a note conveying this rather unoriginal sentiment would almost be expected. By itself, it didn't seem like the signature of a *serial* killer.'

'I suspect all the police departments tried to trace the message.'

'And all came up with the same conclusions.' Matt looked down at his notes. 'Each slip of paper was four inches long and an inch wide, and printed on the most common form of copying paper. It would have been easy for the killer to cut all the letters or words out of magazines, paste them on one piece of paper, then run off as many copies as he wanted. And there are a thousand ways to produce photocopies without anyone else seeing them being made. He could have gone to a copy place and used a self-serve machine – that's normal if you only want to make a few copies. Or he could have had access to a machine where he worked. All the PDs have canvassed their local photocopy shops, but came up empty. Besides, the guy probably copied this material in some other city or town.'

'Did any of the people you contacted act suspicious?'

'Not really. And every time someone told me about the note – it was like pulling teeth most of the time – I acted surprised, like it was the first time I'd heard about it. Besides, I got the feeling all of them would be content to leave their particular case unsolved – forever. It's safe to say that I wanted more information from them than they wanted from me.'

Garland put his feet up on a chrome and glass coffee table, drew on his pipe, and looked out the window. 'So where does that leave us?'

'We know there's a serial killer out there. We know he's never used the same weapon twice. We know he doesn't necessarily live in the same part of the country as his victim – since, so far, we've got Bellevue, Washington, Chicago, Dallas, and Miami. We can assume that he doesn't know his victims personally. The only thing we've got then is a motive.'

'Which is?'

'He believed that all his victims deserved to die.'

'Great. That narrows it down to about a quarter of a billion people,' said Garland sarcastically.

'In *this* country.'

'What do we do now: wait for him to make a mistake?'

'He doesn't seem like a guy who makes many mistakes.'

'Seems to me, he's already made one,' said Garland.

'What's that?'

'The notes.'

Matt looked down at the faxes on his desk and smiled. But it was a humorless smile. 'These're just invitations to the party.'

When Kyle Talbot awoke, it was nearly 10 a.m. He was used to these hours – liked them, in fact. He looked at Cassie Broderick's naked back. She was spread-eagled, face down, on the waterbed, her blond hair just touching her shoulderblades. For an instant the thought of his ex-wife Glenda flashed in his mind.

When he had married her twenty years earlier, Glenda had been thin. Everybody, except Kyle, was always trying to get her to eat. Somewhere along the line, someone had succeeded. When they got married, she had weighed ninety-eight pounds. When they were divorced, three years ago, she weighed 165. Most men were visual in their sexuality. At least, that's what one psychologist Kyle had interviewed on his show a few months ago had said. It made sense to Kyle. The sight of his 165-pound wife failed to arouse him.

He smiled as he walked from the room, glancing back once more at Cassie's lean young body in his bed. She had once complained that she was nothing more than a trophy for him.

He had not argued.

Talbot brushed his teeth with Sensodyne toothpaste. His dentist had recommended this brand because his teeth were so sensitive, and he always made such a baby of himself in the dentist's chair. After brushing, he gargled with fluoride. As he swished and gargled for the required one minute, he turned on his portable TV. Ten o'clock, straight up. *Headline News.*

'In Las Vegas last night, accused child-molester Angus Trent was murdered. In Washington this morning . . .'

Kyle Talbot spit the fluoride into the sink. 'Shit!' He picked up the phone next to the toilet, and pressed Ellis Handy's number on his memory touch-tone phone.

'Yeah?'

'Ellis. Did you hear the news?'

'What are you talking about?'

'Angus Trent was murdered last night.'

'No shit!'

'If our Las Vegas friend calls in tonight, it just might mean *People Magazine*. Look, get Craig from the *Messenger* down to the station tonight. If the guy calls, Craig can get the ball rolling.'

'Should I tell him what's going on?'

'Titillate him, then swear him to secrecy.'

'Gotcha.'

'And, Ellis . . .'

'Yes?'

'Make sure he brings a photographer.'

Carnie sat in the dim light of the electric fireplace, mute button on, drinking a Rolling Rock beer. One of the networks had led with Trent's murder, the other two had run the story as their second feature. The tabloid shows were running teasers about a 'bombshell' regarding Trent's murder.

Carnie almost laughed out loud, because he realized that they knew nothing. And he was sitting there in his living room, a free man.

But he *didn't* laugh. Carnie could not recall the last time he had laughed out loud. He had brooded about that a few months back, and had gone out to rent three comedies that, a few years ago, had him rolling on the floor. Though he had watched all three, he didn't laugh once.

More and more now, Carnie got the feeling that he was just limping through life, since . . . Since that day there didn't seem much point in going on. He had played by the rules, done the 'right' things, never cheated on his wife, put God and country right behind family.

But not everyone played by the rules, reflected

Carnie. And, in a single act of madness, such people could destroy your world and everything in it.

Now Carnie was playing by *their* rules.

Somewhere along the line, Carnie had realized that the world had changed when he wasn't looking. And that change was irreversible. Whatever order he had grown up with – had always believed would be there – was now being devoured by chaos. By violence. One of the reasons violence had become such a potent weapon in contemporary society was because it was so obvious no one could protect the average citizen against it anymore.

Most people were now more afraid than they had ever been.

Carnie *used* that fear now. Used violence. *Playing by their rules.*

Carnie looked at his watch, then pressed the remote control to turn off the TV and turn on the radio. He picked up the phone and dialed *The Kyle Talbot Show*, wondering if he would get through.

'Blow everybody off tonight. I want to make sure this guy gets through.'

'What if he doesn't call?' asked Jill, Kyle Talbot's screener. She was a recent University of Las Vegas graduate. English major. She was thrilled to get the job. Broadcasting – that was where the action was. She had noticed what was going on between Kyle and Cassie. Executive producer, my ass, thought Jill. Had her own ass been a couple sizes smaller, she might have had the opportunity to be, if not in

Cassie's shoes, at least in Kyle's bed. And she would have done it, too. Why not? She was young and hungry. Kyle was someone she admired. What the fuck, she thought. She smiled again. She really did have a way with words. But then, she was an English major.

'He'd better call.'

'Why?'

'Make sure there's always a line open. Give me just the choice calls and get rid of everyone else.'

'What should I say?'

'You're a bright girl. That's why I hired you. You'll think of something,' said Kyle, and he walked away.

Yeah, he thought: a bright girl with a big butt.

Matt had forgotten his tennis shoes, so he stopped by the Barrington townhouse at a time when he figured Laurie and Jarod would be gone.

He was wrong.

'Matt?' Laurie stood at the door with the keys in her hand. She looked very surprised.

And uncomfortable, thought Matt. 'I didn't think you'd be here now.'

'I got home early.'

Matt felt very awkward.

Laurie closed the door, and set her keys on the table next to it.

'I came by to pick up my tennis shoes.'

'Oh.'

Silence. 'You want some coffee?' said Laurie finally.

Fifteen minutes and two cups of coffee later, Matt and Laurie sat in the living room looking at each other. He sat in a chair, *his* chair; she sat on the couch. And they were just about out of small talk.

'I don't know why I feel the way I do, Matt,' said Laurie finally.

'Or the way you *don't*.'

'It's natural that our passion gets less over time.'

'Is it natural for it to go away altogether?'

'I care for you, Matt . . .'

'But you don't love me anymore. Is that it?'

'Not the way I used to.'

'You mean, you don't want to fuck me like you used to. You mean, now that you got some Century City lawyer blowing a little wind up your skirt, our relationship, our marriage is disposable.'

'I prefer to look at our . . . situation as though it were a cocoon from which I'm emerging.'

'That's great. Fucking great. Now I'm just a piece of dead skin you're growing out of. You don't *feel* anything anymore, you know that? I don't mean just toward me. I mean toward anything. You're numb. And some guy ramming his cock inside you a couple of hours a week might give you sensation, but that isn't love, Laurie.'

'I care about you, Matt.'

'That isn't love either. I really don't think you have a clue what love *is*.'

'Do you?'

'Sometimes I think I do. Usually I'm more of an expert on what it's *not*.'

'Did you love me when we got married?' said Laurie.

'Very much.'

'I mean, real love, not just lust.'

'Sure, I lusted for you. But I loved you, too. That's the way it's supposed to work.'

Laurie took out the Marlboro hard pack, shook out a cigarette, lit it, set the pack and lighter down and inhaled the smoke as though it were some kind of sacrament, capable of relieving the hidden pains of a lifetime. She exhaled and, from the look in her eyes, the fix had not quite taken. 'I've always separated sex and love. My therapist says I'm like a man that way.'

'Is this the same therapist who says it's okay to explore your lesbian fantasies?'

'What's your point?'

'I don't suppose this "therapist" had anything to do with your likening our marriage to dead skin to be cast off.'

'I really think you're being a little hard on Cynthia.'

Matt kept silent. He was not about to back off.

'Anyhow,' continued Laurie, 'she says I'm masculine in the sense that I can separate sex and love.'

'Did she say that you *can* separate the two, or that you *do* separate the two?'

'What difference does that make?'

'One implies you're doing it consciously, the other implies . . . other reasons.'

'Like?'

'Like maybe you're afraid to integrate the two.'

'Why?'

'The need to survive is a powerful urge. When you get burned a couple times real good, you learn to protect yourself.'

Laurie did not respond.

'Look, I'm not here to be your therapist, I'm here to be your husband.'

'Even if you're right, I'm not going to change overnight.'

'Maybe, instead of throwing off the cocoon of our marriage, you could just throw off the cocoon of being a slut.'

Laurie thought of about a dozen unkind and combative remarks. What she said, after a moment, was, 'I guess I deserved that. Not that I'm a slut, not that I look at myself as a slut . . . I'm just saying you deserved your shot.'

'And I'm sure your therapist predicted that I, Mr Dead Skin, would react this way.'

'No. She said you'd probably slap me around a little and justify it because your fragile male ego had been damaged. I told her you were much more civilized than that.'

'Is that good? To be civilized, I mean? And, according to your therapist, exactly how civilized is it for a married woman to go around fucking other men?' Matt didn't wait for the answer. He really wasn't interested. 'You know, Laurie, I have no idea who you are anymore. It's a little scary. When we got married, we made promises to each other. I counted on those promises. In my mind they were as solid as the ground I walked on. Now that ground is crumbling under my feet.'

Laurie smoked, tipped ash into an empty glass, and tried her best to look Matt in the eye without looking guilty. It became a balancing act.

Matt stood. 'I trusted you.'

'Is that supposed to make me feel guilty?'

When he was at the door, Matt turned around and said, 'It'd make *me* feel like shit.'

Ten minutes later, Matt was on the San Diego Freeway, heading back to the Valley and Charlie Stratton's place. He turned on the radio and punched a few buttons. Matt recognized Kyle Talbot's voice immediately. He was not a fan, but he knew who Talbot was, had read an article or two about the man, had seen him on one of the tabloid TV shows one night while flipping channels.

Talbot was talking about politicians.

'Politicians at every level of government have sent a clear message – hostility works. Mean is in. It's cool. It's kind of a hellish mutation of the idea that the squeaky wheel gets the most grease. With the media giving the most air-time to whomever shouts the loudest – today that's the only credential you need to become an expert – government has let it be known that if you burn down enough buildings, or rob enough stores, or threaten enough people, we'll give you whatever you want. When I was growing up, if you burned down a building, you went to jail. Today, you're treated like some kind of hero.'

Talbot was on a roll. His coffee was kicking in. Out of one corner of his eye he was watching his slim-hipped honey trying her best to look busy. Out of the other, he was watching Jill.

'It all goes back to leadership, folks; and the people of this country simply do not trust their leader. President Souther lied in order to get elected, then in a series of backroom deals, he arm-twisted the House and the Senate into ramming a tax increase down our throats at the worst possible moment, and he's not done yet.

'We've got to do something about what's happening to our country. I'm telling you, a viable third-party candidate in the next election is becoming a very real possibility.'

That was when he saw Jill signaling madly.

Talbot smiled and said, 'We'll be right back.' He hit the button, killed the microphone, and waved Jill into the booth.

'It's him,' she said, breathlessly.

'Las Vegas?'

'Yes. He verified that he's the one who called last night.'

'Okay, we'll go to him after the break – *immediately*.'

'Right.'

'And tell Ellis to get those guys from the newspaper in here. Especially the photographer.'

'Right.'

'Okay, now move. This could be the big one, Jill.' In his enthusiasm, Talbot leaned over and kissed her on the cheek. She was a little taken aback, but she merely smiled and walked out of the booth. Flattered. All her feminist leanings giving way to the power of the moment. She did not feel threatened.

Outside the booth, Cassie was sitting on a couch. She had watched the entire scene. She was not smiling.

'You're on after the commercial,' said a voice in Carnie's ear.

'Thank you,' he said politely. He considered himself lucky to get on Kyle Talbot's show, his *national* show, two nights in a row. He hit the mute button and the radio went silent.

'You're on with Kyle Talbot,' said another voice in Carnie's ear.

'Hi, Kyle. Great show.'

'Thank you. So, who am I speaking to?'

'Las Vegas. I called you last night.'

'Yes, I understand. Most people give a first name.'

'I know.'

Silence.

Many things understood. On both sides.

'So, if I remember correctly, you said last night that you thought something was going to happen to Angus Trent.'

'That's right.'

'Well, something happened to him, all right.'

'I know.'

This was the pivotal moment. Talbot looked up at the photographer, who was snapping pictures, and tried to look serious. Tried not to look the way he felt: like he was going for a monster, tongue-sticking-out, flying-through-the-air, game-winning, crowd-on-its-feet, slam-fucking-dunk.

'Did you have anything to do with Angus Trent's murder?'

Silence. Waiting. Tick-tock . . . Everything would change with the proper answer.

Talbot knew it.

And Carnie knew it when he said, 'Yes.'

Talbot did his best to stifle the smile. 'What do you mean by that? Are you saying that you murdered Angus Trent?'

'No.'

Suddenly the balloons showering Talbot's victory celebration started to pop.

'No?'

'It wasn't murder. It was an execution.'

Talbot said a silent *Yes!* High-fives all around. He realized that this was a defining moment. Few people had the ability to recognize such moments when those moments actually occurred. Talbot was different, in the sense that he had consciously structured his life so that such a moment could occur.

Which was why he was prepared.

'So, you're saying that Trent's murder was justified?'

'Yes.'

'Why?'

'There are people out there who commit evil acts over and over again, and the justice system no longer protects us from these people. Like you're always saying, someone has to *do* something. Someone has to stop the madness. Some things are just wrong.'

'For example?'

'Some guy rapes my wife, that's wrong.'

'What else?'

'Someone steals money from me, that's wrong.'

'What else?' It was no longer the brandy-laced coffee that Talbot was running on; it was pure adrenaline.

'Someone molests my child, that's wrong.'

'What about the accused getting his day in court?'

'And what if the court turns loose the man who molested my child? What am I supposed to do?'

Silence.

'Am I supposed to just walk away and congratulate the slick lawyer who earned his fee by helping the man who put his penis between my five-year-old's legs go free? Am I supposed to just say, well, gee, our legal system is the best in the world, and, well, if that means that the guy who abused my child is to go free, well, I guess that's okay with me? That's *not* okay with me.'

'What do you mean?' said Talbot. Even though he knew exactly what the man meant. Talbot tried his best to look concerned when he asked the question – as the *Messenger* photographer snapped tomorrow's page-one pictures.

'I mean, most people out there – black, white,

brown, whatever – have more common sense than the men who tell us how to live our lives. I think that's what galls people the most. There's just no common sense in the world anymore.'

'For example,' said Talbot, reeling in the fish.

'I believe a person should be judged by his actions – like you say, Kyle. I don't care what color a person's skin is, I really don't. I *do* care about his actions, when they affect me and my family. I care about that a lot.'

Suddenly, through his window, Talbot saw several uniformed police officers virtually burst through the outer studio door. Ellis Handy tried to stop them. It was at that exact instant that Talbot knew for sure it was really happening. He knew what they wanted. They wanted to know what all America would want to know tomorrow.

'And you care so much about it, that you take it upon yourself to execute certain people?'

'I believe it's time for people to reap what they sow.'

'. . . reap what they sow,' said a voice on the radio.

For Matt Baldwin, it was like being struck with a bolt of lightning from a very dark night sky. Out of nowhere.

He picked up the phone and push-buttoned a special number. 'Clara, this is Matt Baldwin. Get me on a flight to Las Vegas first thing in the morning.'

After a few minutes she said, 'USAir, flight 754, eight a.m.'

'Thanks.'

In Las Vegas, Kyle Talbot sat in the on-air side of the studio booth, surrounded by Las Vegas Police Department detectives and local reporters. 'Reap what they sow, eh? Since you won't give me a name, Las Vegas, I'm going to give you one.'

'If you want.'

'I'm going to call you "The Reaper". What do you think?'

'It doesn't matter. I'm going to hang up now.'

'Wait a minute. When will you call again?'

'When I've got something else to say.'

And the Reaper hung up.

In Los Angeles, Matt Baldwin lay in the middle of the queen-size bed in Charlie Stratton's guest room, an overnight bag packed and on the floor at the foot of the bed. Sleeping by himself in a bed this size made Matt feel even more alone. Made him think even more about Laurie. About what Laurie was doing tonight. And with whom.

And he was thinking that, if his gut was right, he was just about to enter the nightmare.

In his living room, Carnie sat alone in the darkness. But, for the first time in a long while, he no longer felt alone. He was connected. To Kyle Talbot. To the hundreds of thousands of people who understood what he was doing and why, and would not condemn him. One of the reasons Carnie liked listening to

Talbot was because he felt the people who called in were people like himself. People who had *lived* life, not just *thought* about it. If reality was defined by activist groups' hypothetical questions, which was often just another term for the most extreme case possible, then reality would be a strange thing indeed, thought Carnie. America was being destroyed, he reasoned, because the playing field was forever being defined by an ever-diminishing lowest common denominator. Education had to be delivered so that the poorest student in the class could understand. Justice had to be meted out so that even a person who had been captured on videotape walking up to an ATM machine, putting a gun to another person's head and blowing that person's brains out, could exhaust the judicial and financial limits of the system. The government must provide foreigners with brochures, voting information, DMV information, educational information, in the language of each foreigner's choice. Carnie remembered a day recently when he had applied for a driver's license. He could not find a booklet in English. Spanish, Vietnamese, Chinese, yes. English, no. He remembered thinking about what would happen if *he* moved to some other country and demanded that its government and the educational system communicate with him in *his* native tongue, rather than its own.

Nowhere but America.

Land of the free, home of the naive.

But Kyle Talbot wasn't naive. Nor was he a racist.

He was merely a realist whose ideas were shaped by the same kind of common sense that had determined Carnie's philosophy. There was an old line that a liberal was just a conservative who hadn't yet been mugged. The number of people who hadn't been mugged, in one way or another, was shrinking fast.

Carnie sat in the darkness, feeling less alone than he had felt in a long time. Kyle Talbot, a man he respected, had not judged him. Had not told him that he was wrong for *executing* Angus Trent.

Carnie sipped his beer and stared into the darkness.

Wondering how far the dream would take him.

FOURTEEN

Most men were better at starting relationships than they were at keeping them going. But Matt was different. At least he thought he was. Now.

Matt was thinking about this as he sipped a Glen Ellen Chardonnay: the mini-bottle – the three-dollar version they served on the USAir flight to Vegas. The male flight attendant asked Matt if he wanted to sniff the bottle cap. Great wine, vintage two p.m. It was an old joke, but in this case appropriate.

As Matt watched the clouds sliding by slowly beneath him, and observed the great expanse of brown uninhabited land, he wondered, not for the first time, whether there really were too many people on the planet – or just too many people in LA trying to become famous.

The panorama of empty space also made him feel alone. There was no one waiting for him in Vegas. No one had seen him off at LAX. And now, in-between, there was only empty space, unrealized potential. Much like his marriage, thought Matt.

'The FBI . . .' said Vince Brunowski, LVPD chief of detectives. He was young, good-looking, with dark hair and a solid build. Younger than Matt would have predicted. The detective let his comment dangle in the silence, like bait.

It was a complicated scenario, and Matt realized that Brunowski knew the subtleties of the dance. If Matt did not tell Brunowski enough, then he could expect little, if any, cooperation. On the other hand, Matt could not tell him everything. He didn't know Brunowski, or who else he might tell. At this point containment was still important, even though Matt knew the element of containment was slipping away fast. Still, the public didn't yet know that Angus Trent was just one of several men the Reaper had murdered. Part of Matt's job was making sure they didn't find out. At least for a while.

When Brunowski finished running through the facts of the case, Matt knew he was holding back the note, just like the other detectives had done. Partly for the same reasons. Partly because he wanted to hear the big-time FBI man mention it.

'Was there anything else?'

'Like what?' said Brunowski with a poker face.

Maybe people in Vegas played poker better than in other parts of the country, thought Matt. 'Did he leave any physical evidence behind?'

'Like what?'

'Like maybe a note?'

'A note,' said the Vegas detective. It was neither an answer nor a question.

'Was there a note?'

'Yes.'

Silence.

'What did it say?'

'What do you think it said?' said Brunowski.

'Look,' said Matt, 'tell me about the note.'

'Why should I? This case is under my jurisdiction. Some guy got killed in Vegas. That doesn't make it a Federal case . . . unless you know something I don't.'

'Why are you making me crawl through glass?'

'Nothing personal. It's just that I've had some problems before with the FBI. Vegas is a place the FBI takes a special interest in, and they haven't seemed to care much about my feelings in the past,' said Brunowski with the smile of a guy who knows he's holding four aces. 'Maybe you're different.'

'I still don't give much of a fuck about your feelings, but I'm not out to steal any of your thunder either.'

'What are you trying to do, then?'

'I'm trying to catch a serial killer. I think you might be able to help me do that. And I'm trying to keep a PR lid on tight.'

Matt had leveled, to a certain extent. He wasn't positive that it would be enough.

'People've been talkin' about the radio show,' said Brunowski.

This was the beginning. And the end to containment. People, particularly the press, wanted to believe that there was some hero vigilante that had been loosed upon the black plague that was devouring this land. And that this hero was about to make things if not right, then at least more visually interesting to a public that shot up news like a junkie shoots up smack.

One of the differences between drugs and news was that there was more money in news. And its procurers were not as ethical as drug dealers. Matt knew this was true because he had dealt extensively with both.

'I heard the radio show, but I have no idea as to the authenticity of what the caller said.'

'You're here,' said Brunowski. It was a question even though it didn't sound like one.

'So?'

'There's more to it than Angus Trent. Otherwise, it's local, and my case all the way.'

Matt looked at Brunowski. 'What the fuck do you want me to say?'

The Las Vegas detective thought about suggesting 'The truth', but knowing what he did about Las Vegas, the street and life in general, it sounded more realistic to say, 'I want you to give me a fair shake.'

'You give me what you've got, I'll give you everything I can.'

Brunowski wasn't figuring that he was going to hold up the FBI, not in the long run, anyhow. And he knew that a great deal of what he accomplished, the big cases anyhow, depended on the help of others. He could do worse than to make an ally of a high-ranking FBI agent. He had already made his point, proven his worth.

After he had run down the facts and figures of Angus Trent's murder, Brunowski continued, 'I've got a Xerox copy of the note here in this folder.' He opened the folder and handed the photocopy to Matt.

Matt looked it over, but not carefully. He had seen it before. 'No fingerprints?'

'Nope. No way to trace it, really. The original was on the kind of paper you can get at about a hundred thousand photocopy places, coast to coast; and nearly a hundred right here in Vegas. Add to that, it could've been made on a private copying machine, or one where the man himself works. And the letters have been painstakingly cut out of magazines. Each letter could be from a different magazine. Pretty smart, really.'

'Anything jump out at you about this case? I'd like your personal opinion.'

'The viciousness of the act itself. I might expect it from someone close to Betty Womack, but everyone there seems to have a solid alibi.'

'Maybe they paid someone to do it.'

'Maybe. But in Vegas we see our share of professional and semi-professional hits. They're rarely this vicious. They're more . . . I dunno . . . workmanlike, I guess.'

'What exactly did the killer do to Trent?'

'I'd rather have you read the report than tell you.'

Brunowski handed the folder to Matt, who scanned through the report to a page that detailed how Angus Trent had died. He had been stabbed several times in the belly, then he had been castrated and his penis had been stuffed into his mouth.

Matt raised his eyebrows, took a deep breath and tossed the folder back onto Brunowski's desk.

'There are a lot of people out there who believe that repeat sex offenders, particularly child-molesters, ought to be castrated. If I recall, I even heard about a judge offering castration to a repeat child-molester as an alternative to going to prison for life.'

'I know that. But it takes a special kind of person to actually do this.'

'I heard about some shit like that going on in Viet Nam,' said Matt. 'Maybe he's a vet.'

'Maybe. And those knife wounds to the belly tell me that the killer knew what he was doing: that he had seen death up close and personal before. You want to kill somebody, you stab them in the heart, maybe slit their throat. But stomach wounds . . . it takes a while to die that way.'

'Who would know that?'

'Professional killer. Ex-soldier. Somebody who's spent some time in the joint.'

'A cop?'

'Yeah, maybe. Is that where you're going with this, Baldwin? You think the guy's a cop?'

'No. I'm just listing all the possibilities.'

Both men were silent for a moment.

'We ran down a guy who talked to the perpetrator. You wanna talk to him?' Brunowski gave Matt what passed for a smile.

After Matt showed up at his door, Barry Carmen had spent the first few minutes in his bathroom vomiting, before he could answer questions.

'Are you all right now?' asked Matt when Carmen had returned from the bathroom. Matt had heard the dry heaves through the door. He knew what the man was going through, had seen it before. He felt for the guy, but that was not to say that he would not exploit this weakness if he needed to.

'What did you and this man talk about, Mr Carmen?'

'I don't know. Small talk, I guess.'

'Come on, Mr Carmen. I don't imagine you have anything to hide, but I'm going to need your full cooperation.' *Or else* was merely implied.

'Leather.'

'Pardon?'

'I was wearing a leather outfit.'

'A leather outfit?' It wasn't Matt's job to make things easy.

'Leather pants. Leather jacket. Brown.'

'And the two of you were talking about your ... outfit?'

'That's right.'

'What were you saying about it?'

'Honestly, I was saying that I didn't think I looked good in it. I'm a little ... well, it just didn't fit me right. I think it's a little too young for me, you know?'

Matt nodded his head as though he knew. 'Did you talk about anything else?'

'Not that I can remember.'

'Think.'

Carmen sipped a glass of orange juice. If he could, Matt would have filled it half-full of vodka. Carmen needed to relax, and Matt would always rather interrogate a nervous person who got himself drunk to make the nerves go away. But he couldn't play it that way.

'Yeah, I do remember something. He said he works near there.'

'There?'

'The Ruby Slipper bar.'

'He said that?'

'Yes. And I told him that I lived nearby. That I'd been driving by the Ruby Slipper for a long time, and finally took the plunge.'

'Did you notice him looking at Angus Trent while you were talking to him?'

'Not really.'

'Describe this man to me?'

'He was blond, and he had a blond mustache.'

'How long was his hair?'

'Kind of longish. Not quite to his shoulders.'

'Build?'

'He had a good build. Not overweight, not too skinny.'

'Muscular?'

'I couldn't tell. He had on a jacket. A black jacket.'

'How old do you think he was?'

'I don't know. He wasn't a kid, if that's what you mean,' said Carmen defensively.

'That's not what I mean. How old do you think he was?'

'Late thirties, early forties. It was hard to tell because, like I said, he had a good build, like he stayed in shape. Then, with the long hair, it was really hard to say.'

'Did you notice any other distinguishing marks? Like a tattoo, a scar, a mole – anything like that?'

Carmen thought a moment, then said, 'No.'

'Did you notice any distinguishing jewelry, like bracelets, a gold chain, anything like that?'

'He was wearing a wedding ring.'

'You noticed that?'

'Yeah, I noticed it right off.'

'What did that mean to you?'

'I wasn't sure. Some guys wear wedding rings just to throw people off . . . people they're not attracted to. It kind of smoothes the skids of rejection, you know. And some people really are married. Hell, *I* used to be married. Honestly, it's kind of a turn-on to see some guy who's married come into a bar and, well, you think maybe you can seduce the guy. I mean, he's there to be seduced. It's just that maybe you can be his virgin experience, you know?'

Again, Matt nodded his head as though he knew – but he did not. 'Was there anything distinctive about the ring?'

Carmen thought about that for a moment. 'It was a twisted kinda thing.'

'Pardon?'

'It was like twisted bronze. It's hard to describe.'

'Try.'

'It was like two tiny bronze ropes twisted together. Kind of like a hippie thing.'

'What do you mean?'

'Like when people had their own rings made, you know?'

This Matt did know. He recalled a time when people wrote their own vows, putting in quotes from Khalil Gibran's *The Prophet*, leaving out offending words – 'obey' was one that usually found the trash heap – and composed, or at least specified, their own music. It was a time when people made God a generic overlay for whatever philosophy they happened to be into that week. Matt had been the best man at a wedding during which the bride and groom smoked a joint and pledged allegiance to some red-haired kook who thought he was the reincarnation of every great religious figure from the beginning of time.

It had seemed to be the thing to do at the time.

'Was there anything else you remember? Anything at all?'

'Can't think of anything. Honestly.'

Matt noted that Carmen had used the word *honestly* three times already. He really wanted Matt to believe him. But, most of all, he wanted to be left alone.

'May I use your phone?'

'Sure,' said Carmen.

Matt picked up the phone next to him, and push-buttoned Vince Brunowski's direct line.

'Brunowski,' said the detective into the phone.

'Baldwin here. Your guys check the alley behind the Ruby Slipper?'

'For what?'

'Look for a blond wig and a blond mustache for

starters. Check a few blocks in either direction: every dumpster and trash can.'

'Got it.'

'I'll meet you over at the Ruby Slipper in about an hour,' said Matt, and he hung up.

'Am I in any kind of trouble?' said Carmen.

Matt thought about telling the guy that he was standing neck-deep in shit. But Matt knew that the man had nothing to fear from the cops, at least in regard to this case. And he doubted seriously that the killer was going to go after him. What for? Carmen was a perfect mouthpiece, telling police exactly what the killer wanted them to know.

Except for the ring, maybe. Why wear such an obvious wedding band? Two possibilities came to Matt's mind immediately. First, it was yet another obvious clue, like the blond hair and mustache, to get a potential witness's attention. Second, maybe the guy really was married, and he had either made a mistake or felt honor bound to wear it. Matt knew guys like that: wouldn't take their wedding bands off ever – for any reason. Some were superstitious; some just took their vows very seriously.

Matt looked down at his own wedding ring. He thought about whether Laurie was still wearing her ring. Wondered if she had worn it when she . . .

Matt stood. He needed some air.

'As long as you're telling us everything, and everything you're telling us is the truth, then I don't think you have anything to worry about. Here's my card.' Matt handed Carmen his card, then he walked out into the sauna that passed for a Vegas afternoon.

When Matt arrived at the Ruby Slipper, Detective Brunowski was waiting for him inside. He was smiling.

'How'd you know?' said the detective, tilting his head toward a blond wig and mustache.

And a knife.

'The guy we're looking for is good with disguises,' said Matt, recalling his trip to Chicago and the stories about a homeless man camped outside Arthur Camacho's apartment. 'A place like this, low lit, people dressing up in everything from toupees to dresses with matching pumps, it'd be a piece of cake.'

'And we've got the murder weapon. What do you wanna bet we don't find any prints?'

'Sounds like a safe bet. Even in Vegas.' Matt told Brunowski about his conversation with Carmen, and about the ring.

'Think it's anything?'

'I doubt it. How cooperative are the big hotels?'

'Depends.'

'On what?'

'On which hotels, and what I want them to do.'

'How many people do you think were connected with Kyle Talbot's phone-in number last night, when the killer was on the line?'

'The person Talbot was talking to and the callers on hold. Couldn't be more than four or five.'

'How many of those calls do you think originated in Vegas?'

'Chances are, only one.'

'That's what I'm thinking. When I check out of a hotel, the numbers I've called are listed on my bill. Long-distance and local. Even my credit-card calls, which I make through the local line, are listed. Let's find out Talbot's call-in number, and check to see if there's a local call-in number for Vegas calls.'

'Right. Then you want the hotel to run a computer check to see if any guest was on the phone to Kyle Talbot's show last night, at the same time the killer was talking to Talbot.'

'Exactly,' said Matt. 'It sounds like a pretty narrow computer sort. It isn't like the hotels are going to have to go back months. It's last night, during a ten-minute period of time.'

'What if he called from a phone booth?'

'I heard the call. It didn't sound like it was from a phone booth.'

'Could've been a phone booth in a quiet lobby somewhere.'

'Yep. Or he could've used a cellular phone. Or he might have broken into a home and used the phone. Or he might have called from a gas station, or a fast food restaurant. All I'm saying is that he *might* have stayed at one of the hotels. If he did, we can find out fast.'

'I'll get on it right away.'

FIFTEEN

'Watcha' drinkin', darlin'?' said the blond sitting on the stool next to Carnie's.

He looked around, oblivious to her before now. She looked to be in her middle forties, buxom, and filled out her jeans nicely, had capped teeth polished and shining. She wasn't Dolly Parton. She wasn't all that young anymore. But she was a good-looking woman who looked more interested than desperate.

'Bud Dry,' he said.

'Give this man a Bud Dry,' said the woman, who seemed to have the bartender's attention.

'Thank you,' said Carnie.

'My pleasure. Name's Dottie.' She stuck out her hand.

'Carnie,' he said, shaking her hand.

'Interesting name.'

'Yeah,' he said, without explanation. He picked up the bottle of beer, pushed the glass aside and took a swig.

'You know, you remind me of Dwight Yoakam, with that long rider coat and that hat.'

'Thanks,' said Carnie.

Silence.

Dottie was used to receiving more of a reaction than this. She was a looker, especially with this crowd – white male, over thirty. Okay, maybe she wasn't a smash at the singles bars, where men joked about throwing back any woman who could buy liquor without having to show proof they were over twenty-one, but here she was a superstar. Or at least a star. And this guy was treating her like . . . well, like he wasn't interested. But he *was* interested. She knew it. Guys like this just played hard to get.

The big-screen TV came alive with images of the Angus Trent murder. Dan Rather and Connie Chung were talking about the dangers of vigilante justice, while several people sitting at the bar raised their drinks in toast to the killer who was still at large.

'Whatdya think about that?' asked Dottie, raising her vodka gimlet in the direction of the television.

'About what?'

'What do you think about that child-molester getting killed?'

'I dunno. What do *you* think?'

'I think he got what he deserved. I think that if criminals really expected they were going to pay a price for what they did, they'd think twice about doing it. Way it is these days, person can get away with murder.'

'Yeah, I believe that's true,' said Carnie, taking another drag off his beer. 'What do you think they should do with the killer when they catch him?'

'Give him a fuckin' medal.' Dottie sipped her gimlet. 'Yep, a fuckin' medal.' She had a way of using the f-word and making it sound cute. Or that's what several men friends had told her.

'Why?'

'Why?' she said with a smile. 'Because this country needs a hero again. I mean, John Wayne's dead, right?'

Carnie nodded.

'So where is he when we really need him?'

Dottie extended her glass and clinked it against Carnie's bottle.

They drank to heroes dead and gone.

And said a prayer for those to come.

Matt sat alone nursing his Absolut martini, listening to the lounge comedian tell stories about the Sixties. Lots of jokes about smoking dope and the Grateful Dead. Matt's generation was now relegated to the stereotypes of LSD-crazed hippies, wearing love beads and tie-dyed T-shirts.

He and Laurie were both of that generation. But somewhere along the line their philosophies had diverged.

Laurie still believed that if it felt good, do it.

Matt believed that there were lots of things that felt good that should not be done. Mainlining heroin felt good, but that didn't make it a desirable thing to do.

Laurie felt that if it came too hard, then it wasn't meant to be.

Matt knew that most of the things that meant something to him in his life – his career, getting on his feet financially – had required not only great sacrifice, but also a great deal of persistence in the face of sometimes overwhelming obstacles.

Laurie felt that there was nothing inherently right or wrong about anything. The rightness or wrongness of a thing was merely the significance one attached to it.

Matt knew that *philosophically* it was impossible to prove anything *absolutely* right or wrong. Lying, stealing, murder, even child-molestation could be defended if you created bizarre and unrealistic situations that had little, if any, relationship to real life. But Matt believed that life was less a philosophy course than experience's classroom. And experience had taught Matt, after all these years, that some things were right and some things were wrong.

He looked at life as a series of choices. Ideally, the more experience you had, the better choices you made. Unfortunately, he knew that this was not necessarily true. But he had a subjective vision of what was right and what was wrong. He had shared that vision with Laurie. They had made agreements based on that shared reality.

Now those agreements had been broken. Shattered.

The comedian, who was dressed in a tie-dyed T-shirt, jeans, sandals, and with a flower in his long hair, was talking about how, during an acid trip, he had decided that David Bowie was really an alien from another galaxy . . .

When Matt's beeper went off.

Matt and Vince Brunowski got off the elevator on

the twenty-fifth floor. Twenty officers were already in the sealed-off area.

The LVPD detective said, 'Desk says he already checked out, but who knows, right?'

The Flamingo Hilton had run a computer check and discovered that Jack Mason, staying in room 25998, had made a call to Kyle Talbot's show at exactly the time the killer had done so. No one remembered the man. He had paid with cash – left a $300 deposit at the front desk for phone calls, room service, etc. It wasn't common to leave cash instead of a credit-card imprint, but it happened. No big deal.

Matt and Brunowski reached the door at the same time. The two SWAT team members moved away. Brunowski knocked on the door. No answer. He knocked again. No answer.

He put the magnetic piece of plastic into the slot, a tiny green light lit up, and Brunowski turned the handle. He nodded to the SWAT team members, and they rushed inside.

The room was empty.

'Don't touch anything!' said Brunowski.

Matt looked around the dark room. It was freshly cleaned. No sign of Jack Mason.

'Damn!' said Brunowski. He turned to a skinny guy with a rumpled suit and a goatee beard, and told him, 'Fingerprint the fuck outta this place.'

Matt walked over to the window and looked out over the Strip and Caesar's Palace. He wondered what the man who had stayed in this room the night before thought about when he stood here looking down upon the lights. Knowing that he had just killed Angus Trent.

Matt was glad that Brunowski was diligent, but he had a feeling that the LVPD would find *hundreds* of different fingerprints on primary objects – door handles, TV remote controls, telephones, shower knobs, sink knobs, etc.

Or they would come up with none: zero, zip, zilch. Matt realized that either way they were probably fucked. He knew that the man he was looking for was smart. Real smart. And such a man was bound to know that his call would eventually be traced. Matt would like to be pleasantly surprised over this, but surprises rarely occurred in his line of work. By the time Matt got involved, the skill level of this pursuit was already set at *best of the best*.

While Brunowski went about his business, Matt headed across the street to the Caesar's Palace Forum shopping mall. He trusted Brunowski. Besides, the LVPD detective was self-motivated, and cracking this case could mean big things for his career. It was *his* case, and it was getting national attention. Also, Matt didn't want to appear as though he was looking over Brunowski's shoulder.

The Forum was the ultimate mall. It wasn't the biggest, but it was definitely the most decadent. Armani, Guess, Spago, you name it; if it was a designer label, then it had a shop in this mall. On the ceiling was a visual effect making it appear as though clouds were moving through the sky. Day changed to twilight, then to night, then back again, giving the illusion that you were walking outdoors. The decorative motif, of course, was ancient Rome, complete with giant stone columns, water fountains, chariots and gold. Added to that, once per hour huge stone figures of the gods began to move and talk to the crowd, as a laser show shot colorful light beams down from the heavens to the mortals on earth.

Matt walked into the largest sports collectibles store he had ever seen. On display were several baseball cards that cost over a $1,000 each. He remembered the time when he could get every card in a 500-card set for about ten bucks. There were also signed basketball jerseys for up to $500. A Mugsy Bogues jersey caught his eye. Bogues was a guard for the Charlotte Hornets, and stood well under six feet. Guys like Patrick Ewing and the Shaq should be able to put him in their pockets and walk around with him. Should, but couldn't. He was a little guy who played tall in a tall man's sport. Jarod liked Mugsy because he himself wasn't very tall; and, like Mugsy, Jarod used his speed, ball-handling abilities and intelligence to play taller.

Pointing to the Mugsy Bogues jersey, Matt beckoned the young man behind the counter. 'I'll take this one.' After all, it cost only a hundred bucks – signed. The big money in basketball still went to the guy who could fly, and the guy who destroyed backboards.

'Place was wiped clean,' said Brunowski. 'If we catch

this guy, and he gets off, I'll hire him to clean my house.'

Matt noticed how the detective had said 'if'.

'Virtually every surface we could lift a print from was totally clean. We did get a few prints off things I doubt he ever touched, like the curtain rod and the metal runners of a couple of chairs. I'll run them, but I can tell you right now it's shit.'

'You talk to the people at the front desk?'

'Woman who checked him in had this fixation on the word "average". Average height, average weight, average looks; maybe he had blond hair, she wasn't sure; maybe he had a mustache, she wasn't sure. She checked in about a hundred people that day. Same story with the clerk who checked him out. He checked out at a time when there's a line of about fifty other people trying to check out, so the guy doesn't remember him at all.'

'Maids?'

'He was never in his room when they cleaned. All the linen he used is already washed. Drains have been cleaned – probably by the killer. I mean *spotless*. No hair. Hell, the drains look brand fuckin' new. Guy's good.'

He was a hell of a lot more than that, thought Matt.

•

'It's only a matter of time until the local police departments leak the news about those notes,' said Lloyd Garland. He was sitting in Matt's office, smoking his pipe.

'I've called all the detectives in charge of the cases I know about, and asked them to keep a lid on. They said they would do what they could.'

'What kind of reason did you give them?'

'Whatever worked. I told them we were close to someone, and we didn't want to scare him off with all the publicity. I said that if the national media got hold of it, they'd make the killer into some kind of hero, and that might spur the guy on to kill more and faster. And, finally, I told them that if the media starts glorifying the killer, it might cause an outbreak of copycat killings across the country.'

'What did they say?'

'I got the feeling from a few of them that, if the killer continued going after the same kind of scum he's killed in their cities, they wouldn't mind if he killed somebody else every day till the end of time.'

'Yeah, I know.' Garland picked up a folded newspaper he'd brought with him, and tossed it on Matt's desk.

Matt picked it up and didn't need to ask what Garland wanted him to look at. At the top of the page was an article entitled 'VIGILANTE: THE NEW AMERICAN HERO', written by Susan Dornan of the *USA Tribune*, the other national daily. Matt scanned the item, even though he knew what it was about before he read it. Dornan's point was that, since it was clear that the American Justice system had failed the people, and because it was equally clear that the police could no longer protect honest, law-abiding citizens from crime and criminals, it was only a matter of time until people started taking the law into their own hands.

Matt knew this was just the beginning. And when they found out about the rest of the garbage the Reaper had already disposed of, it would be tough to keep him out of the White House.

'What are you going to do?'

'First thing I'm going to do is go back to Vegas and have a talk with Kyle Talbot.'

'You ever listen to the guy?'

'Couple a times. You?'

'Yeah. I didn't like him at first. But he grows on you.'

'So does fungus.'

'I take it you're not a fan.'

'I think he's an opportunist. And that's the nicest thing I can say about him.'

'Lot of people think he's a patriot.'

'Maybe he's both. Wouldn't be the first time.'

'Aren't we cynical today . . .'

The intercom buzzed and Matt punched a button on the console. 'Yes, Mary?'

'It's Laurie on line three.'

'Thanks.'

Garland started to stand, but Matt waved him back into his seat.

'Hello.'

'You busy for dinner?' said Laurie.

After only a slight hesitation, Matt said, 'I can get away.'

'Where would be convenient for you?'

'Four Oaks. Let's make it early – say, seven?'

'Fine. See you then,' said Laurie and hung up.

'Hope you two work things out,' said Garland, as he tamped out the smoldering cherry-flavored tobacco in his pipe.

'Yeah.' Matt hit a button on the intercom. 'Mary, get me on a flight to Vegas tonight. Ten o'clock would be perfect.'

Garland reflected, not for the first time, on what a 'company' man Matt was. He was in the middle of an emotional marital crisis, yet his work crisis, as always, took precedence. He was a man of conviction and priorities, and, in some ways, a relic of another age.

Garland stood and said, 'Good luck.'

'With what?'

'Everything,' said Garland, as he slid his briar into his jacket pocket and left the room.

The Four Oaks was located in Bel Air, a few blocks north of Sunset on Beverly Glen Boulevard. It was a romantic hideaway with French windows, a terrace garden, and large overhanging trees. Inside, it looked like a cozy country inn with warm furnishings and a real fireplace. Matt and Laurie didn't really have a restaurant that was *their* restaurant, but if they had to choose one that they both liked the most, this would probably be it.

Matt was early, Laurie was late. Some things never changed. They had agreed on seven, so Matt had made reservations for seven-fifteen, and she showed up at seven-thirty. Matt was already working on a Glenlivet, neat, when she came through the door. He had not seen her in a few days, and was wearing a suit she had bought him two years ago for his birthday. She was wearing a suit, and it looked as though she had just come from the office.

He stood as she walked over to the table and sat down.

'Hello, Matt.'

'Hi. You're looking . . . well.' He sat down, too.

'Thank you.'

It all sounded very formal.

'How's Jarod?'

'He's fine. I told him you were out of town. Look, Matt—'

'You like a glass of wine?'

'No. No, thanks. Look, Matt, we've got to talk.'

'I know. I've been thinking about . . . about what happened and I—'

'I'm getting a divorce, Matt.'

The emotional hammer fell, and hit Matt squarely in the heart. She didn't say that she *wanted* a divorce. She didn't say that she wanted to *talk* about a divorce. She said that she was *getting* a divorce.

'Look, I know how you must feel . . .'

Matt shook his head, still in a daze. 'No, I really don't think you do.'

'Look, it's not like there weren't any warning signs.'

It was a mark of how traditional, perhaps antiquated, was Matt's mindset about certain things, but he had not even considered divorce. Separation, yes. Counseling, yes. Divorce, no.

'Isn't this kind of quick?'

'Matt, let's face it. This . . . thing with Frank, it's just a symptom of what was wrong with our marriage. Things haven't been really good between us for a long time.'

'What do you mean by really good?'

'Like when we first got together.'

'Do you honestly believe that, in order to have a good marriage, things have to remain at the same emotional peak as when the relationship began?'

'I think that life's too short to settle.'

'Settle?'

'We were settling, Matt. We weren't that happy with each other anymore.'

'Exactly how happy do we have to be in order for us to stay together?'

'Now you're being facetious.'

'No, I'm being honest. I really don't know what you're talking about. You're defining our marriage by a series of bumper stickers. Life, real life, isn't always a happy experience. But that doesn't mean that it doesn't have meaning and value. A relationship has to ride out the ups and the downs. Our vows didn't read "for better or even better".'

'You're bitter. I knew you'd react this way.'

'What did you expect? You come here to inform me that my marriage is over, and then you call me bitter because I'm not ready to buy the house a round of drinks.'

'At least I had the guts to tell you to your face.'

'Gee, that must make you feel really good about yourself,' said Matt, unable to hide his anger. 'You know what I think?'

'No, what?'

'I think you're just rationalizing your behavior.'

'What do you mean?'

Matt tossed back the rest of his Glenlivet and looked his soon-to-be ex-wife squarely in the eye. 'I think you went out and had an affair, felt like a piece of shit about it, then retroactively downgraded our otherwise solid marriage to justify your behavior. That's what I think.'

'You're entitled to your opinion.'

'I'm entitled to more than that.'

Laurie sighed. 'I imagine you're referring to our settlement. Being a lawyer, I have you at a slight disadvantage.'

'Being as how I have proof that you're sleeping with one of your colleagues, don't be so fucking sure,' said Matt. He stood and tossed down a ten-dollar bill on the table.

'Where are you going?'

'I've got a plane to catch,' said Matt, not bothering to look back.

SIXTEEN

The flight took less than an hour and it was about midnight by the time Matt got into Vegas and over to the radio station. His FBI credentials acted like a universal backstage pass and worked their usual magic.

'I'm not doing any more interviews tonight,' said Talbot, as he put on his jacket and picked up a briefcase. 'If you'll leave your name with the girl outside, I'm sure we can work something out.'

Matt flashed his badge, and Talbot put his briefcase down again.

Matt sat down on a black leather couch, and Talbot sat opposite him in a matching chair. On the walls were records – album covers and even some signed .45 rpms. Artifacts of the station's previous incarnations.

'Lot of excitement around here these days, I'll bet,' said Matt.

'Not sure I'd put it that way, but there's been considerable interest in what happened.'

Matt noted that, initially at least, Talbot was reacting the way most people reacted to an FBI badge: he was intimidated. His speech sounded more stilted than usual; on the air the man was smooth. Talbot was anything but smooth at the moment, but

Matt knew things would change as the interview progressed and Talbot noticed that the sky wasn't falling.

'What exactly did happen, from your perspective, Mr Talbot?'

'Some guy called in predicting that something was going to happen to Angus Trent and, well, it happened.'

'You mean he was murdered.'

'Yes. You don't think I had anything to do with Trent's death, do you?'

'Why would you say that?'

'I don't know. I didn't do anything wrong. Look, I'm not used to the FBI showing up on my doorstep. What do you want?'

'I want to ask you a few questions. Do you have any way of knowing who the caller was?'

'None whatsoever.'

'Do you keep tapes of the show?'

'Yes. And you're free to listen to them.'

'I might just do that. Do you remember this man ever phoning in before?'

'He called in the night before the murder – then last night. If he ever called before two nights ago, I don't remember. I take about forty calls a night, five nights a week.'

'How long does a caller have to wait before he gets on the air?'

'It varies.'

'Can *you* vary it? I mean, if you wanted to put a caller on hold for a few minutes, you could do it?'

'Yes. You mean long enough to trace?'

'Yes.'

'I can't do that.'

'You mean you won't.'

'I mean, my credibility wouldn't be worth a plugged nickel if I allowed the cops to come in and trace my callers' phone numbers. People trust me. They trust that they can call here anonymously, and say what's really in their heart of hearts.'

'The man's a murderer.'

'Some people don't look at it that way.'

'How do you look at it?' said Matt.

'I don't think that's the issue. The issue is whether I'm going to let the police trace calls made to my show. And I'm not going to allow that.'

'I could make you.'

'I'm not sure you could. You're not the first person to suggest it. The local cops asked me earlier today, and the station lawyers said I'm under no obligation to comply.'

'Maybe the Justice Department wouldn't agree.'

'Look, I don't want trouble with the government, but I'm not going to just roll over and die here.'

'Let's not confuse this with a moral dilemma. We're asking for your help to catch a self-confessed murderer. Think about that. I'll be back tomorrow morning.'

'You know, I have no problem with you sitting in the studio. Maybe *you* can talk to him if he calls again.'

'I don't think so,' said Matt, realizing that Talbot

was thinking about becoming a ringmaster for ratings points. *Step right up, folks, hear the real live FBI man try to catch a real live killer. It's real, it's live! Come one, come all.*

Matt hadn't been to the circus since he was a kid. And he wasn't in the mood for it now.

Outside in the parking lot the warm desert air was still and comforting. Even though the Strip was about six miles south of the station, it rose in the distance like a neon oasis, promising more dreams than it could ever deliver.

Matt heard a car door slam. A blond was getting into a Buick Regal. He recognized her, but couldn't quite place . . . Susan Dornan. Yes, he had seen her picture above her column in the *USA Tribune* just a few hours earlier.

As Matt walked over to her car, she reversed the direction of her automatic window. She didn't know this man. Quickly he pulled out his ID, and let it hang there until she scanned it. Then she buzzed her window down again.

'I wasn't speeding, was I, officer?' she said with a smile.

'Nope.'

'When did the FBI start handing out traffic citations?'

'You're Susan Dornan, aren't you?'

'That picture gets me into more trouble than it's worth.'

'You look better in person.'

'It was a bad picture.'

'Mrs Dornan—'

'Mizzzz,' she said.

'Ms Dornan, I wonder if I might have a word with you?'

'Don't sound so formal. You wanna go have a drink?'

'Sure.'

'Follow me. If you get lost, it's Alias Smith and Jones, over on Twain.'

Alias Smith and Jones was a working-class bar with a working-class menu and portions to match. Burgers, chili, chicken fingers, potato skins. Booths ringed the central space, and there was a step-down-into bar with a big-screen TV at one end. Matt felt comfortable there.

'Kyle suggested this place to me. Said it's one of the two local hangouts.'

'I like it,' said Matt as a plate of chicken fingers, complete with ranch dressing for dipping, and a Heineken were set in front of him by a friendly waitress. Susan ordered a glass of white Zinfandel, and a plate of chicken wings with blue cheese dressing.

'Why did you agree to meet with me so readily?' asked Matt as he wiped some dressing from his lips with a napkin.

'If a girl can't trust the FBI, who can she trust?'

Matt didn't want to give the impression he was pushing, but he didn't want her to think he was a complete fool. 'Why?' he repeated – smiling to take the edge off the question. He knew the answer, but just wanted to establish some ground rules.

'You're here to find out more about the Reaper – and so am I.'

'I'm here to find out who killed Angus Trent.'

'Same thing.'

Matt wasn't sure about that, but now was not the time to argue.

'Now you know why I wanted to talk with you. Why did you want to talk with me?'

Matt knew that he could not tell her everything, and had no idea how much he could trust her. But he needed to tell her something in order to keep her interested – and get her to trust him.

'I'm concerned about how the press is going to handle this.'

'What do you mean?' said Susan, even though she knew exactly what he meant. She just wanted to hear him say it.

'I don't want the press to turn this murderer into some kind of hero. I think that's irresponsible, and it could lead to a lot of problems.'

'Such as?'

'Such as copycat killers. If the press sanctions people taking the law into their own hands, that serves as a tacit approval for all kinds of maniacs to go out and start killing people they believe deserve to die.'

'Do you think the Reaper's a maniac?'

'I *know* he's a murderer.'

'But do you believe he's a maniac?'

'I don't know.'

'But you used the word. Do you really think he's mentally deranged?'

'I find it difficult to believe that anyone who would purposely plan to kill another person is not at least a little crazy.'

'Soldiers aren't considered insane when they kill to defend their country.'

'We're not at war.'

'I'm not so sure I agree with that, as I live in New York. Where do you live?'

'Los Angeles.'

'More people die of gunshot wounds in a single weekend in our two cities than die in most of the 'official' wars around the world. I believe we *are* at war, and the government won't admit it because they don't know what to do about it.'

'And you believe vigilantism is the answer?'

'I believe that people have lost faith in the system and they're searching for answers. Protecting themselves is one alternative.'

'There's a difference between protecting yourself and going out, tracking someone down and murdering him. The Constitution has always allowed for self-defense.'

'But how can a society protect itself against murderers, rapists and molesters who keep getting put back on the street even though there's a *probability* – not just a ten percent chance – that these people will kill, rape and molest again?'

'You can't execute someone because of what he *might* do.'

'Maybe that's not fair, but is it fair to the public to allow habitual offenders back into the community? I'll tell you one thing: I don't see many tears being shed for Angus Trent.'

'A lot of people are outraged,' said Matt.

'A lot of liberals are intellectualizing their outrage. The average guy on the street is glad that a man who's been in and out of jail all his life for molesting young boys – who was in the company of teenage boys the night of his murder – is dead. Someone finally did what the justice system could not do – they separated an out-of-control pedophile once and for all from innocent children. End of story.'

Matt knew it was far from the end of the story, but he also realized this was an argument he was not going to win. Not tonight, and maybe not ever, with Susan Dornan.

'So,' said the reporter, toying with the rim of her wine glass, 'what's the FBI doing in Las Vegas, investigating a murder? I thought that'd fall under the local jurisdiction.'

'There are national implications. I'm here unofficially to assist local law enforcement, and to try to keep a lid on.'

Susan nodded, but Matt couldn't tell if she was buying that.

'I'm afraid you're wasting your time with me. Part of my job is to take the lid *off* things.'

'What do you intend to do?'

'I'm not here to pour gasoline on the fire, if that's what you mean. I'm really not bad at what I do. You should read more than one of my columns. I'm here to take the temperature of the situation, and to profile Talbot.'

'What do you think of Talbot – from your professional point of view?'

'I'm not sure yet. I only talked to him for a few minutes. I'm going to interview him again tomorrow.'

'First impression.'

'I think he's a guy who knows a good thing when he sees it. He's been around the block a few times, and I don't think he'll let go of this thing until it bucks him off.'

The two ate and drank in silence for a moment.

'You know, I'd love to put *your* point of view into my column.'

'You mean quote me?'

'Ideally.'

'No way.'

'How about "an FBI source"?'

'Absolutely not.'

'You're not very helpful.'

'It's not my job to help you sell newspapers.'

'Yeah, I know. Your job is to bring in the murderer dead or alive. You know, you sound like a pretty boring person, Matt Baldwin.'

For some reason, the comment struck Matt hard. He was ordinarily pretty thick-skinned, and anyhow he was not trying to amuse Susan Dornan; he was trying to get her to cooperate with him – with the Bureau.

Matt looked at his watch. 'I gotta go.'

He stood and reached for his wallet.

'It's on me. I've got an expense account.'

'So've I,' said Matt. He tossed a twenty on the table and walked out.

As he got into his car and started up the engine, he began wondering if Laurie considered him a boring person, too.

SEVENTEEN

The next night saw Kyle Talbot playing to his biggest audience yet. Reporters huddled in the room outside his tiny studio.

'Are you Cassie?'

Cassie turned toward the woman, and smiled. 'Yes, why?'

'My name's Susan. I'm a columnist for the *USA Tribune*.'

'Oh, yeah, I've seen that paper,' said Cassie flatly. Not many people wanted to talk to her. Everyone wanted to talk to Kyle or, when they did speak to her, they wanted to talk *about* Kyle.

'You're Kyle Talbot's girlfriend, aren't you?'

'Yes.'

'Must be exciting being with Kyle through all this.'

'Yeah, I guess.'

'You know what they say, behind every great man is a great woman.'

'I never heard that before.'

Somehow, Susan was not surprised. The on-air red light started flashing.

'I gotta go,' said Cassie.

Susan handed Cassie her card. 'If you ever want to talk, or if there's anything you think I might be interested in, give me a call, okay?'

'Sure,' Cassie said, and pocketed the card.

'Pretty girl like you, maybe we could do some pictures with you and Kyle.'

'Really?'

'Who knows? Give me a call.'

Cassie pocketed the card and eyed her reflection in the glass that separated the on-air and off-air sides of the studio. She *was* pretty. A photo spread in *USA Tribune*? Not too shabby.

Kyle Talbot could see his own reflection in the glass from inside the booth, but he was concentrating on the dogs in the outer studio, nipping at his heels. Some people might have been overwhelmed, but this was a moment he had worked for all his life. One he had waited for, wondering, at the age of forty-five, if it was ever going to happen. Last night as he lay in bed, Cassie serving him with genuinely worshipful sex, he had thought about how to play this moment. Had he been younger, he might have been blasé, but Talbot now knew that such moments came once in a lifetime. If you were lucky – and ready.

Talbot was ready.

'. . . And I appreciate all good wishes from you listeners out there in the heartland. Something's happening here, and I really don't think the bleeding hearts get it. I really don't. But they will, folks. They will. And . . . we go to Marsha in Omaha, Nebraska. Good evening, Marsha, you're on.'

'Hi, Kyle. I'm a little nervous.'

'Don't worry about it. *I'm* not.'

Marsha giggled nervously. 'I think you're doin' a

great job, Kyle. I think you speak for the common man.'

What Talbot really wanted was to hear again from the Reaper. The screeners were keeping one line open at all times, just in case. Everyone was waiting for the Reaper to call in. He was the new star of the show. Talbot was merely the MC, and he knew it. If the star never called back, that room outside would soon be as empty as a beach at midnight.

'My daughter was molested by my second husband – her stepfather. Nothing ever happened to him. I went to the police; I went to a lawyer. Nothing. Then he divorced me and married a friend of mine, and he started molesting *her* daughter. I just feel so helpless, you know?'

'I know. Lots of people feel helpless, and they just don't know what to do,' said Talbot, sipping some coffee from his Kyle Talbot Show mug.

'Anyhow, I just wanted to call in and say I'm glad that someone did what our justice system should have done in the first place. The Reaper has probably saved dozens of families a lot of pain and anguish. If he's listening, I just wanted him to know that.'

'Thank you, Marsha in Omaha. And we'll be back.'

Talbot hit a button and his mike went dead. He looked through the glass at the sharks in the other room. They were waiting for blood. Waiting for the killer's voice to fill the air. Waiting for the story to write itself.

Ellis Handy and Cassie were glad-handing, serving donuts and coffee, and laughing at just about anything any of the reporters said.

One face wasn't smiling. That FBI guy – what was his name? Matt something-or-other. He's not going to rain on my fucking parade, thought Talbot.

After the commercial break, Talbot took a call from Jack, a local blackjack dealer. 'Councilman Torrez is costing us jobs, Kyle. He's taking money out of my pocket. My taxes go to pay his salary, and he's taking food off my table. I'm fed up with this crap.'

'When you're right, you're right. The man's a liberal with a capital L, and that stands for loser and that rhymes with boozer. I'm not telling tales out of school here, folks. For those of you not familiar with the *left* honorable Reverend Torrez, he has been a colorful piece of the local landscape for years. Last year he was photographed walking down the Strip with a prostitute on each arm, wearing no shoes and drunk as a skunk. But don't despair, we are not a heartless people. At the city's expense, the Reverend Torrez – also a mail-order minister in a previous incarnation, who still owns a string of local wedding chapels – has completed an in-patient alcohol-rehabilitation program.

'Recently, the born-again Reverend Torrez, now an anti-vice crusader, is leading a small but ever-increasing faction of Las Vegans who believe that our little town has grown just about enough, thank you, and the last thing we need is another casino. He has been making the permit process so difficult that one Atlantic City-based casino group, which was going to build a two hundred-million-dollar casino, has now decided against it. Meanwhile, unemployment is starting to hit this city like a stake through its heart.'

'I think Torrez should retire and go back to running his wedding chapels.'

'It ain't gonna happen, Jack,' said Kyle. 'Vote him out of office, instead.'

'Elections aren't for another two years. My wife's already out of work, and I'm on the bubble at my job. We're out of options, Kyle. I can't wait. We need more jobs here, and less preaching from the Reverend.'

'From your lips to God's ears. And we'll be back.'

Talbot hit the button and his microphone went dead again. He was tallying up dollar signs. Ellis Handy had told him before the show that he had raised the sixty-second spot rate by fifty percent for the next month, and he had added seven new sponsors. In one fucking day!

'Try the Chinois Chicken Salad,' said Kyle Talbot.

Spago, in the Forum at Caesar's Palace, was kind of California elegant casual. You could show up in jeans, a logoed T-shirt, $200 tennis shoes, or an Armani suit with $500 shoes. Both outfits would gain you admission to the inner dining room. But either way you were going to pay for the privilege.

All the waiters, and the manager, knew Talbot and treated him like a celebrity. In Vegas the kind of treatment one received was very important; it said something to others, if one cared about such things.

Talbot cared about such things, partly because he had never received that kind of treatment before. Even though he had lived in Vegas for more than twenty years, he had been virtually invisible until now.

Now he was somebody. People came over to the table and talked politics. Talked about what was wrong with this country. Talked about how the liberals, led by President Souther, were destroying the country. Then they listened as Talbot held court. To the faithful, he was the guru of common sense. No mystical nonsense, no smoke and mirrors, just good old-fashioned discipline and traditional family values. One of Talbot's amazing strengths was that he could get his audience to believe that there was a consensus on such things, that they were all talking about the same things, the same values. He got them nodding their heads and exchanging knowing glances, as though the knowing looks were some kind of secret handshake of the anointed, the initiated.

Talbot had ordered for the table, which included Ellis Handy, Cassie, Matt and Susan. Three Chinois salads, three Spicy Chicken Pizzas, and two bottles of Acacia Chardonnay, the second of which was on the house.

Midway through what everyone, including Matt, had to agree was a fabulous meal, Talbot said, 'Vigilantism isn't an aberration; it is an inevitability. Don't get me wrong – I don't consider it a solution – but it is part of the process. When people conclude *en masse* that a system no longer works, it is inevitable that they disregard that system and try to create a new one.'

'Vigilantism is not a workable system. It's anarchy,' said Matt.

'To a certain extent, I agree with you,' said Talbot, wiping some mozzarella off his chin. 'As I said, it is not, by itself, a solution. However, I submit to you that where vigilantism exists, there is fear, but in a different segment of the community. In other words, for the first time in a long while, criminals are afraid that there might be some *real* punishment for breaking the law.'

'I agree,' said Susan Dornan, dealing herself into the conversation. 'With dwindling law-enforcement budgets, dwindling prison budgets, spiraling crime, and overworked judicial systems, let alone widespread corruption, the cause-and-effect relationship between committing a crime and paying a penalty is all but erased. Even with deterrents, the system was crumbling. Without them, for all practical purposes, the system ceases to exist.'

'This is all very intellectual—'

'Tell that to the parents of the boys molested by Angus Trent,' said Talbot. 'Real crimc is anything but intellectual. To those without the money to seal themselves off from crime, the system has *already* failed. It is not some subject on a talk show, or an article on the Op Ed page of the *New York Times*, it's real life, today, right now, and they are fighting back the only way they know how.'

The manager walked over to Talbot and whispered

something into his ear. Whatever it was, it made the guru's face turn pale.

Talbot drove, Matt sat in the front seat, and Dornan in the back. They drove into the driveway leading up to the Blissful Bells Wedding Chapel. As soon as the uniformed cops saw Matt's ID, they waved them through.

Brunowski took charge. When he spoke, he spoke to Matt. From what Matt could tell, Brunowski wasn't a fan of Talbot's, nor was he particularly impressed by the fact that Susan Dornan was a national newspaper columnist.

The dead body of Councilman Carlos Torrez was sprawled out between the front pews and the cheesy altar where thousands of drunken newlyweds had tied the knot. He had been shot twice in the head. The scene didn't bother Matt, who had seen his share of newly departed, but Talbot looked a little green; and Dornan did her best to look strong, while not looking directly at the body.

According to witnesses, a man wearing a ski-mask had run into the chapel, where Torrez was just finishing up a wedding ceremony. The intruder had yelled, 'You liberal piece a shit!' Then he began firing.

Witnesses ran out of the wedding chapel when the shooting began and saw the assailant climb into a metallic blue Honda Civic. They also got a partial license plate, which the cops were running now.

When Matt managed to get Brunowski by himself, he said, 'You got a note?'

'Nope. But, with the license plate and the car, I've got a lot more than that.'

Matt nodded and said, 'Maybe.'

When Matt, Susan and Talbot started heading out of the chapel, Brunowski said, 'Hey, Talbot.'

The shaken talk-show host turned back toward the detective. 'Yeah?'

'Next time you go after somebody on your show, make sure they live outta town, okay?' The cop wasn't smiling as he said this.

Neither was Talbot when he turned and walked over to his car.

Talbot, Susan and Matt found a coffee shop on the Strip called the Peppermill and sat in a back corner booth, a semi-circular sectional wrapped around a small round table. Talbot ordered a drink, quickly. Matt could see that the man was still shaking. They had talked little in the car on the way over, but Matt had suggested that they all have a drink before calling it a night. He wanted to take advantage of this first moment he had seen Talbot really vulnerable.

When their drinks were delivered by an attractive Asian waitress, Talbot said to her, 'Bring mc another Absolut martini when you get a chance.' Then he went to work on the first one.

After a while, Talbot said, 'I can't be responsible for every kook with a gun.'

No one replied.

'What's the difference between Torrez and Angus Trent?' said Matt finally.

'Are you serious?'

'Yes.'

'Trent was a criminal. A piece of human scum. Torrez . . . I mean, I didn't like the guy, sure. And his politics were pinching this city hard. But . . . Damn!' Talbot polished off his martini and looked around for the waitress.

'How do *you* feel about it?' asked Matt, looking over at Susan, who was taking things better than Talbot. But, then, her butt wasn't on the line, either.

'I think Kyle's right. He can't be responsible for every crazy person with a gun. Still, it is frightening that, by just mentioning someone's name, you might be signing their death warrant. I don't know what to think. It's scary.'

'You know, maybe we're just jumping the gun on this thing. Maybe the killer was planning to murder Torrez anyhow, and my reference to him on the show had nothing to do with it.'

'What about the killer calling Torrez a "liberal piece a shit"?'

'Yeah, well . . .' Talbot lifted the second martini off the waitress's tray as though it were holy water and he was dying of thirst. And ordered yet another one.

'How do you feel now about a trace?'

'It didn't *sound* like the same guy tonight,' said Talbot, trying to pass this remark off as an answer.

'I know. But if and when the Reaper calls back, I want to nail him.'

'I don't know about this,' said Talbot shaking his head.

'After tonight I think the public might be willing to accept your allowing a trace. Obviously, you won't announce it ahead of time, anyhow. If we don't catch the guy with a trap on the line, no one will ever know.'

'Except me,' said Susan.

'And how do *you* feel about it?' asked Matt.

'This morning I would have been against it. Tonight, I think maybe it's not such a bad idea.'

'See,' said Matt. 'Here's a microcosm of public opinion.'

'Let me sleep on it,' said Talbot, shaking his head again. He was starting to loosen up a little. 'It's really crazy. I just say the magic word, and this Reaper guy goes out and kills somebody. In-fucking-credible.'

'You'll let me know in the morning then?'

'Yeah. I'll talk it over with Ellis and the lawyers, and I'll call you.'

'Good,' said Matt. He stood and reached for his wallet.

'My expense account this time,' said Susan.

'Thanks.'

'Let me finish up here and I'll drop you,' said Talbot.

'No, thanks, I think I'll walk,' said Matt. 'I could use the fresh air.'

Matt walked out of the Peppermill and up to the Strip toward the Mirage. The air was warm at two o'clock in the morning. Time and temperature sign read eighty-four degrees.

The Strip was still going strong, even at two a.m. Thousands of people were waiting for the mock volcano in front of the Mirage to erupt with its regular 'explosion'.

An older couple, carrying large plastic cups full of quarters, sped by Matt in their electric get-around carts. Probably the only muscle tone they had left in their bodies resided in their right arms, he thought.

When he got back to his hotel room, the red light on his phone was flashing. He called downstairs and was told that he had two messages. The first was from Lloyd Garland, asking Matt to call him first thing in the morning. The second was from Detective Brunowski, whom Matt dialed immediately.

'We got the guy about an hour ago.'

'The Reaper?' asked Matt. It was more a wish than a question.

'More like the Weeper,' said Brunowski. 'He's some twenty-two-year-old kid whose father belongs to one of those white supremacist groups. Big fan of Kyle Talbot. Anyhow, we traced the license plate to him, showed up at his place, and the kid broke down bawling after ten minutes.'

'He's got an alibi for Trent's murder. He was in jail, DUI, when Trent was killed.'

'Shit!' said Matt.

'Don't take it so hard, Baldwin. You *knew* this wasn't a match. You didn't think it was gonna be that easy, did you?'

'It never is.'

'You can talk to the kid in the morning, as long as his lawyer doesn't mind.'

'Thanks.'

'Always glad to help the FBI.'

'I'm glad you said that. I wonder if you would do me a favor.'

'Depends on the favor.'

'Don't announce to the press that you know this kid isn't the Reaper.'

'You crazy? The press'll check this kid out but good, themselves.'

'I'm talking about stalling for twenty-four hours. One day. Say you can't decide one way or the other: that you're just checking every possibility before you make an announcement – which will come by tomorrow night.'

'What time tomorrow night am I going to know?' asked Brunowski cynically.

'Any time after Talbot's show begins.'

'Anything else? You want your car washed, shoes polished, anything like that?'

'Thanks. I owe you.'

'You got that right.'

Matt hung up and tried to get a few hours' sleep before he started putting the moves on Talbot.

EIGHTEEN

Matt got up at seven, and ordered a pot of coffee and a croissant, which was delivered with a copy of the *USA Tribune*. He checked the three mutual funds he and Laurie had put twenty-six grand in. They were all down. The Angels had lost 1–0, and the President's approval rating was now in the teens.

Luckily, thought Matt, Torrez's killing had happened too late for the morning papers.

Matt turned on the TV. *Good Morning, America* carried the story, not at the top of the hour, but about halfway through the news.

The local newscasts all gave the Torrez murder a big play. Matt was pleased to see Brunowski – who looked like he'd had about ten minutes' sleep – being interviewed live; saying that the police were still not certain if there was a connection between the Angus Trent murder and the Torrez killing. He finished by stating that he thought they would have an official announcement sometime within the next twenty-four hours.

At eight-thirty Matt returned Lloyd Garland's call.

'Talk about being in the right place at the right time,' said Garland.

'The kid who killed Torrez isn't your guy.'

'I was afraid you were going to say that.'

'But I'm trying to use it to persuade Talbot to go along with a trace.'

'Think he'll go for it?'

'I'll know in a few hours. So, you called last night?'

'Yeah, Laurie called and she was trying to reach you. I didn't know if you wanted me to give her your number or not.'

Matt didn't respond immediately.

'Is something wrong, Matt?'

'Yeah, Lloyd, something's wrong. Laurie and I are getting a divorce.'

Lloyd didn't ask any questions. From Matt's response when he got Laurie's call in the office, and from Matt's response today, it was clear to Lloyd who had initiated the divorce.

'If she calls back, tell her that I asked you not to give out my phone number to anyone. Tell her I'll call her.'

'You got it. How long you think you're going to be in Vegas?'

'I don't know. Keep your beeper on. If I get this trace put on, I've got one night to do the job. Talbot will probably feel a whole lot less guilty when he finds out some white supremacist nut did a copycat killing, and he'll probably lose the trace.'

'Think one night'll do it?'

'It'll have to. Besides, I have a feeling that the real vigilante will be eager to let people know that he isn't some crazy skinhead running around knocking people off. I think he'll try to set the record straight.'

'Let's hope you're right.'

Three hours later, Matt was sitting in Talbot's office with Talbot himself, Ellis Handy and Bernie Feinstein, the station's attorney. Talbot wore a gray sweatshirt with the station's logo on it; Handy and Feinstein were in suits. Matt wore a blue jacket over an unbuttoned white shirt and beige slacks.

'It goes against the grain, against what talk radio stands for, to put a trace on a caller,' said Feinstein. 'It could badly damage, even destroy, Kyle's credibility.'

'So would being perceived as condoning murder, and aiding and abetting a murderer.'

Matt had handled enough negotiations to realize that the lawyer's choice of word 'could' indicated that they were ready to deal. He was not saying no, absolutely not, don't even bother to show up. He was just going on record.

Matt nodded. 'I understand that this will need to be handled delicately. For example, I will not even begin the trace until we know it's the Reaper on the line. No other caller's number will be traced.'

Talbot, Handy and Feinstein exchanged glances. It was clear that they had already made their decision before Matt arrived.

'Under those circumstances, we agree to allow you to trace that specific caller's number. But we reserve the right to discontinue the trace at any time.'

'Okay. I'll make arrangements with Detective Brunowski and my people in LA.'

'Very well,' said Feinstein and he stood, indicating that the meeting had ended.

Matt went back to his hotel room and called Garland, then took a nap before what he figured was going to be a long night. Brunowski meanwhile arranged for the phone tap, which would be triggered by Talbot giving a signal to a technician on the scene, who would immediately employ a tracing device that would instantly register the caller's number on a small LCD screen.

Matt picked up the copy of *USA Tribune*, which the maid had not thrown away but had left neatly stacked on his desk. He turned to Susan Dornan's column. Essentially, it was a puff piece on Kyle Talbot, 'the gruff but charming talk-show host'. Besides the story on Talbot, a couple of blind items ran at the end. Apparently this was a regular feature of her column; Matt had noticed the same type of items in the other column he'd read. Today it was: *'Craig in St Louis: please send me a copy of that book you wrote me about.'*

Matt rang Susan's room at the Mirage, but she was out, so he left a message.

Then he called Laurie. Her secretary put him right through.

'Thanks for returning my call,' she said. Her tone was conciliatory. She didn't ask why he had waited so long to phone her back, nor why he would not allow her to have his number.

'So, what's up?' said Matt, thinking that saying

What do you want? sounded too hostile; as did *What in the fuck do you want now, you heartless bitch?!*

'Things are moving pretty fast. I just didn't want there to be any big surprises.'

Matt knew this was code for *because I'm a lawyer – forget the fact that my lover is a lawyer, too – I'm going to get this divorce so fast it'll make your head swim. And when you get served with papers I don't want you getting so pissed off that you decide to fight the action and prolong the proceedings.*

'I appreciate that,' said Matt. He didn't want to ask the next question, because he was afraid he knew the answer. 'Have you told Jarod yet?'

'No. What do you suggest? You know how much he cares about you.'

Matt knew. And he knew how much he cared for his stepson. 'Let me tell him.'

Silence. Laurie weighed her options. If she said no, she would most certainly antagonize Matt. If she agreed, she knew Matt well enough to know that he would not say anything to Jarod to poison the boy against her. And obviously, she would get custody of her own son. It was a smart play. In spite of herself, she could rarely stop thinking like a lawyer anymore. Even in situations like this. Especially in situations like this.

'Okay. When will you be back?'

'I don't know. Maybe tomorrow. I'm not sure. I'll let you know ahead of time. What have you told him so far?'

'Just that you're working on a case out of town.

But I think he senses something's wrong.'

'Why?'

One reason Jarod sensed something amiss was that even though Frank didn't stay overnight, he was spending a good deal of time with Laurie. Jarod saw this and, coupled with the fact that Matt was not around, Laurie realized that the boy must be getting suspicious. But she wasn't going to tell Matt so. 'I'm not sure,' she said. 'Jarod's a pretty sensitive kid.'

'I'll try to get back as soon as I can.'

'Good. And, Matt . . . thanks for taking this so well.'

'Yeah,' said Matt and hung up without saying goodbye. Before he could say a lot of things.

The phone rang. For an instant, he thought it might be Laurie calling back to apologize for sounding so cold. But then he remembered she didn't have his number.

'Matt?'

'Yeah.'

'Susan Dornan here. You called?'

'You had lunch yet?'

'Yes. But I was just going downstairs to look at the tigers. You want to join me?'

'Sure. Twenty minutes?'

'See you there.'

The two white tigers, Sasha and Noel, lolled on a rock up toward the top of their jungle environment, behind the glass wall that separated them from about

300 spectators taking pictures and gazing in awe at the two magnificent animals that performed with Siegfried and Roy at the Mirage. That was Las Vegas's most popular show.

Standing behind Susan, Matt noticed her blond hair and how the light streaming in from the large terrarium made her hair glow. Then he noticed the fine blond hairs on the tanned nape of her neck. He noticed her thin waist, and the shape of her calves in her high-heel shoes. He noticed her perfume.

And when she turned around suddenly to face him, for a moment he felt as though she had caught him doing something he wasn't supposed to.

'What do you think?' she said.

'Beautiful.'

Susan smiled at Matt and said, 'You wanted to talk to me?'

'Let's walk.'

Matt and Susan headed out of the Mirage and down the Strip toward Caesar's Palace.

'Let's talk about last night,' said Matt.

'What about it?'

'Did that incident cause you to rethink how you feel about vigilantism?'

'I don't know. I still think something has to be done to shake up the status quo. The system just isn't working any longer.'

'But until you have something to replace that system with, don't destroy the only law and order that separates us from complete bedlam.'

'I know. And I have to admit that what happened

last night with Torrez is a point in your favor.'

'I'm not trying to win a debate, Susan – may I call you Susan?'

'Please. And I'll call you Matt.'

'I'm not trying to beat you at anything. I'm trying to catch a murderer, that's all. But I think some people, like Talbot—'

'And me.'

'Maybe. Some people are trying to use this situation to further their own agendas. With some people it might be some political philosophy; with Talbot it's probably just to make a few bucks. Regardless of motivation, people like you and Talbot are in a position to influence people. Take my word for it: there are a lot of people out there who don't need much of a push one way or the other to go over the edge. Glorifying the Reaper puts a seal of approval on the belief that if you think someone is evil, it's okay to go out and blow him away.'

'There *is* evil out there, Matt. And the system is simply incapable of protecting us against it.'

'I understand that, Susan. And I agree that changes, drastic changes, need to be made. But who defines who's evil and who's not? Maybe you and I agree that the world's not going to be a worse place without Angus Trent in it. But who do you think the KKK believe is evil enough to deserve execution? Who do you reckon the neo-Nazis think is evil? How about the IRA, or the militant blacks, or just some guy who thinks his long-haired neighbor is playing his "evil" heavy metal music too loud? Each of those groups will define evil in a different way than you and I do. And once you tell people it's okay to personally exterminate evil, outside the system, you might as well just start wearing a bulletproof vest, because you're going to need it. Somebody, somewhere, some day is going to try to kill you.'

'I don't know, Matt. I hear what you're saying, but maybe I'm just desperate for a hero.'

'Maybe you're just desperate for a simple solution. But you've got to remember that you're more than desperate: you're influential. Right or wrong, a lot of people read what you write and believe that, because it's in print, it must be the truth.'

'I'm not as irresponsible as you make me out to be.'

'I'm not saying you're irresponsible. I'm just saying that this country needs less people screaming into microphones, and a few more cool heads.'

'A lot of people believe that the people in power have been more than irresponsible, that they've plundered this country, serving only their own interests. Now people feel they've got to take responsibility for themselves and their families, and not wait around for a corrupt government, that doesn't seem to give a damn about them except at election time, to do something about it.'

Matt smiled. 'So, I haven't convinced you, eh?'

'Not yet. But I see your point of view more easily today than I did before I saw Torrez's body last night.'

Susan looked at her watch and stopped. 'I've got to be getting back. I need to modem my column in two hours. I hear you convinced Talbot to put a trace on the phone lines this evening.'

'Word travels fast.'

'I'm looking forward to tonight.'

'Me, too,' said Matt. He smiled and walked back to his hotel.

NINETEEN

Detective Ira Levinson first introduced himself to Matt and Talbot, then he attached a small device to the phone bank used by the screener in the outer room. The night before, the room had been filled with reporters and photographers. Tonight, besides Levinson and Matt, it was just station personnel – and Susan – all of whom had been sworn to secrecy regarding the trace. Susan had agreed to the terms, but it wasn't as though she had any real choice: she could be the only reporter inside, or she could wait in the parking lot with everyone else. It didn't take her long to decide.

The Reaper didn't call during the first hour.

Carnie knew he had to make people aware that he didn't kill Carlos Torrez. But he had to do more than that.

He had read the articles, listened to the other radio talk shows – all about him. Most people were for him. They were fed up with the system, and ready to do something about it. He had figured that would be the case. He had assessed the public temperature correctly. But, after Torrez's murder last night, public support was starting to erode.

Tonight would be a pivotal night. He knew it, and

he knew that others anticipated it.

He sat sipping a Rolling Rock beer from the bottle, Frye boots up on the hassock, listening to some bleeding heart going on and on to Kyle Talbot about how 'if everyone decided not to play by the rules, then there would be no law and order'.

'I hate to burst your bubble, madam,' said Talbot, 'but a large segment of this society stopped playing by the rules a long time ago. President Souther not only stopped playing by the rules, he invented new ones: rules that hurt the average working man and woman severely, and have all but destroyed the small businessman.

'Or, if you're deluded enough to be one of the President's admirers, and it sounds like you are, then let's look at some other criminals – excuse me, rule breakers. Take a walk through Los Angeles some night, and when some gangbanger walks up and puts a gun to your head, remind him that he's not playing by the rules. Or how about the guys who bilked the Savings and Loans out of billions of dollars? Maybe you should write some letters to those guys and remind them that they're not playing by the rules, and to send all their ill-gotten gain back to the taxpayers.'

'I think you're over-simplifying,' said the woman.

'I think *you're* overly simple,' said Talbot. He cut her off and went to a commercial.

Carnie had to smile. He thought that was pretty funny.

* * *

Matt thought that was pretty rude, cutting off a caller that way, but apparently he was the only one in the room who thought so. Even Ira Levinson was smiling.

'Still think he's going to call?' asked Susan.

'He'd better.'

It was at that moment that Matt sensed it. There was something electric in the room. An instant later, the screener was waving wildly through the window at Talbot, who scooped up his earphones quickly and put them back on. The commercial ended and Talbot went back on air.

'Hello, caller.'

'Hi, Kyle.'

'Have we spoken before?'

'I'm the guy you call the Reaper.'

Levinson went to work, and in less than ten seconds a number appeared on the LCD screen. It was a number in the 310 area code.

Matt knew that meant Los Angeles. He dialed Lloyd Garland's number, and the phone was answered immediately. 'He's in LA,' said Matt. Then he read Garland the number. 'Go get the son-of-a bitch.'

'Done,' said Garland, and he hung up.

'I think I need to say a few things,' said Carnie.

'This is your forum. We're listening.'

'First of all, I believe in the idea of personal responsibility.'

'How do you reconcile that concept with taking a man's life?'

'Society condones killing all the time – under the proper circumstances. When a soldier kills an enemy in a war, that's not only okay, but they pin ribbons on him for doing it. A cop kills a drug dealer, he might get a citation and an invitation to speak at the local high school. You kill a guy while he's trying to rape some teenager, you're a hero. When the state executes a criminal, it's not only legal, it's the morally and legally correct thing to do.'

'But you're not the state, we're not at war, and—'

'Hold it right there, Kyle. You ask the average guy on the street if he doesn't consider America to be in an undeclared state of war. People are armed, people are killing each other, people are threatening each other over the airwaves. Crime and corruption are steamrollering what used to be called the American Dream. We *are* at war, Kyle. Make no mistake about it. And in a war, you do what you have to do to beat the enemy.'

By the time Lloyd Garland reached his car in the garage under the Federal Building, his people had secured the caller's address. Five federal cars full of agents and ten LAPD black-and-whites were already on their way. Garland was only about five minutes drive from the address.

He screeched out of the subterranean garage, ran the light at Wilshire, and screamed west down the boulevard toward the ocean.

* * *

'It is the job of every citizen here to fight evil wherever we find it,' said Carnie. 'Not just for ourselves, but for our children. What kind of a world are we leaving to our children, Kyle?'

'Are you talking about values?' said Talbot, doing his best to keep the Reaper talking. For several reasons.

'Yeah. I hear people say that we've become a society without any values. But that isn't true. We do have values; it's just that those values are so demeaning, so violent, so narcissistic that they create a world that is morally bankrupt.'

Carnie stopped and set down his bottle of beer. He thought he had heard a noise outside.

'Are you still there?' asked Talbot.

'Yeah, I'm here. Hold on a second.'

Silence. In Carnie's living room. In Talbot's on-air booth. On a million radios coast to coast.

'Okay, I'm back,' said Carnie. 'I want to say something else that's very important. I didn't kill that Torrez guy. No way. I'm not crazy, and I'm not stupid.'

'I believe you,' said Talbot, who was running on one-hundred-proof adrenaline. And forty-proof brandy. 'But how would you convince other people of that?'

'Well, first of all, I figure the cops already know that I didn't do it.'

'Why?'

'Because I left something at the scene of Trent's murder.'

Suddenly the hair on Matt's arm stood on end. *Don't do it!*

'What did you leave?' asked Talbot.

'I'm not going to say. I'll make a deal with the cops – I imagine they're listening. If they tell the public that they know I didn't kill Torrez, I won't reveal what I left at the Trent scene. If they persist in trying to create confusion about my work, then I'll reveal to the public what I left there.'

'And you're sure they'll know what you're talking about?'

'Positive.'

'Okay.'

A knowing, and relieved, smile spread across Matt's face. The guy was pretty smart. He had a unique signature, and now it would remain unique, at least until some low-level law-enforcement grunt decided to cave in to a media payoff. That would happen, but not for a while yet. Matt knew that it would also serve as a deterrent to other law-enforcement agencies who had similar 'signatures'. This would help Matt, in that it would keep the lid on a little longer.

The Reaper was flexing his muscle. *I'm not such a bad guy. I don't go around killing just anybody. And, just watch, in an hour or so the cops will go on record,* have *to go on record, and tell the world that I had nothing to do with Torrez's murder. Because I told them to do it.*

By the time Garland got there, the LAPD had the

place surrounded. No flashing lights, just forty officers ringing a tiny bungalow set back about twenty yards from the street. Garland was not officially in charge of the operation, but the detective in charge had still waited for him to arrive. Besides, they had the area completely contained.

'You ready to go in?'

'Let's go,' said Garland.

And nine men started closing in.

'Anyhow, Kyle, that's really all I wanted to say.'

Talbot looked through the glass at Matt, as though waiting for some direction, or at least absolution. He couldn't keep the caller on any longer without making it look suspicious.

Matt shrugged his shoulders. He knew that by now they either had him or they didn't.

Carnie heard the noise again. 'I've got to go, Kyle,' he said and hung up. He picked up his gun, turned off the light on the side table, hit the power button on the remote control, and the radio went dead.

And he walked to the window where the noise had come from.

Garland banged on the door. 'Police, open up!' No answer. He knocked again. No answer. He nodded at the detective, and said, 'Let's go in.'

A large cop, who looked about two hundred and fifty pounds, all muscle, hit the wooden door and it exploded apart, leaving a large hole for a dozen men to run through, guns drawn.

In the corner of the living room sat an old woman about ninety years old. She was too frightened to speak. Instantly, Garland knew what had happened, but the other men searched the other rooms, anyhow. Nothing was found.

Carnie pulled back the curtain slowly. A cat was climbing on a woodpile outside his window. Carnie laughed at his own nervousness.

And at a scene that was probably playing itself out at this very moment somewhere in LA.

'You can take that fucking trace off the phones, tonight!' said Kyle Talbot, after his show had ended.

Matt and Susan were in his office. Talbot was working on a Johnnie Walker Black he had poured from a bottle in his desk drawer. He hadn't bothered to offer his guests a drink.

'Some local skinhead kid killed Torrez, not the Reaper.'

'Okay,' said Matt.

Matt's calm acceptance took Talbot by surprise. Then it hit him. 'You son-of-a-bitch. You knew, didn't you?'

'What are you talking about?'

'You knew the Reaper didn't kill Torrez.'

'I know the Reaper killed Trent, but apparently I can't make you do what's right,' said Matt, dancing as fast as he could.

'Who the fuck knows what's right? It's my show, and *I'll* decide what's right.'

Matt wasn't in the mood for this. Especially not after Garland's phone call.

'Well?'

'Well, what?' asked Matt.

'Did anything come of the trace?'

Matt stood. 'I gotta get some sleep.'

'Me, too,' said Susan and she followed Matt to the parking lot, leaving Talbot smiling and drinking toasts to himself in his office.

'Feel like a nightcap?' she said when the two were standing beside their cars.

Matt felt exhausted, but said, 'Sure,' for a couple of reasons.

'See you at Alias Smith and Jones.'

Matt nodded and started to get into his car.

'Matt?'

'Yeah?'

'It's your turn to buy.'

'Not exactly the great debate back there,' said Susan as she sipped her white Zinfandel.

'What do you mean?'

'I mean you didn't put up much of a fight.'

Matt didn't respond. He was trying to figure out how to play this. It was a risk, but catching this guy, after what he now knew about him, wasn't going to be easy. And time was going to be an important factor. Such a situation required calculated risks.

'What happened with the trace?'

'It was a phone booth, and we didn't get there fast enough.'

'You want me to believe that?'

Matt smiled. 'Yeah.'

'Let me rephrase my question. Is it true?'

'Now, that's an entirely different question.'

'How about an entirely different answer?'

Matt drained the Heineken and made a decision. 'We broke in on some ninety-year-old woman, who got scared so bad she had to be rushed to hospital. We'll be lucky if she doesn't sue.'

'I take it she's not the Reaper.'

'No.'

'So he rerouted the call.'

'Yes. And in a very sophisticated way. More than just call-forwarding.'

'So, it wasn't any big deal you agreeing to take the tap off Talbot's phone, since it wasn't going to work anyhow. Why not tell Talbot?'

'Why give the son-of-a-bitch the satisfaction?'

Matt poured himself another Heineken from the bottle which the waitress had just set down.

'So, why are you leveling with me? I mean, Talbot will just read about it in my column.'

'*If* you put it in your column.'

'Why wouldn't I?'

'Because you're a concerned and conscientious citizen.'

'Any other reason?' said Susan with a smile.

Matt and Susan sat in the booth, sizing each other

up for a moment. This was high-stakes poker. This was Vegas.

'Let me ask you a question. You know what the Reaper's signature is – the one he talked about tonight – don't you?'

After only a slight hesitation, Matt said, 'Yes.'

'That's the reason you're here in Vegas, isn't it?'

'What are you talking about?' said Matt, even though he knew exactly what she was talking about. In fact, he was deliberately leading her into this line of conversation.

'I figure that before you came to Vegas you called Brunowski, and asked him if the killer had left something – the signature.'

'Kind of a leap in logic,' said Matt, not denying anything.

'Not at all. This is a local matter, so what in the hell are you doing here?'

'Can I speak to you off the record? I mean *really* off the record, and if you can't guarantee me that it stays off the record, I'll respect you for telling me. I need to know.'

Susan took a deep breath. 'Okay. I'll let you know if we're getting into an area where I can't promise anything.'

'I'll make you a deal. You soft-pedal this thing in your column for a while, and I'll give you what I've got, when I get it. No other law-enforcement official is as deeply into this as I am. No one else has put it together.'

'Put what together?'

'The Reaper is a serial killer,' said Matt. This was the risk he had decided to take. She was close enough to the truth on her own, and if she put just another few pieces together, he would have no control over her. She would then be a loose cannon. This way, he filled in a few blanks she would have soon filled in herself, and he owned her. At least, that's the way Matt hoped it would play.

'Incredible. How many?'

'I'm sure of at least four others, maybe more.'

'And the signature?'

'This *has* to be off the record.'

'I swear.'

'It's a photocopied note that reads 'We reap what we sow'.'

'The Reaper.'

'Exactly.'

'And he's killed at least four other people . . . ?'

'Yes?'

'Here in Vegas?'

He sipped his beer. 'No.'

'Good Lord. He's killing people all over the country!' It was not a question. 'And the other people he killed are all scumbags like Trent?'

'Basically.'

Susan ran through the information in her head, and any way she figured it, it came up big. Very big. For the first time in history, the public – if it knew about this – would be rooting for a serial killer to kill and kill again. No wonder Matt looked preoccupied. It wasn't as though he could announce this information to the whole country and ask for help.

The implications for the journalist who could bring this story in were enormous. And she had just been offered it on a platter.

If she would cooperate.

'Okay, I'm in. But I go with you wherever you go until it's over.'

Matt nodded. 'I'm heading back to LA in the morning. Call me at my office in the early afternoon, and I'll bring you up to speed. Remember, if I read a word about this in your paper, or if I find out you leaked anything I've told you to anyone else, the deal's off and I'll take it personally.'

'Which means?'

'Which means that the FBI is not without reach.'

'You're not going to have me killed, are you?' she said sarcastically.

'Worse than that. We'll put the IRS onto you.'

'Okay, okay, I give in.'

Matt paid the tab and walked Susan to her car. As he drove back to his hotel, following behind her, Matt thought about his decision to bring Susan in. Right now, he was playing her more than she was playing him. But he knew that situation could change fast.

And there was something else: something he knew she had not considered. In his head, Matt had played the game out to the end, and he knew that there was another use she could serve – if things didn't break right. And, as Matt knew, they seldom did.

Especially when he was up against someone as smart as the Reaper.

As he watched her turn right into the Mirage valet parking lot, Matt was hoping that Susan hadn't figured out how he had just set her up.

That she hadn't figured out how at risk she had just become.

TWENTY

Matt caught the 10 a.m. USAir flight back to LA, picked up his car at Park One, and was in his office by 11:45. Lloyd Garland was already puffing away when Matt walked in.

'The old lady's out of the hospital.'

'You didn't have her assume the position, did you?' said Matt sarcastically, as he took off his jacket, draped it across the back of his chair, and sat down behind his desk.

'Couldn't. She just passed out.'

Matt shook his head.

'This guy's good,' said Garland.

'We should have already known that. Trent wasn't the first murder he's gotten away with. What did we expect? Of course he's not going to hang on the phone talking to Talbot, and wait for the cops to trace his fucking phone call. Shit!'

'We had to try.'

'Yeah, yeah, yeah . . .'

'You're in a good mood,' said Garland.

'No, I'm not. I'm in a pretty piss-poor mood. Nothing's going my way these days.'

'Laurie?'

'On my list of things to do today is to tell Jarod that his mother and I are getting a divorce. During that verbal high-wire act I'm supposed to tell him how much I love him, that nothing's really going to change between us, and that his mother really isn't the irresponsible slut I know she is. And that the real reason for the divorce, if he really must know, is not because his mother, my wife, is out playing hide the sausage with some low-life lawyer, but because, hey, we're just two good people who've kind of grown apart here. Fuck!' added Matt, 'On top of all that, I just told a columnist for the *USA Tribune* that the Reaper is a serial killer.'

'You what?' Garland nearly swallowed his pipe.

Matt explained his logic and Garland gradually started breathing regularly again. 'You really think you can trust her?'

'I had no choice.' Matt sighed, and tried to get a grip on himself. 'You get anything new on the guy? I mean, was he even in Los Angeles last night, or could he have rigged up the re-route from anywhere in the country?'

'Theoretically, he could've done it from anywhere, but our electronics guy says it was most likely done from here in LA.'

'Great. That narrows it down to about ten million people, most likely. However, in a way it makes sense. We're dealing with a pretty sophisticated killer here. Not just electronically sophisticated. He's street smart. Smart enough to outsmart big-city cops and, so far, the FBI. You don't get that kind of smart from living on a farm. That comes from a city education.'

'More than just *living* in the city. A preliminary profile from downstairs says the guy's killed before.'

'Where and for whom? Viet Nam? For some drug-dealer? Maybe he used to be a cop. Lloyd, get me a list of every city Talbot's show was carried in last night.'

'Right.'

'And Lloyd . . .'

'Yes?'

'Get some new fucking tobacco. That cherry shit smells awful.'

'Thanks for the Mugsy Bogues jersey, Dad.'

'You're welcome,' said Matt.

Jarod toyed with his chocolate milkshake and barely touched his Johnny Rocket's hamburger and fries.

Matt knew Jarod was a bright kid. He didn't know how much he knew, or sensed, about what was going on between Matt and Laurie, but he knew the boy realized things weren't right. It occurred to Matt that Jarod might have actually met Frank Jacobsen, or seen him with Laurie. The thought did something to Matt's stomach.

'Something's going bad between you and Mom, right?'

'Yes. We're getting a divorce, Jarod.' There was no good way to phrase it – at least, no way Matt had yet thought of. And during that afternoon, he had thought of little else.

Jarod nodded and rolled the straw between his

fingers, all the while unable to look at Matt directly.

'Who wanted it?'

'I'm not sure that's really important—'

'Mom wanted it, didn't she?'

After a moment, Matt said, 'Yes.' He didn't want to ask Jarod exactly how he knew that. Suddenly Matt felt that sensation in his stomach again.

'How will that change things between you and me?'

Matt wanted to say, 'Hey, nothing's going to change between us. I promise.' But he didn't want to lie. 'I'm not sure, Jarod. I love you. I love you very, very much. That won't change. I swear to God it won't.' Matt sighed. 'But, on the practical side, I imagine how much we actually go on seeing each other will depend on how things go between your mother and me. And, of course, if and when she remarries would play a part in things, too.'

After a moment, Jarod looked up at Matt and said, 'This is fucked.'

Matt thought about saying a lot of things, but all he did say was, 'You're right.'

'My real father doesn't give a damn about me anymore, my mother doesn't understand me . . . My whole fucking life is controlled by people who don't know who I am.'

'I know who you are, Jarod.'

'But you don't have any control over my life. Not anymore.'

'Look, Jarod, you're fifteen years old. Your mother isn't heartless. She knows what you're going through.'

'C'mon, Matt. You and I both know my mom. I love her, you love her – at least you used to – but, let's face it, she's a very selfish person. She even says so herself, like it's some kind of badge of independence.'

'Maybe it's because of the success she's finally getting—'

'You don't need to make excuses for her, okay. I'm not saying she's a terrible person. All I'm saying is that, for whatever reason, she always, almost always, thinks of herself first. You know something, Matt, I don't mean to be rude or anything, but I think your "me" generation sucks. A person can't just always do what feels good all the time, you know? Especially when it hurts other people.'

From the mouths of babes. Matt had to smile. Fifteen-year-old Jarod sounded a lot like Matt's father. 'Yeah, I know.'

'So, what happens now?'

'Your mother is getting the divorce papers drawn up. I imagine we can iron out most of the wrinkles pretty quickly.'

'I mean, are you . . . You're not coming back . . . to the house, I mean.'

'No, Jarod. I'll probably come by and pick up my things some time in the next week or so. You can reach me anytime at the office. I'll leave word that you can have my number, even when I'm out of town. You're the only one.'

'Thanks. What about custody?'

'What about it?'

'Could you get custody of me?'

Matt smiled. Just to hear Jarod ask the question made Matt feel better than he had felt in a long time. 'Legally, I don't think there's any chance that I could get custody but, as a practical matter, as long as your mother and I remain on good terms, you can come and stay with me any time you want.'

Jarod nodded. 'Can I have my own room where you live?'

'Definitely. When I get a place, I'll make sure it's got at least two bedrooms. And I'll give you your own key, so you can come and go as you please.'

That seemed to make Jarod feel a little better. 'Yeah?'

'Damn right.'

'Thanks.'

'You don't have to thank me, Jarod. I look at you as my own son. Nothing will ever change that. I promise.'

When Matt dropped Jarod back at the Barrington condo, and watched the young man disappear through the gate, he suddenly felt very, very alone. He could not go through that gate now – not without calling ahead first to make sure . . . To make sure that it was okay.

Two weeks ago that condominium had been his home. Jarod and Laurie had been his family. Now the condominium was just a place where some of his furniture and clothes were being stored, short-term.

His son was trying to think of ways to still see him.

And his wife was sleeping with another man.

The Santa Monica Pier had an old Dodgem Car concession, a place where a guy could knock down a few milk bottles to win a stuffed animal for his girl, and a restaurant that served decent soft-shell crabs.

'This is great,' said Susan as she walked along the boardwalk next to Matt.

'I thought you might like to see something besides the inside of a restaurant.'

'I don't get to the ocean much.'

'What do you do in your spare time?'

'I don't have a lot of spare time, really. Most of my free time happens at night, and I just meet friends at clubs or coffee-houses in town.'

'Coffee-houses?'

'They're coming back. Or haven't you heard?'

'Oh, I've heard. In fact, I know a couple of excellent coffee-houses here on the west side. That is, if you like poetry readings, original acoustic music and strong coffee.'

'Three of my favorite things,' said Susan amiably.

'So, how did you get a column in a national newspaper?'

'Pardon?'

'I mean, you're so young.'

Susan smiled. 'Yeah, well, I'm not that young. How old are you?'

'I'm old enough to remember coffee-houses from the Joni Mitchell/Cat Stevens era, and young enough not to remember them from the Beatnik days.'

'Beatnik?'

Matt didn't know whether or not she was putting him on, until she smiled playfully. 'Just kidding. I've read Kerouac. You know the thing I like most about coffee-houses?'

'What?'

'You can go to one and actually talk to someone. You don't have to shout over loud music. Besides, dancing was never my strong suit when it came to impressing men.'

'What was?'

'My intelligence, of course. But then, I'm sure you already knew that,' said Susan, encoring that playful smile.

Matt liked her confidence, liked the easy way they communicated. Still, he knew that she was personally motivated to be nice to the FBI agent who was handling the serial killer story of the century. Matt didn't look at the case that way, but he could see a marketing guy putting that spin on it.

'What about country and western music?' asked Matt.

'What about it?'

'You like it?'

'I didn't use to. But I have to admit I like some of it now, yes.'

'These days I listen to about as much C and W as I do to rock and roll. I can't tell whether country music's getting better, or I'm getting older.'

'Probably a little of both.'

He laughed. 'Probably more one than the other.'

Matt and Susan arrived at the end of the pier, and they both looked out over the Pacific for a moment, in silence.

'So, where do we go from here?' said Susan finally.

'What do you mean?'

'I mean, are you likely to get a break in one of the other cases you're already investigating involving the Reaper? Are we going to just wait for him to commit another murder, or are we going to do something proactive?'

'We?'

'We're partners, right?'

'Wrong. I said I'd give you the story. Exclusively. But you're not going to be at my side when I go through the door.'

'You know what I mean.'

'As long as you know what *I* mean.'

'I understand. But I also want you to understand something else,' said Susan, turning her back to the ocean and facing Matt. 'I'm grateful for your offer, and I take you at your word, but I still feel the same way about this guy.'

'The Reaper.'

'I look at him as part of a something that *needs* to happen in this country. He's not some drug-crazed, out-of-control nut who goes around blowing everyone away. Yeah, I know how you feel about glorifying his behavior, and I'll try to write a story that's even-handed. But I really believe he's a man with a conscience, a man who's been pushed to the wall and doesn't know what else to do.'

'A hero?'

'Our nation's heroes currently consist of rock-and-roll stars I wouldn't want drinking out of my toilet, rap artists who want to kill cops just for kicks, actors and actresses who couldn't relate to the common man if you gave them a two-day seminar on the topic, and sports figures who make millions of dollars a year and charge ten-year-olds twenty bucks for an autograph. Yeah, I think the Reaper deserves some credit for being willing to put his ass on the line: not for money, not for a movie deal, not to get laid, but for principle, for values. If you molest children, you pay a price. Who would you want *your* child to identify with?'

'Me,' said Matt. Without explanation, but not without passion.

'I didn't know you had children. I don't know why I didn't think of it. I just—'

'I have a stepson. I'm in the process of getting divorced.'

'Sorry.'

Matt laughed and defused a potentially tense situation. 'My wife's the one who should say that.'

'I didn't mean to pry.'

'No problem.'

A woman and a little boy strolled, hand in hand, past Matt and Susan. The boy was carrying a balloon. His mother had a Walkman stuck in her ears, and she was moving to a different rhythm. The boy was running to try to keep up.

'You still didn't answer my question,' said Susan finally.

'Which was?'

'What do we do now?'

'You continue to write your column, without divulging any information I've given you, and I continue to work on bringing this guy in.'

'So we – that is, you – have no plan.'

'I wouldn't put it that way.'

'What about my column? Can I say how I feel about the guy and what he's doing?'

'Within reason.'

'I'm not a journalist. I'm a columnist. With a journalist, you pay her to keep her opinion *out* of the story. A columnist, that's what you're paying for – her opinion.'

'Okay, but in expressing your viewpoint, try not to whip up public opinion any more than it already is about this guy. I've got enough to contend with. Besides, there are all kinds of other people out there trying to stir things up. Write about him, express your opinion, but tone it down, and don't, under any circumstances, even intimate that you might be getting inside information.'

'All right. Now I know the ground rules.'

'Good.'

'So how do I reach you, besides your number at work?'

'I'm staying with a friend; I just moved out of my . . . where I used to live. I'm not settled right now. But I can give you my beeper number.'

'Great.'

Matt took his card out of his jacket pocket. 'You have a pen?'

'I've got a pencil.' She handed it to him.

Matt wrote down the number on the back of his card and handed it to Susan. 'You can get me anytime at that number.'

'Thanks,' she said, and pocketed the card.

The two of them headed back along the pier, and Matt walked Susan to her rental car.

'So what am I supposed to do for fun in LA? I don't know anybody here.'

'You know me.'

'Are you fun?'

'If you're bored to tears, call me later.'

'Wow, you're really smooth,' said Susan ironically.

'Maybe I should try harder.'

'Maybe you just need practice.'

Carnie watched CNN, as a local correspondent explained what Detective Brunowski's news conference meant. The bottom line was that the vigilante, dubbed 'The Reaper' by national radio talk show host Kyle Talbot, was not involved. The suspect linked to killing local politician/businessman Torrez was in jail the night Trent was murdered. Plus, the *real* Reaper had called in to Talbot's show to set the record straight.

Carnie wasn't caught up in the circus aspects of what was going on. He focused on what lay ahead. In the future, the immediate future, there were dominoes that needed to be knocked down. Dominoes that toppled in a fluid and unstoppable manner toward an ultimate goal. He wondered if the FBI had been called in yet. It was only a matter of time until they were on this case. Would they know where he was going with all this? Would they guess where the dominoes led?

Carnie knew that he himself was not some kook killing at random, playing out some personal vendetta – except that once. He was not some nut believing that he would never be caught. Carnie knew that he *would* be caught. In fact, it was part of the plan.

He sat in the front yard, looking at his modest one-story, two-bedroom ranch-style house. He had lived there ten years. This last year and a half, he had lived alone.

He finished his Rolling Rock beer, tossed it into a large rubber garbage can – two points – and stood. Alone in the darkness. Looking at the only house he had considered a home.

Visions of another life washed over him like a living and vivid wave of sights, sounds and emotions. Laughter, passion, lust, the excitement of shared hopes and dreams. Eventually the images dissolved into other, more recent, pictures. Tears, loneliness and, on a bad night, screams in the darkness, crying out unanswerable questions into an empty and silent night.

Tonight the only sounds he heard were crickets and the roar of a distant laugh track coming from his neighbor's TV.

Carnie walked up to his front porch, opened the door, and tossed a match onto the gasoline-soaked living-room carpet.

In his rear-view mirror, as he pulled away, Carnie could see his past going up in flames.

And, as he drove into the night, he thought to himself that the fires in Hell would be a welcome relief.

TWENTY-ONE

Matt Baldwin scanned the profile worked up by Donald Straight, a psychiatrist who worked for the FBI. Matt had specifically asked for Straight. He had worked with him before and found the man to be intuitive. Intuitive in the sense that he could connect diverse data and statistics, extrapolate facts into a composite that, more often than not, hit the mark. Never one hundred percent, but more than the other men and women Matt had at his disposal.

It was nearly nine p.m., and Lloyd Garland was working on his eighth pipe bowl of a new mixture he'd picked up at Tinder Box, called 'Keith's Mixture'. It still smelled a little on the sweet side, but Garland had made certain there was no cherry-flavor in the mix.

Donald Straight sat in a chair directly opposite Matt, while Garland sat off to Matt's left, near the window facing west toward the ocean.

'Interesting,' said Matt when he finally looked up at Straight. 'Run it by me again – for Lloyd.'

Garland hadn't read the just-completed profile, and Matt wanted him to hear it. Also, Matt wanted to hear Straight recite it. Perhaps there was something Matt could pick up from hearing the psychologist *say* it out loud.

'All right,' said Straight, clearing his throat. He was much more comfortable with written presentations.

Matt knew this, and was prepared to prompt the man with questions. 'About the possible profession . . . ?'

'Yes, well, either he's a professional criminal or someone in law enforcement.'

'Why do you say that?'

'Well, he's not just some nut out there run amok. He knows a lot about electronics – the re-routing of his call to Kyle Talbot's show indicates that. He knows about disguises. From the very first murder – at least from the first murder you've documented – he has completely eluded police. No fingerprints, no physical evidence of any kind except the note, which in itself indicates a sophisticated knowledge of police methods.'

'But you lean toward our man being in law enforcement.'

'Yes. For several reasons. First, he's killing criminals. He is killing on what he considers to be moral grounds. His note indicates that he is merely carrying out a punishment his victims have brought upon themselves. And his thinking is not abstract, not particularly subjective. What I mean by that is he's probably considered very sane, not only by the people who know him, but, as you can see, millions of other Americans consider his actions sane as well. This is not common with most serial killers. For example, Jeffrey Dahmer could not go on the radio, explain why he killed and mutilated his victims' bodies, and win any sympathy from the public. Ted Bundy couldn't explain his motivation for killing his victims and get sympathy from the public. Yet this man has a conscience and a moral compass pretty much in sync with the public at large. In short, we are probably dealing with an otherwise productive and well-adjusted member of society.

'Second, he seems to be well versed in a variety of sophisticated criminal techniques. Whereas a white-collar criminal might know a lot about electronics, he might not also know about disguises and working undercover – like our guy, who lived on the street with that homeless man. And a white-collar criminal would rarely ever consider killing a man face to face. And, even if he did consider it, chances are he wouldn't have the intelligence, the knowledge or the guts to carry it out.

'No, I feel that this man we're looking for is not only familiar with all these things, but skilled in them as well. As you know, Matt, what I practice is not an exact science, but that's my best guess.'

'What else? Who is this guy? How old is he? Married? Single?'

'We know he's white from the descriptions given by witnesses – but because he was in disguise, that's about all we know about his appearance. He's young enough to be able to perform extraordinary physical feats, yet he must be old enough to have developed the skills I spoke of before. My guess is he's about thirty-five to forty-five. I don't know whether he's single or married, but it's extremely unusual to find a married serial killer. Yet the subject doesn't fit the crazed, out-of-touch serial-killer profile to begin with. And then, of course, there was the ring.'

'So, why now? Why not a year ago? Two years ago? Ten years ago?'

'You probably won't know the exact answer to that question until you know who the guy really is. However, if you look at his targets, they're all people who have escaped punishment by the justice system; punishment, I might add, a majority of people would believe his victims deserved. Add to this a pervasive feeling throughout the country that the average guy is powerless, that the system has failed, and that law enforcement can no longer protect the public – it could just be a question of critical mass. What I mean by that is the killer might have just reached the point where he was so fed up, so cornered by external circumstances, that he felt he didn't have any choice.'

'A lot of people feel that way, but they don't go out and start killing people.'

Straight smiled. 'Quite frankly, Matt, I'm surprised there aren't more people like this guy out there already.'

More and more people were saying so lately, realized Matt, but he kept the thought to himself. 'The difference between this guy and a bunch of vigilantes is that *he* knows what he's doing.'

'That's at least one difference.'

'What about a triggering event?' said Garland, keeping his hand in.

'Very possibly. A lot of would-be vigilantes never act out, because they still have something to lose. But when a traumatic, or triggering event occurs, the person may become convinced that he has nothing left to lose. At that point he becomes very dangerous. He begins to act out behaviour he would ordinarily have suppressed.'

'When you have nothing to lose, there's no reason not to do whatever you want,' agreed Matt.

'Many criminals feel that way. One reason young people and poor people are more prone to violence is because they don't have anything to lose – no property, no long-term relationships to protect. I mean, their freedom is the only thing left to surrender, and for a variety of reasons they don't feel they have much freedom anyhow.'

'So, do you see a triggering event here, Don?'

Straight hesitated a moment, and considered the possibility, not for the first time.

'Yes. And if we're correct and a triggering event has occurred, then he doesn't feel desperate because he believes he has nothing left to lose. He is, therefore, acting rationally. He apparently has very sophisticated knowledge that can be used to kill people and to elude law enforcement. But, even more than that, he appears to have a plan.'

'What do you mean?'

'I mean, he is executing various members of America's "low-life" class, but he's also on some kind of mission – the notes, the calls to Talbot's radio show. Because he's so bright, he must know that he will eventually be caught.'

'What exactly are you saying, Don?'

'I'd say watch out for this guy's end-game.'

'What do you think it might be?'

'I don't know.'

'I know you don't. What's your best guess?'

Straight sighed, looked up at the ceiling, tried not to focus on Garland's sweet-smelling tobacco, and considered the question. 'He believes he's doing something good. Not just for himself, but for other people. In this case, probably even for his country. I don't know. My guess would be, if he could isolate a figure he felt was responsible for what he considers wrong with this country, that person would become his ultimate target.'

'That responsibility seems pretty well spread around, if you ask me,' said Garland.

'True. Another thing you're going to have to contend with – and this isn't in the profile – is the effect the killings are having on the country as a whole.'

'What do you mean?' asked Matt, although he already had an idea.

'A lot of citizens feel his victims deserve to die. The longer he gets away with doing that, and the longer opinion leaders like radio hosts and others in the media condone such behavior, the more other people with grievances will consider this course of action an acceptable way of resolving those grievances.'

Matt nodded. 'Thanks, Don.' He flipped over the cover page of the report and stood to indicate that the meeting, or at least Straight's part in it, had ended.

The psychologist also stood up, smiled at Matt and Garland, and started to leave. When he reached the door, he turned around. 'There's one thing.'

'Yes?'

'This is just some creative extrapolation on my part, but here goes. If this guy really is a "good guy" – that is, if he grew up with a defined sense of right and wrong – then killing other people, even in a "righteous" cause, could create a core conflict inside him eventually. In other words, he may develop a problem of conscience, an inability to reconcile his actions with the core beliefs he's held most of his life.'

'Great,' said Matt with a smile. 'All we have to do is get him to feel guilty enough to turn himself in.'

'It's a thought.' Then Straight left the room, closing the door behind him.

'Well?'

'If he's right about the guy being in law enforcement, this is just the beginning of the nightmare,' said Garland, after removing the pipe from his mouth.

'I know. I want you to do something for me, Lloyd. Check all airlines, bus lines and train lines for a person buying a one-way ticket, with cash, to leave the cities where any victim was murdered, from thirty minutes after the murder took place, to forty-eight hours afterward.'

'You're kidding.'

Matt looked at Garland.

'Gotcha.'

'Airlines will be easier, and frankly I think they're our best bet. I'm giving you those specific sort parameters for the following reasons. First, chances are the guy would buy a one-way ticket because he wasn't certain when he was likely to return.'

'He might have bought an open round-trip ticket.'

'Maybe. Second, he probably paid with cash so he didn't have to use a phony credit card. Third, he probably left each city immediately after the murder.'

'Sounds logical.'

'Sounds desperate, Lloyd. We're dyin' here.'

'If he was trying to conceal his identity, he obviously wouldn't have used his real name. What are you hoping to find, Matt?'

'A break, Lloyd. A fucking break.'

Ten minutes later, Matt was on the 405 heading north toward the Valley, when his beeper went off. He called the number, which he didn't recognize, from his car phone.

'Matt?'

'Yes.'

'This is Susan. You in the mood to show me one of those coffee-houses you were telling me about?'

There were all kinds of coffee-houses in Los Angeles these days, but the one Matt liked most was McGavin's in Santa Monica. It had about twenty small round tables, sawdust on the floor, and a thirty-foot stage against the wall opposite the door. It was just coffee, decaffeinated plus about a dozen blends of exotic brews ranging from Black Bayou Mud to Malibu Mocha. The place made its money from a seven-dollar cover charge, four-dollar mugs of coffee, and a newsstand that sold foreign newspapers and magazines. Every night – every night Matt had been there anyhow – at least four or five poets read from published works, works in progress, or something they happened to write down on a napkin during a caffeine rush before taking the stage. Besides poets, there were usually half a dozen singer/songwriters who played original material.

'This is great,' said Susan.

'I thought you'd like it.'

'Because I'm the Bohemian type?'

'You figure I think you're Bohemian because you're a writer?'

'Yes.'

'I think there's a difference between what *you* do and what's done here.'

'Such as?' said Susan, arching her eyebrow a little.

'This is art for art's sake. No one gets paid, and everyone has a day job; or at least they get a check from the actor's bank.'

'Actor's bank?'

Matt smiled. 'Unemployment.'

'Doesn't make what I do bad, just because I get paid for it.'

'No, and I didn't mean it to sound that way. All

I'm saying is that it's different, that's all.'

'Then why did you think I'd like it here?'

'I'm a pretty good judge of people. Disco, fancy restaurant, ballet . . . I just thought this was more you.'

'You were right.'

Susan had been careful so far not to bring up the case, for a couple of reasons. First, Matt looked exhausted – though he seemed a little more relaxed now than when they had first arrived. Second, she knew that he was probably looking for something to take his mind away from the Reaper, even if just for a few minutes.

When Matt had paid for the first round of coffee, he took Jarod's picture out of his wallet and showed it to her.

'Handsome boy.' Susan smiled and handed the photograph back to Matt.

'He's a great kid.'

'Divorce is tough enough, without children. You don't have to talk about it if you don't want to.'

'Hell, it almost feels good to talk about it. My friends are walking on eggshells around me, careful not to ask me the wrong or insensitive question. She left me for another man. Another fucking lawyer. *She's* a lawyer,' said Matt, 'in case I failed to mention that. Great spot I'm in, eh? My wife is a lawyer and she's suing me for divorce. I might as well just gather up all my assets and start a fucking bonfire.'

'Is it one of those nasty divorces?'

Matt took another sip of coffee. 'It's one of those

very civil divorces,' he said. 'In fact, she seems quite amiable about the whole thing. I think she just wants out.'

'You shouldn't blame yourself.'

'Why in the hell should I blame myself?'

'You shouldn't,' added Susan quickly. 'I was just saying that if you were – because some people do – you shouldn't.'

'Yeah, well, I don't. I was one hundred percent loyal to her – not that I didn't have my chances.'

'I'm sure.'

'Really?'

'What do you mean?'

'I mean, what makes you so sure I had my opportunities?'

'You're a good-looking guy. I imagine you meet people, in your work, especially out of town. And, well, things happen.'

'They didn't happen to me. That's the problem with the world,' said Matt, definitely loosening up now. 'It's fashionable to say "shit happens", as though that's some kind of pop-culture absolution. People still have choices. They make the decision to do something, or not to do something. I chose to be loyal to my wife, and she chose to ignore our vows.'

Neither Matt nor Susan spoke for a moment.

'You ever married?' said Matt finally.

'Once. Guy I met in college. He was a musician. Now, that was a *real* smart choice.'

'Great sex?' asked Matt.

'Phenomenal. Still think about it, now and then.'

'The sex or the guy?'

'The sex. Then I take a cold shower and remember what an asshole he was the other twenty-three hours and forty minutes of every day. You know, I saw him last year. I was in Detroit at some convention, and I stopped into the Marriott downtown. He was playing in the bar, but I hardly recognized him. When we got married, he weighed about one hundred and fifty pounds and he had hair down below his shoulders. These days he's pushing two hundred pounds and he's going bald.'

'How'd that make you feel?'

'Honestly?'

'Honestly.'

'Pretty good, actually,' said Susan impishly.

Matt didn't reply. He knew that, more than anything, she was trying to cheer him up.

'People live through divorces,' she said. 'It's not like it's a terminal illness. When you're on the short end of the emotional stick, you tend to think only about the good times, the good sex. Those things aren't as irreplaceable as they may seem to be right now.'

'I understand that. Intellectually, anyhow. It's just that my attention's still stuck on the *loss*.'

'Maybe you need to focus on something else for a while,' said Susan with a smile. It was not a seductive smile, but it wasn't far from it. It could have passed for one. In dim light. After a few drinks.

'I believe there's no sense trying to avoid pain,' said Matt. 'Do the grieving, feel the anger, get it over with.

If you suppress your feelings, you just delay them. And when you postpone the pain, you'll end up dropping it like poison into some other relationship.'

Matt looked at Susan. She really was quite attractive. A little earlier Matt had noticed that when she got up to go to the restroom, two men had turned their heads to watch as she walked away.

But Matt had to control himself now, for many reasons. First, he needed to focus on the case. People's lives depended on it. Second, despite his obvious feeling of attraction towards Susan, he had to remember that she was a reporter.

Susan, however, sensed that Matt was vulnerable, his ego a bit fragile. She knew he believed he was in control of the situation, yet Susan was confident she knew the buttons to push that could put Matt into her bed that night.

But it was too soon for either of them, so she looked at her watch and said, 'I think I'd better call it a night.'

Matt nodded.

'I had a good time,' she said, catching and holding Matt's eyes.

'Me, too. Let's do it again.'

'Count on it.'

'I will,' said Matt. Being genuinely attracted to a woman other than Laurie, and being in a position to act on it, was something new for him. And as he stood, tossing a ten on the table, and watched Susan walk out ahead of him, he let himself enjoy that feeling.

* * *

'I don't condone killing another human being, whether that human being is a doctor or a fetus. Either way, it's wrong,' said Kyle Talbot. 'Liberals would have us think that fetuses aren't babies, aren't real life. Let me tell you, folks, you take a look at some of the photographs, *real* photographs of *real* aborted fetuses, then you come back and look me in the eye and tell me that fetuses aren't real live human beings.

'But I have to tell you that the liberals just don't get it. I mean, I feel bad for that doctor's family. When I heard that he'd been shot, I really felt sad. But when I heard how many babies the same man had killed over the past ten years, the thought of all those dead babies made me sick, literally.

'We're in a war here, folks, whether you know it or not. And in any war there are going to be casualties. If you're a soldier, you can't back off just because you see someone die. You've got to keep your nerve, keep your eye on the prize – on victory.'

As he drove north along the San Diego Freeway, into the Valley, Matt listened to Kyle Talbot. So far, there had been no call from the Reaper. Matt wondered how many impressionable and desperate listeners tuned in to Talbot, or people like him, every day. How many of them got caught up in his metaphors, and took them literally? How many of them had stopped thinking for themselves, content to let Talbot analyze the world for them? How many were finger-on-the-trigger ready to go?

Matt suspected there were far more Reaper-like vigilantes out there than he wanted to believe.

Perhaps Lloyd Garland would give him something to work with tomorrow. But tonight what Matt needed most was a good night's sleep.

Carnie turned off Kyle Talbot's radio show, and pulled into a parking space in front of a small coffee-shop facing the ocean. Two couples sat at tiny white wrought-iron tables outside.

He got out, went inside, ordered a cup of cappuccino in a Styrofoam cup. Then he walked across the street and stood by the cement wall overlooking the ocean. Across the bay he could see the lights of a large hotel. Beneath him the waves of a chilly sea smashed against huge rocks, performing an ancient ritual, shaping them more elegantly than the most practiced human hand.

Carnie sipped his coffee and looked out across the water. About a half a mile to the left of the big hotel was a house on stilts. A big house. Carnie knew the man who lived there. He didn't know him personally, but he knew a great deal about the man.

Carnie looked to his left, down the street. La Jolla was a beautiful little town. You needed money to live in this place. To live well here.

The man in the big house had money. Lots of money. Other people's money.

Carnie had seen the same man laugh on television when interviewed about how he had stolen money from depositors in his Savings and Loan. He had looked straight into the camera, and claimed that he had done nothing illegal. As though that meant he had done nothing wrong, nothing immoral.

As though taking thousands of people's savings, leaving them penniless, defenseless in their old age, was not wrong. As though putting all his money in his wife's and son's names, shortly before he learned – from a senator he had purchased a few years earlier – that his assets would be attached, was not wrong. As though buying back his S and L's assets at ten cents on the dollar – with money he had managed to hide in off-shore accounts – was not wrong.

Somewhere legality had become synonymous with the word morality: if it was legal, it must therefore be moral.

But Carnie knew the difference between what was legal and what was moral.

Tomorrow night the man in the big house would know it, too.

'What an asshole,' said Susan Dornan, to herself. She hit the remote button on the radio as Kyle Talbot signed off. She had been as nice to the guy as she could, schmoozed him up one side and down the other in order to get her story, but there was no getting around the fact that Talbot was an asshole.

She turned on David Letterman instead, snacked on a room-service pizza, then tried to get some sleep.

'You were great,' said Cassie.

'You really think so?' Kyle Talbot was lying on

his waterbed, with a half-glass of Scotch, watching his big-screen TV. On the local news there was a piece describing how police had officially arrested some skinhead for the murder of Carlos Torrez.

'I like being close to power,' said Cassie. She was dressed in a silk teddy Talbot had purchased for her at Victoria's Secret a couple of weeks ago. She knew he liked the way it was cut up in front. The way it revealed the fact that she was shaved smooth *down there.* Well, almost, anyhow.

Talbot liked the way Cassie catered to him, doted on him, depended on him. At his age, after three marriages and lots of firecracker-and-fizzle romances, Talbot knew enough to enjoy the moment – which he realized would always pass away.

'Damn!'

'What, honey?' whispered Cassie.

'They didn't even mention my name.' The sports reporter came on next, and Talbot winced. He knew that guy when he had real hair. Didn't like him then; liked him less now. Talbot hit the off button, and the screen went dark. The room was lit by a full-moon spill.

'I wish the Reaper would've called in tonight.'

'Don't worry, he will.'

'I suppose.'

'What you need to do is relax.'

Talbot looked at Cassie's smooth skin, how it seemed sculpted in the shadow and light, and decided that she was probably right.

The phone rang in the other room.

'Let it ring,' said Cassie.

'Don't worry. I don't hear a thing,' said Talbot as he kissed Cassie gently on her neck.

In the other room the answering machine picked up, and Talbot's message instructed the caller to leave a message.

Carnie put down the phone, looked around, stepped out of the booth, turned his collar up against the chilly ocean breeze, and started walking, his shadow long in the moonlight, the sound of his boot leather clicking and echoing down empty La Jolla streets.

TWENTY-TWO

'I hate waiting,' said Matt.

'We should have something back from the airlines late today, or first thing in the morning.'

Matt and Lloyd Garland strolled leisurely through Veteran's Cemetery, which was located across the street from the Federal Building in Westwood. At least the pipe tobacco didn't seem so bad here, thought Matt as they walked.

The cemetery ran along the east side of the San Diego Freeway. Joggers went through their paces amid neat rows of manicured landscaping. In the bright sun of a California day, all things considered, it was a pretty good place to take a walk. Matt often spent his lunch hour here, after changing into tennis shoes, shorts and a gray FBI T-shirt, jogging or walking briskly along the road that ran through the cemetery.

'Why is the Reaper doing this?' said Matt, partly to Garland, but partly just to give voice to the unanswerable questions racing around his brain.

'There are a lot of crazy people out there.'

'This guy's not crazy. Oh, I know what he's doing *sounds* crazy, but do you remember what Straight said about a triggering event?'

'Yes.'

'Lloyd, is there anything that could happen to you that would make you completely rearrange your priorities, chuck it all, and use the skills you know to go out and kill people?'

Garland puffed and smoked and walked while he considered Matt's question. After a moment he said, 'I don't think so.'

'I'll bet our guy would have answered that question the same way before *something* happened.'

'Maybe he still would.'

'What do you mean?' asked Matt.

'If there was a triggering event, something that caused a moral sea change, he probably doesn't look at his current behavior the way we do. He probably doesn't think he's chucking it all and going out and killing people. Most likely he thinks that he's achieved some type of epiphany that sets him free to right some of society's obvious wrongs.'

'To be the Reaper.'

'Exactly.'

Matt and Garland walked a while in silence.

'How you holding up?' said Garland.

Matt knew what his friend was talking about. 'I'm okay. I'm seeing an apartment on Federal near Wilshire this afternoon. It sounds nice.'

'So, you're definitely making the move?'

'When your wife starts sleeping with another man, I think it's one of those telltale signs that you should start looking for your own place.'

'It'll work out, Matt. Don't worry about about it.'

The remark sounded weak to both men, but Matt

let it slide. He knew Lloyd meant well. But Matt was in a place where no friend could help him now. What he had to go through, he would need to go through alone.

'I'm going to leave work early tonight. I'm meeting the apartment manager at four-thirty, and Jarod's got a game at five-thirty.'

'Fine. If I get anything, I'll beep you.'

'Okay.'

'Hang in there, buddy.'

Matt smiled at his friend and said, 'What other choice do I have?'

The speaker on the dais was a tall man with white hair. It was difficult to place his exact age, but the seminar literature had listed Douglas Stevenson's age as forty-nine. He spoke and moved with authority, and the 150 men and women in the hotel ballroom stared at him with a mixture of awe and respect. They hung on his every word because, God willing, with enough knowledge and luck, what had happened to Stevenson would happen to them.

The seminar materials stated what most attendees already knew. During the Eighties, Stevenson had amassed a fortune in excess of two billion dollars, most of which was tied in one way or another to investments made through, or money generated by, a string of Savings and Loans owned by Stevenson himself. At one time or another he had been on the covers of most major financial publications. One famous example had a doctored photograph of him, in his trademark running shorts, jogging on water.

The last cover featuring Stevenson appeared on *Time:* an actual photograph of him being led away from a federal courthouse in handcuffs.

But that was three years ago, and money was money. He was a good guy again: 'not a hardened criminal, not the kind of guy who's going to put a gun to your grandmother's head and steal her car', as one interviewer on a financial cable channel had put it recently. Besides, the reasoning went, say what you wanted about Stevenson, the guy knew how to make money. Big money. Fast.

And knowledge about how to make big money in a hurry never went out of style. There was no shame in making money. If anything, there was a stigma in not at least trying to make as much as you could. To 'provide for your loved ones, give them all they deserve', the brochure read.

Eight months after Stevenson's release from prison, he was on the seminar circuit, once again electrifying the masses. The handouts contained two pages of quotes from financial celebrities, Hollywood types, even a couple of retired congressmen and senators, extolling the virtues of Stevenson's strategies.

With a wireless microphone attached to his lapel, Stevenson was free to prowl the stage like an evangelist spreading the gospel of life everlasting.

'People will tell you that money is bad. A man came up to me the other day, after a talk I gave in Houston, and he said that the Bible said money was bad. I asked him to step backstage with me where I pulled a Bible out of my briefcase and referred him to the actual passage which actually says that the *love* of money is bad. Not money itself.

'I want as much money as I can get. But why? I don't shower with it. I don't sleep with it. I don't love it. But I do love what it can do for me. It can provide not only security, but options for my family. Options they would not have without it.

'I've been blessed in my life by the love of a wonderful woman, and by the births of my son and daughter. They were with me in the hard times as well as the good. Is there anything wrong with going out and trying to provide them with all the opportunities and creature comforts I can afford?

'I didn't make the rules, friends. And success in these United States, whether you like it or not, is measured by one thing, and one thing only: money. If you have more money than the next guy, you have more options than the next guy. You can do more, have more, and be more successful.

'There is only one champion of major-league baseball every year. They don't hand out two Super Bowl trophies each year. At the Indianapolis 500, they don't give a runner-up trophy for the second car across the finish line.

'I'm a winner. For three years in a row, I made more money than any other man in the United States. Three years in a row,' he repeated.

Carnie sat in the back row and leafed through the handout. He looked occasionally at the men in blue blazers who guarded each exit. These were not accountants, or students hired to make sure that groupies had tickets. They were beefy football-player types who wouldn't know a mutual fund from a slush fund. And they were there for one reason.

Despite the fact that Stevenson had his admirers, his detractors were even more fanatical. The two years he spent in prison had failed to assuage the mental and, in some cases, physical pain inflicted directly or indirectly on thousands of investors who had lost tens of millions of dollars – money they would never recoup. Stevenson had paid his debt to society, but there was another part of society that was still looking to collect. Any way they could.

'Remember that line from the movie *Wall Street*, about greed being good?'

Stevenson waited for the puppets to nod their heads. They did, and he continued.

'That movie character was ridiculed in the press, but let me tell you something: greed has a royal pedigree in this country. When the framers of the Constitution ruled early America, did they sit down with the Indians and say, "Well, you know, I think we ought to figure out a way where we can share the wealth here"? When a business goes to market with a product, do they sit down with their competitors and try to figure out how they can each share in the proceeds? No. The object is to *win* – and winning includes beating the other guy, and claiming the prize, which is always money.

'There is nothing wrong in using every legal

maneuver possible in order to beat your opponent.'

A ripple of laughter spread through the crowd.

'I know what you're thinking, that I tried to beat my opponents by using illegal means. I'm sure that most of you who have seen or read about my case understand that, in many ways, I was a victim of circumstance. I was too busy making money to watch every move my lawyers and underlings were making. They did some things that weren't right, and I later took responsibility for that – which is right. I am responsible for those who work for me. It was a good lesson, and it is one that I pass along to you.

'We'll take a fifteen-minute break now, then I'll be back to answer all of your questions.'

With that, the audience broke into applause.

Carnie walked out into the lobby, with everyone else. But he did not return for the second half of Stevenson's lecture.

'Not much of a view,' said Matt. The balcony looked out over a courtyard towards another apartment building.

'It's the only furnished apartment I have left.' said Danny, the on-premises manager.

Matt wanted to stay in the Brentwood/West Los Angeles area, but there weren't a lot of furnished apartments available in his price range.

'Any facilities?'

'Well, there's a laundry room on the first floor, and a rec room with a pool table – I play pool myself every day, so if you want to play or take lessons, I'm available. We got a Jacuzzi and a heated pool, but the pool's got a crack in it and it won't be usable for another two months or so.'

'The furniture . . .' Matt couldn't decide on the right word, without sounding extremely offensive.

'Yeah, well, if you've got any furniture you wanna bring in, I can take a little off the rent.'

Matt nodded and looked around. It really wasn't that bad. It was just bad in comparison to what he was used to. And what he was used to was a home. What he needed now, though, was a place that would serve as a transition point. Some place close to work, some place close to Jarod, some place other than Charlie's.

Matt followed Danny downstairs, filled out the paperwork, wrote out a check for the first and last months' rent, plus a deposit. Danny said he didn't have to check any references after he knew Matt worked for the FBI. So he called the Federal Building, confirmed Matt's employment there, and turned over the keys.

'I'm going to need two sets of keys,' said Matt.

'Just so happens the previous tenant had an extra set made. Saves you the trouble, right?'

'Right.'

'No extra charge. It'll be good to have an FBI guy living here. There's this guy down on the first floor, he's always playin' his stereo full-blast at midnight, sometimes two in the morning. Can I call you if I need some, you know, official help? Somebody to flash a badge?'

Matt smiled, picked up the two sets of keys and said, 'No.'

He arrived only twenty minutes late for Jarod's game. Jarod was at bat as Matt sat down in the stands. Stepping out of the batter's box, Jarod glanced up towards the stands, spotted Matt, and smiled.

After the game, the boy sat on Matt's Jeep, sweat dripping off him onto the hood. Matt didn't mind.

'Great game.'

'Good, maybe. Not great.'

'I'm prejudiced. Besides, three-for-four ain't nothing to sneeze at.'

'Yeah, but they were all singles,' said Jarod, using the towel from around his neck to wipe his forehead.

'Got something for you.'

'Oh yeah, what?'

Matt dug into his jacket pocket, took out a set of keys, and handed them over. 'I got a place over on Federal. The address is on the key chain.'

'Great, that's walking distance from . . .'

'Call ahead if you want, but you don't have to. The only rules are the same rules we've always had. When I'm not there, no girls, and only male friends you genuinely trust. Okay?'

'Okay.'

'I want you to feel comfortable at my new place.'

What he really wanted was for Jarod to feel a sense of continuity. There was a good chance that Matt, at his age, would never have any biological children of his own. And even if he did, he felt that he could never expect better than the young man who sat next to him on the hood of his Cherokee.

He didn't want to lose Jarod. Ever.

The two of them talked about the game, specific plays made and not made, other players and the next game. Then Matt sensed a change in Jarod's mood.

'What is it?'

'Nothin',' said Jarod, again burying his face in the sweaty towel.

'C'mon. We tell each other everything, right?'

'Right.'

There was an awkward moment of silence as Jarod collected his thoughts. 'This guy . . .' He didn't know the right words. He was too young to understand it all, but old enough to know that whatever he planned to say would hurt Matt.

Matt tried to make it easier. 'You mean Frank Jacobsen?'

Jarod turned and looked Matt in the eye. 'You know?'

'Yeah, I know. If you promise not to tell your mother I told you, I'll tell you something.'

'Promise.'

Matt then proceeded to tell Jarod what had transpired in Jacobsen's office several days earlier.

It took a few minutes for Jarod to compose himself – he was laughing so hard he fell off the car. It was a calculated risk on Matt's part, to be this honest with Jarod, since there was a good chance that Jacobsen might be Jarod's new stepfather. Matt was not a vicious person, and he would never badmouth Laurie to the boy. But he felt no such obligation to Jacobsen.

'He's an asshole,' said Jarod.

'Yeah, I know. But he's also the man your mother's involved with. She might even marry him.'

'Shit!'

'Don't worry about it. I'll always be around. But if your mother winds up marrying this guy, I'll expect you to show him respect as well.'

'This must be tough for you, Dad.'

'Yeah, it is tough. But I'll tell you, most people go through something like this at least once during their lifetime. You've got to deal with it, and move on. There really isn't any choice.'

'I'm never going to get married.'

'That's a wise decision. And you'll stick to it until you don't.'

'What?'

'Someday you'll meet somebody who's going to make you believe that the rules and laws of averages don't apply. I didn't marry your mother with the idea that we were going to get divorced.'

'I know. It's just .. sad, that's all.'

It was that, and much more, thought Matt.

'You said you'd always be there for me,' said Cassie, another tear making its way slowly down her mascara-stained cheek.

'And I am,' said Talbot, even though he wanted to point out that he had not used the word *always*. He recognized – himself being in his forties, Cassie in her mid-twenties – that it was his job to do the calming down.

'I can't believe you want me to get an abortion,' she continued through her tears. 'That child is the product of our love.'

'Yes, well, but technically it's not yet a child, okay?'

'That isn't what you say on your show.'

'People who march for twenty minutes don't have to live with a mistake for the rest of their lives.'

'A mistake?'

'You know what I mean.'

'I'm not sure I know anything anymore.'

Talbot thought of a rather sarcastic rejoinder but, under the circumstances, decided against it. 'Look, I don't expect you to pay for anything. In fact, after you have . . . you know, have it taken care of, we'll go away for a weekend. Hell, we can go to New York, just you and me, for three, maybe four days. I need a vacation, anyway. What do you say?'

'One of the things that first attracted me to you was your stand on abortion,' said Cassie through her tears.

Yeah, right. What really *attracted you to me was the fact that you could give up your waitress job at the Burger Hut, come to work for me at twice what you were making, live in a beautiful house with a local celebrity, eat at every fuckin' restaurant your girlfriends work at, while you order the most expensive thing on the menu and the wine list. Bull-fuckin-shit, you were attracted to me because of my 'pro-life' position.* What he said was, 'I still believe in the sanctity of all life. It's just that this is very bad timing, that's all.'

Timing was an element of Talbot's life that had never worked out very well in the past, but his luck was changing. And he would be damned if he was going to let an accident stand in the way of getting a fair shake for the first time in his life.

The phone rang.

'Talbot here.' Pause. 'My God, how did you get my home number?' Pause. 'Hold on a second. I've got to go to another phone.'

Talbot turned to Cassie. 'Sorry, honey, I gotta take this in the other room. Business. Hang this one up when I pick up, okay?' he said as he handed her the phone.

It wasn't a question but a command, so she took the receiver. She was used to taking orders. In cheap restaurants *and* in Talbot's house. The only real difference was that the pay was better here.

'Okay!' yelled Talbot from the other room.

Cassie was seething, silently. That was the way powerless people released their anger – slowly, usually in private, and never directed toward the proper target. In the end, not much internal pressure was ever released. She hit the disconnect button on the phone . . . then released it quickly . . . and covered the receiver with her hand. She heard a man's voice speaking, telling Talbot to take notes, to write down all he said. Talbot, the 'big man', was taking orders. Cassie liked that. The more she listened, the more she liked the control this other man had over Talbot. Yet the more she listened, the more frightened she became. She had to listen very, very carefully now, because it was important that she hang up at exactly the same instant Talbot did. She must not let Talbot, or the caller, know that she had overheard this conversation.

'Sorry about that,' said Talbot, as he walked back into the room, some while later.

He didn't look sorry, thought Cassie. He looked exhilarated. And she knew why.

Talbot sat down on the bed beside her. 'Don't be upset, honey. You know I love you. Remember, your job is to look pretty, and mine is to make you happy.'

'Having this baby would make me happy.'

'It's more complicated than that. You're talking about another human being.'

'I thought you said it *wasn't* a human being.'

'It isn't. Not yet, anyhow. Look, forget New York. You said you wanted to go to the Caribbean. Let's go there. Sun yourself in a different string bikini every day, sip exotic drinks on the white sand, dance every night – it'll be great. Whaddya say?'

Cassie knew she was not going to get what she wanted. So now she had to figure how much of a tab she could run up on Talbot's guilt. With something like this, the sky was the limit.

'I'll think about it,' she said poutily.

'That's my girl.' He leaned over and kissed Cassie on her black-smudged cheek, then smiled patronizingly. 'It's gonna be okay, honey. We've got plenty of time for kids.' What he meant was that *she* had plenty of time for kids . . . with someone else. 'I gotta go.'

When she heard the garage door open, and then close, Cassie got out of bed, walked across the room to retrieve a card from the bottom of her purse, push-buttoned the beeper number, left her own number, and waited for a return call.

In less than two minutes, Cassie was talking to Susan Dornan. 'I think there's something you might be interested in.'

TWENTY-THREE

It was Sunday morning. And there were fresh flowers on the grave. Like every Sunday morning.

Carnie sat on a nearby bench while his father, Arthur, knelt next to the grave, talking to Carnie's mother as though she could hear every word he said. Several months earlier, Carnie had started sitting away from his father during these Sunday morning conversations. It was always the same thing: it was not so much a conversation as it was a pathetic and incessant apology. It never ended, because there could never be any absolution or forgiveness.

At least not in this life.

Ever since his mother died, Carnie's father had been in a very dark depression. Some of that depression was to be expected. The depth and length of the despondency was what bothered Carnie.

His father was convinced that he was responsible for his wife's death. Even though Carnie had pointed out many times, that Arthur could not possibly have been responsible for the tumor in his mother's lung.

Carnie looked at his watch. It was noon. They had been there an hour. He walked over and stood beside his father.

'You ready?'

'Your mother says to say hello,' the widower said without looking up.

'Thanks, pop.' It was getting worse. For the first three months the conversation, at least as reported by his father, had been one-way. A couple of months ago, Arthur had started giving Carnie 'messages' from his mother. From the other side.

Carnie never argued, never asked any questions. Just nodded, the way he nodded today.

All the way home, his father talked about what he always talked about – when he wasn't talking about Carnie's mother. Money. Or, more precisely, lack of money. They had been smart, Arthur said. They'd invested conservatively, done the right things. Low-risk mutual funds, bonds, CDs. Planned for every contingency.

The first time his father said that, Carnie had pointed out that it was impossible to plan for every contingency. He had said it, but his father had not heard it. And so, after a while, Carnie stopped saying it.

Carnie had pointed out that no one could ever plan for the kind of illness that, after two lingering and miserable years, finally took his mother's life. His father had argued that catastrophic illness had to be built into every long-range financial plan. And he had mumbled something about the fact that it had been built into his own plan.

Before he was robbed.

In Carnie's father's mind, the person responsible for the robbery was not an intruder who had put a *gun to his head. Not some doped-up thug who had come in the night. It was a rich man, a white and well-respected man who had, using fine print and high-pressure tactics, stolen every penny of their $125,000 savings. Not a lot of money to last them for the rest of their lives. But with Arthur's pension, insurance, social security and interest on their savings, it would be enough – especially since the house was already paid for.*

Arthur had thought he had it all covered. Thought he was shrewd to take their Savings and Loan representative up on a sure thing. Twenty-five percent, guaranteed: that's what the guy had said. The fine print said nothing about a guarantee. Not an illegal *business practice. Lawyers said he should have listened more carefully. Unethical, then? Perhaps, but ethics were not a part of the modern business equation, or so Arthur's lawyer had informed him when they filed the class action suit. And Arthur had figured that if anyone knew about such things, lawyers did.*

Carnie remembered the day his father found out. Arthur had received a letter in the mail that he didn't understand, and he wanted his son to come over and try to make sense out of it. Arthur really had understood it; he just wanted Carnie to come over and interpret it some other way, to tell him that the nightmare wasn't true.

Arthur had put off telling his wife for nearly two months. Finally, when she kept complaining about how grouchy he had become, he had told her. And she wept.

It was not long after that, about six weeks, that the doctors had found the cancer. They assured Arthur that there was no medical connection between the two disasters. But Arthur knew better.

The kind of care Arthur could afford in order to keep his wife alive became an incredible financial burden. But he insisted his wife must have the best care. Nothing but the best, when his wife's health was concerned. Insurance helped, but not to the extent that they had anticipated. The savings, what little they had left, went first. Then the house. Then the car. And – with the last remnants of the possessions collected throughout a lifetime of sacrifice, commitment and love – went the dying woman's hope.

And Arthur's pride.

Carnie vividly remembered that Sunday when he had gone over to the apartment, where his father lived very alone, to pick up the old man to take him to the cemetery. As soon as he opened the front door, Carnie smelled it. Doing what he did for a living, he recognized the smell of death.

It wasn't that he hadn't feared this might happen; it was just that he hadn't known how to stop it. His father had stopped listening to reason a long time ago.

Carnie followed the odor into the kitchen. There on the floor, sprawled on the black-and-white checkered linoleum, lay his father minus the right third of his head – pieces of which were splattered on the nearby wall.

Carnie slumped against the door frame and started to weep silently. On the kitchen table was a photograph of his mother, propped against a bottle of expensive Scotch – Carnie remembered hoping that his father had charged it. Fuck 'em: at least he'd have had his last drink on those sons of bitches.

In front of the photograph lay a handwritten note: 'Please forgive me.'

Carnie wasn't sure who the note was for, his mother or himself.

In the months that followed, he decided that it was probably intended for all three of them.

When she had finished modeming her column to New York, Susan sat back on her bed and took a deep breath. Her mood was a mixture of fear and exhilaration: fear because of the risk, exhilaration because of the potential. She had made a decision, knowing the risk, betting on the potential.

In her next column there would be a hidden message. What she had written would appear to millions of readers as merely another blind item.

To one man, it was an invitation.

TWENTY-FOUR

Lloyd Garland smiled as he tamped down a fresh bowl of Keith's Mixture.

Matt propped his feet up on his desk. 'What do you have for me?'

'Nothin'. Train and bus lines have no matches for any of the nights in question. Lots of cash customers, but no two names are the same. Apparently, more people use cash for trains and bus tickets than for airplane tickets. Makes sense. Some bus fares are as low as fifteen bucks. Lot more one-way tickets, too.'

'When do the airlines check in?'

'Tomorrow morning. Most of them, anyhow.'

'Good.'

'He could have used a different name each time out.'

'He had to show *some* ID when he bought his ticket, at least with the airlines, even if he paid cash. If he used a different ID each time, then we're fucked.'

'Right,' said Garland, sensing his friend's frustration.

'You don't think he'd be stupid enough to use his own ID, do you?'

'No, I don't believe in Santa Claus, Lloyd. I'm just

looking for someplace to start.'

Matt's beeper went off. He looked at the number and dialed it.

'Matt?' said Susan.

'Susan?'

'Yes. What are you doing?'

'Saving the world. What about you?'

'I just modemed my column to New York, and I wondered if you were free for a drink?'

'You interested in helping me pick out some linens?'

He could feel the ocean water through his wet suit – through the clothes he wore underneath the wet suit.

For the average man, a two-mile swim was a goal that would never be accomplished. To Carnie it was like an evening jog. His training during the war, his work with the Special Services, had prepared him for *dangerous* duty. Tonight's mission was a very low risk. Even though it would have seemed an impossible task – for the average guy.

But Carnie was by no means the average guy.

As he crawled up on the beach out of the Pacific Ocean, he was in shadow, but he could clearly see the large, well-lit grounds of Douglas Stevenson's three-story La Jolla mansion. He stripped off his wet suit and tossed it back into the surf. It could never be traced to him – he had shoplifted it when he had purchased two T-shirts at a snorkeling shop in Marina Del Rey a week ago. Fingerprints were not a possibility.

Carnie checked his belt, checked the knife.

And moved barefoot through the sand. Toward the target. Toward death.

Toward justice.

When he reached the outer wall, Carnie grabbed hold of the top of the cement wall, pulled himself level with the top, and peered into the compound. He almost laughed, but he stopped himself.

In the distance two guards were sitting on lounge chairs. Not looking toward the ocean.

None of this surprised Carnie. This was what he expected. Stevenson was not an international lead-story-on-CNN terrorist.

Carnie knew the security guards. Not by name, of course, but he knew them just the same. Ex-cops. Ex-military. Cushy job. Play into some guy's paranoia, nod at the right places during the conversation, make the right kind of faces, it was a done deal. Easy money.

Sure, the guy had enemies, such men thought – who didn't? Some people caved in to verbal threats, some to acts of violence. This Stevenson – or so the logic went – was a guy with a lot of enemies. But these enemies were real people. In other words, not people who knew how to get revenge. They were frustrated little people.

It was easy money to protect some guy from killers that didn't exist.

Carnie pulled himself up and over the cement wall, and fell, unnoticed, onto the wet grass just outside the moving blade of light that cut the darkness and slid slowly back and forth across the grounds, searching for intruders.

In and out of shadows, he worked his way to the main house.

'I've lived in a house or a condo for so long, this seems like a step backward,' said Matt.

'Lots of people live in apartments.'

'I know. When I lived in one before, I would have been offended to think that anyone considered my apartment somehow beneath a condo or a house.'

'So, where is this place?' asked Susan.

'Federal near Wilshire.'

'That means nothing to me. How far is it from here?'

'Five minutes. I like these, what do you think?' said Matt, pointing to the sheets with the baseball scene motif.

Susan tried to look at the sheets as though she was seriously considering them, then said, 'Maybe not.' What she wanted to say was, 'Maybe if you were five years old, but . . .'

'Yeah, you're right.'

Matt bought two sets of sheets and pillow cases, one white, the other peach. With no objections.

The two men sat on lounges looking out over the ocean.

'This ain't a bad gig, you know?' said Ozzie, a slightly-overweight black man.

'Bad? It's fuckin' great, man,' said Eddy, a late-fortyish, chunky-but-muscled white ex-cop. 'I got my pension and I'm collectin' five bills a week under the table to watch rich, tanned women walk along the beach. I tell you about the chick I talked to yesterday?'

'I'm not sure,' said Ozzie, although he had heard the story twice already. But since Eddy was the guy who hired him, signed his time-card and loved talking about his way with women, Ozzie figured there was no harm in hearing it again.

'Oh yeah, she was fine. Flat stomach, long legs, tanned, blond. Little tits, though. She was probably forty-two or so. You know the type. Long as they got access to their old man's money, they can look decent, you know.'

'Yeah,' said Ozzie. He knew what Eddy was talking about, but he wasn't planning to discuss *his* private life with Eddy.

Ozzie'd had enough trouble in his life. Which was why he was sitting with a loaded gun on a rich man's patio, watching for assassins, talking about sex with some bullshit son-of-a-bitch who probably had a pin for a dick.

'Man, I'd like to know what it feels like to be in that kinda shit again, you know?'

'Yeah, that'd be cool,' said Ozzie.

'I'm feelin' the call, Oz. You think you can handle things?'

'No sweat.'

Eddy stood and walked into the light of the big house, leaving Ozzie sitting all alone, his loaded gun on his lap, looking out over the ocean, smiling, remembering what it had been like yesterday afternoon with the fortyish tanned lady next-door. The one with the flat stomach. The one Eddy dreamed about, but could never have. Fuck, man, the only reason she was parading by the grounds was to jog Ozzie's memory. To make him crazy. To get him to come back for more.

Which he planned to do tomorrow.

He sat back and closed his eyes. The flat-stomached woman had a very tight pussy. Man, that felt good. Didn't expect that with an older woman. But she had set Ozzie straight on that. It was all in the 'abs – abdominals,' she'd explained. 'Tighten the abs, you tighten the inner abs.' Maybe she was full a shit, but there was no doubtin' the squeeze. It was *major thang.*

Ozzie was thinking about the exact sensation when he heard the noise. He opened his eyes immediately. But it was too late.

A lifetime too late.

Susan set the shopping bag down on the table, while Matt felt for a light switch, found it and lit the kitchen with fluorescent light.

He put away the groceries he and Susan had bought at Pavilions, a nicely decorated gourmet supermarket/warehouse. Rows and rows of gourmet food he had heard of but never bought. Including something called 'Western Dressing'. Susan had said it was a 'Midwestern thing', delicious but definitely not on the Pritikin menu.

'Nice place,' said Susan, while Matt put perishable food in the refrigerator, and other items away in the cabinets. It was funny, thought Matt – this was the first time he had put groceries away here, so nothing had a particular place yet. It was a disorienting thought.

It was not the only disorienting thought he had at the moment. Besides an entirely new physical environment, there was Susan, and there was a case that was unique in the sense that half the people he discussed it with were rooting for the killer. Nothing made much sense anymore.

'Damn, I forgot a corkscrew,' said Matt.

'Never fear.' Susan withdrew a version of the Swiss army knife from her purse, pulled out one of the accessories and handed it to Matt.

'You are prepared.'

'For just about anything,' she said with a winking smile.

Eddy's walkie-talkie crackled as he pulled the sliding glass door open, careful not to spill the coffee. Jake, the guard at the gate, was just checking in. Eddy set down the mugs and said, 'We're cool,' into the walkie-talkie. Jake's voice crackled, 'Check in thirty.' Then the walkie went dead.

'Eh, Oz, I brought you some coffee.'

Ozzie's back was to Eddy, who picked up a coffee mug and walked around Ozzie's chair till he was facing him. In the darkness it didn't register fast enough. It didn't register that the dark stain on Ozzie's shirt was blood. It didn't register that Ozzie wasn't moving because he was dead.

And when it did register, Eddy dropped the mug of hot coffee on Ozzie's lap. Ozzie didn't mind. Not anymore.

And before Eddy could draw his gun, the man's hand was over his mouth, and a serrated blade was already ripping away the skin around his Adam's apple.

'Why are you doing this?' asked Matt. They were drinking a bottle of Chardonnay that Susan had insisted on buying as a house-warming gift. They sat on the balcony overlooking the deserted courtyard, which was lit by amber spots running along the sidewalk that led from the front entrance to the door that opened onto a parking lot behind the building.

'Why am I doing what?'

'The wine, the company, the drinks . . .'

'I like you.'

'I like you, too. That's why I want you to be completely honest with me.'

'Okay,' she said, raising her right hand as though taking an oath. 'Cross my heart and hope to die.'

'There's no need to go that far.'

'Thanks. Look, Matt, you know I'd be lying if I told you that I'm not interested in the Reaper's story, because I am – very interested. But – and I hope this doesn't come out the wrong way – I'm not a person without options. I know some people here in LA but, frankly, right now I'd rather hang out with you, if you feel the same way.'

'What way?'

'Come on, Matt. Aren't you the least bit attracted to me?'

Matt thought about that before he answered. Such answers could never be taken back. 'I guess.'

'Very smooth. Girl could get a swelled head around you. Look, if I'm out of line, I apologize. I know you're going through a tough time with your divorce, I just thought you could use a little cheering up.'

'And you're the cheerleader.'

'Partly.'

'So, what do you get out of it?'

'That's a very male thing to say. Men aren't the only ones who 'get' something out of a relationship. I'm the kind of person who's used to doing what I want to do, and passing on the rest.'

'Very impressive.'

'Look, Matt, we're not on opposite sides here. I've been where you are now. I've gone through a divorce. I know my experience is not *exactly* the same, but there's always pain, always some second-guessing, always some loneliness. No harm in helping a fellow traveler.'

Matt knew what she meant. He really didn't mind the company. And he *was* attracted to Susan.

'I just want us to keep our personal and professional lives separate.'

'Okay. You're in charge of the professional stuff

and . . .' Susan leaned over and kissed Matt gently on the mouth, then leaned back. '. . . and I'll handle the personal part.'

If he had a choice, Matt would not have put Susan in his life at this exact moment. Despite this cold analysis, her lips on his felt more than good. It was nice to be the object of an attractive woman's desire. His ego had taken a major blow from Laurie's affair with the lawyer.

Maybe he should just relax and enjoy it, thought Matt. Life rarely happened on schedule anyway.

They lay in bed, in each other's arms, making the sounds lovers made. Loud sounds, subtle sounds, moaning sounds. He liked the way she pulled back playfully each time he reached for her. She always stayed within reach, but made him take her. They were lost in each other.

Which was probably why they did not hear the man enter.

Garnette was the first to see him standing at the foot of the bed. She screamed.

Douglas Stevenson rolled off his wife and shrunk back from the ski-masked figure holding the gun.

Carnie tossed a four-foot length of rope to Stevenson. 'Tie her up.'

'What in the fuck—'

Carnie walked over to where the nude man lay, and smacked him hard across the face with the back of his hand. 'Do it or I'll kill her now!'

Stevenson was shaking. Garnette was trying to

scream but nothing came out. Stevenson picked up the rope and began tying his wife's hands behind her back.

Carnie picked up a corner of one of the sheets, tore off a two-foot-square corner, rolled it up into a ball, walked over to Garnette and stuffed it into her mouth. He took her by the arm, checked the knot Stevenson had made, led her into a closet, closed the door, and propped a chair up against the handle.

Then he walked back to Stevenson, who sat cowering on the bed. Carnie removed his ski-mask, and suddenly the rich man knew what was going to happen.

'Oh God, please, no! Don't kill me. I'll give you anything. I can make you rich beyond your dreams. Please don't kill me,' whimpered Stevenson.

Carnie stuffed the mask into his pant's pocket. 'You recognize the name Arthur Martin?'

'What?' asked Stevenson, lost in his own fear, trying to focus on what the killer was asking him.

'Arthur Martin. A little guy, not like you. You're a big man. Live in a big house, drive a big car. I don't suppose a big man like you has time for little guys like Arthur Martin.'

Even through the fog of fear, Stevenson had a pretty good idea what was coming, a pretty good idea who Arthur Martin was. Not specifically, but generally. There were a lot of Arthur Martins out there. He had heard from many of them – in lawsuits, threatening letters, phone-calls, through the media. That was why he had security guards. Fucking security guards, where in the fuck were they anyhow? Fuck!

'Are you Arthur Martin?' said Stevenson finally.

'No. He's dead.'

Fuckin' hell! Where were the fuckin' guards! Then it hit him. Obviously they were dead.

'He was my father.'

Stevenson looked up into Carnie's face: the executioner's face.

'He killed himself when you took all the money he and my mother spent thirty-five years saving. Every penny.'

'I did nothing illegal—'

Carnie kicked Stevenson in the solar plexus, and waited for the naked man to catch his breath.

'What you did was immoral. My mother was sick. That money was supposed to pay for her care. When it was gone . . . my mother died in a county hospital. Six months later my father blew his brains out. I was the one who found him.'

'Look, I'm sorry, really, I—'

'My father was a proud man. He played by the rules. He was just one of those little guys you laugh about with your rich friends. Just sheep to be fleeced. You took my father's money, and his pride. And you hid that money all over the world, and now you're back spreading the gospel of greed to a new generation. Teaching people that anything you do is okay as long as you come away with the fucking cash.'

'Look, I'll stop, I promise. I'll—'

'Oh yeah, you're gonna stop, pal.'

Carnie jerked Stevenson to his feet by the hair and marched him to the window. 'You like money, don't you?'

'I . . . I . . .'

'Say yes.'

'Yes.'

'Open your mouth.'

'What?'

'Open your fuckin' mouth!'

Stevenson did so. Carnie reached into his pocket with his right hand – both hands were covered with surgical gloves – and pulled out a wad of one-dollar bills. He stuffed them into Stevenson's mouth, until he started to gag.

'Turn around!'

Stevenson turned around and looked out of the window facing the ocean. He continued to tremble. What was the intruder doing? Did he have the gun pointed at his head? As he waited for the painful impact that would probably kill him, Stevenson began to weep.

Carnie lifted his shirt and quickly unwrapped the forty-foot length of steel-enforced clothesline, and tied one end of it to the foot of the heavy king-size bed. Then he walked over and stood behind Stevenson. He realized the man could hear his footsteps and knew that he was standing behind him now. Carnie could tell from the other man's convulsive breathing that he was crying.

Carnie picked up Stevenson's trousers from the

floor, removed the Pierre Cardin belt and secured the rich man's hands behind him.

'Don't do this, I beg of you,' pleaded Stevenson.

With the end of the clothesline in one hand, Carnie tied a noose around Stevenson's neck.

And pushed him toward the window.

Placing his foot squarely in the middle of Stevenson's back – the image of his own father's brains decorating a kitchen wall – Carnie kicked Stevenson over the ledge and out of the window.

Stevenson shrieked, but only for a split second.

The king-size bed jerked off its foundation.

And it was over.

TWENTY-FIVE

He felt the bed jerking as he clutched the brass rods at the head of it to pull himself deeper and deeper into her.

When it was over, Matt lay there, Susan's perspiration-drenched hair on his shoulder.

'That was great,' said Susan.

'That was pretty good, wasn't it,' said Matt. He had surprised himself. He had figured that, with the ego-bruising he had just gone through, this might not be the perfect time to test his manhood. He had figured wrong.

Matt kissed Susan and noticed the shape of her bottom in the light filtering in from the courtyard. He caressed her thigh and ran his hand up over her butt. He was just thinking it wouldn't take much to get used to this, when his beeper went off. He got out of bed, padded across the hardwood floor, picked up the beeper and checked the number.

'Shit,' he said.

'What?'

'It's Lloyd, and my only phone's in the car.'

'I've got one in my purse.'

Matt handed Susan her purse. She retrieved the phone and handed it to Matt, who quickly dialed Garland's number.

'Yeah?' Matt listened. 'I'll meet you at the office in thirty minutes.'

Susan sat up in bed. 'What happened?'

'The Reaper just killed Douglas Stevenson.'

'The savings and loan guy?'

'Yeah.'

'How do you know?'

'He just announced it on Kyle Talbot's show.'

Matt stood and walked into the bathroom.

'Can I come?' said Susan.

Matt peered out from the bathroom and said, 'I think we've already established that.'

'Smartass. Can I go with you?'

'Okay. But remember, you're on my turf. If you come along, you play by my rules: no arguments, no negotiable points. You do as I say, or you don't do it at all.'

'I like it when you talk that way.'

Matt smiled and thought, walking back into the bathroom, *I do, too.*

The ride down to La Jolla took a little over an hour, going ninety miles an hour. Garland hadn't challenged Matt about bringing Susan along. In fact, the two of them seemed to hit it off pretty well.

Susan was one of those women – and Matt had known a few in his life – who were more comfortable with men than with other women. She liked men, and they liked her. There was always the spark of flirtatious interplay, but at a safe distance – most of the time. She joked with men, and was not offended by their humor. She had no problem drawing the line when necessary, and knew that she could handle whatever situations arose. She had an air of confidence about her that attracted men like a magnet. Of course, thought Matt, keeping a smile to himself, the fact that she had a great pair of legs didn't hurt either.

The detective in charge of the La Jolla investigation was Thomas Washington, a large African-American who wore a Stetson. He looked like a basketball player who had gained weight, or a defensive tackle who had merely maintained his college bulk.

'Who is this guy?' asked Washington, when he and Matt were alone.

'What do you mean?' Matt had no obligation to provide the local cop with details, but knew he would have to give him something.

'I mean, this guy took out Stevenson's bodyguards like Lawrence Taylor might take out a high-school quarterback. And my guys tell me some nut called a radio show and claimed responsibility for the murder.'

'Where's the note?'

Washington didn't respond immediately, partly because he was aware that Matt had not answered *his* question. Finally, the detective took a plastic bag out of his pocket and handed it over. Inside was the *'We reap what we sow'* note that Matt had seen several times before.

'Where did you find this?'

'In Stevenson's mouth, along with about thirty one-dollar bills.'

'What do you know about Stevenson?'

'One of the most hated men in America. The reason most people didn't know just how much he was hated was because there were only about ten thousand people directly affected by his dirty dealing. I say *directly* because every tax payer has been indirectly affected.

'Anyhow, there was a core group of about three thousand investors who got hurt the most. They hounded the guy with phone calls, and by picketing outside his place, jumping in front of TV cameras every time Stevenson was coming from or going to court. There were lots of threats, but they really didn't amount to much. This core group consisted mainly of people who lost everything: lots of older people, retired people who have nothing to do now except dream about revenge. It's sad, really, these people getting hurt bad – I mean real bad – and Stevenson still living like this,' said Washington, lifting his eyes to take in the palatial splendor bought and paid for with what many considered blood money snatched from those who could least afford it.

'You think one of those disgruntled investors did it?'

'My first thought was that they hired a professional killer – whoever did this has done this kind of thing before. Then, when I found the note, and heard about the radio caller . . .'

'You got any clues?'

'Not yet. Guys like this usually don't leave us much. I was hoping that the note would be helpful, but apparently you've already got a bunch of 'em.'

'Can I talk to the wife?'

'Far as I'm concerned. She's pretty upset now, but she says she wants to help.'

Garnette Stevenson was a looker, even at forty-seven. She had been nipped and tucked in every place a plastic surgeon could charge for, but she had brought the genes and a healthful lifestyle to the party to begin with. She wore jeans and a long sweatshirt, and she was drinking liberally from a half-glass of something amber.

'I noticed him first.' She shivered at the thought, looking up at Matt. He recognized the look in her eyes. It hadn't all sunk in yet. She was as much in a state of denial as in shock. 'You *must* catch this maniac. Those people just would never let us be. Doug went to jail, for crissake. What the hell more do they want?'

The question sat there. Not because it could not be answered, but rather because it had been. About five hours earlier.

'You say "those people". Why do you say that?' asked Matt.

'It's obvious, isn't it? The killer came for revenge. He didn't take anything. He didn't do . . . anything to me. And because of what he said.'

'What do you mean?'

'I couldn't make out the words clearly through

the closet door – it's very heavy oak – but he was talking to Doug about his father.'

'The killer's father?'

'Yes. He talked about how Doug had destroyed his father's life.'

'How exactly? Did he mention any particular investment, any particular bank, or deal?'

Garnette thought about that for a moment, then shook her head. 'No. I'm sorry.'

'Thank you,' said Matt. He stood up and started to walk out of the room.

'You will catch this man, won't you?'

'Yes, ma'am. You can count on it.'

'I am.'

Susan slept all the way back, while Matt and Lloyd went over and over what they knew, trying to see what they had not noticed before.

'What kind of computer sort can we use with the investors who lost money with Stevenson?'

'I don't know. The problem is, it's the killer's father who lost money, not the killer himself.'

Lloyd dropped Matt and Susan off at Matt's apartment about 5 a.m. They went immediately to bed, Susan curling around him as close as she could get.

TWENTY-SIX

Matt woke at 7:30. He showered, shaved, kissed Susan, and told her to lock the door behind him.

She mumbled something that sounded like 'Okay'.

He was in his office by 8:30. On his desk was a note to call Lloyd as soon as he came in.

Five minutes later, Lloyd Garland walked into the room. The broad smile on his face belied the fact that he had only managed two hours' sleep. He handed a sheet of paper to Matt and sat in a chair opposite his boss.

'Jonathan Mason,' said Lloyd with a smile, as he withdrew his pipe and began to go through the ritual.

According to the information supplied by the airlines, only one name met all the criteria outlined by the FBI. *One* man departed by air from each city within forty-eight hours of each murder – the longest time, according to the printout, was six hours afterward. *One* man paid cash for the one-way tickets. That *one* man used the name Jonathan Mason.

And the destination of his one-way ticket was always the same: Los Angeles.

'I think he's our man, but you can bet the farm that his name's not really Jonathan Mason,' said Garland, as he torched his Keith's Mixture.

'I know. Check it out, anyhow. But the important thing is that our guy is here in Los Angeles.'

'That doesn't narrow it down much.'

'It narrows it down a helluva lot further than that. Especially when we make certain assumptions.'

'For example.'

'For example, let's say we assume our man is, or was, in law enforcement, and he's in Los Angeles. Being a cop, he knows where to go for a good false ID.'

'Jonathan Mason.'

'Exactly. Let's get the short list of the best guys in town for providing false IDs.'

'I'll get right on it. I know just who to ask.'

'Great. Let's take somebody to lunch.'

Two hours later Matt and Garland were sitting across the table in a Santa Monica coffee shop from Lester Callaway, one of the best false-paper guys in town – according to Garland's friend on the LAPD, who was in a position to know.

Callaway was dressed in a suit that was all the rage in the Fifties, which, by the smell of it, was probably the same decade in which it had last been cleaned. Callaway, who looked to be about sixty but was really forty-seven, wore a bright yellow ascot that he thought went well with the brown suit. From what Garland's friend had said, it wasn't that Callaway couldn't afford better, it was just that he was what – if you liked the guy – you might call eccentric. If you didn't like him, he was just a nut.

And a very-poorly dressed one at that.

'Jonathan Mason, eh?' said Callaway, scrunching up his wrinkled puss. 'Not a job I did. I remember every one of 'em, and I've done thousands.'

'In your business it might not pay to have such a good memory.'

'Yeah, yeah, I know what you're sayin'. Whether I tell you or not, I'm sayin' I'd remember.'

'You wouldn't hold out on us, would you, Lester?'

'I might hold out on *some* cops, especially if it's chicken-shit stuff. But you, the FBI? Fuck no, I wouldn't hold out on you guys.'

Matt knew Callaway, or at least his type. He was equally at home on both sides of the law. He was too good a resource for a lot of cops to waste, and too much of an artist for criminals to pass up when they needed phony paper.

'You gonna eat your hash browns?' asked Callaway.

'No,' said Matt. He handed his plate across the table to Callaway, who scraped the potatoes off Matt's plate onto his own.

'If you were a cop, who would you go to – besides you – for false ID?'

'Hmmm,' said Callaway as he drowned the hash browns in catsup. 'Couple guys come to mind. 'Cause, if I'm a cop, I wanna keep a tight lid on things. Also, bein' a cop, I know who's good, who ain't, who talks, who don't.'

'Maybe it's a guy the cop has something on,' said Garland.

'Maybe, but that wouldn't be the way I'd play it. Not bein' a cop myself, I can't say for sure. But if I got somethin' on a guy, and I buy some funny paper from him, now he's got somethin' on me, too. What I'd do is I'd go to the best guy in town who don't know me. Don't know I'm a cop, don't know me from Adam. But, then, you guys know cops better than me, right?'

While Callaway dove into the catsup, and the hash browns that lay somewhere beneath it, Matt figured that he would probably play it the way Callaway said.

'So, who's on the short list?' said Matt.

'There's only a couple I'd even consider. Guy named Barney Slade, he works out of the Miracle Mile district. Name's in the phone book. He runs a watch-repair place over on Wilshire. Slade's Watch Repair. And Connie Mauch, he's an old-timer works out of his house in Silverlake. He's in the book, too. I think. If he ain't listed, he lives in a duplex across from the Chevron station on Alvarado and Glendale Boulevard.'

'That's it?'

'That's the cream of the crop. You can go all the way down to people using color copiers, working outta the copy shops in Hollywood. But the guy you're talking about, I don't think he'd go to an amateur. If it was important, that is.'

Matt picked up the tab and left with Garland, while Callaway continued to make the hash browns disappear.

* * *

Matt decided to hit Slade and Mauch later in the afternoon. Back in the office, Matt found messages from Susan and Laurie waiting on his desk. He called Susan first.

'So, do you still respect me?' said Susan.

'You're taking for granted that I respected you to begin with,' said Matt, leaning back in his chair, feet up on his desk.

Susan, who was sitting on the balcony of her room at the Loew's Santa Monica, looking out over the ocean, feet up on the rail, said, 'That's not a very nice thing to say. If I weren't so goddamned sure of myself, I might be shattered.'

'It was nice.'

'Nice? You really aren't much of a sweet talker, are you?'

'I'm an action guy.'

'I noticed. So, anything new?'

'Several things. But I don't have time to talk about them now.'

'Dinner?'

'Fine. I've got a couple of late afternoon appointments. I'll call you, probably about seven. You be at your hotel?'

'Waiting for your call.'

'See you later.'

Matt dialed Laurie's number and got through to her right away.

'You must be pretty busy these days.'

'I am actually.'

'Well, anyhow, I just wanted you to know that we can settle this whole thing—'

'You mean the divorce.'

'Yes, the divorce, with a minimum of angst.'

'And expense.'

'That, too. I'm sending along a basic agreement, or understanding, between us that, essentially, divides our assets fairly.'

'According to whom?'

'Look, Matt, I'm not playing hardball. Take a look at the list and the agreement. I believe you'll think it's fair, too. Besides, if you don't, just make the changes the way you see it, and send it back to me. I'm sure we can work this out. Feel free to have a lawyer look it over.'

'Thanks.' There was no way that he was going to negotiate with his wife, the shark of sharks, without his own lawyer looking over every word of the agreement.

'So, how are you?'

Matt felt the distance in her voice. She was doing her best to be civil. But, as Matt knew, civility was not his wife's strong suit. And the only reason she was trying now was because she wasn't in a leveraged position.

'What about Jarod?'

'What about him?' said Laurie defensively. 'He's my son. I hope you're not considering contesting custody, because if you are . . .' She bit her tongue.

'I just want to make sure I have a legally

acknowledged right to see him, and for him to see me.'

'I'm sure we can work that out. See how easy I am?'

Matt thought that perhaps his wife had employed a poor choice of words, but he didn't say anything. 'Okay, so when can I expect your agreement?'

'Tomorrow maybe. Two days at the latest.'

'I'll look for it.'

'Thanks, Matt.'

He didn't know exactly what she was thanking him for, so he just said goodbye and hung up.

A few minutes later, Lloyd Garland was puffing away in Matt's office, taking notes as the two of them spit-balled another sort parameter for the computer department.

'All right, according to the profile, our percentage play is that the guy is, or was, in law enforcement. Now we believe he lives in Los Angeles.'

'Okay,' said Garland, as he continued to take notes.

'Straight said there could have been some kind of triggering event. My guess is that, if there was such an event, it probably happened in the past year or so – why else would he have waited so long to start killing? Chances are he's no longer employed by law enforcement. So, first, do a sort of law-enforcement personnel in the LA area who have quit their jobs in the past two years; second, of those same personnel, give me the ones who indicated some type of traumatic event as their reason for leaving.'

'What do you mean, exactly? I mean, we're talking about a computer. We're not going to have access, at least not immediate access, to the reasons why individuals quit.'

'Okay, rule out all personnel who took mandatory retirement because of age – that information should be there. What I'm looking for is someone probably between the ages of thirty-five and forty-five. Rule out anyone who took retirement because of physical impairment.'

'What about mental impairment?'

'Keep that person in the sort. What I'm looking for, Lloyd, is a guy old enough to become skilled in sophisticated criminal activity, and young enough to take advantage of that knowledge himself. I'm looking for a guy who suffered some type of physical or emotional trauma over the past two years that caused him to quit his job and become a killer.'

'What if he's just on a leave of absence?'

'Then we're fucked. Look, at this point I've got to go with what I've got, which is a little bit of fact and a couple high-percentage guesses.'

'What about including the data regarding his father losing money with Stevenson?'

'Fine, if you can get the computer guys to factor it in. Chances are, though, we'll only be able to use that piece of information later to verify that we've got the right guy.'

'I'll get the computer department to run what sorts they can; then I'll get people on the phone, following up on the names the computer kicks out. That'll be the only way we can find out if a person quit because of a triggering event.'

'We need maximum cooperation with local PDs, and tell them we need it two weeks ago.'

Garland tamped out his pipe, dumped the ashes in the ashtray on Matt's desk, stood up, and started to walk out.

'When you get that rolling, call me. I want to check out Slade and Mauch this afternoon.'

TWENTY-SEVEN

Barney Slade sat behind the counter in his watch-repair shop and looked up through thick glasses as Matt and Lloyd walked in. Next to him was a rotator-dial phone, a library book on famous stamps, and a couple of old *Sports Illustrated* magazines. He didn't look rattled, nor did he look even remotely surprised when Matt flashed his ID.

'I don't do much of that kind of thing anymore,' said Slade after Matt had explained to him the purpose of their visit.

Which is exactly what Matt figured he would say.

'What did you say the man's name was again?' said Slade, doing his best to appear helpful.

'He had the ID done under the name Jonathan Mason.'

'White guy, you say?'

'Yeah.'

Slade shook his head, 'Nope. Can't place the name. I'd remember. I've got a head for details.'

'So, if *you* didn't do it, who do you think did?'

Slade shook his head again. 'Hard to tell.'

Matt gave Slade the same parameters he had given Lester Callaway – where would a cop go if he wanted to acquire a false ID? Slade mentioned two names: Lester Callaway and Connie Mauch. Matt asked him where both men lived.

Even though he already knew.

Silverlake was a pocket of diverse ethnicity about a mile and a half from downtown LA. It was one of the few parts of town from which the downtown skyline was visible on a typical day. The tall buildings stood in the near distance, like a carrot dangling on a stick that would forever be too long for most of this particular city's residents. The suburb was named for a famous lake that – before gangbanging, graffiti, drive-bys, AK 47s, and making yourself a target because of the color of your skin or clothes – used to be a nice place to spend a Sunday afternoon. A person could once rent a boat and row around the lake, lie back, read some poetry, split a basket full of food, or just take in some sun rays.

Those days were gone forever, and they were never coming back.

Matt and Garland got out of the unmarked car just south of the Chevron station, and walked across the street. A coin laundry was located next to the duplex supposedly occupied by Connie Mauch. Matt noticed a couple of gay men laughing and joking while they did their laundry. He knew the look, the walk, the mannerisms – from being a cop and a citizen of the world in the Nineties. He knew there were a lot of gay-bashings in this part of town. Matt didn't know a lot about being gay, but he knew a lot about human nature. And if he were gay, he wouldn't live in Silverlake. But, if he did, he sure as hell wouldn't flaunt such behavior in a primarily Hispanic neighborhood. A gang neighborhood.

He knew the rebuttal, and had heard it a million times. *Being gay is no crime.* Neither is being stupid, thought Matt. But sometimes people paid for crimes they didn't commit.

Mauch's name was written in pen on a faded piece of paper located just above the mailbox of the duplex located on the right-hand side of the large Craftsman design house. It was an old house not originally designed to be a duplex, but the conversion had taken place so long ago that most people wouldn't be able to tell the difference. Matt could.

Garland knocked for nearly two minutes before a door opened.

'Yes?' said Mauch's neighbor. 'May I help you?'

'We're looking for Connie Mauch,' said Matt.

'He's not home,' said the man, stating the obvious.

'And *your* name?'

'What's *your* name?'

Matt flashed his ID, and something in the air changed.

'Charles. Charles Montgomery. Is there some kind of a problem?'

'Do you know Mr Mauch?'

'He's my neighbor,' said Montgomery, as though it were an answer.

Matt knew that, in Los Angeles, people could live for ten years in an apartment or a condo and not know the first name of the person on the other side of the wall. But he took this man's meaning: he knew Mauch.

'When's the last time you saw him?'

'I don't know exactly. We don't keep tabs on each other.'

Matt wasn't in the mood. 'I didn't ask you if you signed each other in and out. I asked you when was the last time you saw him.'

The mid-thirtyish, thin man considered the question, seriously. 'Well, the last time I actually saw Connie was last Saturday night. I needed to borrow some popcorn. He always has some microwave popcorn, and Jimmy and I . . . well, we ran out. I didn't want to go to the store, you understand. Not at that time of night.'

'Which was?'

'About eleven-thirty. *Saturday Night Live* was just starting.'

'Do you have any idea where Mr Mauch might be now?'

'Not really. He works at home.'

'Doing what?'

'I really don't know,' said Montgomery.

Matt took a reading in the young man's eyes, and decided that Montgomery didn't give a fuck what Mauch did.

'Is there any other way into Mr Mauch's apartment?'

'There's a back door.'

'Thank you.'

Montgomery took that as a cue that it was okay

to close his door. And he did so. Immediately.

Matt and Garland went around back and knocked on Mauch's back door.

No answer. Matt tried the handle. The door was not locked.

It opened into an old-fashioned kitchen. Lots of brown-and-white checkered tile, an old gas stove, an ancient ceramic sink, and cupboards made of stained glass and wood. Spotless – as though no one had been there in some time. Even the dish rack was empty.

Matt and Garland made their way through the first floor, and the second floor, without coming across anything but the fact that Mauch was as tidy as he appeared to be elusive.

But the moment Matt opened the basement door, he knew.

The LAPD descended on the place as though they were boot camp Marines given a free pass to a whorehouse.

'How long's he been dead?' said Matt to the coroner.

'Few days. I need to run some tests.'

Matt walked outside with Garland, who lit his pipe and filled the air with the smell of sweet tobacco.

'Did you really expect that we'd find the guy who provided Mason's ID alive?'

'Could always hope. I thought there was a chance.'

'Why?'

'Because, so far, everyone he's killed has been a

slimeball. On top of that, he let Stevenson's wife live when it would have been easier to kill her.'

'Maybe he's not the saint you're making him out to be,' said Garland. 'Remember, he killed Stevenson's guards.'

Matt didn't reply. Instead he started walking toward the car. He had never made this guy out to be a saint. Matt wanted this guy bad. But even though he believed in his heart of hearts that the man was wrong, he still thought the guy was playing on a higher moral playing field than the average thug.

But that field was being scorched by the heat of the killer's rage. Matt thought about what George Straight had told him – that the Reaper, having played by the rules all his life, could be having a crisis of conscience, finding it impossible to reconcile his recent actions, no matter how apparently righteous, with his moral upbringing. But murder was an irreversible action.

Perhaps, thought Matt, the guy was starting to lose it. Starting to come apart at the seams. That could explain the apparent inconsistencies.

But there was another explanation – the end justified the means. Matt realized the Reaper was building toward something now. Something big. He was leaving a trail, taking credit, pulling the noose tighter around his own neck. Why? Because he knew that he would eventually be caught. But before he was arrested . . .

What would he do? What was he planning for his

grand finale? He had a captive audience now: an audience that lived vicariously through his little victories.

'So, now we know who gave our guy the funny paper,' said Garland, as he and Matt sat in the car on the freeway, heading back to the office. 'We know he probably lives in LA. We know quite a bit about the guy.'

'Not enough,' said Matt. 'Not enough.'

TWENTY-EIGHT

'You're pretty hard on President Souther.'

'You think so, Lenny?' said Kyle Talbot with a sly grin, addressing Lenny Kahn, host of the popular *Lenny Kahn Hour*, an interview show on ANN – All News Network. All the major politicians, movie stars, authors and rock stars of the moment wanted to be on Kahn's show, whenever they had something to sell.

Now me, too, thought Talbot, as he spoke via satellite from a TV station in Las Vegas.

'Every show, you hammer the President about something or other.'

'It goes with the territory.'

'His or yours?'

'Both. Look, Lenny, if people didn't agree with what I'm saying, I wouldn't be so popular. There are a lot of people very concerned about President Souther's "social experiment". This isn't about politics; it's about the lives of our children and, ultimately, the fate of this nation.'

'That sounds a little strong.'

'I believe it.'

'I read in today's *Post* that you claimed the Reaper is just the tip of the iceberg: that maybe we're due for a wave of vigilantism.'

'There's a lot of frustration out there in the heartland' – wherever the fuck that was, thought Talbot. Still, 'heartland' was a word that played well, and everyone nodded as though they knew exactly where you were talking about.

'Do you mean you believe that there are hundreds, maybe thousands of vigilantes ready to follow in the Reaper's footsteps?'

'It's possible.'

'I have to tell you, Kyle, that's pretty scary. I mean, the ramifications could be staggering.'

'I know.'

'Why do you think the Reaper called you and not, say, *this* show?'

'I'm not sure, Lenny. I imagine it had something to do with my philosophy about this country and the direction in which I believe it's heading.'

'Let's talk about that for a moment. One of the criticisms leveled against you is that you're too conservative, and that you don't represent mainstream America.'

'I don't think that's true, Lenny. If it were, I don't think my show would appeal to so many people. In fact, I honestly believe that I represent the frustration of a *majority* of people out there. I just think my views don't represent the views of mainstream *media*,' he added with a smile.

'So, what exactly is this frustration you're talking about? I mean, people have been frustrated with government since the beginning of time. What makes this time any different?'

'It's different for a number of reasons. I think the '92 LA riots played a very divisive role, in that they let people know that violence would be tolerated by city and federal government. In fact, essentially, the government became so intimidated by the violence that they went out and spent tax dollars to get the rioters the verdict they demanded.'

'A lot of people don't agree with that assessment, Kyle. *I* don't.'

'A lot of people *do*. Television brought the terror of that violence into every living room in the country. We have a government that caters to the lowest common denominator because it can no longer afford, politically, to offend *anyone*. History, let alone common sense, tells us that it's impossible to give everyone everything they want, whenever they want it. We live in a country where the word sacrifice is considered admirable – as long as it applies to the other guy.'

'The government has to do *something*. You can't deny this country's in trouble.'

'And why is it in trouble, Lenny? Because the achievers are out there busting their butts trying to attain the American dream? I doubt it. There are a lot of very tangible reasons why this country's in trouble.'

'For example?'

'Okay, let's take a look at California. It costs one half of a *billion* dollars just to house illegal aliens *convicted* of crime in California. Educating and providing medical care for illegal aliens costs many,

many times more than that. What was once a state with a rich economy is now quite literally going broke. But the question of how illegal immigration impacts California's economy cannot be addressed because, if you do, you're attacked as being a racist.'

'Okay, okay,' said Kahn. 'This is not a pulpit.'

'You asked me to tell you why people listen to me, and why I feel that I represent the majority of people. I say what *they* can't say. Don't misunderstand me here. I don't just represent white people with gun racks in their pickup trucks. Black Americans, Mexican Americans, Asian Americans, none of them want violence to rule this country. Ninety-nine and nine-tenths percent of all Americans just want to work a decent job, educate their children, and feel safe at night when they go to bed. The bottom line, Lenny, is that most people have reached the conclusion that the government either cannot, or will not, protect them from a minority of people – black, white, brown and yellow, white-collar and blue-collar – who use criminal means to put the screws to the rest of us. People just don't know what to do about it anymore.'

'And you're saying that the Reaper, or vigilantism, is an option?'

'People who murder with impunity, rape and sodomize our children, steal the savings of our elderly – these people need to know there's a real risk in that type of behavior.'

'They know it now,' said Kahn, a sly smile twisting up one corner of his mouth. 'Have the police contacted you about helping them catch the Reaper?'

Talbot hesitated for a moment. 'The authorities have talked to me, but I don't think I should comment on what was said.'

'So, you're helping them, then?'

'I didn't say that. In fact, I feel a certain sense of obligation to keep a free line of communication open between the Reaper and myself.' He did not say that the major reason he wanted to do this was so that he could continue to take advantage of the free publicity for as long as possible.

'You realize, of course, that there are a lot of people out there who think the Reaper is a lunatic, and that *you're* even worse for letting him use your show as a forum.'

Talbot decided not to point out that the only reason he was on Kahn's show now was because he was letting the Reaper use his show as a forum. 'They're entitled to their opinions. However, from what I'm seeing and hearing, most people agree that something has to change, and that people have to get out there and *do* something.'

TWENTY-NINE

Carnie had arrived in New York the morning after he killed Douglas Stevenson. The papers contained nothing about the murder, but the electronic media were overflowing with information and speculation. From experience on many different fronts, Carnie knew that he could take about eighty percent off the top of the first wave of information about a crime, and just toss it in the wastebasket. Deadlines and the 'need to lead', as opposed to the 'need to know', were responsible for a lot of the inaccuracies in the media. The rest was merely the result of bad reporting and the sad fact that the profession was populated more now by hustlers than genuine journalists.

Carnie sat at the bar of his cheap hotel, among his anonymous empty-eyed confederates, who sat uncertainly on stools staring into the mirror behind the bar, looking for traces of what they used to be, unable to link the liquid in front of them with their various falls from grace. Christmas lights ringed the mirror, even though the Lord's birthday was still a good eight months away. It was thirty-five degrees outside. The bartender slid the glass across the bar and . . .

Carnie drank the margarita and looked out over the desert. Dust. The world was dry in all directions.

A subtle hot wind shifted dust over more dust until it all just lay there in a dead landscape. He recalled reading the guest book at the front desk when he signed in. Visitor after visitor had written glowing accounts of the wonderful time to be had in Mexico at the Jorge's Desert Jewel. But one guest had written that the desk clerk had stolen her laptop computer and jewelry from her room. She gave names, times, places and all matter of detail. Carnie wondered if management had let the entry remain because it never read the guest book, or because it couldn't read English. It didn't really matter, to Carnie at least. He had nothing to steal.

Carnie spotted the man the minute he walked to the front desk, which was visible from the tiny bar. The guy at the desk pointed toward Carnie.

'Howard Haynes,' said the man, as he stuck out a fat sweaty palm toward Carnie, and sat down. Haynes was a large man – Texan, Carnie gauged by the accent. Judging from the crispness of the starch in his collar, the khaki shirt he wore was recently donned, but a man Haynes' size, in his condition, didn't do well in the heat. The garment already looked more like a wet chamois than a shirt. Yet he looked the part of the perfect messenger boy, sent down by the local authorities to do the dirty work.

'So, you're looking for a girl named Faye. A white girl 'bout twenty.'

'Nineteen.'

Haynes smiled. 'Looks the same to me – eighteen, nineteen, twenty . . . Who can fuckin' tell anymore, right?'

'Right.'

'What makes you think the Jane Doe down here is this Faye whatever-her-name-is?'

'I'm not sure, but I can identify her.'

Haynes took a cold Bud from the bartender, who delivered the beer without taking an order previously – or at least not one that Carnie noticed. Haynes pulled on the long neck, twice. He licked his lips. 'So, what's the big deal?'

Carnie just looked back at him. He knew from experience that Haynes was the kind of man you could learn more from by just listening than by asking questions.

'I mean, you come all the way to Mexico. The US government isn't officially behind this—'

'I'm officially behind this.'

Haynes looked away, and ran his finger around the tip of the beer bottle. 'We got a problem here?'

'What do you mean?'

Haynes looked up again. 'This is personal, right?'

'I just want to know what happened to the girl.'

Haynes nodded, knowing that his question had not been answered. Knowing that it would not be.

'You know we don't have a body . . .'

Carnie nodded.

'I mean, there was no reason to keep the body after . . . well, after a certain time.'

'I'm not here to make trouble for . . . the people here.'

Although Haynes tried to conceal it, Carnie saw Haynes sigh visibly.

'You have photographs.' It was not a question.

'Yes.'

Silence. Both men drank. Neither wanted to speak the unspeakable.

Finally Haynes said, 'It's not pretty.'

'Murder never is.'

Haynes nodded. He knew. He had seen the photographs.

'Let's see what you've got.'

Haynes coughed, even though there was nothing in his throat, removed an envelope from his shirt pocket, and handed it to Carnie.

Carnie took the envelope, but didn't open it immediately.

Haynes looked out the window at the empty landscape, wishing it were an escape hatch.

Carnie finally opened the envelope and withdrew the photographs. He had tried to prepare himself – but nothing could prepare him for this. It was an obscene gallery of gruesome intimacy: blood, nipples, stockings, lips, teeth, pubic hair . . . death.

If he could, Carnie would have vomited, but he could not allow that. Reaction, such as personal revulsion, was a luxury he could not afford. Not now, at least. He clenched his teeth and tried to look at the photographs from an objective point of view. What could he learn from them that would help him find the ghouls who did this?

He sucked in a little air, and studied the lower abdominal area of the victim. Swollen. Bruised. There was a great deal of blood on her upper thighs.

He looked at the victim's throat. She had not died of strangulation. There were no bullet holes. No knife wounds.

After a moment, Carnie looked at Haynes. 'How did she die?'

'Well, we think it had something to do with sex because—'

'How did she die?'

Haynes coughed again. 'I don't know.'

'Who does?'

'I'm not sure—'

'I'm going to find out what happened to her, with or without your help. And if you lie to me, you're not my friend.'

'And what does that mean?'

'That depends,' said Carnie.

Haynes didn't ask on what it depended. He knew.

'How can you help me?'

Haynes looked out at the desert again. He squinted a little, as if he saw some kind of a mirage, then turned back toward Carnie. 'Talk to Manuel. He'll know.'

'Manuel?'

'He's a . . .'

'Yes?'

'He's a friend of the police.'

'He discovered the body?'

'Kind of.'

'Kind of?'

'For all practical purposes, yes.'

Carnie nodded. He knew what that meant, and

appreciated its meaning. Carnie also realized that Manuel knew what he wanted to know, and that either Haynes did not or was not willing to tell him. Either way, it added up to the same thing.

'How can I talk to Manuel?'

'I have an address.'

Carnie noted that Haynes did not volunteer that address. He took a hundred-dollar bill out of his jacket pocket and slid it across the table, so that it came to rest under the edge of Haynes' beer bottle.

Haynes coughed again and pocketed the bill. 'He hangs out at a place called the Mañana Cafe.'

'When?' Carnie knew that an appointment had already been set. Terms arranged. Guarantees given.

'He usually arrives there around eight o'clock.'

'Eight o'clock,' parroted Carnie, nodding. He looked out the window into the desert, trying to fill his mind with images of something, anything, other than those in the photographs. But he knew those images would never completely go away.

The Mañana Cafe had no air-conditioning, just a couple of old circular fans that looked old enough to have cooled off Pancho Villa. Carnie immediately spotted the man he was to meet. He was old and bloated. Too much cheap liquor, too much Mexican food, too much time spent in places like this, sweating because he was too hot and too scared to do anything else. His hair was more salt than pepper, and it looked as though he hadn't shaved in a couple of days. A half-empty mug of beer sat in front of him.

Carnie walked over to the table and sat down. No introductions, no handshakes were necessary. The man looked as though he wished he were somewhere else. But Carnie knew that look and that it was a chronic mask, not something he put on for this meeting.

'So . . .' said the man.

'I was told that you knew how a certain young woman died.'

The man's lower lip crumpled into his upper lip, and his head began to shake back and forth. 'Terrible, terrible.'

'What do you know?' Carnie knew that how *the man knew was not to be asked. The answer to that could only cause them both problems.*

'I know it was a sex movie, and that drugs were involved.'

Drugs were always involved, thought Carnie, but he said, 'A sex movie?'

'A video. For sale in your country.'

Carnie nodded, understanding not only the technical distinction the man was making, but the moral one as well.

'The woman was raped repeatedly, and various objects were – well . . .'

'Put up inside her?'

'Exactly.'

'How did she die?'

'This is not a pleasant thing to say.'

'Go on.' Carnie knew that it was going to be much less pleasant to hear.

'Something very, very big was put up inside her and . . . well, it just kept going, deeper and deeper, until it penetrated vital organs and . . . well, there you have it.'

'Why?'

The man shook his head again and took a sip of beer. 'Who knows?'

'You know.'

The man breathed in deeply, raised his eyebrows. 'For money. The whole thing was filmed: the sex and the killing. Very bad. Very bad.'

For Carnie, it was a sentiment that seemed considerably understated.

'Who?'

'I don't—'

'Who?' said Carnie, not raising his voice. But he didn't have to.

'I don't know the names, but it was a woman and a very short man.'

'What do you mean, a very short man?'

'Like a midget, a dwarf, you know?'

'No names?'

'No names that are real. People like that don't want to leave a trail.'

'This woman's death, was it an accident?'

'An accident?' said the Mexican incredulously.

'I mean, did they mean to kill her from the beginning?'

'Yes,' said the man, nodding and shaking his head at the same time.

'What makes you so sure?'

'It was not the first one.'

'First what?'

'Movie. Snuff movie, I think you call it – the kind of movie where somebody dies. For real.'

'How do I find this short man?'

'I don't know. Did you know this girl?'

'Yes.'

The man nodded; he had already realized that. Why else would he be there in a bar and not at the police station? 'All I know is that the short man and the woman had a great deal of money to spend. Money buys a lot, especially in a place like this. A lot of questions go unasked.'

'What else can you tell me about the short man and the woman?'

'They were both American.'

'And they're not here now.'

'No – and I never saw them again. That's all I can tell you.'

It was a code: a code Carnie understood, and expected. The man did not say that was all he knew, *only that that was all he could* tell. *The implication was that his memory would improve when there was some money on the table.*

Carnie withdrew his wallet, took out a hundred-dollar bill and tossed it toward the man, who picked it up immediately and pocketed it.

'The only other thing I know is that both the woman and the midget bought tickets back to New York City, under the names of Mr and Mrs John Smith.'

Carnie stood. He did not thank the other man. He was not grateful, nor ungrateful. It was like purchasing a piece of meat. Both parties considered the exchange fair, but there was no need to say thanks.

Carnie walked out into the hot Mexican night, wondering what to do with his purchase. He had come here to find out – and he had found out. At least part of it. The rest would be easy.

What to do . . . ? He was an ethical man, a man with things to lose. There was no bringing Faye back. Knowing what happened to her was hard but, in the long run, he knew that it would make it easier. When you didn't know the answer to the nightmare questions that haunted such dreams, you usually filled in the worst possible scenario. When Carnie started to track down what happened to Faye, many horrible scenes had played themselves out in his head.

But none was as gruesome or as horrible as the photographs he had seen a few hours earlier. None as unspeakable.

As he walked back to his hotel in the sweltering heat, Carnie wasn't sure what he was going to do with his newfound knowledge.

But as he lay awake that night, looking out at the 100,000 stars scattered from horizon to horizon over a cloudless desert sky, he had the awful feeling that there would come a time when he just might not have anything left to lose. And when that time came, the woman and the short man would pay for what they did – with their lives.

THIRTY

Kyle Talbot was talking to Lenny Kahn about welfare, as Matt walked into Susan's ocean-view hotel room.

'Do you believe this guy?' said Susan, tilting her head toward the TV.

'I believe he's a hustler.'

'Me, too, but it's incredible. The calls he's taking seem overwhelmingly supportive. It's kind of that "we're mad as hell and we're not going to take it anymore" sort of thing.'

'Or else what? "I'm going to blow your head off"?' Matt sat down in a chair near the sliding glass doors that overlooked the Pacific. He picked up the TV remote control and hit the mute button. 'I understand the frustration, believe me. It's just that I'm positive that this solution is worse than the problem it's supposed to solve.'

'A lot of people aren't so sure.'

'I'm calling Talbot tonight to tell him I want Brunowski to put a tap on his phone again.'

'You think he'll agree?'

'I can always ask.'

'What makes you think a tap'll work this time, when it didn't work before?'

'I'm not sure that it will. But I've got to keep trying

everything. Who the fuck knows, maybe the guy'll get careless.'

'He doesn't seem like the careless type.'

'All it takes is *once*. And I'm going to be there.'

As he drove, Kyle Talbot could see in the distance the aqua-colored MGM Grand shining like a small ocean in the middle of the desert, and the Luxor, a modern-day pyramid rising out of the sand like an ancient Egyptian dream. Both were grand ships floating on a neon sea. Caesar's Palace, the Mirage . . . God, he loved this place. Round-the-clock action.

The car phone rang and he picked it up. 'Yeah?'

'That FBI guy called again. He wants to put a tap on the phones.'

Talbot smiled. 'Tell him to go ahead.'

'What?'

'No sense playing hardball with the Feds. Tell him it's okay.'

'You're sure?'

'Dammit Ellis, I said yes. Make me a fuckin' hero.' The Reaper, Lenny Kahn, now this. Things were really starting to break Talbot's way.

Tiny Mahorn could have been a professional wrestler if he hadn't done so well in the porno business. He stood just a little over three and a half feet tall, and had a full red beard. His head was so bald he made a point of sitting where the light wouldn't create a shine off his dome. Twenty years ago, when Tiny was fifteen, he was plucked off the streets of New York City to perform in sex videos. He'd had hair then, no beard, and a decent-sized schlong. It beat working in carnivals, which he had done for years in Jersey and down South.

Tiny had been on his own since he was ten. His mother was a prostitute, at least she had been till she OD'd when he was nine. And his father? Tiny didn't know who his father was. That was one of the few things he had in common with his mother.

Tiny had learned to take care of himself early on. It was a big job and the little boy became a man quickly. The alternative was death.

He had become an instant sensation in the sex business. It had been good to Tiny. He got lots of sex, pretty good money, and the closest thing to affection he would ever find in this life.

As a survivor, he decided that, even though he was making money doing a freak show in front of the camera, the people selling the stuff were making a hell of a lot more than he was. A wealthy Park Avenue widow, bored with straight sex, had collected him for a while. Knowing how to make the most of any angle was Tiny's forte. So he suggested that, with her money and his connections, they might be able to fill a niche market that would give them each what they wanted. Tiny wanted money and the power and freedom it bought a person, of any height. The widow wanted to experience anything she had not yet experienced, and her list was getting pretty short.

So Tiny suggested that they put together movies and, later, videos that were, well, off-beat. Products that would not be found even in adult over-the-counter stores. Products that other collectors would be willing to pay big money for.

Tiny was not concerned with morality, sin or eternal hellfire. He was concerned with how much life he could wring out of the time he had left, how far he could push his luck with a bum hand.

Their first video involved Faye, a young runaway from Kentucky. Fourteen years old, blond, and intimidated by the pimps, weaponry and bright lights of Times Square. Tiny and the widow took her in. Two weeks later, in a drugged state, Faye was tied to a bed, being fucked by a German shepherd.

This video was an instant success, and Tiny's small but loyal market loved it. And they wanted more. Much more.

Several videos later, Faye, now a junkie, was back and begging to do another one. Compassionate and concerned as ever, Tiny and the widow flew down to Mexico with her for a vacation. There, in a small house in the middle of nowhere, with cameras rolling, Faye was sexually assaulted by several men – then killed.

This latest video was an incredible success. It made Tiny and the widow lots more money.

Over the years, even though they knew what Tiny was up to, cops and prosecutors had never been able to catch him in the act. He had done only a total of four months in jail. Tiny was a murderer, he was scum, but more than anything else he was smart.

He and the widow had stayed together. He had his own place now, and she was only occasionally interested in having sex with midgets anymore – but they were friends, confidants and business associates. They could tell each other things they told no one else. It was better that way. It meant they lived longer, and stayed out of jail.

Every Friday night for the past fifteen years, with very few exceptions, they had met at Lucarino's, a neighborhood Italian restaurant within walking distance of the widow's penthouse. It wasn't a pasta place; it was a real Italian restaurant. They served lasagne, capellini, spaghetti, ravioli, and sauces that smelled of aniseed and fresh garlic.

This particular Friday, it was nearly eleven, and there was only one other couple left in the place. The waiters were preparing for the next day, though careful to let their most loyal customers know, with a smile, that they could stay as long as they wished. Everyone knew they normally stayed until midnight, give or take five minutes.

'What was your favorite moment?' asked the widow, pouring the last of the Chianti into her glass.

'You *know*,' said Tiny with a smile that, had she not known him, might be mistaken for embarrassment.

'I just like hearing you tell me.' Because she was now sixty-three, most of the widow's sexual exploits had already been played out. She still had sex: her money and her connections still gave her access to whatever she might desire. But sex at twenty was different from sex at forty; and sex at forty was different from sex at sixty-three. She knew that she would enjoy sex until her dying day, but she did not delude herself that it would be just the same.

'Tijuana. The donkey.'

She knew he would say that; he always did. 'I used to think it was just a myth.' She wiped some marinara sauce from her upper lip.

'You were incredible there. I remember the guy saying he'd never seen anyone as good-looking make it with a donkey.' What the man had really said was that he'd never before seen any broad that old get fucked by a donkey.

'We've had some great times, haven't we?'

'The best,' said Tiny. They raised glasses to toast fifteen years of decadence and illicit sensation. And money.

'You ready?' asked the widow.

'Yep.'

Tiny tossed a hundred dollars on the table, even though the tab came to only about sixty. He didn't care that much about money anymore – not here in this place that had become his home, with the woman who had become his closest friend. He liked the way he was treated here every Friday. And he knew he was not treated with any respect because of his stature or his looks. But because he spent money here, regularly. Real money, not some fifteen percent tip. At thirty-five years old, Tiny knew that money did not buy everything. But what it did not buy, he realized was probably unattainable for him tonight or any other night.

One of Tiny's few memories of his mother was the time she poured alcohol – straight from a Jack Daniels bottle – onto the knee he had scraped during a fall from his bicycle. As she poured it on the wound, she pinched his arm. When he had asked her why she did that, she explained she was just taking his attention away from the pain of the alcohol on his shredded knee.

Money bought him sensation that took his attention away from his real pain.

For a time.

For a price.

The waiters smiled and said, 'Goodnight, Mr Mahorn.' The owner waved from behind the cash register, and said, 'See you next Friday, Mr Mahorn.'

Outside, it was chilly – more chilly than Tiny thought it should be for this time of year. And there was a wind. Newspapers blew up from around wire trash bins. A homeless man stood against a building at the next corner.

Tiny put his collar up, and started walking toward the same corner. Had he been a man of stature, he would have put his arm around the widow's shoulder. But had he even tried, his arm would have gone around her waist instead. No good, that – humiliating. And one thing Tiny had learned over the years was the ropes: the do's and don'ts. How to move through society, when under four feet, and not make a fucking ass of yourself.

Tiny had never seen this homeless man before, and he noticed such things. He had long made an art of details. Knowing the fine print – knowing the lines and when he was about to step over them – was important in his line of work.

'Hey, man, you got a' buck for cup of coffee?' said the vagrant.

Tiny had not been frightened by Mafia hit men. He had not been frightened by IRS agents. He had not been frightened by New York cops, or even the FBI. Yet in an instant, and for reasons that only God would know, the moment the homeless guy looked down at him, Tiny knew that he was a dead man.

The widow started to scream, but the vagrant caught the first syllable of her scream with the part of his hand between thumb and forefinger. He slammed her so hard up against the brick wall that blood immediately began to trickle down the surface behind her head. For a moment he pinned her there, before letting her lifeless body slide down the wall, like thick paint, onto the sidewalk.

Tiny couldn't run; he wasn't sure why. It wasn't as though he was going to save his friend. She was going to die, and certainly he would, too. It was a strange feeling, he thought, as he stood looking up into the madman's eyes. It was as though there was no point in trying to outrun fate.

'Who are you?' asked Tiny. He was not pleading for his life. Not asking for anything other than an explanation. He wanted an explanation because he knew that this was not some act of random violence.

This was not a homeless man. This was a killer.

'I'm the man who's going to kill you.'

'But why? I want to know.'

'Remember that movie you made where a girl gets killed?'

Tiny began to sweat. He had made more than a dozen snuff films in all. 'Yeah . . .' he said, uncertainly.

'You do, eh? Tell me about it.'

Tiny felt his mouth dry up. Words were frozen somewhere between his brain and hell.

Suddenly the other man slammed him up against the building, hard. So hard that Tiny started seeing stars. Funny, he thought: not really stars exactly, but falling points of light.

'You stupid fuck! I know you don't even know which fuckin' movie I'm talkin' about. Too many snuff films, right? You muthafuckin' piece of shit!'

Again he slammed Tiny against the wall. More falling points of light.

'Who are you?'

'You wanna know?'

Tiny didn't answer. Not because he wasn't curious, but because he knew that the man would do and say exactly what he had planned to do and say.

Then, as the man spun him around, grabbed him from behind and twisted his neck until it cracked several times, Tiny thought he heard his attacker say, 'Faye.'

THIRTY-ONE

'Why do you think Talbot allowed you to tap his phone so easily?'

'I don't know,' said Matt. He was thinking hard. He was always thinking. He and Susan were sharing a bottle of Burgess Chardonnay Matt had sent out for. Room service didn't have the Burgess, but their comparable bottle cost fifty dollars. So Matt called a local liquor store known for its range of wines, plus the fact that it delivered. The Burgess, together with the delivery charge and a tip came to twenty dollars. This time Matt was buying. And he wasn't on an expense account, so it mattered.

As Kyle Talbot's radio show droned on in the background, Matt and Susan sat on the balcony looking out over the moonlit Pacific. To Matt, tonight, the moon seemed as though it were an opening to another, better world. Better merely because it would lead him somewhere other than the world in which he now felt himself something of a stranger – disoriented and adrift, physically and morally. This was not the world he had signed up for.

'This is nice,' said Susan, one hand on her wine glass, the other on Matt's knee.

'Yeah,' he said, keeping half his attention still focused on Talbot's radio show.

'Folks, hold onto your hats. My screener is waving her hands wildly, and that means one thing: our next caller is . . . that's right, folks, the Reaper. So, stay right where you are and we'll be back after this message.'

Matt stood up, walked inside and went directly to the phone.

'Yeah, we're ready,' said Brunowski, anticipating his question.

'Call me at this number,' said Matt. He gave the Las Vegas cop the Loew's phone number, Susan's room number and hung up.

'We're back, folks. And with me now on the line is the Reaper.'

After a slight hesitation, the Reaper spoke. 'Pornography has poisoned this whole country, as surely as arsenic poisons a single human being. It has objectified women to the point that, in the 1990s, a woman is merely a collection of body parts to be graded according to the current fashion trends of our time. One need not look to the adult bookstores to see this moral blight. Just watch MTV, which is available to your children on any cable system. Just tune in during the afternoons, and watch g-stringed teenagers simulating sexual activity. Watch women chained in cages. Watch women grabbing their crotches and proudly referring to themselves as "gangsta bitches".'

'It's like he's reading a speech,' said Susan, who had moved inside too, and was now sitting on the bed next to Matt.

'Pornographers hid behind the First Amendment for many years, equating their smut with that freedom of speech fought for by Martin Luther King and others, whose noble and heroic deeds are cheapened when lumped in the same category as these pornographers'. Is his impassioned "I have a dream" speech really to be counted in the same category as a woman pissing in a man's mouth while he is bound up like a dog?

'Of course not, but common sense has been replaced by a million lawyers splitting legal hairs to the point that our nation is now devoid of common sense. Our leaders are impotent, and no one is willing to step up and speak the truth. Right and wrong are not difficult issues to figure out. We're just dazzled by the bullshit.'

Suddenly the Reaper stopped speaking.

'Something's wrong here,' said Matt with a puzzled look.

'You were speaking of pornography?' prompted Talbot.

'There is a man in New York City named Tiny Mahorn. He is one of the most evil men in this country. Not only has his smut polluted the morals of this country for nearly twenty years, but he has drugged and murdered women in the process.'

Talbot started to say something about this not necessarily being the opinion of the station, or Talbot himself, but the Reaper continued speaking over him.

'. . . nothing more. And so tonight I have put an

end to the evil perpetrated upon this nation by Tiny Mahorn. You will find his body at the corner of 57th and Argyle in New York City.'

Silence.

Sounding now a little shaken, Talbot said, 'Thank you for calling.' Quickly he added, 'Look, folks, I had no idea what was going to take place here tonight. I don't know what the Reaper meant by his last remarks, but hopefully I'll be able to get you up to speed before we go off the air.' He coughed nervously. 'And we'll be back.'

The phone rang. 'Baldwin,' said Matt.

'The phone didn't even ring,' said Brunowski.

'It did here. What've you got?'

'An LA address.'

'Shit!'

'What did you expect?'

Matt didn't respond.

'You want that address?'

'Why? He's not there.'

'Maybe he left you a message.'

Matt wrote down the address on a piece of paper, and hung up.

'Matt, Talbot's on with a reporter in New York,' said Susan, walking over to the radio and turning it up.

'You're sure about that?' Talbot was saying.

'Yes, Kyle.'

'Folks, we're speaking now with Trevor Washington of the *New York Tribune*. Who discovered the body?'

'The restaurant owner, Guido Carboni, had just locked up and was walking home when he discovered the bodies.'

'You mean there was more than one?'

'There were two. Tiny Mahorn and a woman in her late fifties. Mahorn's body – he was a midget – was found stuffed in a newspaper vending machine.'

'Good Lord! Are you serious, Trevor? How in the world . . .'

'Apparently, the murderer was trying to make some kind of statement. Mr Mahorn was a well-known pornographer. So, sticking his body into the vending machine of an X-rated newspaper – well, it speaks for itself.'

'This is incredible. I can hardly believe what I'm hearing. The Reaper kills this notorious scum bag, then calls up this show to announce it to the world. What else can you tell us about this Mr Mahorn?'

'He was generally known to have been a purveyor of the most extreme type of hard pornography – even snuff films.'

'For those of you in Clyde, Ohio, a snuff film is one in which a participant, usually a female, is actually killed on camera. The recorded film or video is then sold to perverts all over the world. Anything else you know about the deceased, Trevor?'

'I know the cops have been trying to nail Mahorn for some time.'

'Let me interject here,' said Talbot in a mock-sincere tone, 'that just because any law-enforcement agency has targeted you, that, by itself, does not mean that you are guilty of any crime.'

'That's true, Kyle, and I didn't mean to intimate otherwise,' said the reporter – even though he, and everyone else listening, knew that he did.

'I see. Jeff from Phoenix, you're on the air,' said Talbot. 'What do you think about all this?'

'I'll tell you what, Kyle, I'm sick and tired of lawyers standing up on TV saying that even though you've got a mountain of evidence against some guy, just because you don't have a video of him running away from the scene with a smoking gun in his hand, that the guy is innocent. These lawyers, they know their clients are guilty, and they waste taxpayers' money and hide behind the Constitution trying to get murderers, drug dealers and pornographers off. They know it's wrong. We all know it's wrong. It demeans our system and it sends the wrong message: no matter how badly you hurt other people, as long as you got a good lawyer, you're gonna walk. Well, I'll tell you something, Kyle, this guy Mahorn, he ain't walkin'. I hope it sends a different message for a change.'

'Whoa! Tim in Fresno, you're on the air.'

'If this guy really made those snuff films, like they say . . .'

'Yeah?'

'Then I say good riddance to bad garbage.'

'Thank you, Tim. Hannah in Dallas, you're on with Kyle Talbot. What do *you* think about the Reaper?'

'I say it's about time. I don't agree with everything the Reaper does, but I'll tell you something, I listened to what he said about pornography . . .'

'Yeah?'

'Why can't we get our politicians to call a spade a spade, like that? It seems like nobody can tell the difference between right and wrong no more. Or maybe they just ain't got the guts.'

'All right, Hannah.'

'Bullshit!' said Matt. He picked up the phone and push-buttoned the off-air number of Talbot's radio station.

'WLVG,' said a woman on the other end of the line.

'I'd like to speak with Kyle Talbot.'

'Mr Talbot isn't taking any calls at the moment. If you'd like to leave a message—'

'Tell Mr Talbot that I'll meet him tonight at Shirley's Place at one o'clock.'

'I'm sorry, but—'

'Tell him it's Matthew Baldwin with the FBI, and if he isn't there, at exactly one a.m., he's going to be doing his show from jail for the next ten years.'

'Will Mr Talbot know what this is concerning?'

'You bet your ass, he will,' said Matt. He hung up and looked toward a stunned Susan. 'You wanna go to Vegas?'

On the way to the airport, Matt and Susan stopped off at the address Brunowski had given him on the phone. Because the Reaper had just killed a man in New York, less than two hours earlier, Matt knew that whatever he would find at the Los Angeles address would be whatever the Reaper wanted him to find.

The address was an apartment, rented to Jonathan Mason. The cops were already there when Matt arrived.

'Voice-activated tape recorder,' said the detective in charge, the man to whom Brunowski had given the trace number.

Matt nodded. He had already figured that out.

'Not particularly sophisticated, but the guy knew what he was doing, that's for sure.'

'So, somebody calls here, the machine picks up, and when it hears a voice on the other end of the line it starts.'

'Right. It's the same tape that played on Talbot's show.'

Matt nodded. 'Is the person on premises who rented this place to the tenant?'

'I think so.'

At that moment a woman walked into the room. Lotte Stein looked about sixty years old, with thinning red hair, wearing black glasses with rhinestones on the frames. She was wearing a green and black flowered housecoat, and looked more excited than scared.

She introduced herself to all the men, giving each a special smile.

'When was the last time you saw Mr Mason?' asked Matt.

'Last week. Maybe he's been here since, but the only time I saw him was when he first rented the place. Seemed like a very nice man. Very quiet. Quiet is good in an apartment situation,' she added, wrinkling her face in a you-know-what-I'm-saying kind of look.

'Could you describe him?'

'Is he in some kind of trouble?'

'I'm not sure,' said Matt. 'But if he is in trouble, I'm sure a very good description from you would help him tremendously.'

'Well,' she said, directing her eyes toward the ceiling. 'He had a mustache.'

When he heard that, Matt knew he was in for a rough ride. The rest of her description was full of words like 'average', 'medium' and 'I don't know'. This woman had barely seen the man. Not really.

It took a few minutes for Lotte to leave. She was not used to a lot of men asking her questions, so was not eager to part with their attention.

After she had gone, the detective in charge took Matt aside. 'There's something I think you should know about.'

'The note?'

'Yeah. I bagged it, and it's on its way to the lab, but I thought you might be interested in what it said.'

' "We reap what we sow",' said Matt confidently.

'No.'

The detective took his notebook out of his jacket pocket and read from it: 'All the executions lead to the one. History will prove me right. Harvest time is near.'

* * *

Matt and Susan caught a 10:30 USAir flight to Vegas, checked into their hotel by midnight, and arrived at Shirley's Place ten minutes before their scheduled meeting. Sweet Louis, a Vegas legend, was singing 'Proud Mary' in the lounge.

'It's all building to something,' said Matt. He was sticking with the Chardonnay, while Susan was now working on a Diet Pepsi.

'To what?'

'I wish the fuck I knew. Frankly, I wish he was just some crazy vigilante. We'd get him eventually, no matter how smart he was. But, with this last note, I get the feeling that his next target is the payoff. After that, it's too late. It's what he's been building to all along.'

'Who do you think it could be?'

'I don't know. I'd never previously heard of anyone he's killed so far, except Douglas Stevenson. It's like if you asked me to list the ten men in the world who most deserved to die, my list would be different from yours – or anyone else's. This guy's got his own list. Who knows who's on it. The guy who the Reaper considers personally responsible for the ills of society might well be someone I've never even heard of.'

Just then Kyle Talbot walked in. With his lawyer.

The two men sat down in the corner booth where Matt and Susan were already sitting.

'I don't have to do this,' said Talbot.

But Matt knew that was a lie. If Talbot had spoken with his attorney, and his attorney had told him that he didn't have to do this, Talbot would never have shown up.

'You're lucky I don't have you thrown in jail.'

'Look, there's no need to threaten here,' said the lawyer. 'My client is here of his own free will, ready to cooperate.'

'When did the Reaper call you?' said Matt.

'Tonight. You heard—'

'Don't fuck me around, Talbot. I'm not in the mood.'

The lawyer started to say something, but Matt gestured with his hand in the man's direction, and the attorney suddenly forgot what he was going to say.

'Look, I know tonight's call was a setup. I've just come from the room where the voice-activated tape player was stashed. I know you were given a number to call, and I know you were given a script.'

'How did you know about the script?' asked Talbot. Before he could stuff the words back down his throat.

'Because I'm not a fuckin' idiot.'

Talbot cleared his throat – while his lawyer swallowed a stale peanut from the bowl in the middle of the table.

'He called me at home this morning – yesterday morning, actually,' said Talbot. Because it was now after midnight, technically he had received the call *yesterday*. Talbot was suddenly nervous. 'He had me write down what I was supposed to say, and when. What I mean is, he told me the last sentence he was going to say – and that was my cue, after which I was supposed to read my lines. Then he gave me a number to call, and he told me *when* I was supposed to call. I swear, I had no idea that he was going to talk about killing someone.'

'You know,' said Matt angrily, 'if I could prove that you knew in advance that a man was about to be murdered, and you didn't notify authorities, you could be an accessory to murder. That's a serious ticket, pal.'

'I swear I had no idea. He just gave the last sentences of the paragraphs, so that I'd know when to come in. Didn't you hear me during the show, when he started saying all those potentially libelous things about the guy? I was shocked. I had no idea what he was going to say. You have to believe me.'

'I don't have to believe anything,' said Matt. 'You have to convince me.'

'Technically, that's not the law,' said the attorney.

'Shut the fuck up, Bernie,' said Talbot. Then he turned his attention back to Matt. 'Look, I know you think I'm a . . . well, I know what you think of me. I don't really care about that, as I'm sure you know. However, use a little common sense here. I realize that if I know about a murder ahead of time and don't report it just because I wanna jack up my ratings, then I'm in big trouble.'

'What *did* you think this guy wanted to talk about? The reason people are listening to him, the reason people are tuning into your show, is because this man is out there killing people.'

'He never gave me any specifics before. And he

didn't yesterday, either. I didn't know, I swear.'

'That's why you didn't give me a hard time about putting a trace on your line. You knew the only thing I'd find is a voice-activated tape player.'

After a slight hesitation, Talbot said, 'Yeah. See, I'm honest about that.'

'This isn't third grade, and I'm not passing out gold stars. We're talking about murder.'

'My listeners are talking about justice.'

'Well, your listeners aren't making the laws in this country. Not yet, anyhow. And until they do, they can dress it up in all the fancy justification people wrap around "righteous" violence these days, but it's still murder.'

Talbot had managed to focus himself, mainly because he now knew that Matt didn't really have anything on him, that he was just trying to bust his balls. He also knew that if Matt could prove that Talbot knew about the murder beforehand, Matt would march him off to jail right now. But he was still sitting there. Fuck this FBI prick. Talbot had run the whole thing by Bernie on the way over, and the attorney had assured him that he was in the clear.

'You gonna let me know if he calls again?' asked Matt.

'I don't know.'

'Whose side are you on? A murderer's or the FBI's?'

'You keep calling him a murderer. A murderer is some guy who blows you away because he wants your car or your money, or some drugged-out fuck who needs whatever you've got in order to get his next fix. This guy isn't like that.'

'What do you think about some guy who just gets pissed off at somebody and blows them away?'

'The Reaper isn't like that. With him it's not personal.'

Matt stood and tossed down a twenty. 'You gullible fuck. He killed Douglas Stevenson because he ripped his father off.'

Matt started to leave and Susan followed behind him. Matt turned around and looked at Talbot. 'Just make sure you don't make him mad.'

Carnie stood on the roof of the World Trade Center. It wasn't that difficult to get up there at this time of night – not for someone like Carnie. Besides, not many people wanted to be up there at four in the morning anyhow.

He felt as though he were literally on top of the world, looking down upon the city – the world. He was becoming a folk hero. A real-life John Wayne. He was amused by the coverage. In a New York telephone poll taken a few hours ago, he received an approval rating of sixty-five percent. Forty-six points higher than the President's last approval rating, as one of the local newscasters had pointed out.

Here in New York, people understood that the world was a jungle. They walked among the animals, smelled the danger, sensed it every day. No one *wanted* it that way; that was just the way things were. He laughed out loud at the bleeding-heart commentators who called him out of control. What did they know about it? He had lived it.

Real life had a way of proving theories wrong.

Carnie knew that when violence laid its ugly hand on you, innocence was lost forever. It changed you. It had changed him.

But it would all be over soon. He would have taken out some of the garbage. But, more than that, he would have shown the way. It was a way that he believed and prayed others would follow.

In a couple of days the plan would be complete.

Carnie breathed deeply, and took in the most spectacular skyline on earth. Everything had gone according to plan. Just as he knew it would.

He had right on his side . . .

And he was right on time.

THIRTY-TWO

When Susan awoke sleepy-eyed at 9:30, she saw Matt dressed and sitting at a small round table, looking out over the city. At night, Vegas looked like heaven dressed in neon; in the morning it looked like a bunch of hotels in the middle of the desert. The two croissants and a carafe of coffee they had ordered before going to sleep last night were sitting on the table in front of him. She smiled at Matt, who was still looking away from her. They had not made love last night, but they had held each other close all night. Susan was the kind of person who woke up often, then rolled over and went back to sleep. She had awakened twice last night, and each time found herself still in Matt's arms.

'Good morning,' she said.

Matt turned toward her. There was something in his look that didn't track.

'I don't think so.' He picked up a newspaper from the table, folded it, and tossed it onto the bed.

Susan's heart skipped a beat. She had dreaded this, hoped against hope that she could walk the tightrope and make it safely to the other side. Now, looking into Matt's eyes, she realized that she had just fallen. And there was no net.

'Did you think I wouldn't notice?' From memory

he recited from Susan's column: *'Will the man who called a talk-show host at home about a script, please contact me at this newspaper? I may be able to help you get it produced.'*

Susan got out of bed, put on her blouse and panties, walked over to the table and sat down close to him. 'I didn't betray you.'

'Legally no. Ethically . . . I thought we were close enough so that we didn't have to play the angles.'

'I didn't use any information I got from you.'

'Who told you, then?'

It flashed through her mind to claim confidentiality, but that was only a fleeting thought. She had a lot more to lose than a legal point of order. 'Cassie – Talbot's girlfriend. She overheard the Reaper dictating some kind of a script to Talbot on the phone.'

Matt nodded. Since reading Susan's column thirty minutes before, he had tried to think the thing through before she woke up. He knew there was no putting the genie back in the bottle. He could rant and rave as long and as loud as he wanted, but Susan had spun things out of his control. It was his job to take control again, or at least to take advantage of what he could not completely control.

'Why didn't you tell me you were trying to contact the Reaper?'

'Would you have let me?'

Matt didn't answer.

'Look, Matt, I played by your rules. I didn't use anything in my column that I learned from you. I got this lead from Cassie, and decided to run with it.'

'You're pretty damned ambitious.'

'That's right,' said Susan unflinchingly. 'I *am* ambitious. Is that supposed to be some kind of dirty word?'

'No, I—'

'You have your career and I have mine,' said Susan, taking the offensive – no defense like a good offense. 'I had to do what I did, just like you have to do what you do. Don't take it personally,' she said, even though she knew that he did.

Matt was not beyond manipulating the situation, for several reasons, not least of which was that he felt he had been manipulated by Susan. But he also recognized that it was possible to push too far. He realized that Susan had put herself into the exact position he had debated about – but decided against – putting her in himself. It was a bitter irony that the reason he had decided against putting her in harm's way was because he was starting to care very much about her safety.

'Has he contacted you yet?'

'No.'

Silence. Each was waiting for the other to speak: to make the defining move.

Matt knew that he must be the one to commit. He could not forbid her to go forward, if the Reaper contacted her; but, if he made the right moves, he could tag along for the ride. And, despite his sense of feeling betrayed, he wanted to be there for another reason: he didn't want to see Susan hurt.

'If he makes contact, we'll play by my rules.'

'C'mon, Matt—'

'I can make it official, if you want. This guy is wanted for murder. You knowingly meet with him, and fail to cooperate with the FBI to apprehend a suspected killer, you're in deep shit.'

Susan didn't answer for a moment. She knew that what Matt said was true. Now that Matt knew, contacting the Reaper without him knowing would be practically impossible. But he was not forbidding her to make contact. He had only said that if she did, she would have to play by his rules. 'I'm listening.'

'We wait for him to contact you, then you go wired to the meet.'

'Okay,' she said. Susan tried not to look so happy. She had drawn to an inside straight, and come up a winner.

'This could be very dangerous. This guy kills people, and you're going to betray him.'

Susan didn't like the sound of that word, *betray*. She didn't plan to give the man up. But then, if she knew the Reaper, he was probably smart enough so that he could still play both ends against the middle. Besides, at this point, there was no other way to get to him. 'So, what's your plan?'

'I really don't have one. This is kind of a new idea,' said Matt, gazing at her. 'When he contacts you, he'll dictate his own plan. Hopefully, he'll want you to interview him. If so, he'll set up a meeting. When you meet him, we nail him.'

Susan nodded. It was not her plan to *nail* him.

'He'll search you for homing devices, figuring that we've planted one on you.'

'Why don't you just follow me?'

'My guess is, he'll construct conditions that could make that almost impossible. *I* would.'

'So you're not even going to try?'

'Of course, we'll try. But I've got to stay one step ahead. I've got to plan for every worst-case scenario.'

'So, he searches me for a homing device, and I don't have one.'

'Oh, you'll have one. You've *got* to have one.'

'Let me get this straight: I'll be wearing a homing device, and if he finds it, he'll probably kill me.'

'Right.'

'I must be missing something.'

'You won't exactly be wearing it. You've got two choices: we can put it in a tooth . . . or someplace a little more, shall we say, intimate.'

'You're kidding!'

'Believe me, when you're out there alone, you're not going to give a damn where it is, as long as we know where you are.'

'Would he search me . . . down there?'

'I don't know. I think if you let him search your things and do a body search, at least a pat-down, he'll be satisfied. I mean, your anger and resistance to having him stick a finger up inside you would sound justified.'

'Justified?' said Susan incredulously. 'I'd knock his fucking block off.'

'He wouldn't let you. This guy isn't worried about your feelings or political correctness. If you want my advice, I'd go the whole route. I wouldn't put it up inside your vagina.'

'Thank you very much.'

'I'd put it up inside your . . . well, from behind. That way, if he pushes you for a search and puts his hand up inside your vagina, then you can slap his face and say, with tears in your eyes something like, "Nothing's worth this humiliation!", *then* break down and start to walk away. He might go for it.'

'That *would* be humiliating.'

'If I lose you, and he does find a homing device, he might kill you.'

Susan didn't buy that scenario. She knew the Reaper was dangerous, she knew he had killed, but she did not feel threatened. He killed criminals. He expunged society's stains. She was not a criminal and, in fact, she sympathized with him. She felt certain that he would not harm her. But, most of all, she wanted Matt to feel that he was back in control. So she said, 'Okay.'

'You don't have to do this,' he said.

Despite the risk, Susan saw more opportunity than danger. She was aware that was probably what she wanted to see, as this was the kind of story journalists dreamed about. This was her chance and, despite the peril, she would never forgive herself if she didn't try.

'I want to do this.'

Matt felt a little guilty because he had anticipated

that was exactly how she would feel. Had he manipulated her? Perhaps – but she had forced his hand.

'Is there someone at the paper you can trust to get hold of the message and forward it to you?'

'My secretary, Janice. She's more efficient than most of the editors, as well as considerably more sober.'

'He'll call you and tell you to be at a particular phone booth at a particular time. It'll be in a public place. He'll observe you walking to the booth. As long as he believes you're not being followed, he'll give you instructions.'

'You sound so sure.'

'It's what a smart person would do. It's what a cop would do.'

THIRTY-THREE

'We've got it narrowed down to five guys.'

It was 1p.m. and Matt had just walked into his office five minutes ago. He was still a little groggy from staying up late in Vegas the night before. But Lloyd Garland's words were like smelling salts.

While Garland puffed excitedly on his pipe, he explained that the five men named on the list in Matt's hand had quit the LAPD over the past two years because of emotional or personal trauma, and were aged between thirty-five and forty-five. 'We're currently cross-checking the surnames of the retired LAPD officers against the list of people filing class action suits against Douglas Stevenson.'

'He and his father might not have the same surname.'

'I know, but it's an eighty-percent probability – least that's what the computer guys say. I've got two agents on each of the men whose names are on the list, digging up everything they can.'

'Good.'

'We should have something soon. We're close, Matt. I can feel it.'

'We'd better be. Otherwise, he's going to kill all the bad guys and put us out of a job.'

Garland stood and headed for the door. Over his

shoulder he said, 'Would that be so bad?'

'Not unless he considered us one of the bad guys.'

Two hours later, Garland and Matt sat at a large conference table in a room just across the hall from Matt's office. Also at the table were ten agents dressed in suits and ties, with legal pads full of notes lying in front of them.

'Harlan Clark is confined to a wheelchair,' said one agent.

'Gary North is a drunk, in and out of the local VA hospital. He has trouble keeping track of where he lives,' said another agent.

'Clifford Hanson is divorced, living with his son in the Marina. They run a little charter service out of there. He was running a charter for some Japanese businessmen yesterday when that guy in New York was killed,' said a third agent.

'Ferguson Brown is a bitter man. His partner was shot two years ago and died in his arms. Brown and another officer were sued for police brutality when Brown beat up the guy who killed his partner. Suit went to trial, and Brown lost his house. Eventually he lost his wife and kids. Only thing he's got now is a bottle and a black heart.'

'Possible,' said Garland, who was making notes.

The last agent to speak said, 'Jack Martin. Special Services in Nam in '71 and '72. NYPD, narcotics division, '75 through '79. Moved to Los Angeles in 1980 and joined the LAPD. Worked narcotics, did some undercover work, gang unit work, five commendations. Wounded twice in 'Nam, twice in

New York, and once in Los Angeles. He has experience in wiretapping and other electronic surveillance procedures.'

'Why did he quit?' asked Matt. He could feel it coming.

'A year and a half ago, his wife was murdered. She was kidnapped, in the family station wagon, from the parking lot of a local market. She was raped and murdered.' The agent cleared his throat. 'It was a gang initiation. The kid made his bones by raping and killing a woman. Any woman.'

Matt nodded. He had heard of this type of gang initiation. The first time he heard about it, it took him a while to shake the nightmarish pictures of that happening to his own wife. It seemed less than senseless. It was the kind of evil that poisons a man. And, in time, it could poison an entire society.

'Children?'

'There was a . . .' The agent breathed deeply before continuing. 'The, uh, boy was in the vehicle at the time of the murder – strapped in a car seat. During a police chase, the killer tossed the child out of the window, still in the car seat. The pursuing police car . . . couldn't avoid the child.'

There was complete silence at the table as twelve men privately thanked God for being spared the horror that had been visited upon Jack Martin.

'What happened to the killer?'

'He got away. However, a man named Howard Jones was arrested two weeks later. There was a trial, but he was acquitted.'

Everyone knew what the next question was, so no one bothered to ask it. The agent flipped over a page of his tablet and continued, 'A month ago Jones was found murdered in an alley in downtown Los Angeles. There have been no arrests.'

The phone rang in the conference room. Lloyd Garland, who had left instructions with his secretary not to be disturbed except for two specific calls, answered, 'Yes?' Pause. 'I see.' Pause. 'You're kidding.' Pause. 'Right.' Garland put the phone down. He had everyone's attention. 'Jack Martin's father lost his entire savings in one of Douglas Stevenson's Savings and Loans. The elder Martin committed suicide six months ago. And fourteen years ago Martin's sister used to be a prostitute, in New York. She used to work for a guy named Tiny Mahorn. Before she turned up dead in a snuff film.'

Matt, who had circled the J and the M in Jack Martin's name, wrote down the name Jonathan Mason and circled the J and the M. He looked at Garland and said, 'Bingo.'

Carnie sat in the rental car shaking. His hands vibrated on the steering wheel and he felt his heart beating fast. He took a deep breath. He had never done this before . . . Not like this.

In Viet Nam, after seeing his buddy sliced in half by machine-gun fire . . . after gathering up pieces of the body so that . . . he wasn't sure why he had done that. His buddy wasn't Humpty Dumpty. Carnie had realized that he would never be able to put his friend back together again. It was just that it seemed the right thing to do. The sight of a living, breathing human being being ripped apart like a stuffed doll did something to Carnie. It was a vivid picture that burned in his brain at some primordial level, deeper than what people called gut level. Beyond emotion. Over time, some actions, some acts of violence had been sorted out of the lexicon of human experience to the extent that there was no precedent, nothing to compare them to. No act of movie or TV violence, no act depicted in even the most graphic novel, served as a model. Only in the primitive behavior of the animal kingdom did such acts have resonance. And, even then, the gory spectacle was only a foreshadowing of the level and efficiency of carnage that man was to perfect.

It was perhaps in that latent part of the animal brain, the unconscious, the pre-selfconscious *brain, that what Carnie saw in the hot and humid jungle darkness made any sense at all.*

It was not logic that led him to lie in wait for his prey. Not revenge. It was some primitive instinct that put him in the jungle that night, his face caked with mud – and blood. His eyes burning and staring straight ahead, with a somber and solitary purpose. He was operating on automatic. He could not have stopped himself if he wanted to.

And the thought of stopping had never occurred to him.

When he had lain awake in the jungle that night, waiting for the men who had killed his friend, he had not felt afraid. He had not considered the danger. He was beyond that. His body was animated by a force over and above logic, emotion, or any other standard of behavior he could recall. It was as though there was no other course of action.

None.

And when he had put his gun to the heads of the Viet Cong soldiers that night . . . and pulled the trigger, he had felt no exhilaration of revenge. Nor had he felt any guilt. The only thing he felt was . . . a sense of balance. It was not that he had done the right thing.

He had done the only thing.

Carnie took another deep breath, removed the keys from the ignition, got out of the Cadillac, shut the door, listened to the thick and heavy sound of the door closing, and walked into the bar. Past a homeless man holding a sign that read: For $1, I will not bother you. *Carnie gave him a look: I'll kick the shit out of you if you fuck with me. Two ships, battleships, passing in the night. Neither man smiled. The homeless man just blinked and looked away.*

Carnie walked into the bar. It took a couple of minutes for his eyes to adjust. A Mexican girl, too young to be a woman, too experienced to be a child, sat next to another girl who was both. Both were dressed up like ornaments on a Christmas tree. Except that they were decorating a bar. Five years – fifteen to twenty – that was their time. The ripe years. After that, the life, a couple of pregnancies, it was over. For people in this bar, in most bars, their idea of long-term planning was figuring out what drink to order next. And if they had enough cash, or chips, to pay for it. But that was always an afterthought.

Carnie sat down at the bar. He was dressed in an expensive Lakers leather jacket, jeans, one hundred dollar-plus tennis shoes, and aviator sunglasses – which he kept on. In a dark bar. The Cadillac, sunglasses, the jacket were calculated. Items that, when tallied, came up two ways: either the man was an idiot, or he was to be feared. Such appraisals were part of staying alive down here. If you fell into the plus column, people left you alone. If you came up in the red, it usually came down to violence.

Carnie knew this. Knew this turf. He knew that when hoods and carjackers looked at his ride parked out front, they thought two things: setup, or this was a guy you didn't want to mess with – no fuckin' way. Either way, if you parked that kind of car in front of this kind of bar, you could figure it would be there when you walked out, even if you left the motor running. This was specialized knowledge: the kind of knowledge that came only with a price.

Carnie had paid that price.

'Watcha' wan', man?'

'Gold with a Corona back.'

The bartender didn't nod, he just twitched his lip. It was the same thing. In less than a minute he slid two glasses across the charred surface of the ancient bar. 'Five dollars.'

Carnie reached in his pocket, peeled off a ten and

tossed it on the counter, waving a hand over it to let the man know the other five was a tip. The bartender tried to conjure up a smile, but the muscle memory was gone. What little made it to his face exposed some bad teeth and curled upward his unkempt mustache; it was pretty pathetic. Carnie nodded, like he appreciated the effort.

By now his eyes had adjusted, and Carnie looked around for the young man he had arranged to meet. Out of the corner of his eye he saw four black men sitting at a table near the back door. All wore baseball caps and colors, blue. They were smiling, in his direction.

Carnie tossed down the Gold, picked up the beer and walked toward the foursome. 'You Jones?'

'Yeah, man,' said the black man with the X on his cap.

Carnie looked across the table at Clarence Jones. 'You a cop?'

For some reason the other three in Jones' entourage thought that was funny.

'No.'

'You could be a cop,' said Jones.

'I could be Abraham fucking Lincoln.'

'C'mon,' said Jones. He stood, and his homeboys stood. No one was smiling anymore.

Carnie took his cue and followed Jones into the back room. One of the men locked and bolted the door.

The back room of the Star Room bar was stark. Boxes of napkins, toilet paper, booze and a couple of extra chairs lined the walls. In the center was a round table, around which were five chairs. Two decks of well-used cards sat in the middle of the table.

'Take off yer clothes,' said Jones.

'What?'

'You heard me, muthafucka. Take off yer fuckin' clothes.'

'Why?'

' 'Cause I said so. I know the cops want my ass. If I give you what you want, and you got it on tape, I'm a stupid muthafucka spendin' the rest of my muthafuckin' life in prison. You strapped?'

'No.'

'You better not be, muthafucka. You strapped, you dead.'

Carnie took off his jacket, unbuttoned his shirt, removed it. He took off his shoes and socks and pants. Then his underwear.

One of Jones' associates withdrew a pile of cash from Carnie's jacket. 'All right!'

'Lookin' good,' said Jones.

'Five grand up front. I'm serious,' said Carnie.

'You better fuckin' be serious, muthafucka. You fuck with me . . .' He didn't finish his thought. He didn't have to.

'So, I did my part.'

'Be cool, muthafucka. Chill.' Jones looked Carnie over, head to foot. 'Least you ain't wired.'

One of Jones' associates tossed Carnie's clothes out the back door. 'We put your clothes outside so no microphone in no fuckin' button's gonna do any good.'

Jones sat down at the table, nodded and everyone else, including Carnie, grabbed a chair and sat down at the table, too.

'If I'm a cop, or if I'm the woman's husband, why would I come here . . . like this? Why wouldn't I just wait outside and blow your brains out?'

'You tell me?'

'I wouldn't. The cops already know you did it.'

'They can't prove a fuckin' thing.'

'I know. But the woman's husband's a cop, and he has access to all the information. If I'm the guy, why would I come here alone and put myself at your mercy?'

'Who the fuck knows?'

'It doesn't make sense.'

Carnie knew how it made sense. He had read the reports, talked to his friends. They all believed that Jones had done it. They were certain. But the DA couldn't make it stick.

The reason Carnie was here tonight was to make sure, for himself. There was no margin for error.

'All you have to do is verify a few details – I've seen the cops' reports – and we're in business.'

'How's come you need me, if you know what the cops got?'

'I want this movie to be accurate. You're the only one who can tell me for sure what happened. All the . . . details,' said Carnie, looking at Jones.

'You mean what it was like to fuck that bitch?'

'Exactly.'

'It was cool, man. Real cool.'

'The papers said the murder was some kind of initiation.'

'Yeah. I do some chick and I . . . you know.'

'Show your courage.'

'Right. Takes balls to do somethin' like that, man. Don't let nobody tell you it don't. I was sweatin', man, but you know somethin'?'

'What?'

'When I got to the part when she was beggin' me, whinin' and shit, and I got a glimpse of that pussy . . . man, I wasn't scared no more.'

Carnie saw the veins in his wrist start to throb. He took a deep breath and tried to slow down his heartbeat. He imagined what the veins in his neck must look like now. If he were in their place, he would have noticed. But Jones and his homeboys looked pretty stoned.

'I love it when bitches beg – you know what I'm sayin'?' said Jones with a toothy smile.

Carnie nodded. And took another breath. 'What about the kid?'

'That was just icing on the fuckin' cake. He was screamin' and cryin'. He didn't know what the fuck was goin' on. He only about a year old, right?'

'Yeah,' said Carnie, the inside of his lips so dry that they stuck to his teeth as he spoke.

'Tell the truth, I didn't have nothin' against the fuckin' kid. I didn't wanna kill him, but what the fuck, it wasn't my fault he was there, right?'

Carnie nodded.

'So, can we be extras in the movie?'

'Sure.'

Jones and his three homeboys smiled and nodded, crack dreams of glory dancing in their heads like sugarplum fairies.

Before he had sat down, Carnie knew exactly how it was going to happen. And now the moment of execution had arrived. Carnie took a deep breath and relaxed.

Then exploded.

With his right hand he backhanded the man to his right, sending his knuckles crashing against the victim's windpipe. The man gasped and collapsed in a writhing heap, trying to suck some air through his smashed larynx.

Carnie stood, lifting the table with him, causing Jones, who sat opposite him, to fall backwards in his chair. The other two men looked disoriented and reached for their guns. With a vicious leg sweep, Carnie took down the man to his left. The man's head hit the cement hard, and blood started to spread under his motionless body.

Carnie grabbed the gun hand of the third homeboy, just as he started to aim it at Carnie. A shot hit a crate of whiskey and suddenly the place smelled of booze. Carnie lifted his knee into the man's sternum and he crumpled into a heap, letting go his grip on the gun, which Carnie now held. He dove behind the upturned table just as shots from Jones' semi-automatic started to splinter it.

As Carnie lay still, he saw Jones' reflection in a window. Jones was reloading. Instantly, Carnie leaped over the table and stood above Jones.

'Drop it!'

Jones looked up at the nude man, the assassin, and tossed away his gun. The look in Jones' eye was a mixture of fear, disorientation and drugs.

Carnie grabbed him by the hair and dragged him toward the center of the room. The other men were either unconscious or so conscious of their own pain that they were helpless. There was some pounding on the door leading from the bar to the back room, but the door was locked and bolted. Carnie wasn't afraid. This wouldn't take long.

'How did she sound?'

Jones, who now on his knees, looked up, confused. 'What?'

'You said she was begging and whining.'

The glib gang member was suddenly at a loss for words.

'Do it!' Carnie slapped Jones in the face with his gun. 'Do it!'

Suddenly Jones started to make a sound.

'Beg me, you fuck!'

'Please, man, don't do this,' whimpered Jones.

'Whine!'

Jones started to make a noise that sounded like a wounded animal: a frightened animal in real pain. He started to cry, and the fear began to stretch his face into a pitiable mask.

As the moans filled the room, Carnie saw the real terror in the other man's eyes, and figured that was a lot like his wife must have looked as she pleaded for her life. As Jones raped her, back and front, and strangled her. In front of her son. Carnie's son.

Carnie felt his hand start to shake just before he pulled the trigger twice, and blew Jones' brains all over a cardboard box full of napkins.

Carnie quickly opened the back door, picked up his clothes, dressed, and walked away down the alley. He had stolen the Cadillac. And nobody in that bar would remember his face.

He was a bad dream they never wanted to have again.

Matt stood with Lloyd Garland on the sidewalk in front of Jack Martin's house – or at least where Martin's house used to be. It was now all charred wood and exposed foundations. There was nothing left of the life that Jack Martin had built before his wife and son went to the store one day and never came back.

'What do we do now? We publish his photograph, he'll just wear a disguise. He showed us he can do that. We announce his name, it won't make any difference. He's traveling under false ID as it is. He probably has more IDs than just Jonathan Mason.'

'Let's see if he makes contact with Susan first,' said Matt. 'If he doesn't do that in a day or two, then maybe we'll go public with what we've got.'

Garland nodded. On the way over, Matt had told him about Susan Dornan's column. Garland didn't like it any more than Matt did – having an amateur, a very ambitious amateur, in the middle of an investigation. But it was done, and he would try to turn it into something useful. He could look at it more pragmatically than Matt. Unlike his friend, Garland didn't care about Susan Dornan one way or the other. If anything, he felt that she was an opportunist who was making his job harder, and just possibly manipulating Matt at a time when he was vulnerable. But Lloyd kept these thoughts to himself. At this point, voicing his concerns would serve no useful purpose. Lloyd Garland was a very practical man.

As he stood looking now at the ruins of one man's life, Matt understood that Martin was burning bridges – any connections with his old reality. He wondered how far out of touch Martin had become with the man he once was. How mad had he actually become? Looking at the ashes, the devastation, made Matt even more concerned about putting Susan in the line of fire. But, he reminded himself, he had not put her there; she had put herself there.

No matter what Jack Martin's motives were, or how much he sympathized with the man, Matt knew that Martin was a man who had nothing left to lose. Which made him dangerous, very dangerous. His nightmare had probably driven him insane. Who could blame him, thought Matt. Nothing in this life prepared a person to handle that much pain, that much loss. Still, even if what he was doing made some kind of sense, it was madness to become the self-appointed wielder of 'the terrible swift sword'. Susan was about to walk into that madness.

And Matt was holding open the door.

THIRTY-FOUR

Matt sat in his office looking at the sun going down over the Pacific, sensing that his life was like paint melting and dripping off a canvas. What was once colorful and rich was now either gone or fading. What he could once reach out and touch no longer held the same shape or form.

Two weeks ago his marriage had been there. He knew it was there, felt it like some kind of invisible anchor. He and Laurie had had their problems, but in the Nineties, in Los Angeles, problems not only came with the territory, they were factored into the monthly payments. Unfortunately, that territory was built on the swampland of enough me-first and emotional baggage to sink a ship. Matt's generation had deified feelings and downgraded commitment.

Two weeks ago, vigilantes were black hats riding black horses. Today, articles glorified such behavior. TV talk shows considered the 'situational ethics' of taking another person's life, depending on the reputation and potential danger of the victim.

Matt knew that the world he had grown up in was gone. Norman Rockwell's vision of America was like an old black-and-white movie whose characters were irrelevant to an audience that was more familiar with Rodney King than Martin Luther King.

That old vision had been replaced by a mix of violent images of people lining up on opposite sides of a color bar.

The thing that pained Matt the most was that he had considered himself an American all his life. He had taken a bullet for the America he loved. But the America he loved was changing so fast, becoming, to a certain extent, a whore to fast-talking hustler/activists and gutless politicians. His true love had slipped away.

And, like his wife, the America that Matt had grown up with was never coming back.

'Matt?'

Matt turned around. Susan stood in the doorway. She walked over to him, kissed him on the lips, and looked out at the view. 'Beautiful.'

'Yeah.' Matt wanted to say much more, but now was not the time. And his office was not the place.

'No message yet?'

Matt nodded. He was not disappointed. 'Your secretary knows what to do?'

'I told her I wanted to keep this just between the two of us because the guy who wrote the "script" was an old flame, and I felt guilty about using the paper. Don't worry, I've got my beeper. You hungry?'

'I could eat.'

'Let's stop by the market on the way home, and I'll cook for you.'

'Home?'

'You know what they say: home is where you hang your pantyhose.'

'I didn't know that.'

'Maybe you ought to get out more.'

'Back in a minute,' said Kyle Talbot through the Walkman earphones in the man's ears. Carnie walked along the dark, nearly-deserted streets of Spanish Harlem. Fires burned in barrels, casting the backstreets in an eerie light. Two Hispanic men stood next to one of the barrels, consummating a deal.

As he walked along the street, his shoe leather clicking and echoing off ancient walls, Carnie felt a sense of epiphany, exhilaration. Epiphany because justice was finally within his grasp; suddenly it was all starting to make sense again. Exhilaration because he was living on adrenaline.

And there was also a sense of relief. Everything was in place; all the groundwork had been laid. It was his for the doing. Finally.

'Hey, muthafucka, whatchu doin' down here?'

Carnie looked at the Hispanic man, but said nothing.

Two other Latin men walked up behind the first man.

Silence. Street chess.

After a long moment, Carnie said, 'So, what do you guys think about the Reaper?'

Carnie just stood there, not looking scared.

The man who had approached Carnie stood his ground. He checked Carnie's eyes. It was not what he saw in those eyes that frightened him; it was what he did not see: fear. A white man, walking these dark streets alone at this time of night, confronted by three young Hispanics . . . It was smart to be afraid.

But this man was not. He just stared back.

And asked about the Reaper.

The first man coughed a nervous laugh out his nose, and backed away, never taking his eyes from Carnie until he was around the corner.

Carnie just smiled and walked on. It was nice to see the bad guys scared of the good guys. This was the way it was supposed to be.

This was what he'd had in mind all along.

After they had made love, Matt and Susan lay in bed, the sheets moist from their love sweat. The window was open and a slight breeze tickled the white drapes that covered the bedroom window.

'You don't have to meet with this guy, you know.'

'I know, but I want to, Matt. I know you think I'm crazy, but I'm actually excited about interviewing this man.'

Matt knew that one of the reasons she was more excited than scared was because she didn't really know what to expect. For most people, even journalists, violence was still, for the most part, something that happened on TV or in the movies. And in the movies the good guys usually walked away.

Matt knew that there was a very big difference between real life and the movies. Real violence was ugly. Real murder was a tragedy that family and friends never completely got over.

He knew that Susan was thinking more about the glory of what could happen than about anything else.

He was thinking this when he heard the sound.

'What was that?' said Susan. Her smile was gone.

'Stay here and be quiet,' whispered Matt. He got out of bed, slid his gun out of the shoulder holster which was draped over a chair, and moved toward the bedroom door.

When he reached the doorframe, he could hear a sound in the living room. There was no doubt that someone was in the apartment.

Matt took a deep breath and focused himself as the sound got closer to him.

'Freeze!' he shouted as he jumped out into the living room.

A man screamed and fell to the floor.

Matt hit the lights and . . . felt like a fool. And worse.

'Jarod! What in hell . . . ?'

Jarod's eyes were big, and he looked more terrified than Matt had ever seen him.

Matt reached down and pulled him up. 'Are you okay?'

Jarod tried to speak, but the words wouldn't come.

'Jesus, I'm sorry. Why didn't you call?'

'I don't know your phone number. All I had was the address.'

'Oh, God, I'm so sorry.' Matt put his arms around Jarod and held him close. For a lot of reasons.

'Matt? What's going on?' The voice came from the bedroom.

Jarod looked puzzled. 'Who's that?'

Matt never said, even mentally, *what else could go wrong*? He was afraid he would get an answer.

Later, on the balcony, Matt sat with Jarod. Just the two of them.

'I'm sorry, I should've called.'

'No, no, it's not your fault. I told you to come by any time. By the way, what are you doing here at midnight?'

'Mom's not home yet and, I don't know, I just didn't feel like being alone.'

'She with . . .'

'Yeah. I imagine, after the divorce is final, he'll probably start staying over. I guess they're just trying to be legally circumspect.'

'Strange term for a fifteen-year-old to use.'

'I overheard Mom say it on the phone.'

In spite of his own pain at hearing that his wife was, at that very moment, shining the sheets with Frank Jacobsen, he couldn't help but crack a smile. He knew that he was doing the same thing with another woman, but that was different somehow. Had Laurie not thrown him out, he would not be here in this apartment, not be having a . . . what? Is it an affair if neither party is married? Was he still married, technically, if his wife had filed for divorce and was sleeping with another man? It was all quite confusing. Since the Sixties, it seemed to Matt that the book of sexual etiquette was being updated every couple of months. And he'd been off the mailing list for over seven years.

'Do you love her?'

Jarod's candor took Matt by surprise, though it should not have. He and Jarod had always been very straightforward with each other. 'I don't know, it's kind of new.'

'Have you told her?'

'Told her what?'

'That you love her.'

'No, not yet.'

Jarod smiled. 'Not yet? Sounds like you plan to.'

This revelation seemed more remarkable to Matt than to Jarod. Until that very instant, Matt had not really put his feelings for Susan into those terms. But now, when he looked at it, certainly all the symptoms were present for such a diagnosis.

He decided to change the subject. 'You said you didn't want to be alone. Anything in particular bothering you?'

'Nah. Just a general malaise.'

'Don't tell me. You heard your mother use that word, too.'

'She's a lawyer. She knows words, what can I tell you?'

'Look, despite what happened tonight, don't feel you've got to call in advance. You can come over anytime. You know, I'm going to be out of town now and then. I'm sure that presents a very tempting set of circumstances, but I don't want you using this apartment for things that you can't do at your mom's place. Understood?'

'Understood.'

Matt knew that he didn't have to mention not bringing drugs or alcohol into the place. They had been through all that a couple of years ago. And Matt, being in the line of work he was in, knew what to look for in Jarod's behavior. Substance abuse was not the boy's problem. His mother staying married to the same man was his problem.

'The bed in the second bedroom isn't fixed up yet.'

'All I need is a pillow and blanket.'

'I think that can be arranged.'

THIRTY-FIVE

'Is he gone?' said Susan the next morning as she entered the living room, wearing Matt's robe, still rubbing sleep out of her eyes.

'Yeah, he left for school about fifteen minutes ago.'

'I feel so stupid.'

'You don't look stupid.'

'You're sure your wife wasn't worried?'

'He left a note for her.' Matt put on his jacket.

'I thought we'd have breakfast.'

'No time. There's food in the fridge. Your secretary knows how to reach you?'

'She has my number here, plus she has my portable phone number and my beeper number. Don't worry.'

'That reminds me, what *is* my number?' Matt walked over to his phone and memorized the figures displayed on the base of the phone. Pursuant to an agreement with Matt, the manager had let the phone man in the previous afternoon.

'There's three hours' difference between here and New York. It's almost eleven o'clock there now,' said Matt, thinking out loud.

'If my secretary hasn't phoned in an hour, I'll call her and remind her how important this is. I'll tell her to have lunch in, this afternoon. Anything else?'

'Yeah. Promise to meet me at the door tonight in that robe, and don't wear anything underneath it.'

'I promise.'

Matt kissed Susan lingeringly, then left.

Matt spent the next three and a half hours on the phone filling in the NYPD about Jack Martin, and making contingency plans regarding the possible meeting between Martin and Susan.

He called Susan at noon, and learned that she had talked with her secretary, twice. No calls so far. That made it three o'clock New York time. Maybe Martin wasn't in New York. Maybe he hadn't read Susan's column. Maybe he smelled a trap.

Three minutes later the phone rang, and Matt picked it up.

'He called,' said Susan.

Matt wanted this – but did not want it. 'And?'

'He said he wants to meet tonight. My secretary told him I was out of town, but he said he didn't know how much longer he was going to be in New York, and that I should try to make it.'

'Did he leave a phone number?'

'He left an address.'

'How did he ID himself?'

'He left a name – Jonathan Mason. Mean anything to you?'

The words made the hair on the back of Matt's neck stand up. 'Toss a few things from my closet and drawers into a suitcase, find a taxi, and get over here in thirty minutes. I'm getting us a flight in an hour from now. Move.'

The flight actually left at 1:45, which put them into JFK at about 6:30 – 9:30 New York time. The meeting was set for midnight. An NYPD black-and-white met them at the airport, and they were in Detective John Knoerle's downtown Manhattan office by ten after ten.

'Everything in place?' said Matt.

Knoerle shrugged his shoulders, as though Matt had asked him if he wanted to be rich and famous: sure, but what good was it going to do? 'You say this guy's one of us?'

'He was a cop,' said Matt. This was neither the time nor the place to make distinctions.

'So, he pretty much knows what we're going to do.'

Matt nodded.

Knoerle nodded too, but what he really wanted to say was, *So, if he's this fucking good, and he knows what we're going to do, what the fuck am I going through the motions for?* But what he actually said was, 'We've got everything you asked for.' He was doing his job – didn't want to be second-guessed – even though he was positive that it wouldn't make a damned bit of difference.

'The address is in the South Bronx,' said Matt, repeating what he had been told via the phone on the airplane. 'Tough area.' He knew a little bit about the city.

'Good choice, though.' Knoerle didn't wait to be asked to explain. 'Midnight in that area, there's not much fuckin' traffic – sorry, miss,' he said to Susan.

'I graduated from kindergarten a few years ago. Feel free.'

Knoerle nodded. And smiled a little. He liked tough broads. Even though he knew that they hated being called that. Most of them anyhow. 'So, you go down there in a taxi, get dropped off, he's got a perch on some building he's already sittin' in, and he sees everything. He sees headlights within six blocks 'a there, he's gonna walk. Or maybe he whacks you before he walks.' Knoerle didn't bother to apologize this time, only to gauge her response, in silence.

'What about helicopters?' said Susan.

Knoerle tried not to make it sound as though he were talking down. 'Well, we figure that if he can see a car for six blocks, he'd be aware of a helicopter too.'

It was Susan's turn to nod. And to feel a little stupid.

'The address he gave you is a restaurant. It'll be closed at midnight. But there's a phone out front. He'll call you there at midnight, and tell you to meet him somewhere else – after he tells you to get rid of the cab. He'll tell you to call a cab company of his choosing – that lessens the chance of you being able to substitute a cab driver with a cop.'

'Can't I tell him that I feel in danger down there, all by myself?'

'The irony is, you're completely protected. He'll

be watching you. If anybody tries to hassle you, he'll probably just blow them away.'

'I didn't think of it that way.'

Knoerle smiled and sipped some coffee from a Styrofoam cup. He *had* thought of it that way. And he knew he was right.

'Your men ready to move?' said Matt.

'They've been deployed since thirty minutes after you called me. But then the shooter had at least an hour on that. So, I figure he's in place already.'

'I feel so violated,' said Susan as they sat in a coffee shop across from the cop shop.

'It could save your life. Besides, it's your choice. If you really want to go through with this, putting a homing device there is your best chance. If it was too humiliating, you should have just walked away.'

'You think I'm wrong?'

'I think you're doing what you think is right.'

'That's not an answer.'

'It's not like I'm an unbiased observer.'

'And why is that?' asked Susan, even though she knew.

'Because I care for you.'

'Care for me? What do you mean by that?'

'I care for you. I don't think that needs a lot of explanation.'

'Does it mean you're fond of me?'

'Of course.'

'Does that mean you love me?'

Silence.

'Well?' asked Susan. She recalled the smug look of control on Detective Knoerle's face. She could relate to it now.

'Love means a lot of things to a lot of people.'

'What does it mean to you?'

'What are you looking for here, a definition?'

'I'm looking for an honest answer.'

Matt focused on the question. He no longer felt as though he was trying to cover himself. He was looking for an answer as much as Susan was.

'I'm not sure. I've been married twice. In each marriage, I was initially attracted by looks.'

'But neither one worked out, right?'

'Right.'

'So, you go through this cycle of physical attraction, then marriage and divorce.'

'I never really distilled it to that formula,' said Matt sarcastically. 'Before you get dizzy riding that high horse of yours, *you've* been divorced, too.'

'That's true.' Susan sipped her coffee. 'Let's face it, Matt, we're like most people. When you mix decent sex with romance, we all get a little stupid. But we keep hoping that we're not as stupid as the last time.'

It was Matt's turn to nod – and smile. He raised his coffee toward Susan, and they touched cups.

'To not being as stupid as the last time.'

Susan drank her coffee, looked into Matt's eyes, and said a silent prayer that she would get a chance to find out.

Including Matt, there were at least thirty NYPD and

FBI personnel standing around the cab that was going to take Susan to the South Bronx. An NYPD cop was driving, but that wasn't much of a risk, nor much of a surprise. Everyone, including the Reaper, knew that if the driver was *not* NYPD, *that* would have been a surprise.

Matt leaned in through the back window. 'I'll take you to breakfast when you get back.' It was the only thing he could think of to say. He knew that she knew what he meant.

'I'm looking forward to it,' said Susan.

As the cab made its way through the streets of Manhattan, Susan began to feel swallowed up by the darkness. She tried her best not to question her decision. There was no turning back. Not now. She had made a choice and she could make it work. At least that's what she kept saying to herself, repeating it as though some kind of mantra.

Still, as the lights, the people, the hustle and bustle faded into the rear-view mirror, and the desolation, the distance, the emptiness began to envelop her, there was no denying the fact that her excitement had been replaced by fear. She could taste it.

Finally, the cab pulled up in front of the address listed in the Reaper's message. Susan checked her watch. She was three minutes early.

She got out of the cab, purposefully stepping over a puddle of water on the sidewalk. It had not rained, so the water was there because someone had opened a hydrant, or somebody was using the sidewalk to take a piss.

Susan walked over to the phone booth. She was there less than a minute before she realized that the moisture she had first avoided was human waste. The wind was blowing the wrong way.

The cab driver remained at the curb. Matt had advised her to let Martin persuade her to tell the cab driver to leave. According to Matt, that would be standard operating procedure, but they would learn something if Martin did tell her to have the cab driver leave. Martin would have to be able to see her in order to know that she had arrived in a cab, that it was still waiting for her, and if it really left on instruction. Of course, if he were monitoring the scene electronically, they would arrive at false conclusions.

The phone rang and Susan jumped. She took a deep breath, then answered it.

'Glad you could make it.'

'Who is this?'

'Don't you know?'

After Susan hesitated, the man said, 'Honesty is important from here on out, Susan. And I'm pretty good at this.'

'Jack Martin.' On the plane, Matt had told her the man's name. He had also told her that Martin would expect her to know it.

'Very good. Now, get rid of the cab.'

'But how will I—?'

'Do it, Susan.'

Susan waved to the cab driver, and the cab pulled away.

'Good. A cab will pick you up in a few minutes. I've already given them the address to which you will be taken. Don't think about calling another number. The phone is bugged, as is the booth itself. So if you're wired, and you say anything that doesn't sound right . . . well, let's just say I'd be very disappointed.'

'Are you going to be where the next cab drops me off?'

'You don't need to know. Besides, I'll answer all your questions when we get together.'

The man hung up, and so did Susan. The cab arrived two minutes later, and Susan got in. The ride back seemed very strange. Outside her window, real life was going on just as it always did. Couples walked down the street hand in hand, people yelled on the car radio, and the cab driver sang country and western songs during the commercials.

Yet she knew that the world was not going on as usual. She was on her way to meet a man the rest of the world called the Reaper. An ex-cop who had already killed at least six people that she knew of. She was going to meet him in the middle of the night, alone.

Her only consolation was that she was wired with the homing device. She wondered how close Matt was to her right now. She felt so vulnerable.

The cab pulled up in front of 298 W 72nd Street. Susan paid the driver, got out, and the cab disappeared into the night. The street was dark. The streetlight in front of the address flickered, but mostly stayed off. She walked up the steps of the building and entered a small, dimly-lit foyer. There were four apartments listed on the directory, but none with the name Jack Martin or Jonathan Mason. It was after midnight, so she didn't want to ring every buzzer. What would she say if anyone answered? Think. She realized that Martin would predict her confusion.

She stepped outside, walked back down the steps and peered up at the windows. All the windows were dark. She was starting to wonder what she was going to do next when she felt a tap on her shoulder. In spite of herself, she let out a small scream. Nothing that would wake the neighborhood, but enough to make the bearded man jump back.

'Who are you?' said Susan instinctively.

'Terry Summers, ma'am,' said the man. He was dressed in a tattered sport coat, tennis shoes, very old jeans with holes in them – not the store-bought, pre-holed jeans. From the looks of this man, he had come by the holes the old-fashioned way, he had earned them.

'What do you want?'

'There's a man paid me to take you to him.'

'Where is this man?'

'He told me not to say nothin' about that. I'm just s'posed to bring ya.'

Susan looked up and down the street. It was deserted. If Martin was on top of one of the corner buildings, he would be convinced that she wasn't being followed on foot, by a car, or by helicopter.

Summers started walking and Susan fell in behind him.

In less than five minutes they were in Central Park. A bizarre tableau played itself out around her as she followed the bearded man into the heart of the park. Four middle-aged black men heated a can of something that smelled like beans, over a squat candle. People camouflaged by the night moved in the distance, behind bushes, behind trees.

Susan and her escort walked under bridges, past equipment that loomed like giant beasts in the shadows, past campfires and bodies of people who sat on benches staring blindly ahead, as though waiting for a bus to nowhere. She saw men and women who looked as close to death as a person could come and still be breathing.

Finally Summers stopped under a bridge. The air there was putrid with the smell of human waste. At the other end of the small dark tunnel a man lit a cigarette.

'That's him,' said Summers.

Susan walked slowly toward the other man. Just beyond him a cement path led up a hill toward an ancient lamppost, the light in which still burned brightly.

Jack Martin wore a long black coat, tennis shoes, a New York Yankee baseball cap, a black T-shirt and a pair of jeans. He looked as though he hadn't shaved in a couple of days. He appeared muscular, even under the coat, with the neck muscles of someone who worked out. His face was tanned, his features angular. She could tell that he must have been a good-looking man – at least at one time. Now he was looking old. Maybe it was the beard; maybe life was just starting to catch up with him.

Out of the corner of her eye, Susan noticed that Summers was still standing at the other end of the tunnel.

'We meet at last,' said Susan.

Martin removed a small box from his pocket. A small pen-like device was connected to the box by wire. 'I'm going to ask you if you are wired, or if you're wearing a surveillance device. And I expect you to tell me the truth.'

Susan felt her heart starting to beat faster. 'Why would I be wired?'

'Because that's what I'd do if I were a cop.'

'You think I'm working with the cops?'

'I'm gonna to cut through all the shit right away, because there isn't much time. Of course, you're working with the cops. That's one of the reasons you know so much about me. They told you my name was Jack Martin. Now, I know you haven't been followed, but I still don't know if you're wired. If you don't tell me the truth – which I can verify one way or the other with this machine – then I'll kill you.'

'How do I know you won't kill me even if I tell you I *am* wearing a device?'

'Because even though you'd have betrayed me, like the others, you're more useful to me holding the interview than you would be dead.' Martin clicked on the tiny box, and it started making clicking noises like a Geiger counter.

'Are you wearing a tracking device?'

After only a slight hesitation, Susan said, 'Yes.'

'Remove it.'

'It's—'

'I know where it is,' said Martin. 'I said to remove it.'

Martin kept his eyes level with Susan's while she went through the humiliation of removing the homing device from her rectum.

'Clean it off.'

Susan took a Kleenex from her purse and cleaned off the device. Martin held out his hand and she gave it to him. 'They made me wear it. They wouldn't let me meet with you unless I did.'

Martin didn't respond as he ran the pen-like scanner over Susan's body. When he had finished, he seemed satisfied, and put the box and scanner back into his pocket.

'Wait here.'

Martin walked back down the dark tunnel to where Summers stood waiting.

'I did good, right?'

'Very good. So good in fact, I'm going to give you another job. Here's eighty dollars,' said Martin handing the man four twenties. The man's eyes lit up. He hadn't held that much money at one time in nearly five years.

'I want you to take a taxi that's waiting just up

that hill there,' said Martin pointing out toward the ancient lamppost. 'Tell the driver you want to go to JFK. Tell him you'll pay him forty dollars in advance, and he'll take you, don't worry. Then I want you to wait there for ten minutes, then take another taxi back here.'

Martin took a crisp hundred dollar bill out of his pocket and held it up in the light so that Summers could get a good look at it. Then Martin tore it in half and gave one of the halves to Summers.

'Wow!'

'Meet me back here in an hour and a half, two hours, and I'll give you the other half.'

'A hundred bucks? You got it!'

'Okay, now go on.' Despite the homeless man's odor, Martin forced himself to put his arm around Summers and walk him back up the tunnel toward the light.

Slipping the tiny surveillance device in the man's outer breast pocket as he did so.

'Thanks, man,' said Summers as he walked quickly up the path toward the waiting cab, leaving Martin and Susan standing in the shadows of the dark tunnel.

'Follow me,' said Martin when Summers had disappeared up over the hill and the sound of a car door slamming was heard in the distance.

Susan followed Martin out the other side of the tunnel, down a worn path into what appeared to be a dense patch of weeds. About three minutes later, Martin stopped inside what looked like a small cave hollowed out of the side of a hill. It was a bizarre scene. From the depths of a primordial cave she could see the Manhattan skyline glittering in the distance over the trees, which were swaying back and forth now in the wind that had picked up steadily since she had begun her journey.

'How did you find out about the script you referred to in your column? You must have known about it before the police, otherwise they would have stopped the broadcast.'

'Talbot's girlfriend. She overheard you instructing him on the phone.'

Martin smiled. A small mistake, nothing fatal. In fact, he had used it to his advantage. Martin knew that a person in his position must be able to adapt quickly, very quickly, to changes in the game plan. Survival depended upon that ability.

'Do you believe what you write in your column?' said Martin, leaning against the side of the cave which, as her eyes adjusted, Susan could see was covered with grafitti.

'What specifically?'

'What you write about me. It's as if you really understand me – or at least what I'm doing.'

'If you're asking if I condone your murdering people—'

'You know I don't murder people. I punish people who evade the system. People who don't play by the rules.'

'It started with the man who killed your wife and son, didn't it?'

Jack Martin sighed deeply. 'It started a long time ago, Susan – may I call you Susan?'

'Of course.'

'It started with a genuine love for this country and what it stood for. I'm not talking about some bullshit kind of flag-waving, Fourth-of-July-only kind of patriotism. I'm not like a guy who goes to church one day a week in order to absolve himself of the sins he commits the other six. I mean, I really love this country. I live it, breathe it – always did. That's why, when other guys my age were growing their hair long and trying to evade draft, I joined the Marines. I wanted in.

'I know what some people think. They think I'm some kind of psycho who'll use any excuse to kill people. But that's not true, Susan. Until a month ago, I'd been shot myself more times than I'd shot other people. I killed three people in 'Nam, all three because they killed my buddy. I never shot anyone when I was a cop in New York, and I shot just one person in self-defense in all my years on LAPD.'

'You were saying how you love this country.'

'I grew up believing that there was some kind of absolute right and wrong. I grew up believing that principles and a man's word meant something. The only right and wrong nowadays is store-bought, and paid for by some guy in a suit. Besides, nobody cares anymore. This country is filled with more hate than ever.'

'Do you hate, Jack?'

'Yes, Susan, I hate. I hated the man who raped

my wife, murdered her and my baby boy, then went back to his homeboys and described *every* grisly detail about how she screamed, how she pleaded with him to spare our son, about how it felt to . . .' Jack's voice cracked. He took a deep breath. 'All so he could be considered man enough to be in a gang with a bunch of cowards.

'I hate what's happened to this country. But it seems that nobody *really* cares until it hits their own family.'

'So you quit the LAPD . . . ?'

'Without my wife and son, I knew it was over for me. And since I had nothing left to lose, I decided to do what I could to set things right before I died.'

'What do you mean, set things right?'

'In our society many people, especially criminals, think the law is a joke. The only people afraid of the law anymore are law-abiding citizens. Every person I took out had escaped justice. Every person I executed had hurt other people and gotten away with it.'

'Not everyone.'

'Some things can't be helped. There are always "peripheral casualties", even in a holy war. All my targets destroyed not only the obvious victims, but the victims' families and – because they were not punished for their crimes – society at large.'

'Do you really think violence is going to solve anything?'

'The justice system has so betrayed this nation, there are only two choices left: watch the country go down in flames, or fight back. I'm fighting back. It's like when I went to 'Nam. I was willing to put my life on the line because I truly believed that Communism was a threat to this country. I truly believe that the moral decay here, the lawlessness, the drugs, have created more of a direct threat to this nation than any outside force in our history. We're destroying ourselves from within.'

'But how is being a vigilante going to help save America?'

'It might not. But sitting by waiting for politicians and lawyers to do the right thing ain't gonna get it. And waiting for people to start loving their neighbor ain't gonna get it, either. Someone's got to stand up and say enough is enough.

'I'll tell you something, Susan,' continued Martin, as he walked to the mouth of the cave, the distant city skyline playing in the background like some great Hollywood special effect. 'One of the reasons I love this country so much is because I know that most people here are good and decent. The media have convinced us, with these crazy talk shows and by sticking a microphone in all these screaming idiots' faces, that we're all a bunch of illiterate, racist fuckups. But that's not so. Good people always outnumber the bad people, ten to one.'

'Who defines who's a good person, Jack?'

'It's got nothing to do with skin color, or which god you worship. It has to do with a person's conduct – like Kyle Talbot says. A good person doesn't purposely hurt or cheat other people; he takes responsibility for his actions, for his kids. That's a good person. You purposely hurt and defraud somebody, you run away from responsibility, blame everybody else for all your problems, that's a bad person. That's a taker. Our society is teeming with them. They're like maggots.

'I know in this culture every "bad" person's got some excuse about the bum hand dealt to them by society, the government, the gene pool, whatever. But you know what? Most of the rest of the people have their own problems with alcoholic and abusive parents, with being black, brown, yellow, whatever. The difference between the good people and the bad is that the good people make a decision not to join gangs, sell drugs, steal, rape and murder.'

'There are a lot of experts who say that these people don't have a choice.'

'The experts are wrong – people always have a choice. Might not be the choice they want, might not feel wonderful at the time, but they have a choice. Besides, the experts get paid to perpetuate these myths. As a cop, I saw a lot of therapists who, when it was their own family member who'd been injured or killed, didn't give a flying fuck about the criminal's past. They wanted to rip the guy's heart out just like everybody else.'

Jack took out a cigarette and lit it up. 'I haven't smoked one of these in ten years.'

'What's the special occasion?'

'I dunno,' said Jack looking away, back toward the New York skyline. 'Nobody lives forever.'

He turned again toward Susan. 'You're pretty brave coming here alone – even if you did think the cops would track you.'

'I figured you'd find the bug. Like I said, they made me do it. Besides, I knew you wouldn't kill me. I'm one of the good guys.'

'Are you?'

The question sent a chill down Susan's spine. 'You know that. You read my column and decided to meet with me.'

'I met with you because I want someone to get the facts straight. I'm not some white supremacist freak. I judge people by their actions, nothing else. But if a society is to have order, you must also punish that small percentage of people whose conduct harms the rest of us. If you don't, the whole group loses confidence in the system. When that happens, the group has to protect itself. Believe me, I wish I didn't have to do what I'm doing now. I wish . . .' Martin pulled hard on the cigarette, exhaled and blew a plume of smoke into the swirling wind. For a moment he was somewhere else. Ten years ago. Smoking. Walking hand in hand with—

'You wish your wife and son were still alive.'

'More than anything.' Martin exhaled deeply. 'More than anything. It's tough wishing something so hard, and knowing that it can never come true. You know,' said Martin, taking another long drag off the cigarette, 'it's ironic in a way. I spent my life trying to protect my country, my city, my neighborhood, and in the end I couldn't even protect my own family.'

'It wasn't your fault, Jack.'

'Oh, I know that. It was that asshole's fault who killed my wife and son. And if it was up to the system, he'd still be walking around selling dope, raping other women, and killing other people. But he's dead. End of story. Sometimes I wonder how much tragedy I took out of circulation with two bullets to that punk's head.'

There was a moment of silence while Martin smoked and Susan tried to focus on what he was saying, on the surroundings, sights, smells, sounds, the feel of the encounter. The details would be important later when she wrote her story.

'So, what do you get out of all this?' said Martin finally.

'Truth?'

'Life is too short for anything else?'

'This is the biggest story of the year. Probably the biggest exclusive I'll ever have.'

'Fame and fortune,' said Martin. It was as though he were mouthing the pledge of allegiance to Sodom and Gomorrah. But his smile tempered the sharp edge. 'Least you're honest.'

'But it's more than that. To a certain extent, I think you're right. I think you represent the anger and frustration of a lot of good people in this country, who don't know what else to do.'

'Kind of like a militant Ross Perot?'

'Kind of. Where is all this leading? You've

obviously given it a lot of thought.'

'You really want to know? If I tell you, I'll have to kill you.'

Susan did not respond.

'That's a joke, partly,' he said with a smile.

'The FBI knows who you are, what you look like, everything.'

'Not everything.'

'What do you mean?'

'I can tell you that it'll all be over soon.'

'What's soon?'

'Within forty-eight hours.'

'What are you going to do? At least give me some kind of a hint.'

'You like skating on thin ice, don't you?'

'I'm a pretty good swimmer.'

Martin smiled again. He liked this woman: she was not afraid. Still, he had known it would come to this, and in fact he wanted it to.

'My last target is a well-known senator.'

Susan's blood ran cold, but she tried not to show it. 'Who?'

'I can't tell you that.'

'I take it you have a personal grudge against this guy.'

Martin did not respond.

'Like the grudges you had against Douglas Stevenson and Tiny Mahorn?'

'Not exactly. The decisions this man's made, the speeches he's made, the causes he's backed, have impacted my life. That's about all I can say.'

'You live in California, and there you only have two senators.'

'My hint to you is that I guarantee neither California senator is the target.'

'So your target's in Washington, DC?'

'That's where he works,' said Martin.

'What if I publish this tomorrow?'

'Your newspaper deadline won't allow you to publish it tomorrow. You could tell the FBI tonight, but I still don't think they'll be broadcasting it on CNN.'

'What makes you so sure?'

'I'm not sure. I'm not sure about anything anymore. But it doesn't make any sense. The FBI will mobilize Washington with federal and local cops, and the last thing they want is chaos. They want control. And, like I said, it'll all be over in forty-eight hours, anyhow. Containment and control. Broadcast what I'm telling you, and they'll have neither.'

'So, why are you telling me this now?'

'Because I've planned it out to the last detail. There's nothing you or the FBI can do about it. By the time you figure out which senator, it'll be too late. Like I said, I just wanted you to tell my side of the story, and tell it accurately.'

'What do you gain by killing a senator?'

'Visibility. I'm creating a reality that other people can imitate. They can see how one good man with principles can make a difference. I'm not some nut who's been holed up in his tiny apartment for twenty years and suddenly goes berserk. I'm a man who chooses his targets based on behavior and not ideology. I recognize and respect the rights of others to disagree with me, to protest, to do all kinds of things. But I do not recognize the right of another person to hurt me or my family. Do you?'

'Do I what?'

'Do you believe other people have the right to harm you?'

'Of course not.'

'You say that as though you mean it.'

'I do.'

'Do you mean it enough to be committed to not letting it happen?'

'That's why we have laws.'

'And you really believe that the law protects you from harm?'

Susan did not respond immediately, because she was aware the law did not protect her from those things. 'No, but it's the only alternative we have.'

'Maybe it's time to come up with some options.'

'And so that's what you're doing – presenting options?'

'The American public is brighter and stronger than the media think. Trust me, Susan, it's going to be incredible.'

She thought about saying something like, 'That's a strange way to describe assassinating a senator,' but instead said nothing. Her job was not to argue but to write a column that sold newspapers.

'Is there anything else you want to add?'

'No, that's it,' said Martin.

'When can we get together again?'

'We'll never see each other again.'

'How can you be so sure?'

'Trust me.'

Susan had no choice.

Jack took one last puff on the cigarette, and flicked it out into the wet grass. 'You can go now.'

'Just like that?'

'Just like that.'

'I'm a little surprised.'

'By what?'

'I thought a guy like you wouldn't let a woman walk home alone through Central Park.'

'I'll pretend that you're sincere and that you're not trying to play me for a fool. First, I'm going to lead you out of the park.' Martin looked at his watch. 'Second, there will be a taxi waiting for you. Third, I'll observe you – from a distance, of course – until you're in that cab. Any other questions?'

'One. Are you taking such great care because you're a gentleman, or because you want to make sure nothing happens to me so your story gets told?'

'Maybe you'll never know.'

Susan moved out of the cave and onto the grassy area just outside.

'Follow me.' Martin turned and started walking quickly away from her. She followed, hurriedly, trying to keep up, through bushes and underbrush, until she came to a cement path. When she reached it, she realized that Martin was already gone. So she followed the path toward the city lights and, sure enough, there was a taxi waiting for her.

'You the one who called for a cab?' said the driver.

'Yes.' Susan got in.

'Where to?'

'The Plaza,' she said. Matt had told her that if it went this far, she was to meet him at the Plaza.

All the way back, Susan found herself amazingly calm. At least she thought so after what she had just been through. She was the pivotal point of global news. People in Japan, in Germany, in Great Britain, all across the United States, would want to know about the Reaper. Even if she did not know exactly what he planned to do, she would be the one person in hot demand. All the talk shows would call. There would be a major book deal. There would be a movie deal. At least one TV-movie deal.

The taxi pulled up in front of the Plaza and stopped. 'That'll be three dollars,' said the driver.

Susan handed the man a ten and didn't ask for change.

THIRTY-SIX

Matt and members of the NYPD spent the next four hours debriefing Susan. The only humorous moment came when one of the NYPD cops described picking up some derelict named Terry Summers at JFK.

By 5:30 in the morning every available FBI agent was on his or her way to Washington, DC.

Even though they took separate rooms, for several reasons, propriety being not the least of them, by six o'clock Susan was sitting in the window well of Matt's room, sipping black coffee, watching dawn break over Central Park. 'It doesn't look so dangerous in this light,' she said.

Matt had collapsed in a chair next to her, his feet up on the writing desk. 'I was scared last night. Really scared. I thought . . .'

'You're not going to get rid of me that easily.'

Neither had caught a minute of sleep, but they were both still wired: ten percent strong coffee, ninety percent adrenaline.

'What should I do now?' said Susan, turning away from the park and looking at Matt.

'About what?'

'I'm sitting on the story of the century – well, the last couple of years, anyway.'

'Fame can wait a day or two.'

'Timing is everything, Matt. You know that.'

'Hold off until he makes his move. It's either today or tomorrow. Then you can start lobbying for your Pulitzer.'

'What about an Oscar? This'll make a great movie, don't you think?' said Susan, only half kiddingly.

'I think it'll be made into a movie, yes. Whether it should be, whether it'll be great, who knows?'

'You think I'm wrong for cashing in a lottery ticket?'

'I don't know what's right anymore, Susan. All I know is what is – that people act exclusively out of self-interest.'

'That's human nature, Matt. Nothing wrong with that.'

'There's something wrong with it when it works to the detriment of the whole. I really believe the media are partially responsible for the deterioration of this country. They have focused our attention almost exclusively on the worst among us, on the worst in each of us. They've made it okay to be greedy, made it more attractive to be a rap music star than to be a doctor. Every fucking night it's serial killers or strippers on these tabloid shows. If all you did was watch TV, you'd think America's made up of fifty percent mud-wrestlers and murderers.'

'So you think that's what I'm going to do with this story – exploit it irresponsibly?'

'I don't know. I realize that people want to know about this guy. I realize you risked your life to interview him. I realize people are fascinated by vigilantes, especially now, and I think that there's a danger in making this man into some kind of hero.'

'If I don't write about it, someone else will.'

'C'mon, Susan, that's a cop-out and you know it. You've got to have some personal integrity. You can't just do or not do something because if *you* don't someone else will.'

'I'm sorry you feel that way about me, Matt.'

He sighed, picked up his tired body and snuggled it up beside Susan's in the window well. 'I'm tired, Susan. I know you've got a job to do, and I really believe you'll act in a responsible manner.'

'You want to believe that.'

'Yes, I do,' he said, touching her cheek gently, then kissing her lingeringly on the lips. 'Besides, if I'm not nice to you, you'll probably demand that some fat old fart plays me in the movie.'

Susan smiled. 'Were you really worried about me?'

'Very much.'

'What do you think that means?'

'I don't know. What do you think it means?'

'Sounds to me like you might be in love.'

'Really, doc. I was hoping it wasn't that serious.'

' 'Fraid so.'

'So, what do you recommend?'

'I'd advise bed rest. Lots of it.'

'Think so?'

'Definitely. Tell you what. I think you should take two of these,' she said, as she took Matt's hands and placed them on her breasts, 'and call me in the morning.'

Matt picked up Susan and carried her to the bed. It proved to be just what the doctor ordered.

The car picked them up out front of the hotel at 8:45. They sat in the back while the FBI agent drove.

'Mind if I listen to the radio, sir?' asked the young man.

'As long as it's not rap music or polka,' said Matt.

'Don't worry.' The agent turned on the radio and Kyle Talbot's voice filled the car. Matt thought about objecting, but decided against it. It was a taped 'Best of the Kyle Talbot Show', and he was talking about how 'liberal' President Souther was and how his policies were bankrupting the country, not only financially but morally as well. It was an old tune: easy for Matt to tune out.

'What's wrong?' asked Susan. She had not known Matt long, but her instincts about people were good. Especially when she was interested in that person.

'Nothing.'

'Come on, tell me.'

'Something's not right.'

'What do you mean?'

'I'm not sure. Something's wrong and I can't quite put my finger on it.'

'Wrong with what?'

'This whole set-up.'

'Could you be more specific?'

'For one thing, why should Martin stay in New

York? After he killed Tiny Mahorn. Every other time he's killed somebody, he's left town within a few hours.'

'He used to live here. Maybe he has friends here.'

'No, he's on a mission. This isn't a vacation. And when he calls you, he knows you're writing columns about him. He knows you're on the scene on the west coast. Why doesn't he go home to LA? If he's going to orchestrate a meeting with you, why not do it on his own turf?'

'I give up. Why?'

'I don't know.'

'The obvious reason is that he's going to Washington to kill a senator.'

'So why not meet you in DC?'

'Maybe he knows New York better and felt more comfortable meeting here.'

'Maybe he's not planning to go to DC.'

'But he told me that's where he's going. I distinctly heard him say—'

'So what?'

'I don't think he'd lie to me, Matt.'

'Why not? Do you think it's more important to tell you the truth, or to accomplish his goal?'

Susan didn't respond. She was starting to feel frightened again.

'What would he accomplish by lying to me?'

'Are you serious?'

'Yes.' Even though it was all starting to dawn on her like a bad dream.

'He knew you were wired. He knew, when he let

you go, you would go back and tell the FBI and the NYPD everything he told you. If his target was in New York, he would have then accomplished the monumental feat of sending every available FBI agent in the country to Washington DC.'

The car was silent, except for the radio.

On it, Kyle Talbot was saying, 'Folks, I just don't know how much more of this the country can take. I gotta tell ya, I heard this joke the other day. A group of people want to put President Souther's face on Mount Rushmore. So they approach the proper people about this idea and the people in charge say no. Reason is, there's no room for two more faces on the mountain.' Talbot laughed at his own joke – one that had been doing the rounds for some time.

'But seriously, folks, something has to be done. We are a country in crisis. We need a leader. A real leader. I've heard talk of impeachment and, I'll tell you the truth, when I first heard it, I thought no, that's not possible, and it's not good for the country. But after what we've been through, and considering the immediate future of this country, I might just be wavering on the possibility of impeachment. Back in a minute.'

'Good thing the President isn't going to be in Washington,' said the driver.

Although the Reaper's threat was not common knowledge to the general public, it *was* common knowledge throughout the FBI, which had pulled every possible agent back from vacations and sent them to Washington.

Matt nodded. He had been so preoccupied that he hadn't kept up with Souther's schedule, that not being his immediate concern. 'Where is the President?'

'He's off to Japan today.'

'Good,' said Matt. At least that was one problem he didn't have to worry about. His mind turned to possible targets in New York. The mayor was a liberal, so that was a possibility, but it would seem odd for Martin to target a New York City mayor rather than his own Los Angeles mayor, who was equally liberal – at least that was the perception. Who else was in town? Maybe it wasn't a politician, but just someone high-profile. Maybe an actor involved in liberal causes. Maybe a civil rights leader. Who the hell knew? Matt saw the *New York Times* on the dashboard.

'Hand me the paper, Al.'

'Sure.'

The driver handed Matt the newspaper. He unfolded it and looked at the headline.

'Oh, my God,' was all he said.

'What?' said Susan.

She took the paper from him and studied the headline: SOUTHER IN NEW YORK TO INK INNER CITY FUNDING ACT.

'My God!' said Susan. Suddenly she realized how she had been manipulated into helping a madman assassinate the President of the United States.

On the radio, Kyle Talbot was saying, 'I'm telling you, folks, someone's got to *do* something.'

* * *

'It's nice seein' you again, man.'

'Hey, I'm in New York, so why wouldn't I look up my old partner, right?'

'Right,' said Eddy Marconi. Marconi was fifty-five years old, retired NYPD, divorced, an alcoholic with a plan to give up the booze next year when circumstances would be right. He had an apartment in New Jersey not a whole hell of a lot smaller than the house he and his wife raised their kids in. The kids were grown now. The wife was married to a car salesman. And one of the kids even called him on Father's Day. Sometimes.

'So how do you like working airport security?'

'You really wanna know?' said Marconi.

'Sure.'

'It's a fuckin' check, Jack. I mean, the most exciting thing I do is order some suit to turn on his fuckin' laptop computer. But I can't complain.'

'Yeah.'

'Kind of a coincidence, me working at the airport and you needin' a ride to the airport today.'

'I like coincidences that work in my favor. So, this Pam person you work with . . .'

'She's a fuckin' barrel 'a laughs. She keeps me laughin' all fuckin' day. Hell, if she wasn't around, I don't know how I'd make it through the day. You know what she does?'

'No.'

'All these people walk through the X-ray machines, right? She makes up a story about each one of them. She's such a fuckin' riot. We'll be standin' by the X-ray screen, she'll see somethin' in the luggage, look at the person and she'll say somethin' like, "Bet that's a fuckin' dildo." It's funny when you see the person she's talking about, you know. Yeah, Pam's great.'

'Sounds like it.'

'Weirdest fuckin' thing I ever saw was this guy who came through the machine. Took out his keys, took off his rings, and the machine still kept goin' off. All the time I'm seein' that the guy's lookin' real nervous. He had long hair and a beard. I thought we caught ourselves a whacko. Guess what it turned out to be?'

'What?'

'Guy had a fuckin' ring through his penis. Shit! Makes me shiver just thinkin' about it. 'Side from shit like that, it's a pretty fuckin' boring job.

'Well, here we are,' said Marconi as he pulled his car into the parking garage.

He parked the Ford Escort in his space, and turned off the engine.

He never saw it coming.

Matt was on the phone as soon as he figured it out.

Unfortunately, all the extra law-enforcement personnel he had access to were already on their way to Washington. He placed a call to the Secret Service, and got through to a top level officer who said, essentially, 'Thanks for the speculation. We're capable of taking care of the President, and fuck you.'

Even though Matt was thoroughly convinced that Jack Martin was now planning to kill Souther, that was still only Matt's best guess. He had no facts.

During his phone calls, he learned that the President was not actually coming to the city, but was meeting Mayor Robbins at the airport. He would sign the legislation, pose for a few photographs with the mayor, get back on Air Force One, and head off to Japan. That photo opportunity was set to take place in forty-five minutes.

THIRTY-SEVEN

Jack Martin took the escalator up toward the security area. His heart was beating very fast. He was now twenty yards from the X-ray machine. Carrying a gun in his duffel bag.

Ten yards. Five . . .

'Pam?'

The large black woman turned to look at Martin, as he moved *around* the metal detector and reached out his hand. 'I'm filling in for Eddy today,' he said matter-of-factly, setting down the bag.

Pam Smith looked the man over. The uniform was right. He clearly knew Eddy. And he seemed to know her.

'See that guy over there,' said Martin.

Pam eyed a large man who could barely fit through the metal detector.

'What do you make of him. Eddy says your assessments are the only thing that make this job bearable.'

Pam smiled and studied the fat man for a few seconds, then started to give Martin her opinion. But Martin wasn't listening.

His mind was on other things.

'We're driving a black company car,' said Matt into

the car phone. He was speaking with the head of the Secret Service ground team. The President was still in the air, but Air Force One was due to land in twenty minutes. 'I'll have the driver blink his lights twice when we come onto the runway. I don't want your guys blowing my fucking head off.'

Matt hung up, and told the driver what he had said to the Secret Service.

'I'm coming with you,' said Susan.

'Out of the question.'

'I just spoke with Martin a few hours ago. Do *you* know what he looks like?'

'I've seen photographs.'

'I've seen him up close, and personal.'

Matt had to admit she had a point. Even if Martin was in disguise, he probably would not be heavily disguised. The photo op would be open only to the press and a few politicians, so a man with a heavy beard or other obvious facial disguises would stick out, especially in this heat. Matt needed to get a quick read.

'Look, Susan, I'm in charge. You have to remember that.'

'Okay.'

'What I'm planning is to get as close to the scene as possible, but staying in the car. You try to spot him, and I'll do the rest.'

'I got it.'

'I think I've got a problem,' said Martin.

'What's the trouble, baby?' said Pam. Though she

had only just met this guy, she liked him. She liked any guy who wasn't seriously overweight, or seriously married.

'Stomach flu. I've been living in my bathroom. Maybe it's the same thing Eddy's got.'

'Hope you didn't catch it from kissin' him on the mouth, now,' she said with a grin.

Martin smiled back. 'Man, I gotta go.'

'No problem. I'll catch the terrorists till you get back. Run along, now.'

'Thanks, Pam.'

Martin picked up his small duffel bag and walked off toward the restrooms.

Instead of going into one, he continued toward the gates. He kept walking until he found the right one: a gate with a flight in a pre-boarding state – where the plane was at the gate and the portable entranceway was connected to it, but the passengers were not allowed on yet.

'This country is in crisis. Someone has to *do* something,' Kyle Talbot repeated on the radio. As he walked through the airport, Martin could hear Talbot's words on his Walkman.

He was thinking about those words, and what they had meant to his life, when he spotted the Mid-Atlantic Airlines flight that met his specifications.

Martin walked past a blond in a MAA uniform, who was involved in handling some problem with a passenger's ticket. She didn't take notice of the security guard walking past her.

He headed into the entranceway and down the

long portable corridor. He stopped just before it veered sharply to the left to connect to the plane. He peered around the corner, but saw no one.

He then stepped forward, just as a stewardess emerged from the plane. They looked at each other, surprised.

'Hi,' he said.

'Hi. Anything wrong?'

'The President's plane is landing in ten minutes. It's a security nightmare. You notice any problems, any suspicious characters?'

'No.'

'Good. If you do, report it immediately.'

'I will.'

'Nothing out of the ordinary is too small. It's better to be safe than sorry.'

'Right,' said the stewardess, nodding. Then she walked back into the plane.

When he was certain she was back inside, Martin moved toward the open seam created when the portable entranceway butted up against the plane. Just enough space for a person to squeeze through. In an instant, he dropped the twenty feet and rolled – as he had done many times from planes in Viet Nam. That had been a long time ago, but he had practiced recently by jumping from higher and higher levels, until he could predictably drop and roll off his roof. The roof of the house he had burned to the ground before coming here.

No turning back.

Someone has to do something. Kyle Talbot's words

rang in his ears like a battle cry.

'Police! Freeze!'

The adrenaline was mainlining now. Every muscle in Martin's body was tense and ready. 'Don't shoot, I'm a cop!'

'Turn around!'

Martin put his hands up and did what he was told. A uniformed NYPD cop was pointing a gun at him.

'I'm airport security, man. Why are you busting my balls?'

'Why did you jump down from this plane?'

'Check my ID, man. I'm clean. I'm just doing my job. Maybe I'm a little overzealous but, hey, how many times do I get to protect the President, right?'

The NYPD cop approached Martin. 'Where's your ID?'

'In my inside jacket pocket. You want me to give it to you, or do you want to get it? It's your call. You've got the gun.'

'Take it out, real slow.'

Martin reached inside his jacket, slowly, and handed the cop an ID billfold.

But it wasn't the ID that caught the cop's eyes. It was the uniform he saw when the man opened his jacket. The man was wearing NYPD blues underneath. He was wondering why that was when Martin's hand exploded upward, knocking the cop's gun away, and grabbing him by the throat. The impact crushed the cop's vocal cords so he could not cry out.

Martin knew what he was doing. He had done it before – in Viet Nam.

'Can't we go any faster?' said Matt.

'I'm going as fast as I can, sir.'

'Calm down, Matt,' said Susan. 'We'll be there in five minutes.'

Matt didn't say anything more, but the thought running through his mind was: I hope the President will still be alive when we get there.

Martin left the cop's body under a piece of heavy machinery that looked as though it hadn't been used in a while, and headed toward the gate that he knew the mayor's car would soon be entering. He knew this because it was the gate the mayor's car always came through. Martin himself had been involved in protecting the New York mayor on six occasions while he was serving with NYPD. In fact, one of the bullets he had taken had come while protecting the mayor. Some Puerto Rican drug dealer had gone a little crazy one New Year's Eve, and figured the mayor was responsible for everything wrong with New York – which, quite frankly, wasn't that far from Martin's own view at the time. Regardless of that, Martin took a bullet for the mayor.

An NYPD cop stood at the gate. Martin could see the temporary dais set up on one of the runways. He didn't see the mayor's car, nor Air Force One. He walked over to the cop, who now saw a fellow officer dressed in NYPD blues.

'Anything?' asked Martin.

'Everything's cool.'

Martin nodded, turned and looked away from the officer, away from the gate, toward the dais. When he turned back toward the cop, he was holding a knife.

Which he thrust into the man's heart. Martin caught him before he hit the ground, and quickly dragged the dead man into a small shack located next to the gate.

Inside the airport terminal, word had spread about the President's visit, and people were jockeying for position. One woman was asking a security guard if she would be able to take a photograph through the window. He assured her that would be okay.

The mayor's car pulled up, a contingent of motorcycle cops surrounding it. Jack Martin waved them through, purposely making a comment to one of the cops in the motorcade.

The mayor's car passed through, and Martin closed the gate.

'Will I see the President from here, Mommy?'

'Yes, honey.' Inside the terminal the woman had trouble hearing her daughter speak because, through Walkman earphones, she was listening to Kyle Talbot saying, 'President Souther is either a stupid man, or he knows what he's doing. I don't think he's stupid. And if he knows what he's doing, dragging this country into the gutter with policies that will put our children on a par with the Third World, then somehow, some way, he must be stopped.'

Matt pulled up to the gate through which the Secret Service had instructed him to enter the airport. As it was unmanned, his driver got out, opened the gate, got back inside and drove them through.

'Isn't that odd?' said Susan. 'Leaving a gate unguarded?'

In that moment, Matt knew. 'He's here.'

Martin rode on the motorcycle that belonged to the dead cop who had been guarding the gate. Wearing the dead man's helmet, he purposely rode over and spoke to the motorcycle cop he had purposely addressed a few minutes earlier.

'Everything okay?'

The officer said, 'So far. But I hear we've got company.'

Martin nodded, turned off his motorcycle, and got off to join the rank and file, his eyes turned away from the dais, as if looking out for the assassin.

Air Force One landed on schedule, coming out of the sky like some regal bird, and coasting to a stop less than fifty yards away from the temporary dais. The door opened and the crowd inside the terminal bristled with expectation.

On the runway, photographers started taking pictures, and the mayor checked his notes.

Matt told the driver to pull up near the ring of security personnel and reporters, as he searched the crowd for Jack Martin.

The assassin put on his sunglasses. His heart was beating fast, but he looked outwardly calm. Inside his head the mantra kept rolling: *Someone has to do something*.

'What are we going to do?' said Susan. 'I can't really see from in here.'

Matt instructed the driver to stop. He and Susan climbed out and started walking toward the dais.

President Souther, flanked by his wife Joan as well as a number of Secret Service men, walked up the steps of the dais.

'What do I do if I see him?' said Susan.

'Tell me, and then get out of the way.'

She kept looking.

'As mayor of the greatest city in the world, it is an honor for me to welcome the President of the United States.' The mayor checked his index card, then proceeded.

President Souther stood behind the mayor. No seats were set up on the dais, because it had been made clear that this would be a *very* quick stop, its sole purpose being to provide a couple of photographs of the two men together. The mayor's speech was not to last more than three minutes. What would be the point of anything longer? The news programs would only broadcast ten seconds of it anyhow. Besides that, the President didn't much like the mayor, and was doing this only because his party chairman had pressured him.

Suddenly Susan's blood ran cold. 'There he is,' she whispered.

'Where?'

Even though Jack Martin hoped to hide behind sunglasses, Susan had found him.

'You're sure?'

'Positive.'

'Okay, back off.'

Susan stood perfectly still as Matt made his way through the crowd toward the assassin.

Someone has to do something. As the words kept playing in Martin's ears, he no longer heard the mayor speaking. He was now only remotely aware of his immediate surroundings, and he knew what he was there to do. Knew that he would not walk away from here today. But knew that he was doing something noble. Something that had to be done.

Someone has to do something.

As Matt closed in on the assassin, the mayor was finishing up his speech. And because Martin was wearing sunglasses, Matt would never know if the man's actions were triggered as some reflex to seeing Matt moving in on him.

In slow motion . . .

Jack Martin turned away from Matt and faced the dais. In a single fluid motion, he drew his gun and pointed it directly at President Souther's head.

Matt also drew his gun, aware that there was a good chance he would be taken out by Secret Service agents doing their jobs.

Jack Martin fired . . .

And blew President Souther's head apart.

Someone has to do something.

Simultaneously, Matt fired. What else could he do?

Martin took bullets to his back and neck. As he lay dying on the tarmac, images of his wife and son replayed in his head. Along with the thought that he really had *done something* – for them, and for his country.

Matt stood holding his gun, and shaking. Realizing that, in a single horrific instant, the world had changed – and that he himself was a small part of that irreversible change.

Then all sight and sound drained away.

Into chaos.

THIRTY-EIGHT

In an era of live-action wars, action-cam police pursuits, and video-replay-news-at-eleven-blood-and-gore murder, the assassination of President Souther became the media event of the century. Tears flowed, commentators commented, editors editorialized, and conspiracy theorists starting hitting the talk-show circuit again.

Item: Washington – President McClain, who was sworn in within minutes of President Souther's assassination, announced that the President's body would lie in state in the Rotunda all day Tuesday, from nine until midnight. The casket will be closed.

Item: New York – A woman claiming to be Jack Martin's lover signed a six-figure deal with a New York book publisher. She said that she had met the assassin at a Los Angeles country and western bar. Her agent announced that film rights would be auctioned within the week.

Item: Topeka, Kansas – Jack Martin's sister-in-law, who owns a bar in Topeka, appeared on a national TV talk show and intimated that she'd had an affair with her brother-in-law several years ago.

Item: Los Angeles – Enterprising neighbors have started a unique mail-order business. They are selling charred pieces of Jack Martin's recently burned house for ten dollars an ounce.

Matt watched and listened to the sound of a country gasping for air. The world, he concluded, was not going to hell in a hand basket, but rather in an armored truck full of stolen money.

The night of the assassination, the press was camped on Kyle Talbot's doorstep as he arrived at work. He had no comment.

Inside his office, he watched yet another replay of Souther's head exploding.

With the door shut, in his own private hell, Kyle Talbot wept.

Ellis Handy knocked on the door, but didn't wait for Talbot to tell him to come in.

'I don't want to talk to anyone, Ellis.'

'I know, Kyle. But I wanted to give you something.' He handed Talbot a letter with the presidential seal on it, and also an overnight package.

'What're these?'

'I went through the mail. One is a letter hand-delivered by the Secret Service.'

'From?'

'The First Lady. The former First Lady, that is.'

'Good Lord.'

'And the other one's from Martin.'

'What?!'

'It was overnighted yesterday from New York.'

'My God!'

Talbot opened the letter from Mrs Souther first.

Dear Mr Talbot,

I would like to make a special request. Please do not say further derogatory things about my husband until after the funeral. My son and I will be leaving the country for some time following the ceremony, and then you can resume your assault on my husband if you wish. My son is taking this very badly, as his friends listen to your show. If you could see it in your heart to grant this request, I would be most grateful.

Sincerely,

Joan Souther

Talbot handed his partner the letter. 'What does she think I am, some kind of monster?'

'To be fair, Kyle, for the year leading up to his election, and for every single day since Souther took up office, you've targeted him on every show.'

Talbot didn't respond at first. Finally, he said, 'Does she think she has to ask me not to say anything bad about the man . . . under *these* circumstances?'

Handy did not speak – but the unstated answer was that she did.

Talbot picked up Martin's overnight package and

opened it. Inside was a manuscript, whose cover page read: *The Bill of Responsibilities.*

'What is it?'

After leafing through a few pages, Talbot said, 'It's Martin's view of life. It's like some kind of manifesto.'

'You're kidding!'

There was a note clipped to the cover. 'He wants me to read it out on the air.'

'Good Lord! What are you going to do?'

After a slight hesitation, Talbot said, 'I don't know. It doesn't seem right somehow.'

'Kyle, that manuscript is worth ten million dollars if it's worth a dime. You know, I've been hanging out with the press people all day. Sure, people are pretty broken up about the assassination, but there are still a lot of people out there who think the Reaper performed an act of patriotism.'

Talbot looked up at his partner. 'Do you really believe that?'

'It doesn't matter what I believe, Kyle. Nobody's ever given much of a fuck about what I think. You either, for that matter. This is the opportunity we've been waiting for all our lives. You don't have to endorse the fucking manuscript. Preface it with some kind of disclaimer.'

'But do you know how many crazy people out there would take this shit seriously?'

'That's not your responsibility. You didn't write it. You're just . . . setting the record straight. This is history, Kyle. It's bigger than either one of us.

Besides, if *you* don't do it, someone else will.'

Talbot did not respond. He sat looking at the First Lady's letter on his desk. Right next to Jack Martin's manuscript.

'So, what are you going to do?'

Kyle Talbot closed his eyes and tried to think.

THIRTY-NINE

Susan accompanied Matt back to JFK. On the ride out there, she said that her agent had told her that there was already a one-million-dollar movie offer on the table, and that he could probably get her a 'based on the book by' credit. She did not seem excited, but Matt could tell that she was pleased.

Susan then said she would try to get to Los Angeles as soon as she could, probably within a week or so, and that they could discuss their relationship at that time. They both seemed numbed by what had happened. They had been players in a pivotal moment in history. A tragic moment.

Matt kissed Susan and waved to her as she walked onto the plane.

And, he knew, perhaps out of his life.

He wasn't in touch with reality now, so therefore he was not in touch with his feelings for Susan. He prayed that he would be again. And soon.

Matt called the office. Laurie had left a message. Apparently their divorce was coming along 'very nicely', and she wanted to know if he minded taking Jarod for the weekend. She had left her message before the assassination.

The next call Matt made was to a friend who

owned a fishing boat. He chartered the boat for the weekend, then he called Jarod.

In one minute Kyle Talbot was supposed to go on. He stared down at the manuscript in front of him. And at the former First Lady's letter. He had still not made up his mind what to do.

The On Air sign went on . . .

It just didn't work anymore.

The rules he had grown up with, abided by, no longer applied. Order and justice, even a conscientious attempt at justice, seemed to be a quaint notion from another time and place.

These were strange times, thought the man, as he took a pull off his beer. He sat in the dark room, the only light coming from the amber radio dial. The only sound was Kyle Talbot's radio show.

He wondered what Kyle would say about the assassination. He knew Talbot couldn't come right out and say it was wonderful news. But people knew the truth.

'And, now, the Kyle Talbot Show,' said the announcer's voice.

The man nodded in the darkness. He shifted in his chair. And set down his bottle of beer.

Right next to his .357 Magnum.

More Thrilling Fiction from Headline

EDWARD STEWART
MORTAL GRACE

THE NEW HIGH-SOCIETY THRILLER FROM THE BESTSELLING AUTHOR OF *DEADLY RICH*

New York in the 1990s is in decay and its youth have no hope, as they lose their minds and lives to drugs. The powerful and wealthy pretend to charity but when one of their own is threatened they close ranks to justice.

When the mutilated body of a long-dead teenage girl is discovered buried in a basket in Vanderbilt Gardens, Lieutenant Vince Cardozo of the New York Police Department is called in. Strange and sinister clues begin to emerge which narrow Cardozo's investigations on to one suspect – Father Joe Montgomery, a charismatic and influential priest with friends in very high places.

Out of the blue a convicted murderer confesses to the killing, and though Cardozo is unhappy with this apparent conclusion – the case is personal to him, as his own teenage niece is a still-missing runaway – he reluctantly moves on to solve other crimes. Months later, another – more recent – victim is discovered. And the hunt is on again.

Also by Edward Stewart from Headline Feature
DEADLY RICH
'A tasty, gossipy, suspenseful read' *Publishers Weekly*
'A stunning suspenser' *Publishing News*

FICTION/THRILLER 0 7472 4369 7